ARTEFACTS OF THE DEAD

6

ARTEFACTS OF THE DEAD

Tony Black

BLACK & WHITE PUBLISHING

First published 2014
by Black & White Publishing Ltd
29 Ocean Drive, Edinburgh EH6 6JL

1 3 5 7 9 10 8 6 4 2   14 15 16

ISBN: 978 1 84502 776 6

ALBA | CHRUTHACHAIL

A CIP cata[logue record for this book is available from the British] ibrary.

[Typesetting,] Newtonmore
[by Grafica Veneta S.p.A.]

For Cheryl and Conner

ACKNOWLEDGEMENTS

I'd like to thank Dr Robert Ghent for sharing some of his extensive medical knowledge and putting up with my persistent queries whilst I tried to understand some of the specifics of Valentine's trauma. Likewise, a huge debt of gratitude is due to John Geates for his assistance in some of the technical matters relating to the police investigation, and for sharing personal anecdotes. Finally, praise by the bucketload goes to my first reader, and unpaid editor, Cheryl McEvoy, for reassuring me that I was on the right side of the lynch mob.

PROLOGUE

THE BULLDOZER EMITTED a drone, chugging noise as its caterpillar tracks pushed through the hill-high mounds of refuse. White parcels of cardboard and ubiquitous plastic carriers toppled into the broad, fresh footprint of the earth mover. A grey-to-black cloud of smoke hung in the wide trail, fresh bursts from the vertical exhaust pipe adding to a slug-line smear hugging a blue skyline. The jagged sawtooth of the Isle of Arran and the rough jut of Ailsa Craig looked a long way out at sea as the driver crunched the gears a final time and brought the vehicle to a halt.

In the cab, a shabby portable radio – it looked like a tip-find – sat on the dash, blaring a West FM jingle as Davie ferreted for a pack of Embassy Regal. He whistled something from the terraces, a line about 'honest men' that had been stuck in his mind since Saturday.

'What's this, now?' Davie clamped the filter tip in his mouth and lit up. As he did so, he eyed the fast-approaching quad bike, the orange light flashing above on its pole.

'Bastard, won't give me a moment's peace.' He turned the key in the ignition and felt a shudder as the bulldozer came to life again. As Davie tucked his cigarette packet into the top pocket of his shirt, he smashed a tightly balled fist into the grubby dash. 'Five minutes, for a fag ... I was only after a bloody fag!'

As the crawler-tracks bit into the ground, the dozer blade

caught the refuse piles and ripped them apart. A blunt line was sheared from the side of the tight-packed cardboard and plastic waste, fresh spills of carrier bags and bottles toppling to the cleared ground. A dirty cloud of fly-ridden effluvia escaped into the air but was soon swallowed up by the bulldozer's own emissions.

'I see you, I bloody well see you!'

Davie kept his eyes front and tried to ignore the intoning from his supervisor on the fast-moving quad bike. He bit the cigarette between his teeth and tucked his head further towards the filthy windscreen. He felt the smoke rising; his eyes smarted.

As Davie's supervisor edged closer his driving became more erratic, aggressive almost. He clearly wanted to say something to the man at the earth mover's controls; he wagged an arm to attract his attention, but the act merely increased Davie's resolve to ignore him.

'Aye, I can see you . . .' He smiled to himself, the cigarette on his lips jostling up and down as he rasped. 'Can't have five minutes for a fag, eh. Out that trap like a bloody greyhound, you were.'

Davie crunched the gears again and dug a fresh swathe through the crumbling debris. A broken door clattered off the edge of the bulldozer's side-panel. For a moment it startled him; his stomach lurched, then tightened in expectation of more landslips from the same location. Nothing came, and he collected the cigarette in his fingers, sucked the nicotine deep into his lungs, then flicked the ash onto the floor of the cab.

'Davie . . .'

He heard the supervisor's roars, closer now.

The driver pretended to be oblivious to the commotion that was rapidly drawing near his open side-window. It was one small victory he was allowed in the game of life: to be able to play dumb and irritate the boss. He was never normally in a position to put one over on his supervisor, but he pretended to be ignorant; after all, that's what was thought of him.

'What's that . . . ? Slow down, is it?' Davie felt a glow in his cheeks as he slammed the gears again and forced the dozer blade deeper into the rubbish tip. What would he want, anyway? A few more hours out of him moving this muck; a weekend shift at time-and-a-half when it should be double-time. No chance.

'Keep up, mate,' he rasped beneath his breath.

Still, he didn't seem to be giving up. Davie saw his supervisor haring over the mounds of trash, sending the scavenging gulls back to the sky to circle and squawk. Up and down the terrain he went, in and out of the garbage gulches. He wasn't normally so committed. A niggle started in Davie's conscience. He allowed himself another gasp on the cigarette; the grey-white ash had formed itself into a slender poker-point and threatened to fall on his lap at any moment. He squinted to the left, towards the high-revving quad bike. He was still there, still moving, still at speed.

'What's he up to?'

As the bulldozer's blade cut through a fresh stack of high-piled black refuse sacks, splitting them open and spilling the contents, a flurry of brown rats ran for cover. Davie watched the rats; he knew they were smart creatures and held a grudging respect for them, even if they did churn his guts. The sight of them running from the bulldozer always made him leap in his seat, try to catch a glimpse of a long tail being caught in the caterpillar tracks: he'd never seen a single one caught yet. As he raised himself, his gaze was drawn to the horizon. He kept a hand on the wheel as he eased the earth mover down the gears. The noise from the gulls and the quad bike, the revving of the engine and the crunching of the gears,

3

all faded into oblivion as he stared through a gap in the fly-splattered windscreen.

'What the hell is that?'

In the midst of the collected detritus of Ayrshire's homes sat an unfamiliar object. Davie craned his neck and thinned his eyes to better discern the sight before him.

'Wha—?'

The sudden high-pitched din of the quad bike revving to a halt at his side broke the spell, but only for a moment.

'Davie . . . get out the way!'

He heard the call, but didn't register any interest.

'Davie . . .'

He sensed movement beside him, his supervisor gesticulating with his arms wide in the fly-thick air.

'Yeah, yeah . . .' he said, flagging his boss aside. Workplace rules were abandoned in times like this: those rare occasions when the outside world stepped inside and levelled everyone to the same status. This moment was far more important than any bawling his boss was capable of delivering. Davie wasn't sure what it was that he was seeing – the shape was too indistinct – but he knew this much: it wasn't something you should see on a council rubbish tip.

'Davie, Jesus Christ . . .'

He let the bulldozer roll a few yards, clearing the now-established route through the wasteland, towards the shape. It seemed to be a collection of familiar objects, but none in the right order. There was a central pole, like a flagpole or a spike in the earth, but there was something attached, tethered.

'Stop!'

He rolled the bulldozer further forward. It was a tangle, like a tangle of limbs – arms and legs – was it a scarecrow? Had someone dumped a tailor's dummy?

4

'Davie, please!'

He depressed the brake and stilled the engine. The sun was high in the noon sky, a rare wide blue offering that filled the line of rooftops and stopped just shy of a shimmering yellow band of sunlight. Davie cupped his hand above his brows and stared front. No, it wasn't a dummy.

'Christ above . . .'

At his side, Davie suddenly felt a whoosh of air as the cab door was swung open and his supervisor jerked a hand towards the dash to grab the keys from the ignition.

'What in the name of God are you playing at, Davie?'

The driver turned to face his interrogator; his lips parted and the lower of the two suddenly became heavy.

'Is that . . . ?'

'Yes, it's a body!'

'A what?'

His supervisor's eyes widened; the red shine of exertion showed in their corners.

'A body! A man's body . . .'

Davie's words faltered now. 'On the tip?'

'Yes, yes . . .'

He hung out of the cab and pointed with both his arms in the direction of the corpse, pale white against the bright blue of the sky.

'It's a dead man . . . Can't you see someone's put a bloody great spike through him?'

1

THE ANTIQUATED-LOOKING exercise bike in the corner of the gymnasium was about all DI Bob Valentine could bring himself to tackle. There was a noisy game of five-a-side going on beyond the wall; the shouts and roars of rowdy recruits would once have proven too tempting an opportunity to go and knock off some arrogance, show them who was boss – after all, he had once been a very useful inside-left – but those days were now over. Reluctantly, he stuck to the bike and the slow revolutions of the pedals that emitted a whirring, hypnotic burr from the gyroscopic wheel.

The DI's brow was moistening. It had been – what? – ten minutes of low-impact cycling. The doctor had called for more, much more, but it didn't seem right to push himself. He didn't like getting out of breath, didn't like straining the muscle in the centre of his chest that was forced to do all the work. He knew his heart had been through enough. He watched as stiff arms attached to prominently knuckled hands gripped the handlebars. His hold was weaker, less sure than it had once been. He couldn't imagine hauling himself over the Tulliallan assault course now. His whole body seemed to have attenuated; it was as if some vital force within him had been removed, supplanted with a strange, ethereal mist that he had yet to adjust to, or even comprehend. He knew it was there, could almost see it, certainly he sensed it, but the old mind patterns – they hadn't altered – refused to acknowledge it.

'How you doing, Bob?' The voice seemed to come from nowhere, an eruption amidst the plains of his thought.

'All right, how's it going?' He drew the reply from a store of stock answers. The man's face still hadn't registered with him.

'You're still with us then?'

Valentine had to search deeper for an answer to that question: did he mean at the training academy or did he mean in the land of the living?

'Yeah, for now.'

He eased off the pedals and leaned back in the saddle of the bike. For some reason he found himself folding his arms over his chest as he took in the broad man in the red Adidas tracksuit. He looked older than himself, a bald head with short-trimmed grey hairs sat above jug-ears and eyes deep lined with creases as straight as the radial of an Art Deco sunburst. Fulton, his name was Fulton, he remembered now.

'Don't know what their plan is for me . . . long term.'

Fulton thinned his eyes; the folds on his face deepened and he became jowly as he dropped his chin – he looked like a pug-dog for a moment. 'Right . . .' he nodded, and the image was so complete he might have been sitting on the parcel-shelf of a Ford Mondeo.

What was he doing here, thought Valentine? It was the incident, he knew that. The incident that he had been unable to alter, could do nothing to halt. Except, perhaps to have been a little more lucky. But he had never been that.

'So, we could be keeping you, then?' said Fulton.

Valentine shrugged. 'Who knows?'

A hand was extended, placed on the DI's shoulder; it made Valentine flinch, he didn't like the contact. It felt invasive, it felt threatening. He knew in his mind it was nothing of the sort, but he couldn't alter how he was feeling at any given

8

moment. There was thought, reasoning, for after the event, but in the moment . . . Hadn't someone said 'the heart has its reasons that reason knows not of'?

He rose from the exercise bike. 'Right, well, I better be going . . . hit the showers.'

Fulton smiled, a wide rictus that made him look more of a fool than the PT instructor's garb. 'Aye, aye . . . hit the showers.' He leaned forward to slap the DI on the shoulder, but somehow inferred that it would be an intrusion on Valentine's space. He retreated a few steps, grinned again, then said, 'Catch you later, Bob.'

'Yeah . . . see you later.' He raised a hand and waved the instructor off. He watched him pace a few steps towards the door and waited to see if his suspicions would be proved right: they were. The man turned and put a stare on Valentine that he took as the last look of the utterly perplexed.

'See you, Fulton . . .'

The DI had made the same impression on Fulton as he was having on everyone lately: they thought he was losing it. Maybe he was. He shook his head and made for the changing room.

Tulliallan academy was housed in a nineteenth-century castle but it felt more like any other college or learning institution to Valentine. The sweep of the place, its history, was wasted on him. He didn't like the blonde-wood gymnasium and he didn't like the in-house Starbucks or the two trendy bars that would look more at home in some overpriced boutique hotel. He felt like a fraud just being there, but then what was the option?

A door opened and a stream of smiling, gallus recruits poured into the corridor, pinning Valentine where he stood. They seemed wholly oblivious to him as he held up his elbows

9

and shrunk into the wall, waiting for the crowd to pass. When the mass of bodies had evaporated before him, Valentine lowered his arms and took deep breath.

'Christ.'

He felt like he'd just stepped out of the path of a juggernaut, but he was deceiving himself. He was overreacting. As he made a point of placing his hands in his pockets, Valentine gripped fists – weak fists, not the fists of anger he had been known to clench in the past, but more of determination. He didn't want to carry on like this. He didn't want to be a shadow of his former self.

In the empty changing room, he rested his head on the locker door and sighed.

'Together . . . keep it together, man.'

He repeated the paean to himself over and over until he heard the hinges of a door swinging open; he was no longer alone. The armour needed to go on. He drew back his shoulders and retrieved the key from his shorts. The contents of the locker were neatly packed, his grey dogtooth sports coat on the hanger, his trousers beneath. He removed them one by one and then placed them on the bench behind him. Last to come out were his black shoes, Dr Martens – he had got used to them on the beat. He placed them on the floor and then retrieved his mobile phone from the locker. He'd missed a call.

The sound of showers running started as he checked his messages.

'Martin . . .' He shook his head. 'What the bloody hell does she want?'

Chief Superintendent Marion Martin had been the officer responsible for Valentine's secondment to Tulliallan. She had kept a close eye on him since the incident, but all his requests for a return to the detective's role had been steadfastly rebuffed. A list of options, reasons why she might be calling, raced through his mind: being put out to grass at Tulliallan on a permanent basis topped the list.

Was this what his career had come to? he wondered. His mind spooled back to the youth he had burned up in pursuits he now questioned. Had the effort, the exertion, been worth it? Certainly, he would not chase the same chimerical dreams again. Ambition had been his flaw. The desire to make something of himself, measure his worth against others on the force had filled his life, once. But life was too short for that, surely. Yet Valentine still measured himself against the likes of Martin. Who was she? A careerist, an underwhelming police officer who had fashioned an overachiever's job and responsibility for herself. And what did she have that Valentine didn't, aside from a nice rack and the positive-discrimination policymakers on her side. The answer didn't matter, because the answer counted for nothing. He knew those like Martin had success for one reason – because it was there for them.

Valentine knew success, the dizzying high-wire type, wasn't on the way to him. It didn't come down to ability, achievement, worth – nothing like it. That success was random and disparate; it arrived at the doorstep of some who no more deserved it than desired it. When it fell to people like Martin it engulfed them, changed them completely, took over their personalities and made them anew. She was fighting to sustain an image of superiority – an outward expression of the opposite – and everyone on the force knew it. She was merely acting like the chief superintendent that she imagined herself to be, or thought she should be. The reality was not even a consideration for her. The thought of such a waste of a life struck Valentine as tragic.

11

The time you had was too precious, he had learned this only recently, but it had struck him instantly and decisively. He couldn't be jealous of Martin's success, or anyone else's, he knew this viscerally, but part of him – the old part, the Valentine before he had learned life's lessons – still wanted to roll up sleeves and compete. In his youth, the young boy with the lionheart who strutted with his chest out through the lower ranks thought the garlands of success were his right. He was better than everyone else, the competition, so why wouldn't he be conceded the privilege of lofty regard?

Valentine smirked, inwardly at first, and then gave a replete grin. Had he really once been so stupid? So naive? So utterly dispossessed of any notion of reality, the world and its workings and just how insignificant his role in it mattered? Yes, he conceded. He had been that stupid, once, and it had taken twenty more years of staring at the most blatant of life's facts to realise it.

He held up the mobile phone, looked at the screen for the count of a few stilled breaths and then dialled Chief Superintendent Martin's number.

The sound of ringing filled the line.

A brusque voice. 'Hello.'

'Boss, it's Bob . . .'

A pause entered their exchange; he heard movement, the sound of clothes rustling.

'I called you nearly an hour ago, what the hell have you been doing down there . . . ? Not another bloody happy hour at the Cooper Lounge?'

Valentine held his voice in check; his tone came low and flat. 'I think that place only opens on a Sunday . . .'

She bit, 'Never mind that . . . I need you back at the station. How quickly can you get here?'

Valentine's pulse quickened. 'The station . . . King Street?'

'I don't think they've moved it.'

He lowered himself onto the bench. He was sitting on his sports coat, but he didn't care. 'Is there something I should know about?'

The chief super's voice pitched up an octave. 'I have Bryce, McVeigh and Collins either on annual leave or tied up on other cases, so you are back in business as of today. Unless you're going to tell me you're unfit or some such crap.'

Valentine sensed a smirk creeping up the side of his face. It lingered there for a moment – exactly the time it took him to realise that if he was returning to the fray it was not for a good reason.

'What's the SP?'

A sigh. The sound of a telephone receiver being shifted between hands. 'We have a body in the tip . . . good enough for you?'

Valentine's mouth dried over, the roof first but then his tongue followed as he widened his jaws. 'The tip?'

'Battered into next week, and just to put a cherry on top, impaled on a sharp bit of 4x2 . . . up the arse.'

'That's horrific.'

'If you wanted candy floss every day, Bob, you should have joined the bloody circus. Can I see you back here before close of play?'

His reply was on his lips before he realised the chief super had hung up.

'Yes, of course . . .'

2

THE TILED FLOOR BENEATH his bare feet began to feel cold after a few moments, so DI Bob Valentine started to move his toes. A tingling sensation – like low-wattage electricity – worked its way along the arch of his foot and buried itself into the thick of the heel. Had he missed something? The debates about his fitness to return to active policing seemed to have been instantly swept aside. For so long now he had held the quandary in the back of his mind, removed it to the front once in a while to examine the finer points of both sides of the argument; it had become a practised undertaking. The neural path was a deep one.

'Never . . .'

He said the word, but it didn't sound like his voice. For a moment he stared at the cold feet below him, they were getting colder now. That meant something: he needed to move.

Valentine raised himself from the bench. He was still holding his mobile and he placed it on the brim of the locker shelf in front of him. As he turned, he noticed the crumpled mass of his sports coat and grimaced; it was then that he caught sight of his reflection in the tall, floor-to-ceiling mirror. He saw his face first, the dark hair above his temples – still thick, that was something to hold on to – and the smooth but clean-lined block of forehead. The tight grimace of his mouth subsided as he dropped his gaze onto, first, his neck and then to the expanse of white that sat between his shoulders. He had a broad chest, a barrel some would have called it; the covering of skin was almost hairless, save one or two stray insect-legs that sprouted around his nipples and at prominent points along the line his clavicle: his chest had always looked that way, except for the thick red-brown line that ran vertically through the centre of the sternum with an undoubted surgical precision; this was a recent addition.

Valentine let the lids of his eyes hang heavy as he tipped back his head slightly. It was a look some would have reserved for staring into the middle distance, or further yet, but the DI's focus was squarely on the ridge of unwelcome flesh that sat as thick as his index finger. The geometric line was more than a scar; the thinner white markings where the stitching had tightened the invasive hole could be called a scar. This was something more. A scar suggested an injury, a trauma perhaps, but the object of Valentine's gaze – and its location – proclaimed here was the point of a violent incursion, a beacon blazing the message that this was a man who was lucky to be alive.

A clamour of voices broke from the shower cubicles and a group of recruits, white towels circling their waists, burst into view. Valentine drew back his shoulders and stood before them for a moment.

'Sir . . .' said the first to see him.

He nodded back.

'Sir,' the others followed.

The DI reached for his grey sports coat and started to shake it out; he had creased it when he sat down, but the call had taken him by surprise. He was still in a state of disbelief, his thoughts swaying between his readiness to return to the station and the particulars of the murder that Marion Martin had relayed to him.

He smirked to himself. They called her Dino, after her namesake, but also because it was a dog's name, and she was of the ilk that station smart-arses loved to ridicule by appointing them a derogatory moniker. As he amused himself, he glanced at the mirror – one of the recruits was nudging the other, drawing a line down the centre of his chest with the tip of his finger. Valentine didn't need to second-guess what was passing between them.

'Want a better view, lads?' He turned and put his hand on his hips.

The recruits looked away; as the DI eyed them fully now he saw they were only young lads. Two big shots – chancers – and an 'aye man' – the type that's there to nod and gravely intone 'aye, aye' while the others boasted and prattled about themselves.

'No, I was just . . .' said the nudging recruit.

'I saw you.' Valentine stepped forward. 'You were drawing attention to this . . .' he pointed at the thick line of darkened flesh in the centre of his chest.

The recruits looked away. The air in the changing rooms seemed to have altered. If there had been a pitch of bravado, it had been flattened by the steamroller Valentine was now driving over their egos.

'Don't for a second think this is some badge of honour.'

'No, sir.' The voices were weak, meek. The three lads stared at the water dripping from them as it fell to the tiled floor beneath their bare feet.

Valentine raised his voice. 'Look at this . . .' – he tapped his chest – 'I'm not proud of it.' He raised his voice, flitted looks between the three. When he felt sure he had their full attention, he spoke up again. 'When I was first in uniform, an old sergeant of mine said your tongue's more useful than your baton . . . Just you remember that.'

The DI kept a firm stare on them for a moment longer and then returned to his locker and began the slow ritual of dressing himself. He never felt comfortable bawling out those beneath him in rank, but he was an experienced enough police officer to know when a mind was receptive to a lesson that might make the job a little easier.

On his way out, the 'aye man' turned his head away but the two chancers painted thin smiles on their faces and nodded like they had somehow all now become friends. Valentine looked through them and continued to the door as if he had never spoken a word.

In the car park the sun was high in the sky, painting a hazy red wash over the day. The DI's cheeks flushed as he walked into the heat, and then he cut his stride as the unusually clear and bright light silhouetted the frame of a black dog. The animal stood statue-still, its ears pinned up with angular precision, obviously perfected for the earnest task it had currently set itself. Valentine was gripped by the beast – he had never seen a stray hereabouts – and then suddenly it bolted. The dog crossed the grass at speed, slowed only by the paving flags it had to cross before jinxing round the wall and out of sight. Valentine wondered what strange secret of nature the animal had been privy to. He found himself looking around, trying to discern a clue as to what the dog knew, and then he shook himself and headed for the car. He had been thinking far too much about that sort of thing lately, he told himself. 'Pack it in, Bob,' he muttered as he pointed the key in the direction of the Vectra.

As he started the engine his old preoccupation returned, and he tried to douse it with logic: he was entering into a murder investigation. He needed his attention to be on that, not the events of these last few months, not his self-doubts.

17

'Dogs in the street . . .' he told himself. 'What next?'

As he engaged the clutch and started out of the car park, he turned his attention to the words the chief super had uttered: 'You're back in business.'

There was no denying the fact that he felt good about that. He needed to get back to what he was best at. He was a murder-squad detective and nothing that had happened changed that.

'No Bryce, McVeigh or Collins, eh . . .' He let his thoughts turn to words as he drove back to Ayr. 'King Street must be like the bloody *Mary Celeste*.'

The steering wheel was still warm after sitting in the glare of the sun; he gripped lightly as he spun the wheel through his palms. It was good to be driving back to the station, to be back on the proper force – not messing around with wet-behind-the-ears recruits and has-beens. The likes of Bryce would be falling over themselves to get a murder case like this, so why was he filled with apprehension? He was going back to the place he knew best – the sharp end. The thought made his throat constrict slightly, but he brushed it aside; there really was no place for doubts now.

3

THE ROAD INTO AYR WAS tightly packed with cars. It was that time of the evening, thought Valentine, but then he remembered when the rush hour in town had lasted only ten minutes. He had left the A77 to take the arterial road towards the airport and, after travelling only three car lengths, found his vehicle hemmed in by open fields on one side, all the way to the town of Troon, and by runways on the other, reaching to the outskirts of the village of Mossblown. Ayrshire was a collection of small villages interspersed with fertile farmland, the produce of which was famed the world over. Beef, potatoes, dairy: the region served our tables well. Industry was less prevalent now: a lone paper mill, a shoe factory and some light engineering works were all that remained of a once bustling 'Silicone Glen', and mines with a hundred years of coal. You couldn't look back, Valentine knew that; the district he had grown up in was gone. He tried to imagine how it might feel to be a school-leaver now and have his expectation of life reduced to a supermarket job or a seat amongst the battery hens in a call centre's serried ranks. It was no life for a man, but then it had not been a man's world for a long time. Was that such a bad thing? He doubted it, but at the same time felt a drifting, deepening nostalgia for a lost era when he knew his place and felt comfortable there.

The tailback on the road told him he was not getting to King Street station in time to meet with Chief Superintendent

Marion Martin. She wouldn't be pleased, but he held to the knowledge that she would have no choice: experienced staff were a luxury in short supply. The journey from Tulliallan had given the DI time to think, to take in the news that he was an investigating officer once again. It had also allowed him to regain perspective; he had no room for self-doubt in a murder investigation. He was either on his game – one hundred per cent – or he was assuredly off it. The victim deserved as much. Throughout the length of his time on the force, the ability to apply himself fully had never before been an issue; it was what he was there for. Valentine had had cause to question his choices, from time to time, but he had never doubted his duty. His father – a miner who had channelled his considerable vehemence into deterring him from joining the police – had taught him that duty was everything. It was never so much expressed as shown. The Calvinist dirge sang to him still.

The queue of cars nudged ahead a few inches and Valentine released the clutch; the tyres almost completed a full revolution before the brake went on again. The slow, jerky progress persisted all the way to the Heathfield Road traffic lights, which showed red just to affirm their role in the road's hesitant drama. As he was stopped again, Valentine found himself drawn to a black limousine. It was a long, angular Mercedes driven by a man in a dark coat and tie. The driver possessed the time-worn mournfulness of an undertaker. His hands fed the steering wheel slowly, carefully. His eyes shifted almost imperceptibly as he gauged the camber of the road on the turn. There was something about the way the man negotiated his movements – the practised reverence for the cargo of a single pine box behind him – that made Valentine's nerves tense. He didn't know how many people he had known who were now dead; he had lost count of the corpses he had seen – cadavers on mortuary slabs had long since ceased to be anything more than meat to him – but the image before him of a slow-moving hearse jolted a new impulse.

'Poor bastard.' He ran the tips of his fingers over his lips. He wanted to take back the words: the dead deserved more reverence. But where had this new set of mores arisen from? They were inside him, he felt them, but he had never before been struck by such an intense shift in his own make-up; the change had sneaked up on him, caught him unawares.

A car's horn sounded; Valentine shook himself into action and turned onto Heathfield Road. The wheel was slippy in his hands now; he wiped a palm on his trouser-front, then repeated the action for the other hand. He was past the hospital and at the next set of lights before his thought-patterns turned inside the kaleidoscope his mind had become. It was a shape he recognised, like one from the Rorschach ink-blot test that the force psychologist had presented him with not so long ago. The fact that he identified the shape – where his mind had led him – was not a solution, however; it was more like another problem to add to the growing list that now worried him.

Valentine made a reach for his mobile phone and inserted it in the hands-free dock. It was an action designed to halt the runaway train of his thoughts. As the phone rang he made narrow apertures of his eyes in an effort to firm his concentration. He counted the drill of the line as the sun's waxy sheen painted a yellow reflection on the tarmac of the road; the call was answered on the fourth chime.

'King Street . . .' It was Jim Prentice, the desk sergeant. Valentine recognised the voice at once.

'Hello, Jim, son . . . How's tricks?'

'Oh, it's yourself . . . To what do we owe the pleasure?'

21

The DI smirked into the dash. 'Later, Jim . . . Tell me who Dino's got down at the tip site.'

A gruff clearing of the throat echoed down the line. 'The tip, oh Christ, that was some caper. Got the fellow on a plank, I hear, up the bloody arse as well.'

Valentine hoped the station foyer was empty. He grimaced uncomfortably as he replied, 'Aye, Jim, I've heard the details . . . Who's desking the bag-ups?'

'Hang on . . . What do you want that for?'

The car ahead started to move again. Valentine engaged the clutch, then the gears. 'Look, Jim, sorry pal, I thought I was talking to the desk sergeant. If they've shunted you up to divvy commander in the time I've been away, I'm very sorry.'

'Aye, very good . . . cheeky bloody swine!' An audible smile crept into his voice. 'I was only asking.'

'It's my case, Jim. Dino gave me it today, so if you can tell me who's been chalking up the scores so far, I'd appreciate it.'

Jim sighed, and the sound of a mouse clicking passed down the line. 'Looks like Big Paulo's there just now . . . Christ, he'll not be selling many ice creams on the tip!'

Chris Rossi was an Italian-Scot who had been fortunate, in Valentine's opinion, to have reached the rank of detective sergeant. He was not the only one on the force with that opinion, but the DS seemed to possess an extra layer of skin that helped him retard the endless jokes that had fallen under the politically correct brigade's radar; being Italian, it appeared, was fair game.

Valentine knew better than to bite. 'Is he on his own?'

'No, no . . . he's got three million flies with him.' The desk sergeant found himself hilarious. 'Jesus, a murder on the tip, eh? You've got to wonder about some folk.'

Valentine nodded sagely. 'What about herself, is she off?'

'Aye, oh aye . . . she'll no miss *EastEnders*, Bob!'

The traffic suddenly opened; a full lane had been freed up in the wake of a bus moving off. Valentine found himself racing through the gears on the way to the crime scene.

'Right, Jim, I'll catch you tomorrow morning . . . If Dino asks, I left a message for her an hour ago.'

'You bloody chancer!'

He hung up.

The entrance to Old Farm Road had been blocked off by two patrol cars, and uniform were already there behind a strip of blue and white tape that had twisted into a thin strand of rope with the wind. There were children patrolling the bournes of the cordon on bicycles and a scattering of women stood, backs on walls, arms folded. They were all blethering, passing comment on the goings-on. Valentine knew that if the murder hadn't already made the television news, it would be blazoned in headlines across the morning papers. The gravity of the event of murder was never wasted on him, but a bolt twisting in his gut told him this one was going to test him – and everyone – in ways that they had never been tested before.

The DI wound down his window and nodded to the uniform at the roadside. The PC seemed to do a double take when he caught sight of Valentine, like he was the first to greet Lazarus of Bethany. 'Sir . . .' He gulped the word, then steadied himself. 'I wasn't expecting . . .'

Valentine held up a hand. 'Just lift the tape, son.' He had no time for reunions.

As he drove towards the tip entrance he spotted the SOCOs' white tent, the officers in their spacesuit livery, and the usual hubbub of hangers-on and dicks-in-the-wind.

'God almighty . . .' He tried to locate DS Rossi, but the first to hove into view was the fiscal depute, then as he turned the car towards the crime scene he caught sight of the DS talking to DC McAlister and DS Donnelly.

Valentine stilled the engine and removed his sports coat from the front seat beside him. As he exited the vehicle he was approached by the fiscal.

'Bob . . .' He put a raised inflection on the word that made him sound like an Antipodean schoolgirl.

'Indeed I am.' Valentine walked past the fiscal, patting him on the shoulder. He muttered, 'Later, Col . . . when I've spoken to my lads.'

The first to approach the officer in charge was DS McAlister. He slit his eyes, then took two firm steps in the direction of DI Valentine.

'I heard you were joining us, but I didn't want to believe it.'

'Look, spare me the welcome party . . . What have we got?'

DS Rossi dismissed the white-suited SOCO and made for the newly formed enclave of officers gathering around Valentine like autograph-hunting boys on the gates of Somerset Park.

McAlister spoke. 'White male, late fifties and dead as dead gets.'

'Is that a medical opinion, Ally?' said Valentine.

'You could say that . . .' He tipped his head in the direction of the village. 'The doc's been and gone, by the way.'

'No surprise there, can't get a happy hour on the tip.'

Valentine took hold of a small cardboard box being held out by one of the SOCOs that contained clear-plastic gloves. He removed a pair and quickly snapped them, one after the other, onto his hands.

'I won't ask you to wear the blue slippers,' said the SOCO, waving a hand. 'Seems pointless in this mess.'

Valentine nodded, 'Right, lead the way.'

Rossi was just arriving as they took off again; he called at Valentine's back, 'Hello, sir.'

The DI suppressed a smirk at the thought of Jim's ice cream remark. 'Move your arse, Paulo!'

As the murder squad headed towards the white tent, the refuse crunched and squelched beneath their feet. An omnipresent hiss of flies followed with them. The group, almost in unison, raised their hands towards their mouths and noses as they walked through air gravid with pestilence.

'This is rank,' said Valentine. 'Almost makes you want one of those wee B&Q masks.' He pointed to the SOCOs up ahead.

'They're in short supply, apparently; we asked,' said McAlister.

'You are kidding me.'

'Wish I was.'

Valentine stopped in his tracks and turned to survey the crest of the rubbish mount that they were standing on like the advance party of some perverse colonial incursion. He pointed to the edge of the site, to a concrete wall. 'Where did our man come in?'

DS Donnelly spoke. 'Over there, side of the wall, got blood and fibres from the squeeze.'

'So what's that . . . a hundred metres?'

Donnelly flicked the pages of a spiral-bound notepad – the action shooed flies. 'One-sixty-odd.'

Valentine put himself between DS Donnelly and the view of the concrete wall; he widened his arms. 'That's a path – as the crow flies – of about three metres wide, yes?'

The remark was greeted with nods; his use of the Socratic method had triumphed. 'Right, Paulo, where are you?'

The DS pushed through the bodies, 'Here, boss.'

'Aye, I see you . . .' Valentine pointed to the wall. 'From there, in a direct line to the tent, I want everything.'

The team looked at each other, then back to the DI. McAlister spoke first. 'Are you saying you want it bagged, boss?'

'Do I have to say it twice?'

'But it's rubbish . . . piles of crap.'

Valentine shook his head, as the team stared at him he pointed to the ground and stamped his foot on the detritus. A cloud of grey dust erupted from beneath his shoe.

'Ally, this could be a goldmine of clues we're standing on, so get the lot of it bagged and stored and not another gripe out of you.' He pointed at Rossi. 'Paulo. You're the senior officer on here, why the hell have you not been bagging this?'

'Boss, the chief super will do her nut if she hears you've bagged that lot; do you know how much it'll cost? I mean in man-hours, never mind the storage.'

Valentine smiled; two neat chevrons appeared either side of his mouth. 'I couldn't care less about the cost.' He edged forward and fronted up to the assembled group. 'Do you know the only economics I care about?' He pointed to the tent. 'I care why a group of paid civil servants are standing in the middle of the local tip with a white tent pitched over a dead man . . . That is all I care about.'

Valentine stretched out for the tent; as he went, a dirty cloud of tip stour was released by his heavy footfalls. 'Come on, let's get a look at our victim.'

4

THERE WAS NOTHING TO indicate that the white tent, its sides fluttering like the sails of a pleasure boat, contained anything untoward. If the familiar ingress and exit of men in white bodysuits had not been relayed on television screens a thousand times before, no one would have had cause to be in the least squeamish at the sight of it. Granted, the fact that it was pitched in the midst of a rubbish tip was a surreal factor to consider, though no less incongruous than the flurry of soberly attired bodies clambering over the mounds of Sainsbury's carriers and an assortment of burst mattresses, empty paint tins and myriad plastic containers of household products.

The seagulls seemed to be the most interested in the hurried, ant-like formicating that was underway. They circled overhead, swooping occasionally; the bravest of them even set down and spread wings in proprietary fashion. They were arrogant birds, thought DI Bob Valentine, as he made to kick a king-sized one from his path. 'Flying rats.'

'They're bastards, aren't they?' said DS McAlister. 'Should see them down the shore flats where I stay – think they run the place!'

Valentine let the conversational gambit pass, but McAlister wasn't finished.

'See the roof of the baths, the Citadel, or whatever they're calling it these days . . . That's where they're nesting. If I was

27

on the council I'd be getting a squad of workies up there and burning them out.'

'Burning them out?' said DS Donnelly.

'Too right I would . . .'

Donnelly tipped back his head and laughed. 'What with, flame throwers?' He was still laughing as McAlister began his reply.

'Listen, mate, you don't have to live down there – the noise and the car covered in shit every morning – you can bloody well bet I'd be taking a flamethrower to them . . . I'd be bombing the bastards if I could.'

The conversation had taken on a combative tone. Valentine knew there was a danger of the ante being increased; if he didn't intervene, the seagull topic would become a boxing match between the DS and the DC that threatened to draw attention from the task at hand.

'Christ above, Ally, you truly regret missing out on 'Nam, don't you!'

Donnelly laughed and pointed at McAlister. 'Fancies himself as Chuck Norris.'

'More like Steven Seagull.' Valentine's remark was greeted with an instant burst of cruel laughter. It took him by surprise – he never thought of himself as that amusing, that much of a joker. 'All right, enough's enough.' He asserted his authority. 'Let's try and remember why we're here.'

The squad had reached the entrance to the tent. The front flaps had been secured with a loose knot, which always struck Valentine as wholly insufficient: a light breeze might raise the flaps and expose the contents to those who didn't want to know what was inside, or worse, reveal something to exactly the prying eyes that shouldn't see inside.

The DI reached for the knot.

'It's not pretty, sir,' said McAlister.

Valentine peered over his shoulder. 'When is it ever?'

As they walked into the tent the temperature was the first thing that the DI noticed; it was several degrees higher than he had expected, but at once he realised that the heat was compounded by the foetid air. The stench from the tip waste was intense inside the tent. The SOCOs had put up ultraviolet fly traps but they were ineffective against the plague proportions of insects packed beneath the canvas, which, though white on the outside, had accumulated great black patches of shifting swarms inside.

'It's got worse in here,' said Rossi.

'A statement of the bleedin' obvious,' said McAlister.

It didn't strike Valentine as at all unusual that not a single member of the squad had made any remark about the reason for them being there: the freshly mutilated corpse of a middle-aged man.

The DI was calm with the murder victim in sight. He couldn't explain this: for reasons he was utterly unable to fathom, the first sight of a body on his patch always intensified his obligation to the job. It was as if the mortal remains signalled to those nascent, adolescent parts of his nature, those first forays into near-adulthood that had called him to become a police officer. This was why he had joined up: not to spend all those years in uniform lifting drunks or wrestling with football hooligans – those were social problems, political failings – this murder victim symbolised an act of evil, a killing, and those who plied that kind of malevolence needed to be met by someone like Valentine. He was a born hunter: a finder of the sociopaths and psychopaths who had no place in a civilised world. Their capture, the removal of evil, was Valentine's reason for being – he knew this because his pulse quickened at the thought, every time.

'I'm thinking he's a stoat-the-ball,' said McAlister.

Valentine waited for another reaction from the squad, when none came he put forward his own. 'You think he's a paedophile because he's been impaled . . .' – he waved a hand towards the wooden shaft – 'like this.'

'Aye . . . up the arse.'

The DI straightened his back. 'Go on.'

McAlister seemed less sure of himself when tested, rocking on the balls of his feet. 'Well, from a motive point of view, if he was a stoat then a victim would want to, you know . . .'

'Return the favour in kind,' said Valentine.

'Stick it up his hole, boss.'

The DI let McAlister bask in his opinion for a moment, then dispossessed him of any illusion. 'I think you're just giving your mind a treat, son.' Valentine shook his head; his voice came firm and flat. 'That's a reach; you have not one iota of a fact to back it up with. Pure conjecture. Now, if you'd told me you'd ID'd him and he had a record for fiddling with kiddies I'd say you could be on to something, but a plank of wood up the crack does not a paedo make.'

The squad fell into a lulled silence; the sound of swarming flies filled the febrile air. Valentine knew the rest of the team would be reluctant to voice their opinions so freely now – if they were of the same calibre as McAlister's assumptions, then he was glad of that. He lowered himself onto his haunches and returned to the corpse before them. The mouth, its grey lips contorted, drew him; he removed a yellow pencil from his pocket, and with the eraser-end he pushed the lip towards the gumline. He stared for a moment and then extracted the pencil; the lip stayed in its new position with the gumline exposed. Valentine was uneasy with his incursion now; he seemed to have altered the expression of the corpse in a manner that seemed to heighten an already anguished appearance. He shook the pencil like a doctor with a mercury thermometer and then began to fervently rub the eraser-end in the crook of his elbow.

'We have no ID, I take it?' he said.

Donnelly spoke. 'No, boss . . . the SOCOs have printed and swabbed, but they were hanging off on the dental cast . . .'

Valentine cut in. 'Why?'

'Erm, they were waiting on the OK to move him.'

The DI shook his head. 'I want that done now, not tomorrow morning. Now. And I've seen him, so you can get on that right away.'

'Just hang fire there, Bob.' The fiscal depute was crouching under the tent flaps. 'You can't move this corpse until I have a death confirmation; come on now, you know the rules, not being one of the *tabula rasa*.' He applied a phoney horseshoe smile to his face as he stared down Valentine.

McAlister and Donnelly turned to eyeball the DI, anticipating a reaction. DS Chris Rossi started to speak. 'Colin, the . . .'

Valentine flagged him down and took a step towards the fiscal. 'Keep up, mate . . . Did you miss the episode of *Dr Finlay's Casebook* shot at Ayr tip this afternoon?'

'What?'

'The doc's been and gone . . .' Valentine turned to Rossi. 'Paulo, get him a death cert' faxed over, eh.'

'Yes, boss.'

The fiscal was left standing in the middle of the tent as Valentine headed out, the other officers following behind him in a linear formation, trying to keep pace with the DI's quick step. As he descended the mound of rubbish, Valentine grinned to himself at the thought of the fiscal – alone in the white tent with the bloodless corpse – then he turned to see him throwing back the tent flaps and hitting a jog.

Valentine allowed himself a discreet laugh as he widened his stride towards the car, content in the knowledge that he had exploded a myth Colin Scott held about himself. The fiscal was from the Castlehill council houses; his father had been a joiner who liked a drink in the Chase most nights and his mother was a nice wee woman who held house and home together cleaning offices. Valentine knew Col's type – he had been a bright boy in school who had grown up with the power to shock all the adults around him with his bursts of intelligence and occasional displays of knowledge. In adulthood he still felt that the carefully chosen octosyllable should afford him the same adulation, but he was mistaken. To Valentine it marked him as merely a pompous prick: the Scots had a phrase for dismissing those like Colin – 'I kent yer faither.'

Valentine pointed the key at the lock and the blinkers flickered; he was opening the driver's door as McAlister caught up.

'So, what's your guess, sir?'

'Haven't you learned a thing . . . ? I don't deal in guesses.'

The DI removed his sports coat and placed it on the passenger's seat; he was putting the keys in the ignition when McAlister spoke up again. 'OK, bad choice of wording . . . but you must have some ideas.'

'It's a single perp, our victim isn't a big lad or in any way fit, so one mid-build male could have handled him. Two would have made a cleaner job of squeezing the body through the gap in the wall . . .'

McAlister interrupted. 'So he was killed somewhere else?'

'I'd say so . . . The pathologist will confirm the time of death, but I don't think our killer would have wanted to attract

32

any more attention to himself when he already had the stake to hammer into the ground and the corpse to position on top of it.'

Valentine started the engine and engaged first gear. 'There's something else to consider: our victim's a married man, according to the ring on his finger, and he has some expensive-looking dental implants – not to mention those shoes that weren't picked up at the Barras . . .'

'So he's well off.'

'Well off, and in my experience that always means well connected. People like that don't end up on a tip with a great spike up their backside unless they've made a very big mistake somewhere along the line . . . and somebody else wants the world to know all about it.'

5

DI BOB VALENTINE KNEW that something wasn't sitting right with what he had just observed. It was a crime scene, a brutal murder, and nothing was supposed to sit right, but the information – the sights and sounds, even – were working on an altogether different part of him than usual. As he drove, a shrill chime started to emanate from the dashboard and he noticed the petrol gauge flashing. He had an instinct to curse, to slap the rim of the wheel, but he halted, held himself in check; the days of anger – either inwardly directed or outwardly expressed – were over. He couldn't risk elevating his blood pressure or pitching a spike in his stress levels: not now, certainly not now that CS Martin would be watching him so closely. And she would be watching very closely. There was a line from Burns – the Ayrshire bard – about what a gift it would be to see ourselves as others see us; it came to mind as Valentine drove. He had no desire to see, or even glimpse, how the chief super saw him. He knew what he made of her assessments, her opinions, and they mattered little to him. But in one very important regard her views did indeed matter: she had the ability to pass judgement on his future on the force.

Valentine had been questioning just that recently – his place on the force – and had found himself wanting. The desire was still there, but he had his inner detractors: the little devils on his shoulders that poked fun at him, told him he'd lost it, that he'd lost his bottle. After the incident he wondered if he had,

34

but more worryingly than that, he knew others – like Martin – worried also.

The car slowed as Valentine applied the brakes at the roundabout next to the old cattle market – it was a supermarket now, but he still referred to this end of the town as the old market. Most people did: it was still Auld Ayr to those who had connections with the place and it would take more than concrete to flatten the place it held in their imaginations. Valentine pulled up – there were three rows of cars now, nudging imperceptibly towards the nozzles on the forecourt. He remembered walking past the high walls of the market as a boy on his way into the town centre. Old images flashed by like he was unpacking long-lost photographs for the first time in decades. They were fond memories, they made him smile, but the act of memory was brief, short-lived. Valentine soon found himself replacing kindly thoughts with the harsher light of reality. His neatly stacked store of memories – the photographs he had piled high in his mind – was suddenly introduced to a gale-force wind and scattered.

A car's horn blared.

The detective engaged the clutch and slowly rolled the vehicle forward. As he got out the car, he resisted the desire to have a low word with the driver of the vehicle behind him – a man in his thirties wearing a Glasgow Rangers top and with a seething, petulant grimace above hands flagging aggressively towards Valentine. He knew the type, identified him straight away as one of the gruff Ayrshire lot – evenly balanced with a chip on each shoulder. They betrayed their true selves with the continually simmering rage that was a hair-trigger for a tirade, or even violence. They were common; the talking heads said their problem was a combination of a drink culture, poverty, a criminal subculture and west-coast genes . . . whatever they were. Valentine knew he had west-coast genes, but he was not one of their stripe: they were the unhappy, the let-down, the dissipated, the trapped, all bitter in the knowledge that their lot was their lot and nothing they did in this life would change it, ever.

The man still gesticulated; he pointed a finger at Valentine and mouthed words behind the windscreen that he couldn't hear but could definitely make out. To the others – McAlister and Donnelly, even Rossi – it would have been enough to see a warrant card flashed and a threat to have him locked up in the cells for the night, but Valentine had moved beyond those days. He had reached the stage of opting for the easy path – ignorance. If nothing else, it kept him from unnecessary conflict, and he was all for that.

On the road out to Maisonhill, the sun's fading light bounced off the rooftops and clouds began slow white trails across the blue sky. The last dregs of commuter traffic hissed by as Valentine drove, his eyes focussed on the road but his thoughts intent on other matters. Ayr, the town, was dying. What had once been a bustling centre of activity had fallen into decline. Boarded-up shops and crumbling, derelict buildings lined the periphery, their paintwork peeling, windows shuttered, a fresh canvas for graffiti artists. From the Sandgate, at the foot of the High Street, the ruins marched, stopped occasionally by a branded charity chain or a new pound store. There was no inward investment, nothing to restore pride or even alleviate the wounds of recession. Ayr was moribund – an historic township on its knees, coughing and wheezing as it entered its death throes. It would only take one more high-profile store closure – a big name like Marks & Spencer perhaps – to deliver the *coup de grâce* and see Burns's Country turned into a ghetto populated by zombified drug addicts and an underclass of the impecunious and hopeless. It was pathetic, in the true sense of the word, thought Valentine; he felt nothing but the deepest pity for Ayr and its inhabitants, and a growing shame to count himself amongst their number.

The detective massaged the back of his neck as he worked the wheel with the other hand, but the action provided little benefit. Soon the window was wound down, and then to follow it, the radio turned on, then off again.

'Christ al-bloody-mighty . . .'

He was allowing his thoughts to play tag. And he knew why.

As Valentine pulled into his driveway, he killed the engine and sat listening to the components cooling beneath the bonnet. He inhaled deep breaths but resisted a glance towards the front window. He became momentarily, dimly aware of a figure in the front room, but he refused to acknowledge it.

The sound of the seatbelt being pulled into the inertia reel jolted the detective, pressed the fact that he was home – Chloe and Fiona would be in there, and also Clare. He opened the door of the car and eased himself out. It was still warm, perhaps even warmer outside than inside the car. Valentine tugged the knot of his tie free and loosened off the top button of his shirt as he moved to the back door of the vehicle to retrieve his case and folders. The dark patch on the back seat stared out at him as he lifted the items and for a moment it held his attention. He stared at the marked fabric, the blotch of ingrained staining – no scrubbing or chemical wonder-product had been able to shift it. Why not? He knew what it was – where it had come from, the black mark the size of his head he carried everywhere with him now – surely it should have been removable. At least, by this time, shouldn't it have faded?

'Bob . . . Are you coming in?' It was Clare.

'Yes, of course. Just picking up a few files.' He slammed the car door and directed the key ring, which locked the vehicle with one click.

'What are those?' Her tone was pitched higher.

As Valentine turned towards the house, he caught his wife's stare full on. There was no hiding the fact that he was carrying case notes; she recognised the familiar blue files, knew he had been to King Street station. He halted where he stood, brought the folders up to his chest and dipped his chin towards the rim. 'Well . . .'

He didn't get any more words out. Clare turned from him. He watched her blonde hair flounce off her shoulders, catching a momentary tail of sunlight, and then she was gone. The front door of his home stood open wide and the long, carpeted corridor lay in darkness, a clear, untrammelled route but not a welcoming one. Valentine's shoulders tensed. For a moment he stood unmoving, like he had been carved from stone, and then he turned his head towards the sun-warmed street and shook himself.

Inside the house, Clare sat on one of the kitchen's bar stools with a long cigarette in her fingers. She seemed content to ignore her husband, staring out into the garden through the open window as he walked in and placed his case and folders on the worktop. He watched her for a moment as she poked the inside of her cheek with the tip of her tongue – her angry gesture – and then he reached out for the cigarette.

'Come on, you don't need that.'

Clare recoiled quickly. Her eyes burned like match tips. 'Just bloody leave it!'

Valentine watched as his wife jerked away the cigarette and showered the distance between them with a trail of amber sparks from the burning tip.

'OK . . . It's only you I'm thinking about.'

She huffed loudly, rolling her eyes towards the ceiling. 'Is it really?'

Valentine squinted towards her. It was quite a performance from Clare; he'd been deprived of the petulant turns of late and her sudden return to form was a shock. 'I don't get it.'

She rose. 'No, you don't, that's for sure and certain.'

Valentine recognised the fact that he had walked into one of Clare's ambushes now. It didn't matter what he said, or how he said it, almost certainly it would be the wrong thing. In their battles she had covered the entire house with lethal tripwires and he knew when he had sprung one. He didn't want to upset Clare either, he was grateful for how she had acted these last few months, but the return to their familiar routine now felt like everything they had been through was for nothing.

'Clare, I have a job to do . . .'

She bit. 'Not that job.' She dangled the cigarette over the blue folders; her voice quivered above the jumble of words. 'You said after what happened you'd be . . . what was it? Put out to grass!'

Valentine watched his wife paint on a knowing smile; two sharp arrow-tips appeared either side of her mouth. It was the look she wore when pointing out that she had outsmarted her husband, outmanoeuvred him. It was the glib look of a smart-arse, the kind of expression that, outside of the immediate family, no one would contemplate trying on him.

'I do what I'm told, Clare.' The reply was weak, and he regretted it the second it came out. What was worse, however, was that it was a blatant lie and he knew that Clare would see that.

She exhaled a long trail of smoke and started to stub the

cigarette in the ashtray. Valentine waited for some kind of rebuttal, but none came, and that was worse. Clare knew when the situation had gone beyond words because the silence said so much more.

'Clare . . .' As he spoke, the mobile phone in Valentine's pocket started to ring. He ignored it for a moment. 'Clare . . .' His wife started to move away from him as he looked at the caller ID. 'I'm sorry, I have to get this.'

Clare steadied herself on the rim of the sink and looked out towards the garden. She bit down on her lower lip for a moment and then began to speak. 'I was an idiot to think anything had changed.'

Valentine watched his wife walk from the kitchen and close the door behind her; it bounced loudly off the jamb and swung open again.

In a second or two, Chloe's head popped from the living room. She glanced at the blue folders. 'Oh, back to work!'

Valentine gave a weak wave to his daughter, then retrieved the swinging door and enclosed himself in the kitchen. He pressed a green button on his ringing phone and spoke. 'Hello, boss.'

'Well?' the chief super's voice came shrilly down the line.

'White male, middle to upper, with a serious grudge against him.'

'ID?'

'No, not yet anyway . . .'

She cut in. 'Why no ID?'

'Well, I'd say it's in the post . . . Expensive dental that will be somebody's handiwork.'

Valentine heard the chief super shuffle the phone into her other hand. A television set was blaring. He smiled to himself as he remembered Jim's *EastEnders* remark.

'Have you picked anything else up?'

'Yeah.' He slapped the back of his neck for effect. 'Enough fly bites to last me this lifetime.'

'Stick to the case, Bob.'

'I'll know more tomorrow, when we do the post-mortem.'

Another interruption. 'Christ's sake, why's that not being done tonight?'

'The usual reasons . . . personnel.'

'Well, put your foot in that pathologist's bloody arse!'

'It's not the pathologist, it's his team . . . They won't be with us until first thing. After that we'll be rolling.'

'Is there nothing sticking out?'

'Apart from the dirty great plank, you mean?' Valentine regretted the incursion into humour: CS Martin didn't posses a sense of humour.

'I'm glad you seem to be enjoying yourself so much since I've brought you back onto the squad, Bob . . . I think you and I should have a little chat before you start enjoying yourself a wee bit too much.'

Valentine's facial muscles conspired to form a scowl. 'Meaning?'

She snapped, 'Meaning make your way to my office first light tomorrow morning before you do another bloody thing.'

'But I have the post-mortem first thing . . . in Glasgow.'

'Send Paulo. Be at my desk for nine.'

'Yes, boss.'

He said the words but no one heard them; she had hung up.

6

As VALENTINE WALKED around the mutilated corpse of the murder victim, he had the strangest feeling that he should be elsewhere. He remembered agreeing to meet the chief super, but the pressing urge to take one last look at the crime scene had supplanted that instruction. There was a heat inside his chest that shouldn't have been there, a pressure that sent his heart rate racing. For a moment he looked around for somewhere to rest, to take the strain off his body weight, but there was nowhere. The flies had gone now. He didn't know where, or care. It was dark, too. Night-time.

Valentine started to run fingers nervously through his hair. He heard his throat wheezing and then his state of self-absorption exploded. 'Who the hell let the child into the crime scene?'

The detective felt like steel had been tipped in his spine as he pushed aside the assembled mass of milling bodies. He saw the child, a small girl of maybe five or six years old, in a bright red duffel coat. She was blonde, that pale-to-white colour like Fiona's and Chloe's had been, and was dancing around inside the SOCOs' white tent like it was a kiddies' playground.

'Paulo, who let the bloody kid in?'

Valentine felt eyes burning into him; they seemed to think he was the one that had the problem. No one seemed in the least bit bothered about the little girl. It made him wonder if they had been struck blind and dumb; was he alone in sensing the deeply inappropriate nature of the situation? It was hard to imagine a more unsettling scene – and he had seen a dog mauling at the guts of a day-old corpse that was riddled with wounds.

'Get her out of here! Get her away from that body!'

The child was laughing, smiling. She had been picking daisies and held a bunch of them in her hand. She was a sweet wee thing – a cutie, his wife would say – but she should have been away feeding the ducks or picking out a sweetie for herself; not here, not anywhere near here.

'Hey, hey . . .' He was being ignored. His indignation lit, his nostrils flared – he expected the reek of the tip's mouldering refuse, but instead he smelled flowers, daisies. 'What are you doing here?'

There were too many people, too many officers and uniform, too many SOCOs. They were all trespassing on his crime scene. He was the officer in charge, but his authority was being ignored. The detective lunged out, reached for the girl that no one else seemed to have even noticed. Valentine was caught by his arms and shoulders; he was held back.

'Get off me . . .' He started to lash out. 'Get your bloody hands off me!'

The girl giggled. She watched the others holding Valentine back as he shouted out. He could still see her; she had bright-blue eyes that burned into him. Was she familiar to him? He didn't think so, but she seemed to recognise him. It was all a game to her.

'Get off me . . . Get the girl. She's playing round the corpse.'

The little girl stood over the murder victim and for a moment Valentine caught her expression change. She looked unhappy now. He knew it was wrong; he didn't want the girl to see the dead body, the blood. He wanted to pick her up and take her away, back to her parents, but he couldn't move. His thoughts mashed; ideas of right and wrong collided with a surging, torrential anger as he was held back.

'Get away!' He lashed out with his arms. He just wanted to help the little girl. 'Get away! Get away!'

He was flailing, his heart pounding hard against the inside of his ribcage.

'Bob.'

Valentine heard his name called and the little girl slipped out of view. He saw her bunch of daisies resting on the corpse's chest, left there like a memorial to the dead, like the child had completed a bizarre but completely innocent ritual only she understood.

'Bob . . .'

He recognised the voice now. When he saw Clare's face, the arms constricting him let go. He pushed forward with the release and then the picture changed.

'Clare . . .' He was at home, sitting upright in bed.

'Jesus, you were screaming.'

'What?' He felt lost, even though he knew exactly where he was.

Clare sat up and turned on the bedside lamp. 'It must have been a dream.'

'No, it wasn't a dream . . .'

She touched his back. 'You're absolutely soaking wet.'

Valentine turned away, draped his legs over the side of the bed and lowered his head into his hands. His hair was stuck to his brow.

'I don't know what the hell that was, but it wasn't a dream . . .'

'What was it, then? A nightmare?'

Valentine turned towards Clare. His mind was still full of the images of the little girl. He knew if he held his eyes tight shut he'd see her again, but he was too scared to do so.

44

'It wasn't that either. I was there. I was somewhere else.'

Clare made a sly smile and squinted at her husband. 'Get back to sleep, Bob.'

'I'm not kidding you, Clare. There was this girl . . .'

'Oh, yes . . .'

'No, a little girl. Like five or something. She had white hair, like the girls had at that age, and she was . . .'

Clare started to rub at her bare shoulders. 'She was what?'

'I – I don't know . . . Just, she had flowers and was putting them on my murder victim.'

The mention of the case signalled a shift in Clare's attentiveness. She turned away from Valentine and reached for the lamp. 'Get some sleep, Bob.'

As the light went out, Valentine rose from the side of the bed and made his way towards the bathroom. The brightness of the main light hurt his eyes, but in a moment he steadied himself against the cool tiles of the wall and drew deep breaths. His heart was returning to a normal rhythm now. As he opened his eyes he saw himself in the bathroom mirror. His irises were lined in red; dark shadows sat in pockets beneath them. As he removed his sweat-soaked T-shirt, his eyes were drawn towards the thick ridge of scar tissue that sat in the centre of his chest. He never liked to touch the mark – it didn't feel like a part of him – but he allowed his fingertips to dab at the edges of the fatty tissue that surrounded the scar.

'Oh, Jesus . . .'

Valentine wondered what was happening to him. He felt like he had been given another chance at life, but he doubted whether he deserved it. Why would he be given another chance at life? What had he done to receive that great gift? He thought about Clare and how she had begged him to leave the force, to take a desk job – administration, pencil-pushing, it didn't matter. She knew he was lucky to be alive and she didn't want to take the chance on losing him again.

Valentine started to run the cold tap and, slowly, to douse the back of his neck with water. The first splash made him shiver, and a few beads escaped down the side of his chest and flanked the scar that kept grabbing his gaze. He didn't want to look in the mirror, but this alien object that signified a new right to life demanded his attention.

He picked up the hand towel and dried himself down. As his breathing eased into a slow, steady rhythm, he reached for the light switch and clicked it to off, then he began to move back towards the bedroom and his wife. He knew he needed to attempt some type of explanation, to give Clare some reason as to why he had changed his mind, why he had gone back on everything he had told her he would do.

The bedroom was in blackness; only the orange fizz of the street lamps burned beyond the strips of blinds. He lowered himself down on the edge of the bed and placed a hand on Clare's bare back. She murmured for a moment and then patted his side of the bed.

'Clare, I need to talk to you . . .'

'Tomorrow. I need to sleep.'

'It's important.'

'Can't it wait?'

Valentine got into the bed and drew up the duvet. 'I'm not doing this for me.'

'Doing what?'

'Taking on this case . . . I can't explain it.'

'Well, good. We can talk tomorrow.'

Valentine reached over to turn on the bedside light; Clare grumbled and sat up.

'Right you have my attention, can we get this over with?'

'About earlier, when you saw the case files, I knew you wouldn't be pleased.'

She tutted. 'And you knew why.'

'Clare, please, I'm trying to explain ... I feel like I've changed, been through some kind of life crisis after ...'

'It was a crisis all right, you nearly died, Bob! Jesus Christ, you nearly left me a widow and ...' She looked away.

Valentine's emotional-response signal flared. 'And who'd have cleared your Visa bills then ... Was that what you were going to say?'

He watched his wife raise a hand to her thinned lips. 'That's not what I was going to say at all.'

'I'm sorry. That was a low blow.'

Clare looked towards the ceiling and shook her head. 'I couldn't tell you when I last bought a thing.'

Valentine sighed. 'I don't want to bring that up again ...' He ran his fingers through his wet hair and turned away from Clare. 'I'm just not myself at the moment.'

'You're bloody right you're not. I don't understand you any more, I used to think I did. I look at you now and I ...'

He interrupted. 'You just don't see where I'm coming from. I feel I have this new chance and that I should make a difference. I can't properly explain it, Clare, I feel like a different man.'

Clare put her head in her hands. She held herself on the edge of the bed for a moment and then she turned to face her husband. 'Well, you're certainly that. You just look through me and the girls now. There was a time when you wouldn't have put us second best to some vague notion or late-flush of ambition ...' She met his gaze for a second but couldn't hold it. 'Oh, just forget it. Forget everything.' Clare reclined in the bed, turned over and switched off the light.

As the darkness of the room enveloped Valentine, his spirit shrivelled inside him. He thought about reaching out and touching his wife's bare shoulder, saying sorry again and trying to talk. But he didn't want to be rebuffed. He lay down on the bed and closed his eyes, but knew sleep was going to be hard to find in his current state of mind.

7

VALENTINE ARRIVED AT King Street station before the early shift had sorted itself out. He saw the youngish bloke who sometimes filled in for Jim behind the frosted glass, but he avoided eye contact. The bloke was one of those he didn't know but who would definitely know him, or of him. It was becoming tiresome being a kent face. Valentine caught the desk sergeant grabbing a sly stare – he likely wondered what he was doing there – but he held himself in check and kept to his early morning rituals of shuffling papers and pinning up rotas.

On the stairs, Valentine thought about the rest of the murder squad. They would now be heading up the A77 on their way to the morgue in Glasgow – to the dead place. Under normal circumstances, Valentine could take or leave a visit to the morgue but today would have traded places with any one of them. Of course, he didn't like the accompaniments of the trip – the place seeped into the very fibre of your clothes and hair and colleagues came to sense it on you. A few liked to remark on the observation, but he could never understand the fascination that people who dealt with the dead every day had about an exaggerated storage facility. There were no souls stirring in the air; the dead did not sit up and speak or reveal their secrets.

In the canteen, Valentine paused with his finger over the button for black coffee, removed it, and selected white tea.

If he was being honest about his tastes the caffeine would have been more welcome, but he knew his nerves would soon be tested enough by Chief Superintendent Marion Martin. He took his tea, his case notes and briefcase, and made for the corner of the large, open room. The tea was hot but not scalding. He rested the styrofoam cup on the lip of the folder and watched as his fingers commenced an involuntary tattoo on the tabletop.

The detective's synapses were sparking with a familiar preoccupation now: he despised the games people played with their lives – never talking the truth to power – always toeing the line, even if it meant suffering for it. His meeting with Dino would be a farce, he knew that too. It would play to a script because that's what the world dictated of such scenarios. We were all slaves, and few of us contented; knowing it made him no better than the rest of the world. We all shuffled into the corner when the light of authority shone on us. Just once Valentine wanted to be in an assured position: to be able to speak his mind cleanly and clearly and know that the consequences mattered not an iota. It was all a dream, of course – even those who had the chance to speak up, the retirees and the escapees, they held back for fear of perhaps losing the gold watch and the Fraser's hamper that the wife was so chuffed with. The exchange that awaited him now would be no different. He was old enough and experienced enough to know that he was more likely to get the outcome he desired by playing dumb. Power liked dumb: it meant pliable and he was all for that – he would be as pliable as putty to get his way.

'Bob . . .' His name came uttered under breath. As Valentine looked up he saw the chief super stationed at the door with her coat slung over her shoulder, a broad flank and hip pointing in his direction; it was a look Mae West might have worn had she missed her calling and wound up a scrubber of floors.

'Oh, hello.' He rose from behind the table and collected his possessions. A sliver of grey liquid evacuated from the rim of the white cup as he raised his tea.

'Leave it, Bob, I've some good stuff in my office.' The wink she tailed off her remark with seemed wholly unnecessary to Valentine – unless the intention was to see him fetch up his last meal.

He smiled – deeply ironically – and followed in the chief super's wake; she stretched out with a purposeful stride that looked strong enough to rip the carpet from its fixings. Valentine swallowed a threatened laugh that a sudden cartoon image pressed on his mind of her tearing the place apart like a spinning Tasmanian devil. Was she really so macho, he wondered. Did she go home at night to wrestle with her children and blast tirades at the football results on the television? He didn't know why he was suddenly so concerned with the person beneath the veneer, though he had a sneaking suspicion that it was all part of the same broader reassessment he was making of life. These patinas of familiarity were being excoriated daily.

'Shut the door, Bob,' said the chief super. She walked over to the window. A jug kettle sat on top of a small filing cabinet. She raised the kettle, shook to test its water content, then pressed down the red button. 'Coffee or tea?'

Valentine lowered his briefcase beside the chair in front of the chief super's desk. 'Tea's good for me, thanks.' He didn't really want a drink; he wanted the rigmarole over with. He wanted away from the cold, clinical office that didn't contain a breath of life between its walls. He wanted to stride down to his incident room and get to work on the case – to find out

51

who the poor sod with the expensive dentistry and the large stick up his backside was. But he knew it was never going to be that simple. The chief super wanted to put him through the mill, she wanted to test his mettle – perhaps for no other reason than she could and the simple act of the assessing would, as a direct consequence, assert her authority.

'So how's Clare?' she said. It seemed a standard opener, a starter for ten.

'Fine, all good, thanks.' His voice sounded like someone else's to him. His words were of the sort of slippery dinner-party patois that he despised.

'She'll be glad to have you in one piece, I suppose . . .'

He smiled, reaching over to collect his cup of tea. She droned on, something about the girls – she didn't know their names – and how it must have been a terrible shock. She used the words 'terrible shock' like their father receiving a cold blade in the heart had been no more than another day at the office.

'Fifty pints of blood . . .' She jerked herself back in the chair, retrieved the note from the file she was reading. 'That can't be right, surely?'

Valentine worried at the handle of his cup; it was hot, too hot for his fingertips. He placed the cup on the desk as he looked at the chief super. 'It was fifty, yes.'

'Jesus Christ . . . How many pints are in the human body?'

'I'm not sure . . . Eight, I think.'

She leaned forward, peering over the bridge of her nose as she spoke. Her voice was a shrill whine that echoed off the walls in ways that suggested she knew how to play the acoustics to their best effect.

'I can't believe they gave you fifty pints of blood, Bob . . . Fifty! There wouldn't be any of your own blood left in you after that, then.'

52

Valentine scratched behind his ear, shuffled in his seat uncomfortably. He had spent so long reliving the trauma that it had taken concerted effort to shift the images from his mind – but here they were again.

'What there was of my own blood ended up on the operating-room floor.'

The chief super tipped her head cockily to the side. 'Must have been black pudding on the menu that night, eh?'

She began a laugh that mounted a full-scale assault on Valentine's senses. He watched her meaty shoulders quaking under her already broad shoulder pads and something like pity for her lack of compassion entered his consciousness. He wanted to tell her that he had been stabbed in the heart, in the line of duty; it was not any source of amusement to him or his family. The pain of recall was nothing compared to the event, yet the prolonged agonies of its aftermath – the tears he had watched his wife and girls shed – were something he would never be greeting in even the remotest neighbourhood of laughter.

She continued to read from the notes: 'Left ventricle stab wound from below, through diaphragm. Angiography on arrival at A&E, followed by thoracotomy ... Oh my God, this is just horrific reading, Bob ... Thick-walled ventricle contracted and closed the hole.... Heart-lung bypass for repair ...'

She put down the notes and made an apse of her fingers. Had she somehow imagined that reading the medical notes embayed her with the honorific of doctor? The sudden shift in her sense of self-import suggested it. If she had been wearing glasses, thought Valentine, she would have removed them for effect.

'And how are you now?'

It took all Valentine's girded composure to resist firing a burst of mocking laughter in her face. The detective raised his open palms, weighed the air. His thoughts had been scattered like the contents of an upturned bin. 'Right as rain.'

'Come on, don't play the bullshitter with me. You took a knife in the heart, on the job . . . You officially died, at least twice from what I can make out.'

'I'm here now.'

She picked up her cup of tea and sipped at it. The liquid vanished like rainwater in a gurgling gutter. The taste didn't seem to agree with her; she replaced the cup on the desk.

'I can see that. What I'm getting at is, how much of the old Bob have I got here in front of me?'

He cut in. 'And how much was lost?' He leaned forward, balancing the point of his index finger on the rim of her desk. 'And how much of the old Bob was left on the operating table, is that what you're getting at? None. Let me tell you that for once and for all. None. I am here in one piece and raring to go.'

The chief super ran her tongue over the front of her teeth. Thoughts were queuing behind her green eyes. Valentine read the thoughts as easily as if they had been displayed in a PowerPoint presentation. She was going by the book, making sure she had done her due diligence. If there had been any other option available to her then he would still be at Tulliallan teaching new recruits how to lace their shoes and she wouldn't be worrying about the possibility of drafting in officers from another force to work her patch.

She rubbed at the bridge of her nose and slowly shook her head from side to side as she returned to the file in front of her. 'It says here you had some psychotherapy.'

'I was stabbed in the heart; they're not going to let me back on the force without looking at my head.'

The chief super's cheeks flushed; they looked like plumped cushions as she exhaled a long, distilled breath. 'It might be an idea to keep the therapy up for your return to active duty.'

'I don't think it's necessary.'

'I didn't ask if you thought it was, Bob . . . I'm telling you it's coming and you're going to jump at it with both hands if you want to handle this investigation.'

Valentine reclined in his chair. There was a reply on his lips, but he swallowed it.

'Good,' said the chief super. 'We'll see how you go with this. Any signs of stress, I want to know about it, do you hear me?'

'Yes, boss.'

She closed the folder, returned it to the inside drawer on her desk and flagged Valentine towards the door.

'Get yourself into the incident room and brief your team.'

'Most of them are at the post-mortem this morning, but I'll need to brief the others . . . and the press office.'

She blinked her eyes towards the ceiling tiles. 'Oh God, yes. I do not want to have the media jumping up and down about this today. Give them nothing . . . no, less than nothing.'

'That's all we have at present.'

Valentine reached out for the door handle, and as he grabbed it the chief super called out.

'Oh, Bob, what did he get for the stabbing . . . ? Young Darren Hainey, wasn't it . . .'

'What do you think he got . . . ? A slap on the wrist with a feather.'

8

DETECTIVE INSPECTOR Bob Valentine's jaw tightened as he walked from the chief super's office; his teeth would be grinding next. He knew there were good reasons for him not to play up the emotions he was feeling – the strain it placed on his heart, that hard-pressed, overused and badly damaged muscle, was one good reason – but he also knew he had never been very good at containing his anger. It was as if there was nowhere for it to go; once created, the anger had to find an outlet, like the letting of a valve on the side of a dam – you didn't turn the handle and expect to keep your shoes dry. He was not an angry man, he knew that much about himself; he had once been called proud and didn't understand what was meant by that. He was proud of his job, his position, that was a fact, and when he examined his inner workings it was always this fact that seemed to be beneath most of his problems. But Valentine was getting older now and his physical diminution was a consideration he had to examine more closely. Dealing with Chief Superintendent Marion Martin suddenly felt like an unnecessary and unwelcome weight to add to the load he was pushing uphill. Throwing him under the watch of a psychotherapist was a low blow, though; anyone in his position would have objected to that, he told himself.

Valentine halted mid-stride and checked his watch, tapped the face. As he tried to clear his thoughts and assess what he needed to do – more than bemoan his boss – he thinned his eyes into tiny slits. One of the civilian staff passed by and glanced his way; he felt his skin prickling as he made a poor attempt at a smile. He gripped tight to the handle of his briefcase and walked on. The diversion of the everyday seemed to free him from the tangle of angry thorns he'd taken from Martin's office, but he knew there were still one or two sticking in him. It had not been a good start to his return to active policing.

The incident room was bare. Valentine strolled between the rows of tables towards the broad window that looked out onto the town of Ayr, collecting the view like a postcard. Amethyst clouds sat high above the rooftops, and a white chalk line from a passing aeroplane dissected the cumulus into two distinct camps: those drifting to and those drifting from the horizon. The detective felt a sickening turn of his guts as he followed the pull of familiar sights: Wallace Tower was where he remembered it, the vast carbuncle that was the multistorey car park still stuck out and the King Street bus stop was stacked full of dafties and druggies from the nearby flats. He felt like he had never been away.

He didn't know how long he'd been staring out the window, hands in pockets, just contemplating the day and his duties when the heavy doors clattered off the top wall and two female PCs giggled their way into view. He didn't like the peace of his incident room being disturbed at the best of times, but today was not the day to test his better nature.

The two young officers seemed wholly unaware of his presence at the other end of the room. Valentine felt invisible as he watched them dislodging photographs from the blue folders in their arms. They laid the pictures out – as they'd obviously been told to do by the SOCOs – but something about the manner in which they went about the duty sent the red mist swirling inside Valentine's mind once more. He walked slowly over to the young girls; neither noticed him, and that surprised him because he felt like there was steam emitting from his ears and nostrils.

'Big Rab knows what you're like after that night in the Treehouse,' said the taller of the two. She was clearly the more recessive, because the other one had a sharper line in riposte.

'Bugger off . . . That's the last time I take you howking for men!'

Valentine managed to bring himself within their ambit without either of them noticing him. He raised himself on his toes for a moment or two, scanning the pictures of the crime scene – close-ups of the victim's facial contusions and wider shots taking in the sweep of the landfill site. They were colour photographs, they spared no detail and yet their content had failed to derail the women's pub chatter. There was a time and a place for everything, and Valentine knew the time had come for the girls to meet their new boss.

He folded his arms and made a deeply guttural noise that might have been taken for throat clearing by an imbecile, but to anyone with a modicum of intelligence it yelled trouble.

'Oh.' The taller of the two spoke first; she had the decency to appear embarrassed.

The other officer fronted it out, painting a wide smile on her face and presenting an open hand to shake. 'Hello, sir, I'm Kirsty Duchar.'

Valentine kept his eyes on the PC, then lowered his gaze towards her hand and spoke. 'Do you believe in miracles?'

The girl's smile faltered, slackened a little. She kept her hand out, directed towards the detective, but a few seconds more and she would be in the avenue of looking very silly.

'Winged horses ... angels ... alien intervention in human affairs?' said Valentine.

The smile dropped off her face completely. 'I–I ...' the proffered hand began to tremble a little. Her head stayed front, but her gaze lunged towards her friend as if she was begging for help.

Valentine kept still; his voice was low and calm but backed with a confidence that boomed like a marching band. 'Because you've as much chance of seeing any of those in here as me remembering your name, love. By the end of today this room will be chock-full of uniforms like yours, and if we're here next week you can think of another number and double it.'

He unfolded his arms, placed one hand in his pocket and with his other he gently lowered the PC's outstretched arm. 'I'll call you "love" or "dear" if I'm in good fettle ...' He paused and glanced at the other girl – she had her gaze fixed firmly on her shoes. 'If I'm not in good fettle I'll call you what I bloody well like and you can bet that'll not be something you'd like to repeat to your granny.'

He raised his head, but kept his steely gaze on the pair of them. He appraised them for what they were – a pair of daft lassies. He had been young and daft himself, it wasn't a crime, but this was a police force and he was conducting a murder investigation. There were far too many new recruits who saw the job as a stepping stone to middle management; they spent a few years on the force to make their CVs look interesting. Valentine had nothing against people bettering themselves, he had nothing against ambition, but he had everything against wet-nursing other people's children through the adult world he lived in. The job required more diligence, more respect, and if that wasn't made clear from the outset then some painful shocks were likely to be had along the road.

'I'm a moody bastard, in case you hadn't guessed,' he said. 'And the mood between me calling you "love" and calling you out is me pointing to the coffee machine and expecting you to read my mind.'

He pointed to the coffee machine.

The officers turned away and started to disassemble the filter from the coffee jug.

'Milk, one sugar,' said Valentine.

'Yes, sir.'

As he walked around the table the detective ignored the flurry of activity, but was grateful for the lack of bawdy conversation. He'd set the tone; he knew they'd call him a bastard for it, but they'd think twice about trivialising his investigation. If they had any nous, he thought, they might even think about what they were there for in the first place.

Valentine leafed through the photographs from the crime scene. The first one to strike him was of the victim's face – the expression he wore looked different from how the detective remembered him. It was strange, he seemed almost contented, but it was the camera playing tricks. The next picture was a close-up of the main entry wound – it would take a perverse mind to be contented by a wooden spike inserted where the sun didn't shine, he thought.

'Jesus Christ.' He took the pictures and started to tack them to the noticeboard.

'Your coffee, sir.'

'Put it on the table.'

The girl retreated, looked as deferential as a punkah wallah. The image poked at Valentine for a moment, but there was no retreating from his earlier stance now; that would merely make a mockery of him and what he had said. He raised the cup of coffee and placed it to his lips; it was warm and welcome.

DC McAlister was the first of the officers to show, sauntering through the door and nodding to Valentine. 'Morning, sir.' He moved towards the table and picked up a paper cup. 'Coffee, nice one.'

Valentine turned back to the board and started to loosen off his collar. 'What are your thoughts today, Ally?'

The DC laughed. 'Oh, no . . . Caught me with that already. Not making any guesses.'

Valentine smirked. 'How's the sweep-up going?'

'They got the lion's share of the tip bagged last night, take a wee while for them to sift through it . . . You know Dino's going to do her nut when she hears about that.'

'Leave her to me.' Valentine lowered his cup. 'I'm the one calling the shots. How many uniforms have you got sifting through the rubbish?'

'Plenty, about twenty at least.'

'Double it.'

'What, sir?'

The DI tilted his head towards McAlister. 'You're not going to make me ask you twice, are you?'

'No, sir.' He placed the paper cup on the table and reached for the telephone. As he spoke into the receiver, Valentine returned to the folder containing the photographs and looked for the accompanying paperwork.

There was a list of items that the SOCOs' photographer had seen fit to draw attention to: scrapes on the wall of the tip; red markings that may have been blood on a sheet of corrugated iron; a fresh splinter of wood that had detached from the wooden stake. He matched the list to the pictures and tacked them to the wall.

McAlister raised the paper cup to his lips and nodded approvingly. 'That blood splatter's in for testing.'

'Know it's blood, do you?'

'Looks like it.' He took another swig from the coffee cup, then altered his voice to a more matter-of-fact tone. 'Right, that's the Stigs' Department doubled.'

Valentine smirked. 'Tell me about the door-to-door last night.'

McAlister sighed. 'Well, it didn't turn up much. There was a white van in the locus around 9 p.m. and . . .' He put down his cup again and removed a spiral-bound notepad from his jacket pocket. 'Yeah, around 9 p.m. and it was seen again about 9.30-ish. It could have been a delivery – y'know, no one in and he's leaving it with a neighbour.'

Valentine scrunched his brows. 'At 9 p.m. . . . . working late for a delivery man. Did anyone get a number plate?'

McAlister shook his head.

'Nobody ever does,' said Valentine. 'Right. Check it out, check if anyone on the street got anything delivered, or a tradesman called between 9 and 9.30. You know the drill.'

'Way ahead of you, sir. Got uniform on that this morning. Got the whole area gridded off and being checked.'

'Good.' Valentine knew they were searching for the slightest lead, anything. A chance encounter, a strange-looking manoeuvre in the street, just something that stuck out as unusual and could be examined more closely. This was the vital time: the chances of solving the case depended on the information that came in during the first forty-eight hours. After that, clues withered, got washed away, and singularly human traits like memory and waning interest came into play.

Valentine and McAlister were returning to the folders when there was a thud on the swing doors of the incident room and a rush of movement sent a gale to upend the paperwork.

'Do you want the good news or the bad?' It was the chief

super, marching towards them as the doors passed each other in an out-of-sync motion that caused a chain of jarring, clattering collisions.

Valentine sensed McAlister turning towards him, but he looked away at the quick-stepping chief super.

'What do you mean?' he said.

'ID on your corpse from the tip.' She spat the information in a staccato burst. 'Oh, and you'll love this as well . . . he's a banker wanker!'

Valentine let himself pause for breath, for a moment to digest the sudden turn of events. As he watched the chief super draw up to within inches of his stance, he became aware of her heady perfume. He didn't like the scent, it was overpowering. 'And the bad news?'

She reached out and flicked Valentine's tie. 'You'll need to smarten yourself up . . . The news hounds are on the sniff.'

9

IT WAS ONE OF THOSE strange, seemingly disconnected groupings that the human mind made. Since the winter months – these two years past – Valentine had known his home in Ayr's Maisonhill needed a new boiler. It wasn't a consideration, something he just fancied: it was a necessity. The boiler broke down, repeatedly. In the summer months it wasn't too much trouble, but in the winter it was a disaster. He recalled the first time that it had broken down he had received a quote of several thousand pounds to replace it and he'd decided to delay. It wasn't that he couldn't afford the outlay, as such; it was about choice. He chose to let the girls go on their school holidays instead, and he chose to pay off Clare's store cards and spiralling Visa debts. It was about this time, he recalled, watching a banker on *Newsnight* trying to justify his CEO's £20 million pay packet while at once handing redundancy notices to ten thousand office staff. The hypocrisy struck him as breathtaking, yet to the banker it was all in a day's work.

Valentine felt the same anger surge in him again now – but it seemed to be suffused with a stronger charge. He knew he was balancing his lot against that of others, and that was never a wise move: there were always better and worse off; the process of comparison only made you bitter or egotistical. He could see, however, he envied no one. It was one particular issue that galled him: what was 'all in a day's work' for that banker? He conceded he didn't know, but he doubted it came close to wrestling with junkies, delivering late-night death knocks, retrieving decapitated heads from bramble-strewn side roads (as he had done), or being knifed in the heart by a little scrote who wanted to make a name for himself.

It irritated Valentine that he had to postpone a replacement boiler for his home while earning his keep in an honest and honourable fashion. It gored him deeper that there were others who needed to place no consideration on their spending while at the same time foreclosing on the livelihoods of thousands. As he rolled over these thoughts, the detective had an urge to laugh out. He resisted, but only because he knew the joke was on him. He was bemused by his repeated indignation at the world's injustice.

'When was it never thus?' he said.

'What's that, sir?' DC McAlister glanced over from the driver's side of the car.

'Nothing . . . Just thinking aloud.' Valentine closed the blue folder that was sitting on his knee and rested his elbow on the window's edge. The road out to Alloway was quiet, only the odd 4x4 on the way back from the school run. He remembered when the girls were younger, how he would catch them counting the Ayr number plates whenever they were on the road out to Alloway. The scenery certainly changed the closer you got to the big houses.

'Did you catch the look on Dino's face when she came in with the news . . . ? Thought she'd nabbed a string of sausages.'

Valentine removed his face from the breeze blowing in from the window. Outside, the sun was a dull copper penny being bullied from the sky by bulky rain clouds. 'That'll be short-lived, knowing her.'

McAlister stole a glance at the DI. 'Yeah, she's rarely pleased for long.'

'I mean if you think this is going to be an open-and-shut case, you're deluded. It's never simple where money's involved.'

McAlister rounded the bend at Alloway Church and depressed the clutch as he took a lower gear. 'At least we have an ID.'

Valentine sneered over the brim of his nose. 'We've a report of a missing person who fits the bill – let's wait and see if the family formally identify him.'

McAlister over-revved the engine and then managed to grind the gears; he was shamed enough to look embarrassed. 'Sorry, boss . . .'

'Don't worry about it, I think we've already drawn enough attention to ourselves driving a mere Ford around here.'

'Yeah, it's Beemer country.'

The officers drove past the small, thatched cottage that had once been the home of the poet Robert Burns and had since been transformed into a tourist attraction. The stone walls were painted white and a large plaque sat above the door. To the rear was a decorative garden and a large gift shop. A car park sat to the side, where touring coaches dislodged day-trippers close to a kiosk with the price of entry on a turnstile.

'You should know there's money in muck, Ally.'

'Yeah, well, we see enough of it . . . Muck, that is.'

'Not the money, that's for sure; look at the size of these houses.'

The normal procedure of planning regulations seemed to have been abandoned, with red-brick mansions sitting next to slope-roofed nods to modernism. Valentine knew he was entering another world to the one he inhabited, and the discomfort he carried in his gut about the case started to make itself known again. He rolled up the window and returned to the blue folder to read the notes that had been hurriedly printed off before he left the station. If this was their victim, then he was called James Urquhart and had been a former head of a stockbroker's that had been bought out by the Bank of Scotland before the financial crash of 2008. He hadn't hung about to get cosy with the new company but had opted for early retirement. The notes didn't say much more, but the grainy photograph that had been taken from the Internet was a definite likeness for the man Valentine had seen at the tip with a spike in him.

The car started to decelerate as they turned into Monument Road.

'Right, I think this is us, sir.'

The driveway was gated, and as the car slowed to a halt McAlister leaned out from his window to press the intercom button – but the gates were already in motion.

'Bingo, we're in,' he said.

The car's tyres scrunched over the gravel as the pair rolled up the long drive towards the mansion house.

'Looks like they gave him a hefty payout,' said Valentine.

'Come again?'

'Urquhart was the boss of a stockbroker's that was bought out three months before the crash.'

'Lucky timing.'

'Yeah, very.'

As they reached the end of the driveway, a youth in jeans and a T-shirt waved them to a side entrance. The pair parked up behind a Range Rover that looked to have been abandoned after braking heavily in the loose chippings.

Valentine was first from the police vehicle; he strode round the front of the car and nodded to the young man. The detective watched the youth dig his hands into his pockets and raise his shoulders awkwardly. He didn't make eye contact, but Valentine was close enough to see the pitted declivities that bordered his hairline in a sad echo of once-rampant acne.

'Hello, I'm Detective Inspector Bob Valentine and this is my colleague Detective Constable McAlister.'

The pair were greeted with a nod but no introduction.

Valentine resisted the usual politesse in favour of a more direct approach. 'And you would be?'

'Adrian.' He removed his hands from his pockets and brought them together across his chest, pressing a thumb into the flat of his palm.

'Urquhart?'

He nodded. 'My mum's inside.'

Valentine raised a hand towards the door and started to walk. The wind was picking up and thin, dark rain clouds scythed the sky. The home was airy; some muddy footprints that looked like they had come from Wellington boots covered the floor, but everywhere else was neat and tidy. Adrian ushered the police officers through to the lounge and directed them towards his mother, who was sitting next to a ruddy-cheeked man with his arm around her shoulder. As the officers were introduced to the man called Ronnie, he removed his arm and leaned back in the sofa.

Valentine approached the pair, which prompted Ronnie to distance himself further. 'I'll leave you be,' he said, rising and turning to face Mrs Urquhart. 'I'll drop in again later. Just to see how you are.'

She nodded and sucked in her lower lip.

Valentine kept his eyes on Ronnie; he thought about engaging with him but decided it wasn't the time or place. As the neighbour hurried out the door, Mrs Urquhart made to stand, but her balance didn't seem to be functioning – she flounced onto the sofa's arm and Adrian ran to her side to support her.

'It's OK, there's no need to get up, Mrs Urquhart,' said Valentine. He watched her steady herself on the couch once more: her face was saturnine, the droop of heavy eyelids accentuated by dark hollows above the cheekbones. A prominent white crease dissected her brow with almost clinical precision and then erased itself as black irises gave way to an expanse of white, rimmed in red. As she took in Valentine, he felt her searching stare: it was a look that spoke to you without words; it was such a knowing look that Valentine wondered if his own thoughts were as discernible as the pages of a book to her.

He shifted himself sideways, sat down on the adjacent seat and crossed his legs. 'Hello, Mrs Urquhart.'

'Hello . . .' She had the look of someone whose life had been a trial of hurts: not broken, or ever defeated, but a woman who had known considerable miseries and had grown to live with secrets.

'I believe you called the station . . .'

She nodded. 'Yes.'

'Can you tell me when you first became aware that your husband was missing?'

Adrian squeezed his mother's hand. 'I think it must have been sometime yesterday afternoon.'

'I take it Mr Urquhart has never been missing like this before?'

'No. Never.'

Valentine cast a glance at McAlister, who was walking around the room. 'You will be aware of the television news bulletin.'

Mrs Urquhart nodded again, she scrunched up her eyes as she spoke. 'Yes.'

Valentine shuffled uneasily on the chair, the woman was in no fit state for questioning, but it was one of those moments where the demands of the job overrode etiquette. He lowered his voice. 'I have to ask you, are you capable of making an identification?'

She looked towards her son and buried her head in his chest.

Adrian spoke. 'Can I do that?'

Valentine's mouth widened, but he didn't have time to answer.

'No. No. I'll do it, detective,' said Mrs Urquhart.

Valentine rose from the chair and beckoned to McAlister. It was pointless pressing her: very little of any value could be obtained from someone in such a profound state of mourning. There was a prominent thought impressing itself upon Valentine's mind, though: most murder victims knew their killers. She might indeed be in shock, but her gut reactions would be difficult to fake.

'Mrs Urquhart, if I may ask just one question before we progress . . .' The DI paused for a moment. 'Can you think of anyone who would have a cause to harm your husband?'

Mrs Urquhart looked to her son and then turned on the detectives with steel in her eyes. 'No, no one.' Her cut-glass vowels seemed even sharper now. 'Why . . . why would anyone want to do such a thing?'

10

ON HIS RETURN TO King Street station, Detective Inspector Bob Valentine collected a stack of notes from the front desk of the incident room and retreated to the glass-partitioned end to be alone with his thoughts. He was haunted by the look on Mrs Urquhart's face as she had taken in the growing realisation that her husband was not coming home. No matter how many times Valentine saw the look – and it was the familiar look of death visiting – he could not adjust himself to it. He remembered what it had been like to see his mother on her deathbed. She was still, and the almost imperceptible taking of breath signalled a closer proximity to death than he had ever encountered. All previous introductions had been impersonal – random incidents didn't count, he soon realised – not like this. When he saw his mother, held to life by a pin, the sudden realisation of mortality, of finite time, entered his own life. It wasn't that Valentine hadn't always known about death – not at all – he had, and that made his altogether new consciousness the more palpable. Seeing his mother encircled by death made him realise he didn't know a thing about the end of life. All his assumptions were trite, unthinking, unfelt. He could no more express in words the true gravity of death than he could put the ebbing life back into his mother.

To see someone he loved dying, to know they were going to leave him for ever, had marked death as permanent in his own existence for the first time. Valentine sensed the cold shift immediately. He never wanted death to be a personal matter again, because it was all too personal as it was. He knew the only way to continue living was to ignore all notion of a personal death: it could happen any minute of any day, be all around you in every form of hurt and misery, but the trick was to ignore it, to sublimate it. For the mass of people this was possible almost without thought, but to Valentine – who was surrounded by death – it took conscious effort. He knew he had to obliterate death, before it obliterated him.

The detective turned over the cover of the blue folder that he had positioned in the middle of his desk and stared at the first page. The post-mortem report was not a voluminous document; it always surprised him how little information the ending of a life seemed to generate. He ignored the contents section and scanned quickly over the succeeding pages, which detailed the procedures of the pathologist. For a moment he had a vision of the morgue in Glasgow's Saltmarket area – he saw the murder squad stationed around the corpse of James Urquhart, their looks of dour solemnity and the perplexed impatience with the type of jargon that was used to determine the cause of death.

Valentine turned the pages and scanned to the section where conclusions, of a sort, were made. He had tried to prejudge the pathologist's outcome; in his gut he felt that the victim had been killed a certain way – the scene of the crime suggested much of his assumption – but Valentine knew better than to jump to conclusions.

The first term to attract his attention was 'traumatic brain injury'. There had been a depressed skull fracture, the result of blunt force. More detail was given: acute subdural haematoma, cerebral contusions, dramatically increased intracranial pressure. They were all terms familiar to the DI, terms he classed as necessary evils, but they all mounted up to the same thing in his book: James Urquhart had been hit on the head by someone who wanted him dead.

Valentine was hunched at his desk, poring over the pathology report when the hinges on the door called out and DS Rossi and DS Donnelly walked in.

'Sir . . .' Donnelly was the first to acknowledge the officer in charge.

'Come in, lads.' He turned over the final page of the report and closed the blue folder. 'Just going over the post-mortem.'

Rossi nodded. 'Hammer or a crowbar . . . something like that.'

'Well, it was pretty clear it wasn't done out at the tip. There wasn't enough blood . . . or anyone picking up on a struggle on the boundary street.'

'He wasn't alive when he was squeezed through that fence, that's for sure,' said Donnelly.

Valentine placed his fingers on the rim of the desk and slowly pushed the wheels of his chair back. He was talking as he rose and walked over to the window. 'There's no evidence of a struggle, not so much as a fingernail scraping . . .'

'Not one, no battle scars at all, sir.' Rossi kept his eyes on the DI. 'So he's been whacked and then moved . . . But why to the tip?'

Donnelly folded his arms, then quickly removed one to illustrate his speech with wild, looping gestures. 'That's a message for somebody right there, Rossi. The tip's where the rubbish goes; he's been dumped there because someone wants the world to know exactly what they thought of James Urquhart.'

Valentine's thoughts were building to a fog inside his head. He had been content to sift through the facts in the report, to analyse and to draw his own conclusions. He felt now like he was being sidetracked by the officers – it was as if he had set out for a leisurely stroll and the sudden incursion into his office had resulted in a cross-country run.

'OK, OK . . . Let's keep the party clean. We don't know the first thing about this victim yet, we can't be jumping to the conclusion that the place we found him is a marker to his murderer's state of mind.'

Donnelly flared up. 'But it's an option, boss.'

Valentine nodded, allowed a slight indicator of doubt to play on his face, and then delivered a puncture to the DS's ego. 'It's one option, I'll give you that: our killer might indeed have thought his victim to be trash. But, he might have thought the exact opposite. We don't know what the hell he was thinking. Keep to what we can confirm, Donnelly. The options are endless at this stage . . . our killer might have thought the worst about Urquhart, or the best, or any one of a million other perceptions you could list. Just because you can put options on a list, it doesn't validate a single bloody one of them.'

Donnelly rubbed at the stubble on his chin and clamped his jaw tight. He didn't seem to have any more to add to the debate at present. He looked deflated, like a boy who had kicked a football further than he had ever done before and had expected to be rewarded for his skill – despite having broken a window in the process.

Valentine needed to rally his troops. 'You're right about one thing though, Phil . . .' Donnelly's head lifted as he eyed the DI. 'We need to keep our options open. At this stage, all ideas are worth investigating.'

The remark seemed to be enough balm to cover Donnelly's pride. 'Yes, sir.'

'Right, I think it's time we put our heads together,' said

Valentine. 'Paulo . . . Get Ally and the team together round the board. I want to talk to them in ten minutes.'

DS Rossi pinched his cheeks as if he was about to exhale lavishly. 'I think Ally's upstairs at the press office, there was something said about a statement.' He shrugged his shoulders and levelled a palm at Donnelly.

'Search me,' said DS Donnelly. 'That boy's a law unto himself.'

Valentine made a circular motion with his index finger at the side of his ear. 'If he thinks he's going to be standing in front of a camera this afternoon, he's dreaming . . . You can tell him from me if he's any ambitions on that front then he better be preparing to streak down King Street.'

DS Rossi and DS Donnelly took their cue to laugh up their colleague and exited the DI's office.

When he was alone again, Valentine returned to the blue folder and opened up the front cover. There was an ancillary section that detailed a few more findings from the post-mortem examination. The detective always felt like a voyeur reading these medical records of the deceased, but they had the advantage of embaying a level of familiarity he found useful in bringing him closer to understanding – if not bonding with – the deceased.

James Urquhart had been suffering from cardiomyopathy, according to the report. His arteries were blocked and there was evidence on his heart of previous cardiac arrest. On reading about the victim's diseased heart, Valentine felt a cold shadow pass through him. He had read so many doctors' and surgeons' reports about his own heart that it was almost impossible not to feel a deep, visceral identification with the case notes. Was it sympathy, he wondered, and if it was, then for whom: Urquhart or himself?

He closed the folder and leaned back from his desk. Since the stabbing, the DI had been forced to alter many aspects of his life. His morning ritual now entailed taking a multitude of prescription medicines – tablets in various shapes, sizes and colours – to keep him alive. That itself wasn't the issue, he could cope with that, it was the way his life had been restructured that bothered him. Each pill taken was a fresh reminder that he was a different man from the one he had been before the stabbing. He felt different inside and he knew that on the outside it showed too. Clare had said it only the night before and it riled him again now. Even the chief super had remarked – as early as this morning – that there couldn't have been much left of him after the surgery. Perhaps more than any statement, or observation, that remark had wounded the most. But why? Was it because he knew it was true or because he resented giving Dino credit for having any insight, especially insight into himself?

Valentine drew back into the moment, removed himself from the claustrophobia of thought, and immediately turned his gaze on the two fingers he was rubbing against the shirt pocket on his chest. Was he checking his heartbeat? Trying to massage sympathy into the damaged muscle? As soon as he became cognizant of his actions the detective jerked his hand away and rose from the desk.

'Christ above,' he muttered, wiping at the edges of his mouth. He knew he'd come dangerously close to losing focus and that worried him, perhaps more than anything else.

He looked out towards the incident room: the team were gathering.

11

As Valentine closed the door on the partitioned office in the corner of the incident room, he saw the doors at the far end swing open. There was a flourish of long dark hair and a thudding of high heels that came backed with such force they still registered solidly even on carpet tiles. Here was an Ayrshire heifer – all beef to the heels – stampeding into his midst. As the detective stared at Chief Superintendent Marion Martin, he observed a numbness in his throat that he knew was caused by the automatic locking of his jaws. She stomped through the mass of bodies with all the grace of a bulldozer and made straight towards the noticeboard where Donnelly stood with a photograph in hand. As the chief super halted, she dropped her barely perceptible chin onto her fleshy neck and swiped the picture from Donnelly's outstretched fingers. She started to speak as she waved the photo like a baby's rattle in the DS's face, but Valentine couldn't hear her words – it was not that they weren't audible, more the fact that he seemed to be blocking her utterances out. He had seen the chief super carry on like this before; she came into investigations and stood in the corner like a headmaster who'd come to oversee a less experienced teacher. It wasn't on, he thought. There was a part of Valentine that she stoked like a blast furnace; he was tempted to tap her on the shoulder and ask what the hell she thought she was doing, but he had met her type before and knew the drill.

In Ayrshire, there was a breed of woman that showed themselves up in any crowd by a singular trait: combativeness. They were beyond gruff, verging on bellicose, and there was no getting around them with politesse, put-downs or any of the many options in between. There was no sweet-talking – because that in itself was mere incitement to them – they couldn't be buttered up; swayed by cajoling; manoeuvred into a more amenable frame of mind; be influenced by facts or reasoning; or by showing the glass as half-full and not half-empty. They were beyond all that, beyond all help, all intervention. Their *raison d'être* was to spark up – or, to be more exact, to find an excuse to spark up. It didn't matter what the instigation had been – the object was to be seen as someone who, with the slightest provocation, would lunge into tirades. It was like a self-defence mechanism, a variant strain of the get-your-retaliation-in-first philosophy that had its roots in innate insecurity. It had been this way for decades, centuries likely. It was inter-generational. A blight on the region. A plague no less. In Glasgow, just a few miles inland, it didn't exist. They had hard-faced women, but they possessed humour. The Ayrshire type, being earthier, closer to the soil, had no redeeming features and Chief Superintendent Marion Martin could have been their standard bearer.

Valentine pressed his tongue on the roof of his mouth and tried to release his locked jaws. He could sense the familiar copper taste that precipitated anger; it was enough to alert him to the off switch. As he walked, he put his hands in his pockets and tried to remind himself that he had a bigger aim than playing office politics with Dino. If she wanted to sit in on his briefing then she was entitled, if somewhat less than welcome; he just wouldn't be affording her a front row seat.

'Right, everybody.' He made sure his voice was heard. 'Can I have your undivided attention?'

There was a rustle of paper; a filing cabinet drawer was closed loudly and a ringing telephone cut off by dumping the receiver on a desktop.

'Well, I'm not shouting to the four corners of the station, so you can gather round here.'

As the squad started to assemble, the detective leaned towards DC McAlister and laid a hand on his shoulder. He kept his voice low as he leaned towards him. 'Ally, what did uniform turn up on the delivery van?'

McAlister shook his head from side to side. 'Not good, boss. No deliveries in the locus and no tradesmen uncovered on the door-to-door.'

Valentine huffed. 'So we can rule our white-van man out as a potential to move the case forward.'

'Unless we turn up another lead, I can't see how the van's useful to us.' McAlister turned his gaze towards the board. 'Might have been nothing, sir.'

Valentine patted the DC on the back and moved with the rest of the room's occupants as they gravitated towards its centre. The chief super was left out on the periphery of the group, by the noticeboard, holding the photograph she had snatched from DS Donnelly. Valentine was keenly aware of her displeasure at being dispossessed of cynosure status; from the corner of his eye he watched her suck in her cheeks and drop the picture on the desktop. She folded her arms as the others booked their front-row seats.

'OK, you'll all have seen the pictures and the SOCOs' reports – for what they're worth – by now. The post-mortem report is on my desk through there and you can have a shufti at that if you haven't already. I'm not going to try to prejudge anyone's opinion at this stage; what I want is to make sure we're all singing from the same hymn sheet and make sure we're all aware of our role . . . understood?'

Together: 'Yes, sir.'

'Good,' said Valentine, edging himself onto the side of a desk, taking the collected gaze of the squad with him. 'So what are we looking at? A brutal, almost ritualistic murder on public ground – if not carried out there, certainly the intention was to make people think so – and of a figure who might be described as privileged, perhaps . . . extremely wealthy, certainly.' He halted, drew breath. 'A point in fact: our victim's social status will be a bone of contention with the media – bear that in mind.'

A hand went up in the middle of the crowd. 'Are you approaching this from a financial perspective, sir?'

The DI shrugged. 'We don't have a motive at this stage, but am I willing to explore blackmail or a monetary grudge . . . maybe even resentment or jealousy? Yes, of course . . . I want everyone to keep their minds open. This is not the time to be jumping to conclusions, but it's also not the time to be ruling anything out.'

DC McAlister leaned forward in his seat and held up a pencil. 'If it's related to cash, then why the impaling, boss? Seems a bit . . . unusual.'

Valentine smiled at McAlister. 'Good point. It's unusual all right, unless it's a distraction . . . Make it look like a psycho-killing because you want to draw attention from the fact that the motive is money.'

'They could be linked, though,' said DS Donnelly. 'I mean, say the motive is money but also a grudge.'

'You mean murder's not enough to settle a grudge?' said the DI.

'What I mean is, say our killer wanted to do more than settle a score, say they wanted to pour shame on the victim.'

'Or their memory . . . or the entire family for that matter. Good point, Phil.'

Valentine felt like the focus of the team's attention; he could tell by the way they sat forward in their seats, on the edges of desks that they were as engrossed in the task as he was – and that they wanted to engage. In contrast, the chief super seemed to be uninterested. She stood leaning on the edge of the wall, arms still folded and long earrings swaying in time with her shifting eyes. She seemed to have had enough.

'Right, I don't think I need to be around for this . . .'

Valentine drew his eyeline level with hers. 'Come again?'

She pushed herself away from the wall and stood square footed. 'I'm off.' She turned for the door. 'But I'll see you in my office when you're done, Bob.'

The DI followed the line of her steps for a few seconds, then returned to the group, without answering the chief super.

'OK, I'm glad you're keeping your minds open. Let's recap then: a ritualistic impaling, on public ground, of a wealthy banker. Where do we start? A grudge, maybe . . . Given the nature of the victim, possibly financial. Given the nature of the execution, possibly sexual or an attempt to make it look that way. I want you all to start thinking about James Urquhart in three-dimensional terms. Who was he? What did others think of him? And what had he done?'

DS Rossi lifted a blue folder. 'Boss, the firm he worked for was the subject of a buyout . . . we should be looking into that.'

Valentine nodded. 'You take that, Paulo. Let me know what it turns up. I want to know who was for it, who was against it. If there was a significant benefactor or, more importantly, a significant loser . . . I want to know their inside-leg measurement.'

'Yes, sir.'

'And, Phil, I want you to dig even deeper into Urquhart's business history: was there an affair? A disgruntled partner, maybe? If there was bad blood between an employee or a client or a bloody delivery boy that didn't like the look of him, I want to know what they had for breakfast the day Urquhart copped it.'

'OK, boss.'

Valentine pressed his palms together; he exerted enough pressure to feel his shoulder muscles flexing. 'Ally, you and I will talk to the victim's next of kin; we've already made contact so they know our faces, but I want you to go beyond that: find out what Urquhart did with himself . . . Did he belong to any clubs? Play cards on a Saturday night or go out on the pish? Was he passionate about anything?'

'Maybe he was in a cult, sir?' said DS McAlister. 'One that put spikes up your arse.'

A low hum of laughter passed around the room.

Valentine kept his face firm and pointed at the DS. 'You're joking, Ally, but you never know. Check him out, thoroughly . . . and talk to his neighbours, all of them. Not just the ones he lives beside now, but if he lived anywhere else. And talk to his colleagues, are there any that he's kept in touch with? All of them, Ally . . .'

'Yes, sir.'

The detective started to punch at his open palm with a fist. He could feel the energy spreading throughout the incident room. There was a moment at the outset of every case where the team took up the challenge, and he felt it now. If they were lucky, some of them would return with salient facts, leads that could be pursued. Valentine caught the wave of spreading energy and turned towards the group.

'Right, get on with it. Anything that you turn up, I want to see it straight away. However insignificant you think it is, I want to know. If you can't get hold of me then go to Ally or Phil ... or in emergencies, Paulo! Though you'd have to be bloody desperate to do that.'

Ally aimed a weak punch at DS Rossi's arm; he brushed it away.

'Only messing, Chris,' said Valentine. He clapped his hands together. 'Right, get to work.'

12

SOME PEOPLE WENT THROUGH life hoarding misfortunes. They collected gripes and let-downs like stamps and delighted in displaying them as testament to their hard treatment from an oppressive universe. These were Valentine's worst kind of people – they caused him the most trouble – and they were everywhere. A cleaner rarely rated her station and could be the most difficult to deal with – a freshly mopped floor was a minefield you could dare to cross, but you would encounter the explosion of a lifetime's worth of contempt for authority if you dared. In the wider world it was no different – Chief Superintendent Marion Martin had such an extensive cache of grudges that they had grown arms and legs, become sentient and now bore grudges of their own. A venomous strafe from one of her inner army was never far away – the whole point of which being to subjugate her opponent, to defeat through superior firepower and restore a fractured pride.

It was pathetic and it was draining, thought Valentine. When he looked back on his career he could count numerous occasions where bitter and vindictive types – for no logical reason beyond their own fragile self-esteem – had simply deposited their dumper-truck loads of grief on his doorstep. They weren't happy with their place in the world, their colleague had a bigger office with more rubber plants, or their neighbour had a newer car with a higher spec and a leather interior. Perhaps their sister married a more successful man, or that girl they used to go clubbing with in their teens had popped up on Facebook, inflaming an old slight about imperfect teenage skin. The situation, the cause, didn't matter. It was the effect that Valentine was forced to deal with: the consequence of a world full of neurotic drones who were too consumed by their own sense of lack to ever consider what they were doing to those around them.

Valentine smiled to himself as he went over the markers that the chief super dropped about her state of mind. None of her solar flares could be avoided. The workplace was always a forced union of opposites, a crucible for the embittered, and he knew he had to be on guard lest the collective malaise enveloped him. It was just another daily difficulty to be navigated, an unpredictable chore. Like encountering road works on your regular route home, it was a sapping reminder of the imperfections of this life. But Valentine also knew like attracted like – the bastards got theirs in the end – their problems weren't his, even though they came his way from time to time. He had the last laugh because there were others like him too: he knew them well. They might be a minority, but they existed, and that in itself was enough of a thorn in the side of those like the chief super.

He clattered his knuckles off the wooden door, just shy of the brass nameplate, and walked in. 'You wanted to see me?'

The chief super was sitting behind her desk, the chair in full recline, her stockinged feet balanced on the brim of a blue folder. In her hands was a copy of a paperback book, grey and glossy – Valentine couldn't be sure, because she quickly buried the book in her lap, but it looked like *Fifty Shades of Grey*.

'What the bloody hell are you doing breenging in here leaving Desperate Dan shapes in my door?' She swung her feet down from the edge of the desk and lunged forward on her elbows. The sound of the book landing on the floor was unmistakeable, but she ignored it.

Valentine's stomach fluttered and the muscles of his neck constricted as he pulled back his head. 'If it's not a good time . . .'

She was rattled, her mouth cinching into a tight little knot and her eyes forcing a dart between her brows. 'Shut up and sit down.' She raked her fingers through her hair and then grabbed at the edges of her scalp and started to rock her skull to and fro like an angry wasp was trapped inside her head.

Valentine casually withdrew the seat in front of the desk and sat down. He crossed his legs and made a point of straightening the crease of his trouser leg. He let his eyes rove around the room while the chief super clawed a blue folder towards her.

'I can come back if you'd prefer,' he said. The remark was a prod for her.

She pointed to the chair he sat in. 'Stay put . . .' As she turned the pages in the blue folder, her index finger bounced on the table. Valentine noticed how scalloped and short her fingernails were. They'd been bitten to the flesh in a manner normally reserved for adolescents. 'Right . . . here we are.' She seemed to be calculating something; he imagined she normally counted on her fingers but was trying to appear wise before him. 'Perhaps you can tell me why I have a lab chit here requesting I facilitate storage for half a ton of bloody rubbish?'

Valentine held firm, he kept his eyes locked with the chief super's. 'I'm investigating a murder scene.'

CS Martin turned over the folder and slapped the desk. 'You put forty uniforms on this, Bob? Forty?'

'I didn't count the exact number, but if you say so . . .'

She pushed herself away from the desk and the castors of her chair sung out. 'Oh, I do say so . . . Forty officers bagging Mars bar wrappers and empty Persil packets on time-and-a-half – does that sound like a good spend of budget, Bob?'

He brought his fist up to his mouth and cleared his throat into it. 'Like I said, I'm investigating—'

He was cut off. 'Yes, I heard you the first time.' The chief super tipped back her neck, stared at the ceiling for a moment and then swung forward, balancing her elbows on the desktop. She was pointing at Valentine as she spoke. 'You better hope some vital piece of evidence emerges from this midden that we're creating downstairs, Bob, because if it's not I'll be calling you on a very grave error of judgement.'

Valentine folded his hands and started to play with his wedding ring. He was being belittled for no good reason other than the chief super's egocentricities; the net result – he told himself – would be the opposite of what she expected. He would continue to carry out his duties in the same manner; carpeting over the costs of preserving a high-profile murder scene was as pointless as it was embarrassing.

'Is that everything?' he said.

'No, it's bloody not.' She reached out for the blue folder again, raked it towards her and started to turn pages over. 'I'm warning you now, Bob, don't think about testing my patience. You won't win and your coat's already hung on a slack hook, remember that.' As she spoke, she scanned the contents of the page she had alighted upon. Her tone seemed to harden as she changed tack. 'Right, what does the name Cameron Sinclair say to you?'

The detective raised his eyebrows. 'Bit pretentious giving a kid two surnames.'

Her tone rose. Her eyes burned. 'Does it ring any bells, Bob?'

'Should it?'

She released the folder like it was a piece of litter and sat back in her chair. 'He's a hack . . . works for the *Glasgow-Sun*.'

'Not one I've run across before.'

'Aye, well, I'd like you to run across this wee bastard now . . .' Her words trailed off into vehemence.

'What's he done?'

The chief super started to swing her seat from side to side. 'It's not that he's done anything . . . but if you can find something, that'd be bloody useful.' She seemed to regret revealing her inner thoughts and lurched forward in the chair once more. 'Cameron Sinclair has been badgering the press office about our latest stiff.'

'Well, I haven't released any information yet and neither has anyone on the squad.'

'Well, he's been calling a few people, and a few people have been calling me.'

'Like who?'

She turned down the corners of her mouth. 'People, Bob . . . people.' She let the implication of her words hang in the air between them.

Valentine allowed a pause to enter his thoughts. 'The murder scene is on the edge of the tip, there's public housing a street away, and we've got a team of SOCOs with a white tent pitched out there . . .'

She cut in. 'All right, no need to draw me a bloody picture. I don't care if this Sinclair character has got a tip-off from Joe Public, what I'm more concerned about is if he has an inside track.'

Valentine closed his mouth and breathed out slowly through

his nostrils. He resented the implication that she was making but it was just the kind of thing he'd come to expect of the chief super. He watched her crease her eyes at him and knew that his own stare was a notch above threatening, but didn't bother to alter it. He felt the arm of the chair on the palm of his hand and gripped it tightly beneath the desk. Valentine knew if he was the first to speak then he would relinquish too much ground: it was a classic stand-off.

'Be it on the squad, or elsewhere.' She had to add the 'elsewhere' to get herself out of the bind she'd created.

'I'm not responsible for the entire west coast of Scotland, but no one on my squad talks to the press without my authority and at this stage no one has been given authority.'

CS Martin made a half-smile. 'All right, Bob, don't give yourself a heart attack.'

It was a low blow, but she was all about the low blows.

'If the cat's out the bag, I think we should call a press conference,' said Valentine.

'Oh you do, do you?'

'It would seem the smart thing to do, don't you think?'

Her mouth shut like a zipper, then sprung open again. 'As ever, Bob, I'm one step ahead of you ... I've called a press briefing and you're fronting it up ...' – she looked at her wristwatch – 'in forty-five minutes.'

The response the chief super would have expected, Valentine knew, was complaint.

'Brilliant,' he said. 'I'll tie in with the media department then.'

As he rose from the chair, Valentine delivered the widest smile he could muster and then made a brief, almost mocking, salute before exiting the office.

In the hallway he started grinding his teeth – it wasn't

that he resented being spoken to like a third-rate moron, or the ridiculous assumption that Martin was in possession of superhuman policing prowess, it was the grim realisation that this was in fact his situation. Valentine understood that he was the officer of last resort – she hadn't wanted to give the case to him – but he now saw that she clearly thought he would live up to her expectations.

As he walked back into the incident room, Valentine knew his sense of pride was pushing to the fore. He wanted to prove the chief super wrong, but more than that he wanted to prove to himself that she was wrong. The case wasn't only about him finding a killer now; it was about finding the strength inside him to restore his wounded pride. He could live with his lowly status in the ranks, the feeling that somehow he had not gone as far as he should – but he couldn't live with the knowledge that there were people like Martin who thought he was exactly where he deserved to be, that he couldn't do any better. He'd been pigeonholed before and it hadn't affected him like this, but that was then, thought Valentine; the times were changing, he was changing, and people like Martin were going to have to open their eyes to that.

As he entered the incident room, the detective scanned the rows of desks for a familiar face. He raised a finger and beckoned. 'Ally, get yourself over here.'

DC McAlister closed the cover on a blue folder and eased himself out of his seat. As he rose, Valentine noticed the squint tie and the hanging shirt tails.

'Can you not smarten yourself up a bit?'

McAlister's mouth drooped; he looked down at his tie and grabbed the knot. 'I'm only reading reports, sir.'

'Aye, I can see that, Ally . . .' He shook his head. 'I don't expect you'll ever be heading up Paris Fashion Week, but I want you looking at least presentable if you're going to be standing beside me on the press conference.'

'The telly?' said the DC.

'Don't get excited, son, I don't expect you'll be getting introduced to Pamela Anderson.'

The room's attention had focussed on the conversation now. A ripple of muted laughter spread around the place as the pair turned back for the door. Valentine sensed the shift in the axis and stopped in his tracks. 'We're only going to deliver a statement.' He homed in on Donnelly and Rossi. 'So you can put the petted lips away. I need you lot here holding the fort.'

On the way to the press office, Valentine watched McAlister making a show of tucking in his shirt tails, and he quickly moved from fussing over his belt buckle to flattening the stray edges of his fringe, first wetting his fingers on his tongue and then full-scale slapping his forehead.

'Will you get a grip, Ally?' said Valentine.

The DC gave him a glance that seemed to suggest he thought the remark was a bit harsh; Valentine stored the look away and conceded that he might indeed be correct in the assumption. It was not something that was going to bother the DI, though; his mind was now focussed on the task in hand.

'What are you going to reveal at this stage, sir?'

'As little as possible.' He grabbed the handle of the press office door and walked in. The media manager was standing over a table reading what looked like the prepared statement.

'Hello, Coreen,' said Valentine.

'Oh, it's yourself . . . How's the eh . . .' She ran a finger up and down the length of her breastbone.

Valentine gurned. 'Just fine. Is that the statement?'

'Yes, I thought it was best to keep it as general as possible at this stage . . .'

The detective's eyebrow rose in her direction; he squinted at her and then took up the piece of paper. The statement was full of police speak: in the locus, between the hours of, appealing for any witnesses. Valentine knew better than to follow the script to the letter – there was nothing that marked a policeman out as a sodden-earth plod worse than the kind of language that she was suggesting. Still, he had lived long enough to know the battles that were worth fighting and those that could be avoided without casualties.

'That's fine, Coreen. Are they *in situ*?' he said.

'Yes, more or less . . .' She turned away to the young girl who seemed to be her assistant this month – they changed with the weather. 'Is there anyone else coming, Debbie?'

The girl shook her head. 'I think they're all in.'

Valentine nodded. 'Right, let's get this bloody thing over with.'

'Is there anything you want to ask?' said Coreen, the suggestion seemed loaded with the assumption that she would be able to add anything to what the detective had already discerned for himself; his pulse was racing at the inference, but he let it pass and declined to answer.

On the way to the press room, Valentine turned to McAlister. 'Just sit beside me and look pretty. I'm not opening the floor up to questions, so I'll read the statement and leave. Got it?'

The DC nodded. 'Yes, sir.'

As they walked in, the pair were greeted by a wall of chatter. There seemed to be more journalists that Valentine had expected; it made him wonder where they had all come from and what they expected to receive. There were one or two familiar faces with whom he exchanged nods, but the press pack was a mutable group, constantly changing. The journalists seemed to get younger every time he saw them

– some looked to be ages with his eldest daughter – and he wondered what possible weight they could bring to a news piece on a murder as harrowing as that of James Urquhart.

The officers settled themselves behind the desk and Valentine adjusted the microphone. He watched McAlister fiddle with the water carafe and put out a glass for each of them. As it was slid along the table in his direction he frowned with derision, for no reason he could fathom. He accepted the glass with a curt, 'Thanks.' And then they were off.

'OK ladies and gentlemen, if I can have your attention please,' said the DI. The room fell into a suitably poignant silence. 'At the Ayr municipal refuse site yesterday morning, a member of the public raised the alarm with police about a possible deceased white male.'

A few of the reporters started to rustle notebooks; others adjusted recording equipment.

Valentine continued: 'After investigation and having fully secured the site, officers from King Street station confirmed the presence of a white male in his late fifties who had been left on the tip. As a result of that initial investigation, a post-mortem was carried out, which confirmed officers' suspicions that we are dealing with a murder inquiry.'

One of the reporters leaned forward in his chair and called out, 'Can we have a name?'

Valentine started to shuffle the papers in front of him. 'As I said, this is a murder investigation and we would appreciate your patience with regard to what information we can release at this stage.'

The reporter called out again. 'Is there any truth in the fact that the deceased is a stockbroker called James Urquhart?'

Valentine stood up and pointed to the reporter. 'Are you Cameron Sinclair?'

The reporter tapped the ID badge on a lanyard round his neck. 'Of the *Glasgow-Sun* . . . yes.'

Valentine collected up his notes and cut the air with the blue folder. 'That's the end of the press conference everyone. I'm not taking questions, so if you'd like to make your way to the door please.'

He moved out from the desk, took brisk strides towards the front row of reporters and laid a firm hand on Sinclair's shoulder. 'I think I'd like to turn the tables and ask you a few questions, Mr Sinclair.'

13

LEANNE DUNN WOKE WITH a humming in her head and a dull, persistent ache in her stomach. As she eased herself off the edge of the bed, she felt her cold foot touch the bare floorboard and jerked it back. At once she knew this was a mistake, as it sent the bed shoogling and waves of nausea coursing through her already delicate digestive system. She tried to right herself, placing her body weight on her elbow, and vomited onto the bedspread. The sight of the dark, liquefied bile made her retch again and more malodorous fluid was expressed from her mouth. As she rocked on the bed's edge, sharp pains pressed into her clenched stomach. She leaned forward, elbows on her knees, and watched as the floor swayed beneath her.

Leanne felt worse than she had felt in a while, but she knew that was coming to an end because Gillon was due to arrive and collect the night's takings. He always brought a few wraps – and she'd had a good night, scoring a ton-fifty – so she'd be clear of the nagging symptoms of withdrawal soon.

Leanne found the strength to attempt another rise from the bed. At first she placed her hands either side of her, but the give in the mattress threatened to disrupt her already shifting centre of gravity. She brought her hands together and wrung them like lathering soap; her mouth was dry now, she needed water. She looked down at her thin, bruised legs; they were as pale and white as her feet, the only indicators of colour being the blackness between her toes. Gillon would castigate her for that: he didn't like his girls looking like street trash. She knew she had to wash before he arrived or he'd remind her of the rules with his fists or, worse, withhold the precious wraps.

Leanne found strength enough to plant her feet and stood holding the door handle like an old woman with a walking stick. The expanse of floor between her room and the kitchen seemed an endless savannah – a familiar territory but one beyond her – and no matter how hard she tried to summon the determination to move she couldn't find it. Her back ached where she stood and the calf muscles beneath her screamed with the pressure of body weight. Leanne's knees buckled, sending shocks through her thin thighs. She knew she couldn't support herself any longer; a wave of pressure from an invisible avalanche above suddenly descended and she was floored.

The sound of Leanne's bony frame landing on the bare boards was a pathetic thud, like shopping spilling from a burst bag. Her eye socket had connected with the floor and the stinging sensation told her that there would be swelling. Gillon wouldn't like that: black eyes were against the rules. When he belted his girls, he made sure the consequences stayed out of sight. The thin, pain-wracked bag of bones that lay on the bare floor with the swirling balls of dust and the smattering of condom wrappers didn't resemble a human being. There was no life force on show, no strength or even a dim indicator of breathing. It took some more time for Leanne to summon the courage to attempt a move – which, when it came, transpired to be a shuddering of shoulders as she sobbed into the pale, dirt-wreathed floor of her Lochside flat.

An hour or so after Leanne passed out, she awoke shivering again with a thin tendril of drool tethering her mouth to the

96

floor. The incessant whooshing of her gut seemed to have passed, supplanted with the empty feeling that she carried inside her most days. There was still a persistent thud in the front of her head, but the debilitating cramps had eased enough to at least make crawling along the floor an option. She reached the bathroom door slithering on her belly like war wounded and hauled herself into the shower cubicle, grabbing the handle to release welcome jets of water.

As the shower came to life, Leanne gasped for air. She gulped a few mouthfuls of water as she tried to adjust to the assault on her senses, but it didn't take her long to feel the soothing effects of the water on her weary body. She was still cold and riddled with aches and pains, but as she curled in the base of the shower cubicle she began to feel like a return to the real world was possible. She let the water pour over her, allowing herself to believe that rejuvenation was taking place, but all the while knowing she needed to face the world outside. When she released herself from the shower, Leanne found there was no towel, so she draped herself in a bathrobe, retrieved from the floor. She was cold and shivery, but there was no place to hide from her responsibilities. Gillon would be arriving soon and she would have little time to herself before the day's punters started to appear. She ran her fingers through her wet hair and tried to focus on her face in the mirror's reflection. Her eye had started to yellow after connecting with the boards earlier, but she could cover that with make-up; it would be another day or so before the actual shiner showed and Gillon had anything to complain about.

Leanne's feet were dragging as she made her way through to the kitchen. The flat was cold and bare. There were chairs in the living room, but they were hard-backed – the remnants of a discarded dining set that Gillon had made her stack into the back of his white van after spotting them at the side of the road. She didn't want them in the flat, it made the place look like a dentist's waiting room, but Gillon told her he wasn't supplying the flat for her to get comfortable in: it was where she worked, it was where she turned tricks.

Leanne felt her body's functions returning. She poured herself a glass of water and turned on the portable television that sat on the kitchen worktop. The picture was hazy, flecked with snow, but she wasn't overly interested in the content anyway; it was merely distraction she wanted. She leaned over and reclaimed her packet of ten Club and the blue plastic lighter. As she lit up, she leaned on the side of the sink and watched the news playing. She didn't know why the news had her attention until she realised that she was staring at a familiar scene – the town of Ayr.

'Holy . . .'

Leanne moved closer to the television screen and turned up the volume. The newscaster was the same one she had seen a hundred times, but it seemed strange to see her so close to home.

'Police have confirmed the recovery of a body from Ayr's tip and that they are dealing with a murder investigation.'

The reporter sounded so formal, not like the people Leanne knew. There were some people she spoke to – punters – who could speak posh, but they tended to keep their mouths shut.

The journalist continued with the report: 'Police have refused to confirm the victim's name until family members have formally identified him, but a number of unofficial sources have claimed the victim is a local man, believed to work in the banking industry . . .'

Leanne jumped away from the sink as a loud knock sounded on her front door. She placed her cigarette on the rim of the sink and looked away to the other side of the flat, but felt herself drawn back to the television screen.

'Leanne . . . open up!'

She heard more knocking on the door.

'Leanne . . .'

She recognised the voice, but it wasn't Gillon's. She had expected Gillon, but this voice was a shock. She made her way to the front door and stood with her hand pressed hard against the jamb.

'You need to go away, Danny's coming and he doesn't like you here . . .'

'Leanne if you don't open this bloody door, I'll knock it down and I'll go through Danny Gillon next!'

Leanne's hands were trembling as she removed the chain from the door and turned the key. There was a sudden gust of stale air from the close as Duncan Knox pushed in. The large man was sweating, his hair mussed and his cheeks ruddy and bulging as he stomped past Leanne and made his way into the kitchen.

'This . . . this . . . you've seen it then?' he was roaring, his voice pitched high and bursting with emotion.

As Leanne entered the kitchen, she saw Knox standing in front of the television screen with his hands pressed tight to his face. She had never seen him that way before; he was always so calm: threatening, but calm. Knox was a large man and he liked to throw his weight around: as Leanne appeared at his side, he reached out and grabbed her, and the dressing gown she was wearing opened up and exposed her scrawny breasts. She shrieked out theatrically as Knox pulled her towards him.

'Shut up! Haven't you seen what's going on?' He pointed to the television screen, but Leanne's eyes were pulled towards his face; his jaw jutted forward, exposing broken and cracked teeth that poked up like tombstones. 'Look, look!' he roared.

As Leanne turned to look at the screen once more, she retraced her earlier viewing before the knock at the door and pieced the two ends of the report together. It was a murder investigation in their hometown, that much was certain.

'What's that got to do with me?' she said.

Knox pushed her away and stamped his feet towards the other end of the kitchen. 'What's it got to do with you – are you kidding?'

'I don't . . . understand.'

The man in her kitchen seemed beside himself. He slapped his palm off the side of his face and then ran it over his stubbly chin in one sweeping, nervous gesture that signalled his state of mind like a flare. He kept walking, pacing, as he spoke. 'Don't you know who that is?'

'No . . .'

Knox halted. He brought up his hands and waved them either side of his head as he raised his eyes to face the heavens. 'It's James Urquhart.'

The name took a moment to register on Leanne's memory, but after a few seconds, the realisation of who he was, and what the name meant, sent a spasm of shock through her thin frame. 'James . . . It's . . .'

'Yes. Yes . . .' Knox's voice was thundering now. He crossed the floor towards Leanne and grabbed her by the shoulders. He was shaking her to and fro as he bellowed into her face. 'And you better pretend you never laid eyes on him! Do you hear me? Do you hear me?'

Leanne had no words. Her voice was a part of her that she had lost access to. Her throat was constricted by her own emotion. She was frozen, all over her body; she felt cold.

100

'Leanne ... Do you hear me?' Knox shook her shoulders, and her head lolled on her neck. 'You never knew James Urquhart. I mean it: you better keep your hole shut about him! For the first time in your bloody life you better learn to keep that hole in your stupid head shut!'

14

VALENTINE HAD OBSERVED Clare for long enough to know what was at the root of her personal problems. Her unhappiness – and it was an all-consuming soul weariness – was caused by her own shallow vapidity. She had surrendered early to the ideals of consumerism and progressed to the point where she measured her daily victories in goods purchased. A takeaway coffee might yield a five-minute high, but a dress or a new pair of shoes could deliver a week's worth of inner gratification. However, no matter what she bought or how the thrill was pipetted out over a lengthier period of time, the impact on her long-term self-esteem was always negligible, if not outright injurious.

Valentine had watched over the years as his wife regaled herself with glossy magazines that portrayed a lifestyle truly alien to her – an alternative reality where the beautiful people frolicked under holiday-brochure blue skies. The inference to be taken was always that an Amex with unlimited credit would deliver you from the woes of reality. It was a myth. The world Clare aspired to didn't exist outside of an ad man's imagination – it was a creation aimed at those who were wracked by the keenly felt emptiness of their own lives. The real genius was to slot products around the images of supposed happiness: conferring an inanimate object with transformative powers was, on the face of it, absurd, but people like Clare jumped for the brass ring every time.

Valentine knew his wife had always obsessed about the family home. At first it was interior furnishings and then, when the inside could not be altered any more, the exterior. The need to extend the family home had become a recurring theme for Clare – and one that had come to exhaust Valentine. If they could not afford to extend the home further, it didn't seem to matter to her. That they had enough space for their needs was of little relevance to Clare either. It seemed the mere act of planning to extend the home was in some way a stepping stone towards the conclusion of the aspiration. Valentine knew if the dream itself was ever realised, it wouldn't be enough – it was a flame that couldn't be extinguished. A bigger project or a newer home would soon become his wife's preoccupation.

It disturbed Valentine that his wife's inner life had become so unhealthy, so prosaic. There was no spiritual side to Clare, no intellectual depth. She possessed no desire, it seemed, to expand her life's reach beyond accumulating material possessions. She was like a woman who had been shelled out and her innards supplanted with a robotic desire to consume. It was a desire that was incapable of ever being quenched, because there was always a new range of clothes to buy or a newer catalogue to leaf through. No matter how many armfuls of purchases she returned with, they didn't fill the emptiness, meet the need, which it seemed to Valentine grew deeper and deeper by the day. When she became stressed, like she was now, the obsession intensified. It was as if problems with the girls, or his job, became submerged under mounds of packing foam, crumpled paper, carrier bags, clipped labels and the mountainous remnants of Clare's shopping sprees.

As Valentine sat down to dinner, he watched Clare fussing about the kitchen. The dress she wore was new, but the time when he would pass comment on a new item of clothing worn by his wife had passed; now any remark would be met by defensiveness or recriminations. He stored the fact of the dress away, though; if Clare was seeking solace in shopping then it was good to be forearmed with the knowledge.

She placed his food down in front of him and pulled out her chair.

'What's this?' said Valentine.

'It's dinner,' said Clare. She sat down beside him and began to pick at the food on her plate.

'Salad, I recognise . . . This looks like chicken or pork, but it's neither.'

Clare's jaws went to work on a mouthful, and when she was finished she spoke. 'It's tofu.'

'And what the hell's that when it's at home?'

'It's good for you is what it is . . . Eat it.'

Valentine stared at the contents of his plate and turned over a few pieces of tofu. He raised some on his fork and began to chew. He didn't like the taste. 'This is pretending to be something . . . but it's not.'

Clare shifted her gaze towards the wall and then turned on her husband. 'No, it's not. Now eat it.'

Valentine took a few more desultory mouthfuls and then began to roll the fork around his plate. 'I saw a pig's head in the butcher's once.'

'Really?'

'It was plastic.'

Clare sighed. 'That's nice.'

'Is that what we've got here?'

His wife dropped her cutlery on the plate; the clatter was ear-splitting. She lowered her head onto her chest and then pushed out her chair and left the room.

'Clare . . . Clare . . .' Valentine called to her. 'I'm only having a joke with you. I'll eat it . . .'

She turned on her heels in the kitchen and stomped back into the dining room. 'I bought it because it is good for you, lower fat, healthier . . . better for your heart. Perhaps I shouldn't have bloody well bothered.' She left the room again and closed the door behind her.

Valentine dropped his own knife and fork and stared out into the garden. He could see his neighbour's sprinkler spraying a wide arc of lawn. The sun was low and flat in the sky. For a moment the scene felt calm and familiar, and then the realisation of recent events hit him. Valentine was suffused with a strange kind of sadness. It was the type of feeling he'd had when watching the girls grow up: a pride tinged with loss, the realisation that each day they were getting further away from him. There would be no more first birthdays, no more first steps; so many good times had passed and the future was so filled with uncertainty that it was hard to focus on the good times that were still to come. He knew Clare was not dealing well with his return to active policing; she was handling the situation in her usual way, and he knew what that might mean. Valentine had a well of guilt swelling in him because he felt sure he couldn't give Clare his full attention and still devote himself to the case. But what option did he have? A man had been killed, in brutal fashion, and now the press were circling – he would need to find answers.

The detective removed his mobile phone from his trouser pocket and scrolled the contacts for DS Rossi's number. The phone was answered after only a few seconds.

'Hello, sir.'

'Paulo, I've been waiting for the update on what happened with Mrs Urquhart.'

'Oh, yes, sorry boss . . .'

Valentine cut in. 'Well?'

'I was having my tea . . .'

'Well, you can get back to your bloody spaghetti in a minute, Paulo. Tell me the details, eh.'

The sound of shuffling and the creaking of a door came down the line. 'It's a positive ID, sir. The wife, er, Mrs Urquhart, picked him out at the morgue no trouble.'

'She did . . . and what was the response like?'

Rossi cleared his throat before speaking. 'She seemed a bit, erm, stony-faced, I suppose you would say.'

'Not emotional?'

'Well, yes and no: there was some dabbing at the eyes with a hankie, if that's what you mean, but there was no big outburst or the like.'

Valentine tried to spool the image in his mind: it seemed to fit with what he had come to expect of Mrs Urquhart. She was too high up the social ladder to put on any outward display of emotion in public. They were a reserved lot, the upper classes. The act of keening over the dead was something reserved for the lower caste.

'I wasn't expecting suttee, Paulo.'

'What?'

'Never mind . . . And the son, Adrian, how did he appear?'

Rossi's regular tone returned. 'He wasn't there, sir . . . It was the neighbour . . .' The pause in his speech was filled with the sound of pages turning in a notebook. 'Ronnie Bell's his name.'

'I know who he is, Paulo, we've had the pleasure . . . What I want to know is what he was doing running Mrs Urquhart up to the morgue when her own son was on hand and there's no shortage of luxury motors sitting in the driveway.'

'Erm, well . . .'

'It didn't strike you as just a wee bit odd?'

'Now you mention it, sir, I suppose the boy would have been the likely one to go and hold his mother's hand, but maybe he was too upset or something.'

'Aye, maybe . . . or maybe not. We don't know, Paulo, and that's the problem here. This is a murder investigation and we don't know anything.'

'Yes, sir.' Rossi's voice registered the fact that he had absorbed some of the DI's disapproval.

'Right, I want you to start a file on this Ronnie Bell character, and in that file I want to see everything, including his preference for Ys or budgie-smugglers, and it better all be there the first time I pick the file up, Paulo. Am I making myself clear?'

'Yes, sir.'

'Good. And in future, Paulo, the second anything comes in you pick up the phone, do you hear me? I don't care if you've got a mouthful of spag bol made by the wee granny off the Dolmio ads herself, you let me know what you know right away.'

'Yes, sir . . . I'm sorry about that.'

Valentine hung up. He could feel the throbbing of his vocal chords from when his rant had reached a rasp.

He scrolled down his contacts of his phone again and found DC McAlister. The DI's mind was still sparking as McAlister answered.

'Yes, boss. . .'

'Ally, we have our ID.'

'She picked him, then?'

'Aye, it's officially James Urquhart. I don't see any point in keeping it from the press when this Sinclair hack has so much information.'

107

'What was his explanation?'

'He said he got an anonymous tip-off from someone claiming to be an ex-employee of Urquhart . . . Plausible, I suppose.'

McAlister made a dismissive huff. 'I don't know . . . anonymous. Sounds like one from the hack's rulebook to me.'

Valentine felt the skin tightening on the back of his neck. 'We'll see. I don't think there's any point going in too hard on Sinclair at this stage. It might just be one lucky bit of information that fell into his lap. If he starts sprouting them on a regular basis we might need to look a bit more closely at him . . . and those around him.'

'Understood, sir.' McAlister paused, seemed to hold his breath for a moment or two, and then spoke. 'You don't suspect anyone on the squad, do you, sir?'

Valentine's response to the same question by the chief super had been swift and decisive, but after talking to Sinclair and seeing the whites of his eyes he wasn't so sure of himself.

'I suspect everyone, Ally. Always do. One thing's for sure and certain, though: if we have a mole on the team feeding biccies to Sinclair, then I'll be feeding them into a mincer.'

McAlister's voice rose. 'For what it's worth, sir, I'd be stunned if anyone was that stupid.'

'Ally there's no shortage of idiots in this world.' He cut the conversation off at the knees. The point had been made and he could rely on Ally to circulate the salient facts. 'Anyway, get in touch with Coreen in the morning and tell her to give the victim's name to the press pack at close of play tomorrow – not before. I want a clear day for us to get our ducks in a row before we have to start answering press queries again. But at the very least we'll be raining on Sinclair's parade.'

McAlister bit. 'What do you mean?'

'I asked him not to release the name in tomorrow's paper for fear of prejudicing the investigation.'

'And he agreed?'

'Ally, if he's smart he'll play fair by us.'

'I don't know, boss: like you say, there's a lot of idiots in the world.'

15

VALENTINE AWOKE FROM AN uneasy sleep, and troubling dreams, to an empty bed. Clare had been there when he'd decided to slink upstairs the night before, but she had slept with her back to him. He reached out to her side of the bed and touched the linen sheet: it was cold. For a moment Valentine stared at the ceiling, allowing his thoughts to swirl around, but then he started to feel them gather there like dark clouds above the bed.

'Get a grip,' he mouthed to himself.

Valentine lay for only a second or two longer and then flattened his palms either side of him and pushed away from the mattress. The bedsprings wheezed beneath him. He knew it was becoming difficult to avoid dark thoughts about Clare, even though he tried to fend them off. When he thought about her issues, they seemed so ridiculously trite compared with the issues he dealt with in his working life – but he understood they were very real to her. He knew he couldn't allow his wife's neuroses to dominate his thought patterns for fear they would distract his attention from the case. But there was a bigger picture too: he didn't want to see the children affected by a problem that was nothing to do with them. The DI dressed quickly and took himself downstairs. Clare was in the kitchen reading the newspaper and smoking a cigarette when he appeared.

'Good morning.'

Clare turned towards her husband and plucked the filter tip from her mouth. 'Morning.'

Valentine watched the blue stream of smoke spiral upwards and declined to comment. He filled the kettle with water instead; he was removing the coffee jar when Clare spoke again.

'Isn't this what you're working on?' She held up the newspaper: it was the *Glasgow-Sun*.

Valentine squinted towards the page – along the top, not quite a page-lead, was the story of the Urquhart killing. He read a few words from the first deck of headlines and then his brain started to hum.

'I don't believe it . . .' He reached out and snatched the paper from his wife.

'What is it?'

Valentine stood over the newspaper, shaking his head. The kettle started to roar and steam beside him. His temper was just as hot as the kettle when it pinged. 'This bastard's only gone and released the name of my victim . . .'

'Who?'

Valentine was gripping the paper, scrunching it in his hands. 'Cameron bloody Sinclair . . .'

'And who's he?'

'A reporter . . . or likes to think he is. I told him not to print this name and he's only gone and done it.'

Clare pinched her cheeks. She seemed to be searching for the right words, but pouring oil on troubled waters had never been one of her strengths. 'Maybe it just popped out . . . like a mistake or something.'

'What?' He couldn't believe what he was hearing. 'Are you trying to be funny?'

'No, I'm just . . .' Her mouth sat like an open gutter.

'Well, just don't!'

Valentine balled the paper in his hands; he was wringing it

like a rag as he stomped from the kitchen and collected his coat and case. On his way towards the car, his mind surfed the channels of consequence. The chief super would soon be on the hunt for someone to blame, if she wasn't already. He checked his phone as he got in the car to see if he'd missed any calls from her: he hadn't. He threw the mobile on the dash and groaned audibly as he sat, resting his forehead on the rim of the wheel.

'Bloody Sinclair . . . I'll string him up.'

He turned the key and pulled out of the drive.

On the way through Maisonhill, the commuter traffic was just starting to make its presence felt on the Ayrshire roads. There was a tailback outside the Spar shop where people were stopping off to stock up on sandwiches they'd eat at their desks in place of a proper lunch break. The scene wasn't wasted on Valentine: he knew now his own workload had just got a lot heavier. There would be a queue of hacks looking for confirmation of the details released by the *Glasgow-Sun*. There'd be recriminations to deal with too, and that was before he got to work on the proper business of finding James Urquhart's killer.

This wasn't about the actions of an over-ambitious journalist, thought Valentine; it was a blatant swipe at his authority. Sinclair intended to plant his flag in the case and claim it as his own. Valentine had lost the first skirmish, and the fact that he wasn't going to be able to usurp Sinclair by releasing the victim's name to the rest of the press later was another blow that had been landed without any effort.

At King Street station, Valentine locked the Vectra and walked towards the door. There was some heat in the morning air now and the dew on the grass by the sides of the road was evaporating. He looked out over the skyline towards the flats and saw an old man positioning a deckchair on the balcony of his property. The sight of the man settling down in the chair stirred something like envy in the detective, and he checked himself. He knew, of course, he wasn't envious of the old man's leisure time – the day ahead in the sunshine – it was the wearisome thought, recurring now, that his own life had been shortened by a job that he continued to give more to than to anything else. He knew he had stored up more conflict for himself with Clare with his reaction to the Sinclair headline, and the realisation gored him now. The job just didn't leave room for anything else: it required everything he had to give.

Jim Prentice was on the desk when Valentine walked through the door. He wore a grave expression as he balanced on one elbow and tapped the buttons on a telephone with his other hand. 'Oh, just about to give you a ring . . .' He put the receiver down and at the same time dropped his voice several octaves. 'Herself is up and about early this morning.'

Valentine manoeuvred towards the desk, raised up his briefcase and attuned himself to Jim's frequency. 'What's up?'

The sergeant inverted a smile. 'A paddock out at the track . . . something going on there.'

Valentine shrugged. 'What are you saying to me, Jim?'

He played with the lobe of his ear as he spoke. 'I'm not saying anything because I've been told nothing.' He leaned forward and let his gaze thin. 'But if you were asking me to guess – from the way she's acting – it's not bloody pretty. Got uniform on the way out there now.'

Valentine eased himself from the desk, retrieved his briefcase and made for the stairs. On the first rung, he spun and called to Jim. 'Anything comes on that radio – you shout me.'

'Aye sure . . .'

'I mean it, right away, Jim.'

As Valentine bounded up the steps, his pulse quickened. His thoughts were eddying; he had started the morning with a shock in the paper, but if his worst fears about Jim's announcement were realised then the newspaper issue would be overtaken. On the top landing, the DI felt his temperature rising beneath his dog-tooth sports coat and loosened his tie. He was removing his sleeve and switching his briefcase to the other hand as the chief super's door opened and she stood in the frame. He wondered if she'd been listening for his footsteps.

'Bob – in here now.' Her voice was immediate, certain.

'Yes, boss.'

He watched her turn away from him and return to the office. She had a look that unsettled him. Martin was usually so full of her own self-importance, so assured, but she seemed to be on edge in a way that indicated panic.

She spoke again as he entered. 'Close the door.'

Valentine took a few steps towards her desk and lowered his briefcase onto the ground. He was laying his sports coat on the back of the chair when she caught his attention by slapping her palm off the desk.

'What's the worst possible nightmare you can imagine?' Her voice bled anxiety, edging into a shriek.

Valentine held himself together; it was a trait he was adopting more and more at the sight of rising tensions. 'Are you looking for a list?'

The chief super turned away from him and dropped into her chair. She sat deflated and slumped for a moment and then leaned forward. Valentine removed the chair in front of him and sat down. Martin was grimacing as she spoke.

'We had a call from the racecourse about half an hour ago.' She brought her hands together and looked as if she was about

114

to start praying. 'It was from one of the maintenance blokes . . . He reckons there's a white male impaled on a stake in the middle of the track.'

Valentine sensed cold pustules of sweat standing out on his forehead. His eyes studied the chief super's face for more information, but it was clear she had none. He knew what this latest turn of events meant and didn't want to believe it: he had a strange compunction to object.

'Are you sure?'

'No, Bob, I'm making it up for a laugh . . .' She slumped back in her seat and a truculent gleam entered her eye. 'I've got uniform out there taking a look now, but it sounds genuine, so you'd better get yourself prepared for a day and a half.'

It seemed like a good time to bury bad news. Valentine made to rise; his chair legs scraped on the carpet tiles as he stood. 'By the way, in case you haven't seen the paper . . .' – he retrieved his case and grey dog-tooth sports coat – 'our man Sinclair shafted us well and truly.'

'What?'

Valentine was at the door when he replied. 'Gave our victim's name away. When the hacks get wind of today's turn of events, I think they'll be having a day and a half as well.'

16

VALENTINE WONDERED WHAT it was that had kept him in the job all these years. It wasn't his progression through the ranks or the feeling of moving onward with life in other ways. The job afforded you so little status that it was hardly worth counting; to most, their rating of a police officer was somewhere shy of used-car salesman. The job certainly didn't open any doors to rarefied echelons, or if it did, it was for all the wrong reasons.

There had been a moment at the outset of his career when he thought that he was doing some good. Rounding up rowdies at Somerset Park after the Killie games, or scooping up the Saturday night dafties before they went scripto, felt like a job worth doing. It was physical too, and he remembered a time when he was fit enough and fond enough of his own chances to get a buzz from it. He smiled inwardly – a lot of the boys had joined up because they knew, as he did then, that it was very hard to lose a fight in uniform. But somewhere along the line he'd realised that the task was a thankless one: he was merely working to keep the prison service supplied. He didn't want to be a social worker, picking up the detritus left by political failings: 'an instrument of the state' was the term his father had used to galling effect. It always felt like doing someone else's dirty work: someone better paid, higher up the corridors of power, someone who didn't want to get their own hands dirty.

Valentine knew he remained a police officer for two reasons: because it kept his attention after all these years, and because he had passed the point where there was any other option on offer. He was too old and too set in his ways to switch lanes now – and where would they lead? A private security firm? Nightwatchman? At his age the choices were thin, so he resigned himself to the fact that he still took an interest in the job and its challenges, but more so in the complexities of human foibles. He conceded that, along with the criminal flotsam and jetsam, some complex situations washed up. At their margins of endurance, when pushed, people acted to their true type, and this fascinated Valentine. It confirmed the blackest thoughts he harboured about the human race: we were all, each and every one of us, capable of heinous criminal acts. All that we needed was circumstance. Unravelling the motives, the causes and the triggers that led to crime showed the DI the real people he shared the planet with, and he could think of no other job that would afford him that insight.

Valentine stood in front of the whiteboard in the incident room and pressed the flat of his hand on the blank area to the left of the photograph of James Urquhart. He drummed his fingers momentarily and then he removed the red marker pen from the shelf and circled the picture. When he was finished, he drew a thick horizontal line leading from the circled area and ended the task with a question mark. As he stood staring, he contemplated what was likely to cover the question mark and approached the board again, circling the area in heavy red ink. He was placing the cap back on the marker pen when the telephone to his rear started to ring.

'Yes, Valentine . . .'

It was Jim Prentice on the desk. 'That's the call from the track . . . It's a body. White male, same MO as the tip.'

Valentine felt a chill, like a shadow had crossed him. 'You sure?'

'Certain . . .'

The DI was still digesting the information when the doors to the incident room were flung open and the chief super walked in. Valentine lowered the telephone receiver and turned to face Martin.

'I take it that's the bongo drums?' she said.

Valentine blinked; it seemed to prompt him back to life. 'We have another one, then.'

Martin positioned herself on the rim of the desk and folded her arms across her chest. She bunched her lips and then raked fingers through her hair. For a moment she seemed to be thinking, tapping the leg of the desk with the heel of her shoe; Valentine watched her and tried to detect a germ of optimism in her stance, but found none.

'The press are going to have a field day,' she said.

'Well, that was already on the cards . . . Look, I should get out there now.'

The doors to the incident room opened once more as Valentine spoke; DC McAlister stood in the doorway and stared at the chief super – he seemed to intuit something. 'What's going on?'

'Ally, don't take your jacket off . . . We've got another body out at the track.'

'What?'

The chief super raised herself from the desk. 'SOCOs are on their way. I'd suggest you get out there now and start to make yourself useful.'

McAlister nodded. 'Yes, boss.'

As he turned back towards the door, Valentine called out. 'Can you give Paulo and Phil a holler?'

'Aye, sure . . . You want them out there?'

The DI scratched behind his ear and exhaled loudly; it was an expression that indicated thoughts were fighting for prominence inside his head. 'Erm, no . . . Just Phil. Keep Paulo back here, I want someone looking after the phones.'

As McAlister left the room, Valentine felt the chief super's stare burning him. 'Are you OK, Bob?'

'What do you mean?' He dropped his hand. 'No need to worry about me.'

'We both know I've every need . . .' She tapped her tongue off her two front teeth. 'Don't think just because the workload has doubled you can skip out of the therapy sessions. I need you on the ball, Bob, more than ever now.'

Valentine painted a smile on his face. 'Like I say, you've no reason to worry about me.'

The chief super turned away, flagging the detective off with the back of her hand as she went. He knew she was merely pressing the point to assert her authority – to undermine him – and the thought struck like a winding. He watched her leave, listened to the doors' batting motion and snatched his sports coat from the back of the chair.

On the road out to the racetrack, Valentine felt the morning sun press itself on the window of the car. He was stiff and tense behind the wheel, gripping the gearstick in his left hand like it was a cudgel. Outside, the street was weary, a row of houses that had lost all charm since the giant supermarket had relocated just up the road. The detective rowed the gears back

119

and forth as he passed through the traffic lights. He could see the racetrack on the right, but turned away to check the clock on the dash. He tried to keep his mind open, but assumptions about a double murder on his patch pressed themselves again and again like mosquito bites on his mind.

Valentine parked the Vectra outside the track and made his way towards the collection of uniforms. He was ahead of the SOCOs, but the site had already been cordoned off by the first on the scene. He roved the surrounding area with his eyes and caught sight of DC McAlister walking towards him. Clouds crossed the sky above and dim sunrays fell like ticker tape on the stand before slipping towards the track lanes.

'It's the double of the last one, sir,' said McAlister.

Valentine gave the DC a look, then walked past him and made for the crime scene. When he got behind the cordon, his shoulders tensed beneath his coat. He took a few steps closer and then walked around the victim. The man was heavier than James Urquhart, a bigger individual all round; he had a sports top pushed up around his neck, exposing a prominent stomach. The skin was pale, verging on white, and streaked with dark-red blood. Below his abdomen, a wooden stake poked skywards, streaked in blood that covered the genitals and the ground beneath.

Valentine walked towards the uniforms. 'What's the word from the track staff?'

'No idea who he is, sir . . . Groundsman found him just as you see him now.' The uniform waved a hand over the scene.

The detective beckoned McAlister towards him and stepped away from the uniforms. As he took a few steps further, he hooked his hands below the tails of his sports coat and gripped the edges of the pockets with his thumbs. 'What do you think?'

The DC turned towards the victim. 'He's bigger than Urquhart, but I think it could still be one man that moved him.'

Valentine nodded. 'There's no fence, no wall . . . no obstacles from here to the car park, so it's possible.'

'He doesn't look like a banker.'

'The tattoos and the fingers . . .'

McAlister thinned his eyes and tilted his head. 'Fingers?'

'Yellowed with nicotine: I'd say he was a rollie smoker.'

'I don't see the number one crop being a good look in the board room either.'

Valentine unhooked his thumbs and folded his arms. 'There's got to be some connection, though, someone has executed the pair of them in an identical fashion.'

'We might know better when the SOCOs get here . . . Certainly if we get an ID we can explore links.'

Valentine scratched beneath his chin. He started to shake his head as he spoke. 'Why, though? Why put them up on a spike like this?'

'It's obvious . . . to give a message.'

'But why draw so much attention to yourself? If you want to kill someone, you hide the body, give yourself a chance of getting away with it . . . This is insanity.'

'You're not kidding . . . We're obviously dealing with a psycho.'

'Or somebody who wants to get caught.'

'Or somebody who thinks he's too smart to get caught.'

The DI spotted the first of the SOCOs' vans to arrive; the fiscal and the pathologist would be next. 'Ally, I want you to stay put. Anything crops up, get on the phone.'

'Yes, sir.'

'I want the time of death and how long he's been out in

the cold as soon as you get it.' Valentine removed his car keys
from his pocket and started to rattle them in his hand. 'I want
swabs and prints, and if we have him on file, I want to know
right away.'

'Sir.'

17

ON THE ROAD BACK TO THE station, Detective Inspector Bob Valentine sensed his spirit collapsing inside him. He was queasy and couldn't think clearly – it was as if the whole situation had the unreality of dreams. His mind wandered back to the nightmare he'd had when he saw the little girl with the white-blonde hair laying flowers round the corpse of James Urquhart. He knew the mind worked in unusual ways – that it was likely his unconscious creating an image of a situation that troubled him – but he wondered now what situation could be more worrying than that image? He thought of the girls, Fiona and Chloe: they had been that size once – was there a connection? Chloe had been most like the girl in the dream – she had been a chatty child, though, and this girl had seemed so withdrawn, taciturn. When Chloe was very young she would stay in her room and hold conversations with imaginary friends, always happy, always benign. But when asked who she was talking to, she would go quiet and cross her lips with fingers as if forbidden to say. It puzzled Valentine then and it made him think about the situation again now: children possessed something special at that age, almost preternatural, which was lost in adulthood.

As Valentine drove towards the station, he was bothered by an irritant. A thought was lodged in his mind like a splinter, and he was avoiding it, trying to take an oblique view in the hope that if he snuck up on the thought then it would lose its power. But there was no getting around it. He was being bothered by this case in a way he hadn't been before – he felt it more, but the feelings the case triggered were not ones he had ever encountered.

'Get a grip, Bob,' he mouthed as he rounded the bend towards King Street and took the entrance to the station car park.

As he pulled up and killed the engine, Valentine sat drumming his fingers on the dash for a moment. The sight of the latest murder victim had lit a fuse in him. He felt it burning away inside his gut. Valentine had allowed his intuition to play a part in the job before, but this was something altogether different: he felt as if he was being led by outside forces rather than by his own knowledge and experience. He rolled up the window and let his breathing still as he tried to focus. There was a wider picture – a broader purview than he had – something was tugging him away from the obvious, but even the most mundane and pedestrian of assumptions seemed to be swept aside by the latest victim.

He slapped a palm off the wheel and opened the car door. On the way into the station he nodded to Jim on the desk and then made straight for the incident room. The first person to catch his attention was Paulo, who had his back to him and was speaking into a telephone.

'Aye, put that on and give me another two hundred on the nose.'

Valentine moved in front of the DS and stood with his hands in his pockets, making it perfectly clear that he had caught the gist of the conversation.

'Got to go . . .' said Paulo. 'Er, sorry, boss.'

'That wasn't what I think it was, because if it was then you'd have my foot in your arse and a new role mopping out the kennels for the dog handlers, Paulo.'

He dropped his gaze and painted a contrite look on his face. 'Yes, sir.'

Valentine let his indignation burn into the DS for a moment longer and then he called out to the room. 'Right, can I have all of you round the board, please.'

There was a shuffle of chair legs and some muttering as the squad made their way towards the whiteboard. Valentine picked up a pen and removed the cap; he was writing a description of the latest victim as he began to speak. 'White male, middle aged, blue-collar worker and spiked through the backside with a sharpened plank of wood.'

'It's the same MO, then . . .' said DS Donnelly.

'Ah, Phil, you're here.'

'I was just on my way out to the scene, sir.'

'Leave it. Ally can handle that lot; you'll be more use to me here if they get an ID.' The DI put the cap back on the marker pen and walked in front of the board. 'There're obviously striking similarities to the murder of James Urquhart, so I'd be expecting to uncover links between the two victims . . . What those links will be at this stage we can only guess.'

Paulo asserted himself. 'They must have known each other.'

Valentine tapped the board at the description of the latest victim. 'Do they look like the kind of people to be friends . . . ? See James Urquhart going for a game of darts with our latest victim?'

'Maybe casual acquaintances: he could have been a gardener or tradesman, odd-job man?' said Donnelly.

'Better . . . Get on that, Phil.' He laid the flat of his shoe against the wall and reclined in the chair. 'Anyone get anything on James Urquhart's movements yet?'

DS Donnelly spoke again, reeling off a list of regular activities. 'He was a member of the Rotary Club but not a regular by any means, and there was a model-railway club that according to their website meets on a Wednesday night in the town.'

'Check it out with the club, and with his wife. See if they tie up.'

'Yes, sir.'

'Anyone got anything else to report at this stage?'

DS Rossi raised a hand. 'I looked into the neighbour . . . Ronnie Bell.'

'Oh, aye.'

'Well, on paper anyway, he's clean.'

'Most folk are, Paulo . . . I'm not interested in his parking tickets or if he takes too many plastic bags at Asda. Pay him a visit, get under his skin. How friendly was he with Urquhart? And how friendly is he with his wife?'

'Yes, sir.'

Valentine clapped his hands together. 'Right, that's it for now. Get back to work and let me know the second anything comes up.'

The DI returned to the board and stood with his hands on his hips, taking in the details that had been put up. They had little to go on. He looked at the photographs that showed James Urquhart's brutal injuries, and he thought of the latest victim and the pictures of his injuries that would soon be added to the board. He caught himself tapping a thumbnail off his front row of teeth – the clacking noise seemed to indicate nervousness to him, and he halted it at once. As his thoughts zigzagged, he wondered how long it was going to be before the chief super started to goad him with the possibility of turning the case over to the Glasgow Murder Squad. He knew that he would need to get a lead, to stake a claim on the case to ward off that eventuality, but there was nothing presenting itself. He closed his eyes in an effort to summon inspiration, but the process was immediately droned out by the ringing of a telephone.

'Hello, Valentine . . .'

It was DC McAlister. 'Sir, you're not going to like this, but the SOCOs have ID'd our stiff.'

'They have?' He paused. 'And why wouldn't I like it, Ally?'

'Well, for starters he's known to us . . .'

'Go on.'

'Sir, he's a stoat-the-ball.'

'Convicted?'

'Yes, he's a convicted paedophile, sir . . . Name's Duncan Knox.'

The name didn't register in Valentine's memory banks. 'I take it you've run him through the system.'

'Yeah, and it's a list of convictions as long as your arm . . . If you were looking at a revenge killing, you could be pulling potentials from all over the country. I'd say he's spent more time inside than out.'

Valentine eased himself down into a chair. Pressure was building in his chest and he started to rub the palm of his hand down the front of his shirt. As he looked up, he noticed the chief super walking into the room, eyeing him cautiously.

'OK, Ally, get yourself back to the station when you're ready. Good work, son.'

18

LEANNE DUNN PRESSED HER head against the wall and started to moan, indistinctly at first, and then her slow trail of wails became a lament. She hadn't done anything to bring this upon herself and the feeling of self-pity made the burning sensation in her head sting all the more. She turned over on the floor and laid the palms of her hands out in front of her, and as she kneeled there her head drooped. She was slipping, falling into a stupor that threatened to engulf her when her head was violently jerked backwards.

'I told you I didn't want that stoat round here!' Danny Gillon roared directly into Leanne's ear. He had hold of her hair in a clump, which he tightened like a knot.

'I–I never . . .' Leanne's words came on the back of sobs.

Gillon pushed her towards the wall, pressed her face into the plaster and roared again, 'How many times . . . ? Eh? How many times have you got to be told?'

'But, he wasn't . . .' Leanne felt the dim glow of energy within her being extinguished. Gillon was too strong for her. She wanted to collapse in a heap on the floor and let him tire himself out with roars like he usually did, but this wasn't the usual situation, she knew that much.

'You let that stoat in here again, though . . . Was he paying?'

'No . . . No, he wasn't here . . .'

'Was he after a freebie . . . just like the old days?'

'No.' Leanne felt her hair freed from Gillon's grasp, and she

128

sat upright and pushed herself away from him with the balls of her feet. 'I didn't . . .'

Gillon stepped forward and levelled the back of his hand towards her face. 'Don't you lie to me, Leanne . . . Don't even think about that, because I'll burst your face wide open if you're lying to me.'

Her hands shot up to protect her face. 'Don't.'

The pimp took two steps back and stood watching Leanne where she sat on the floor. She was cowering, her knees locked together and her shoulders trembling. He watched her for a moment or two, and then he withdrew a packet of cigarettes from his pocket. As he lit up, he called out to her, 'Right, c'mon . . . on your feet.'

'Why? Where are we going?'

He flicked his lank fringe. 'C'mon, into the kitchen . . . Have a wee seat.'

He seemed to have changed his tone, but Leanne wasn't fooled. He had done this before: it was his way of lulling her into a false sense of security. He offered her the cigarette; Leanne took it and pressed it to her thin lips.

'There, see . . . We can be friends when we want, eh?' said Gillon.

Leanne nodded and followed him through to the kitchen. She watched Gillon filling the kettle with water. 'You hold onto that fag, doll.' He dipped into his pocket and produced the pack again. 'I'll fire up a new one for myself.' Gillon lit the cigarette and placed it, tip out, on the side of the sink. Leanne watched the blue stream of smoke swirl towards the ceiling as her pimp made tea. It was an unusual situation: they had moved from her being battered near senseless in the hallway to now being made a cup of tea. It worried her; Gillon clearly wanted something from her, but she didn't know what it was.

'There you go, doll.' He placed the cup down in front of her. 'Nice cup of char, eh.'

Leanne watched the cup, steam rising from the liquid that was still swirling in the wake of the spoon's rapid revolutions. She couldn't bring herself to drink the tea; it sat there like a challenge to her, taunting her to take up the cup, to drink – the consequences of which worried her more than anything.

'OK, Leanne, I can see you're wondering why I'm so curious about that big fat paedo,' said Gillon. He leaned back in his seat and reached out his hand to retrieve his cigarette from the edge of the sink. 'See, I know you had him round here the other day, because I know you.'

'What do you mean?' Leanne drew deep on the filter tip; the ash was nearly an inch long now.

Gillon smiled, a mean smirk that showed the yellowed staves in his mouth. 'See, every time that paedo's round here you become a bag of nerves . . . It's like you're a wee lassie again.'

Leanne looked away. She was reminded of that part of her, the place deep inside, that had died. She watched cars hissing by the window on the street below. There were people walking on the pavements, birds swooping in the sky. It always felt strange to know that there was a world of ordinary people and ordinary goings-on and yet Duncan Knox existed within that same sphere. 'He came round.'

Gillon withdrew his cigarette and pinned back his lips; two hollows either side of his mouth became pronounced. 'There, see . . . Wasn't so bad, was it?' He flicked his ash on the floor. 'Now, what did he want?'

Leanne kept her gaze on the street. 'Why? What does it matter what he wanted?'

Gillon's voice rose. 'It just does. Look, Leanne, tell me what he wanted.'

She turned her head and caught sight of Gillon's anger growing behind his eyes again. 'He told me someone had died.'

'Who?'

'Nobody really, just someone I used to know.'

'And why did he tell you this? Why did he come round here?'

Leanne shrugged. 'I don't know.'

'Tell me the name of the person who died, Leanne.'

Her throat constricted; it was as if the words wouldn't pass. She wanted to say them, to get the name out in the open to show that he meant nothing to her. He couldn't harm her: he was dead. 'James Urquhart.'

Gillon pushed the chair back; the legs scraped loudly on the floor. In a second, he was on his feet pacing the kitchen. 'That's him . . . the man on the telly.'

Leanne watched her pimp, flapping his arms and walking the length of the room again and again. 'Gillon, he's dead, what's the matter?'

He stopped still, moved towards Leanne and planted his hands on the table. 'He's dead all right, and so's our fat paedo friend.'

'What?'

'Knox copped it out at the track . . . Place is heaving with filth, right now.'

Leanne felt a tingling sensation behind her eyes. It was as if she had been given a drug that released a sudden burst of energy. 'Dead?'

'Aye, Leanne . . . Both your wee pals have been knocked off; what do you make of that then?'

She watched the ash fall from her cigarette – the tobacco had burned nearly all the way to the filter tip. She raised the

131

cigarette to her lips and drew deep. She tasted a burning sensation that chimed with the heat building inside her. 'The police . . . They'll want to speak to me.'

'Why?' said Gillon. 'How are they going to know anything about you?'

Leanne touched the sides of her face, pressed her cheeks in. 'The police will want to know who killed them . . . He was just here, Knox, he was here.'

Gillon closed down the space between them and threw his arms onto Leanne's shoulders. He was shaking her as he spoke. 'You just stay away from the police. You hear me? I'll tell you how to play this. I've got other ideas and they don't involve the police.'

19

DI VALENTINE RUMINATED on the latest victim's identity for a moment and found his train of thought suddenly hijacked. The death of a paedophile – what was really so bad about that? He caught himself just before the notion became a more solid philosophy; he knew it was the act of murder he needed to focus on, not the murdered. He was a police officer with a duty to protect all – his own personal animus had no place in the investigation, unless of course it coincided with the views of those who paid his wages. He shook his head and saw the tracks shifting again: his thoughts rolled over once more. Knox was still dead; however he assessed it, there were some who would say it was good enough for him, but was it really – what was so bad about death? He had been thinking about death a lot lately, but he recalled a time when death was no more a cause for thought than sleep. Valentine laid down his head each night and fell gratefully into the stupor of sleep, thankful even that the sentient part – life, living – was over for another day. How different was death? Wasn't it something to be welcomed, like a well-earned sleep? It struck him that people had it all wrong: they should be grateful for death; the endless tribulations, tests, daily meetings, the unforeseen challenges of life were the things to be afraid of. In life there was no escape, no release. Knox had been released from it all.

Valentine thought of his father – arthritis-wracked, lungs scarred with emphysema – a prisoner in his own mortality who had come to beg for the release of death. The detective thought of his father in the pits of Cumnock digging for coal. They said he could face down a seam and locate the one point where a single blow from a well-timed sledgehammer would release tonnes of the black gold. They – those who said such things – had admired his father's skill as a miner, but what was that worth now? What use were his great skills, hard earned though they were in the bowels of the Ayrshire earth, when they closed the pit? When his father was on strike and the family starved, when the miners fought hand to hand with the police or when the uniformed officers came on horseback and struck them down with batons – where was the benefit of an accumulated life's experience? This death wasn't to be feared, it was to be embraced. Life was the thing to be afraid of. Valentine shuddered as the realisation came to him in waves of recognition – a perspicacity that was new to him, and yet he recognised every nuance of every word as though they were long-worn truisms of his very own.

In the corner of his eye he caught sight of the chief super approaching. He turned to face her and flagged her towards the glassed-off office at the end of the incident room. As he turned, he felt as though a heavy burden was weighing on him, as if he was dragging the contents of the incident room along with him. He knew, of course, it was a fallacy, but he knew also that there would be a new timbre to the conversations he would now have with CS Martin.

Valentine held open the door and watched the chief super walk through. She avoided eye contact, but once inside, behind the closed door, she fixed him with her gaze.

'Well?'

He placed his hands on his hips as he spoke slowly. 'We have an ID for the victim out at the track . . . Duncan Knox.'

134

She shrugged. 'Who?'

'He's a paedophile, long list of convictions . . . mostly time-served. I haven't pulled the file yet, I just took the call.'

The chief super folded her arms and twisted her mouth. She seemed to be thinking, but Valentine knew the look was more practised: she was battling her true reaction. 'And it's the same MO?'

'Almost identical.'

She unfolded her arms and started to pace the confines of the small room. 'Jesus . . . What the bloody hell's going to tie him to Urquhart?'

Valentine eased his hands from his hips and weighed them in front of him. He had the chief super in his sights as he spoke. 'If there's a link, we'll find it.'

She looked out to the incident room – her gaze seemed to fall on Paulo – and shook her head. 'You're not exactly blessed with a full compliment of detective genius out there . . .'

Valentine resented the statement. His first instinct was to react with a rebuttal, but his second instinct was to say nothing and let the burn of her censure be felt in his silence. She spoke again: 'I think it might be time to talk to Glasgow about the case.'

The DI knew the last thing Martin wanted was another area's officers on her patch – it would be humbling, just shy of humiliating, and the chief super liked to be able to strut around her territory with impunity.

'Let's not be too hasty, we haven't even cracked the seal on this Knox death yet. Who knows what the next twenty-four hours will hand us? It would be a shame to serve everything up on a platter for Glasgow.'

The chief super gnawed on her bottom lip, halted her pacing and stood tapping the toe of her shoe on the ground.

'All right, Bob, I'll give you the benefit of the doubt ... but if you're telling me you can handle this with the team you have, then there better be something more than white space to look at on that board the next time I come in here.' She removed her gaze from the detective and walked past him on the way to the door. 'And tomorrow, Bob, first thing ... you have a therapy session. Hope you can fit them around your workload.'

The muscles in Valentine's arms tensed as he watched the chief super walk out into the incident room and back towards her office. He held himself in check for a moment longer, until she was out of sight, and then he reached for the door handle.

'Paulo ... get your coat.' The roar startled even himself.

DS Rossi rose from his desk. 'Are we going somewhere, sir?'

'Out to see the Urquharts.'

Rossi looked perplexed. 'Shouldn't Ally be going with you, then?'

Valentine's voice became a growl. 'Ally's at the scene, so I'm making do!' He started to walk towards the door, and the police officers in the room dropped their heads to avoid eye contact. 'And anything comes in, I want to be informed straight away ... Call!'

There was no reply, but the message was duly received. DS Rossi wrestled himself into his jacket as he caught up with Valentine on the stairs. 'So, are we running the Knox killing past them, boss?'

The sound of the DS's voice had started to grate on Valentine already. 'What do you think, Paulo?'

He shrugged as he pulled his collar down. 'Will I drive, sir?'

The DI nodded. 'Well, I didn't bring you for your repartee, son.'

By the time they got to the car park, Valentine was several strides ahead of DS Rossi, who depressed the remote locking; the blinkers flashed momentarily to indicate the car was unlocked. As he got inside Valentine had to tip a pile of folders onto the floor. He picked up a mobile phone that rested on the seat and noticed there was a missed-call notification. Valentine registered the caller's ID just as DS Rossi opened the driver's door. 'Is this your phone, Paulo?'

The DS looked at the phone in Valentine's hand and seemed to clam up. 'Erm . . .'

'Simple question: is it or isn't it?'

Rossi nodded. 'Yes, sir.'

'Then you better take it . . . Was sitting on the seat, lucky it wasn't nicked.' Valentine kept a stare on the young detective. For a moment there was an uneasy silence in the car, and then Rossi turned towards the windscreen and put the key in the ignition.

On the road out to Alloway, Valentine allowed himself a few snatched glances at Rossi; he knew he had something on the DS now and that he would have to act on the information, but didn't want to let himself believe it was true. For some unknown reason, Valentine felt the need to observe Rossi: it was as if his own temper was too hot, as if any action taken in the immediate future would be weakened somehow by the anger it would ride on. Valentine closed down his thoughts and stared ahead at the road, the swish of trees that passed the windows and the cold grey of the Scottish sky. By Maybole Road the atmosphere in the car seemed to have lost its foetid air, but then entering the rarefied and well-heeled streets of this part of town always made Valentine ease a little further back in his seat. It was as if the broad, expansive boulevards, meandering driveways and high-pitched roofs dictated it. This was where people came to enjoy the rewards of a good life – and to them it was a very good life.

'How the other half live, eh?' said DS Rossi – his voice faltered a little on the conversational gambit.

Valentine returned the glance. 'Not on your wages, Paulo.'

The remark lodged itself in Rossi's expression like a blow. 'I wasn't suggesting . . .'

'Oh, no.'

They had reached the Urquharts' home in perfect time for Rossi to brake and drop down the gears; he made an elaborate turn of the wheel and changed direction from the main road. In the driveway, he pulled up behind Mrs Urquhart's Range Rover and stilled the engine. Valentine already had his seatbelt off as the driver removed the keys.

The moment he stood outside the car, Valentine was assailed by a faint breeze: it swirled towards him on the path, carrying stray grass cuttings and mulch then surrounded his frame in a tight grip that sent a shiver through him from head to toe. For a moment he halted his stride, grabbed a deep breath and then forced himself to walk on. The mere act of putting one step in front of the other broke the spell of the breeze and by the front door of the property the detective was left wondering what he had just experienced.

'Everything OK, boss?' said Rossi.

'Yes, why shouldn't it be?'

Rossi dipped his chin towards his chest. 'You're as white as a sheet.'

Valentine dropped his tense shoulders and turned back towards the door; he was pressing the doorbell as he spoke. 'No need to worry about me.'

In a few moments the door was opened by Adrian Urquhart.

He paused before opening his mouth, but released no words until Valentine introduced himself.

'Oh, yes . . . Would you like to come in?' he said.

As Valentine stepped into the vestibule, his eyes devoured the home: he knew more about the former occupant than he had on his last visit and the knowledge dredged up James Urquhart's spirit for him. It was as if the banker was suddenly everywhere he looked. The rug on the floor, the paint on the walls, the ornamental lamp on the side table – they all bore his signature.

Mrs Urquhart was standing in the middle of the lounge when the detectives entered the room. 'Hello, gentlemen.'

Valentine nodded and accepted the offer of a seat. 'I hope you don't mind us calling round like this . . . It's just we've had some developments.'

'Oh . . .' She lowered herself into the opposite chair; Adrian followed at her side.

For a moment Valentine toyed with the idea of slowly building up to the revelation of Duncan Knox's murder, but as he eyed the Urquharts sitting before him in calm comportment there seemed no need for soft-soaping.

'There's been another killing, in much the same fashion as before.'

The pair sat, unmoved. Valentine checked them for a flinch, the gripping of hands perhaps, but nothing came. He turned his eyes towards DS Rossi, who was looking at the Urquharts with a perplexed expression playing on his face.

Valentine spoke again. 'I have to ask . . . Does the name Duncan Knox mean anything to you?'

This time there was a reaction: Mrs Urquhart rose from the chair and stood behind her son, then she placed her hands on his shoulders and squeezed tightly. 'No, why should it?'

Valentine registered how she snatched her words. 'You seem very sure.'

'Certain.'

DS Rossi turned in his chair to face the detective and made a taut wire of his mouth. Valentine rose to face Mrs Urquhart. 'Is there something you'd like to tell me, Mrs Urquhart ... This isn't the reaction I was expecting to the news that your husband's rather unusual death has been mimicked.'

Adrian shot from his chair and walked towards the middle of the room where the detective stood. 'I wasn't aware there was a grieving widow's handbook that my mother was supposed to be acting out.'

'That's enough, Adrian ...' Mrs Urquhart walked round beside her son. 'Mr Valentine, we are still in shock.'

'I appreciate that.'

'Then why on earth are you questioning us when you could be out hunting a killer?'

Valentine caught sight of DS Rossi rising from his chair; in the space of a few minutes the cordial atmosphere had turned nasty. 'It's very important that we ascertain any links between your husband and the latest victim, you must be able to see how that could assist us.'

'What makes you think there are any links?' said Mrs Urquhart.

'Well, if there aren't then it's important that we eliminate that line of inquiry.'

Mrs Urquhart's glass-smooth skin reflected the light from the window where she stood; she looked pale and fraught as she spoke to her son. 'I don't know this Duncan Knox, do you, Adrian?'

Adrian Urquhart shook his head. 'No.'

A scowl settled on Mrs Urquhart's face and then she

touched the seam of her blouse nervously. 'Well, there, that seems to be an end to it, doesn't it now, Mr Valentine?'

DI Valentine's facial muscles conspired against him as he eased out a slanting smile. His words came bluntly. 'I suppose it does.'

'Good. Then I'll show you both out.' She turned to the door and stood with one hand on the handle and with the other – palm outstretched – gesturing towards the hallway.

At the door Valentine halted. 'Thank you for your time.'

'You're welcome.'

The detectives walked through the doorway and followed the hall into the vestibule before being shown out the front door. As they stood in the driveway buttoning their coats, Valentine spoke. 'I'm afraid, Mrs Urquhart, there are one or two other formalities that I'll have to . . . address with you.'

'Formalities?' Her tone was clipped.

'Regarding the investigation . . . I'll be back in touch.' Valentine dipped his head and made for the car; as he went he could sense angry eyes burning into his back, but his attention fixed on the sight of Ronnie Bell peering over the neighbouring wall. The detective turned to see if Mrs Urquhart had registered Bell, but she was already heading indoors.

'More neighbourly concern, or was it the sight of the police that brought him out snooping around?' said Valentine. As he spoke Bell turned away from the officers and gripped the handles of a wheelbarrow, which he started to push along the path – a squeak on each revolution – towards his home.

Inside the car, DS Rossi turned the key in the ignition and depressed the clutch, then started to shake his head and curse. 'What the hell was that all about? Couldn't wait to get us out of there . . . Jesus, you'd think we were the ones that murdered him, not the ones investigating the case.'

Valentine waited until they had left the Urquharts' driveway and crossed the first of the broad Alloway streets before he spoke. 'Don't you concern yourself with that, Paulo; you've got other things to be worried about.'

The DS jerked the wheel. 'What do you mean?'

Valentine raised his arm and made a show of exposing the watch face on his wrist. 'By my guess, it'll take you about nine minutes to get back to the station ... That's as long as you have to explain why your phone was dinging a call from Cameron Sinclair when I got in this car.'

20

DS CHRIS ROSSI PLAYED the bluff card because it was instinctual: a remnant from a childhood when pleading ignorance to gullible parents had once paid dividends. Valentine didn't buy the dummy, though, and was vaguely aggrieved by the insult to his intelligence until he realised who he was dealing with.

'And you can take that glaikit look off your chops, son,' he yelled. 'It's not going to get you out of this hole.'

Rossi closed his mouth and his Adam's apple rode up and down in this throat before he parted his dry lips once more and tried for words. 'I'm sorry . . .'

'I don't much like apologies either – the damage has always been done by the time they come out.'

Valentine took his eyes from the detective and watched the road ahead for a suitable place to stop; he selected a calm stretch where the road tapered off into a bus lane. 'Just pull up there.'

Rossi looked in the mirror and put on the blinkers; even his driving had become more cautious now. When he pulled up and halted the car he seemed reluctant to still the engine – it ran on for a few moments – and then he turned the key in the ignition and the juddering stopped.

Valentine looked straight ahead but said nothing. He knew the crucible building in the car would have to be addressed, but it wasn't going to be by him. He had tested this approach, many times, in the interview room; the silence was no threat to him, it provoked no fear, but to those on the receiving end it was a real and palpable force backed with all the weight and import of consequence.

DS Rossi turned to face the DI. 'What do you want me to say?'

'You can say what you like, Paulo; at this stage it's unlikely to make a blind bit of difference.'

He slapped at the wheel: it was a petulant gesture. 'You know what it's like.'

Valentine had a bolt of energy balling inside him. 'Do I?' He had no idea what Rossi was implying: that they were all blokes together, perhaps? Or, that he should sympathise with a fellow officer who had been tempted in ways he had never been and never would be?

Rossi exhaled a long breath. 'Look, do you mind if I smoke?'

'Yes, I do.' Valentine placed a hand on the dash and tapped gently – an almost effete trace of the instructor's emergency-stop signal. 'You have until I tap here again to say something that might help you or mitigate the fact that you are in some serious bother . . . If I like what I hear, I'll do all I can for you. If I don't, you're on your own.'

The DS scrunched his eyes and grimaced. His complexion settled on a shade just shy of white, though his eye sockets were grey and sunken. He was sweating, his brow damp and his top lip glistening. 'Look, sir, you know I've had some financial problems and I'm not about to use that as an excuse, but . . .'

Valentine turned in his chair to face him. 'Go on.'

'I have a family and it's tough on a copper's wage.'

'I've got a family too, son. But I've never been tempted to put my fingers in the till.'

144

Rossi wiped his brow and then fingered the edges of his mouth. 'I've never done anything like this before . . . I got into debt . . . The money was put out there and . . .'

'You took it?'

Rossi nodded, then clamped his mouth shut.

'Tell me, I need to know: did Cameron Sinclair make you an offer or did you go to him?'

The DS kept his eyes fixed on the middle distance but didn't answer. He'd told Valentine all he needed to know.

'You bloody idiot, Paulo.'

On the way back to the station, the pair sat in silence until Rossi parked up in the King Street car park.

'Go home,' said Valentine.

'What?'

'You heard me . . . You're off the case and almost certainly suspended. When I relay this to the chief super there'll be an investigation, a tribunal likely, and you'll get a chance to explain yourself . . . But my advice to you, Paulo, would be to use the next few months to start polishing up your CV.'

Valentine got out the car and slammed the door; he didn't look back as he headed for the station and climbed the stairs all the way to the chief super's office.

The detective's thoughts collided as he stood facing the brassy nameplate, and then he knocked twice on the door and walked in. Chief Superintendent Marion Martin was sitting at her desk eyeing the contents of a tuna-fish sandwich as he appeared.

'I found our mole . . .' he said.

The tone of his voice was so matter-of-fact and the content of his words so at odds that he seemed to confuse the chief super; she lowered the sandwich and thinned her eyes. 'Come again?'

'Chris Rossi tipped off Cameron Sinclair . . . He's up to his neck in debt. I caught him on the phone to his bookies earlier – he tried it on with Sinclair for a few bob.'

'Is this a joke?'

'Do I look like I'm laughing? I've sent him home while we get the suspension proceedings going.'

'What?' CS Martin shook her head and touched her temples with her fingertips as if testing whether the perception was real. 'Jesus, Bob . . . Couldn't you have let me know sooner? At least given me some kind of warning . . .'

Valentine turned away from her, towards the door he had just walked through. 'I just found out myself. Look, what was my option, put him in a cell?'

'What if he goes back to Sinclair?'

'My next call's to the editor of the *Glasgow-Sun*. I think Sinclair will be joining Paulo in the dole queues before long.'

'Unless they stand by him.'

'After bribing a police officer . . . He'll get his marching orders and we'll be shot of him. I could almost thank Paulo, it's his greatest contribution to the whole investigation.'

Martin stood up, shaking her head as she spoke. 'Bob, get real, if the *Sun* punts Sinclair he'll just go freelance and chase us but with an axe to grind this time . . . And what about the squad? It was bare bones before you shunted Paulo out the door.'

Valentine reached for the handle and jerked the door open. His voice was rising too; he knew it wouldn't be long until they were upping the volume even more. 'I think we'll get by without Robocop, don't you?' He walked through the open door and yanked the handle firmly behind him – the door hit the jamb like a full stop on the end of the conversation. In the hallway, Valentine's neck tensed and a firm pulse began

146

to beat beneath his collar. He started to loosen his tie as he walked back to the incident room to break the news to the squad that not only had he no idea how Duncan Knox and James Urquhart were connected, but that they were now a man down too. He knew the impact on morale would be severe. Valentine didn't want the group to suffer for DS Rossi's sins, though. He had been on the receiving end of harsh treatment for others' mistakes in the past and knew the resentment it caused. If there was to be a way forward for the team, it would be by maintaining focus on solving the case.

He opened the door of the incident room and stepped inside. 'Right, listen up everyone . . .'

The place seemed to still, like a low-voltage shock had been passed through the furniture, and then suddenly everyone regained composure and started to mill towards the inspector.

'Something up, boss?' DC McAlister had returned from the crime scene at the track.

'Aye, you could say that.' Valentine's voice signalled another jolt to come. 'I'm just back from talking with the chief superintendent and have some bad news for you, I'm afraid.' Valentine's gaze was on one of the PCs: she held a blue folder tight to her chest, as if looking to put a barrier between her and what was about to come. 'Detective Sergeant Chris Rossi has been relieved of all duties as of today . . .'

A low barrage of muttering buffeted Valentine. 'That's enough . . . The DS is suspended pending a review of his actions of late and in the meantime I'm raising DC McAlister to the post of acting detective sergeant.'

McAlister's eyes widened for a moment and then his face cracked into a grin. 'Thanks, sir.'

'Don't get overexcited, Ally. I'll be wanting my pound of flesh from you – you'll be taking on Paulo's workload, so that's looking at the buyout and Ronnie Bell to add to your duties.'

DS Donnelly crossed the floor to pat McAlister on the back and shake his hand.

Valentine spoke up. 'Right, I haven't heard my phone ring once since I was out, so I'm presuming there's nothing to report . . .'

Silence settled in the room and was punctured by a woman's voice. 'There was a call from your wife, sir . . . I left a message on your desk. It wasn't to do with the case.'

Valentine looked at the officer and nodded, then turned back to the others and clapped his hands together. 'OK, back to work. Come on, move it!' As he walked through the shifting bodies Valentine called out to Donnelly and McAlister. 'You pair – in my office, now.'

The detectives looked at each other and set off in the wake of Valentine's heavy footfalls. At the office door he reached out for the handle and swung it open, and as he stepped inside the DI stood pressing the glass front with his fingertips and ushered the others through. He let them get inside and then closed the door firmly and headed towards his desk to retrieve the telephone message from his wife. It was a short note in looping, large handwriting that reminded him of his daughters'; the contents were, however, all his wife's. He lowered the note onto the desk, then quickly retrieved it before crushing his fist around the thin paper and dropping it towards the wastebasket beneath his desk.

'More good news?' said McAlister.

Valentine set eyes on the newly appointed DS and held his mouth tightly shut. He straightened his back, pressing his hands onto his hips, and then removed his chair from below the desk and sat down. Donnelly and McAlister followed his lead.

148

'I'm presuming neither of you knew about Paulo's . . . addiction?' He spat the last word like it had left a bad taste.

The detectives looked at each other. Donnelly spoke. 'Well, I wouldn't say we never knew exactly . . .'

Valentine raised a hand and cut him off. 'You misunderstand me. I'm not asking you, I'm telling you. I know neither of you are so bloody stupid as to jeopardise your careers like that, but . . .' He leaned forward on the desk and pointed his index finger back towards the chief super's office. 'Some people will be asking just those questions and you better have your answers ready. Do you understand me?'

'Yes, sir.'

'Good. Paulo's been a clown, every circus needs one, but no more than that.' The DI shook his head and exhaled a long breath. 'He's dug his own grave, but if either of you let on you had suspicions that might be looked at as a tacit approval . . . Am I painting a clear enough picture?'

'Yes, sir.'

Valentine was growing tired of the staccato responses; he felt like an officious teacher admonishing the behaviour of errant pupils. He eased back in the chair and the castors squeaked beneath him.

McAlister spoke. 'Can I ask about the shape of the squad, boss? We're a man down now, and . . .'

'I know, and Dino's been threatening to bring in some Glasgow boys since day one.'

'We don't want them coming down here and big-footing the lot of us. Be just like them to steal the show.'

Valentine scratched his chin as he replied: 'It's bad enough on Glasgow Fair having Weegies doon the water for an ice cream.'

'We'll be seeing a few more of them if Rangers ever claw their way to a promotion,' said McAlister.

The three men laughed, but it was short-lived. Valentine's grave expression signalled the true import of the situation.

'If she brings in Glasgow, we're in the shit . . . but at least we know the territory.' Valentine sat forward again, picked up the receiver from the telephone on his desk and started to search his blotter for the number he'd written down earlier. He nodded the others towards the door; they rose and left the office. When he was alone in the room, he drummed his fingers on the keypad of the phone for a moment – the call to the editor of the *Glasgow-Sun* with the Sinclair allegations would have to wait a few minutes longer. He dialled another number.

'Hello, Clare . . .'

His wife sounded stressed on the other end of the line. He surmised she had been busy juggling her shopping addiction with the housework and grimaced into the phone.

'Oh, you got back to me then . . .' she said, her tone smothered in sarcasm.

'I'm sorry, love . . . had a lot on. What's this about my dad?'

Clare sighed down the line. 'I gave him a call today, just checking in . . .'

'Yes, and . . .'

'Well, he didn't answer at first.' She shuffled the receiver. 'I thought he might have been out in the garden or something, but then I called back and he was still in bed.'

'He's retired, he's entitled to a long-lie.'

'It was eleven o'clock, your father never sleeps that late . . . Anyway, he sounded . . . Look, he wasn't himself is what I'm trying to say. I was concerned enough to call you at the station . . .'

Valentine stepped in. 'OK, leave it with me.'

'What does that mean?'

'It means I'll look into it.'

'Will you go round?'

Valentine's eyes roved towards the ceiling in exasperation. He had far too much on to be entertaining his wife's insecurities, even if they were well intentioned. 'If I've got time . . .'

Clair sparked up. 'Look, I would go round myself but he's never keen to have a woman fussing over him, you know how he is . . . and he's your father, Bob.'

'OK, Clare, I'll pay him a visit.'

'Today?'

'Yes, Clare . . . today.'

As he put down the receiver, he glanced towards the clock on the wall and sighed. He still had time to make the call to the editor of the *Glasgow-Sun*. He reached out for the telephone and tapped in the number he had written down beside the name Jack Gallagher. As the line began to ring, he knew it was a call that wasn't going to make him any friends.

21

EVERY DAY WAS A STRUGGLE for the things we decided we couldn't live without. Valentine remembered his father had worded it differently: he'd said it was about 'putting steam on the table'. However you worded it, the struggle started somewhere around the time you left the cover of your parents' home and met the stark realities of the adult world. The game was afoot. And it was a game: a tawdry, shallow, callous and pathetic game. We traded our immortal souls for a place at a feeble table. One where there was no proper competition, no winning or losing; it was all about simply keeping going, keeping playing because the second you stopped that's when you realised there was also a forfeit attached. You gave the game everything for nothing.

Valentine remembered being old enough to leave school and go out amongst the great monetised masses – he had watched those from rich families take a year out or start a business bankrolled by their parents: options beyond the dreams of avarice to him at the time. And his life since had been nothing but graft: hard, sometimes dangerous graft. He wondered how it had been for those others who went off to Peru to follow the Inca trail or took the cosy sinecure, discreetly secreted under Daddy's wing. He knew for sure none would be sitting alone now, wondering what had become of Bob Valentine. And why was that? Because he had come from nothing. And what had he risen to become? A middle-grade public servant, badly battle-scarred and clinging to a notion of respect for his position that was likely ten years out of date. The world had changed very little in many regards since he'd formed his opinion of the force, but all the changes that had been made were ineluctably in the wrong direction.

If there was a point, a focus of Valentine's thoughts – apart from the most obvious form of self-flagellation – he knew it was Urquhart. He was the diametric opposite of the detective, who was the rough to the smooth in the equation. It made him wonder how different a life to him Urquhart must have lived. Valentine did this because it was his job, but also because it was a natural preoccupation of his: he put himself into the mindset of others like some people tried on new clothes for a holiday. Valentine could see the banker had moved in rarefied circles and enjoyed the security of excessive wealth, but what had that done to him? The detective knew his own shortcomings had resiled him to certain choices, but when choices where endless, when the game of life had no dice, how did this influence the making of a man?

Urquhart was one of the masters of the universe the media were so fond of pillorying – the banking elite were so lampooned it had become a cliché, but Valentine knew even clichés had once been fresh and full of insight. Their impact lingered for a simple reason: they were apt. It was a fact then, cemented in Valentine's mind by his own hard-won experience of playing the game, that Urquhart's thoughts, actions, reactions and every nuance of human behaviour in between would have been formed and informed by his sense of self. He was demonstrably a superior sort of person: he couldn't deny that to himself or anyone; who, indeed, could deny it? He was fortified by the adulation the world showered on material wealth. It was of no doubt to the DI that Urquhart, and others like him, felt empowered by their status. The question the detective wanted, and needed, to answer now was: how had the innate human need to exert status manifested itself in this instance? In simpler terms: what did Urquhart think he had a right to get away with that lesser mortals had obviously taken grievous exception to? If he could answer that, find the root of the first murder on his books, then the killing of Duncan Knox would, he had no doubt, become clear. He hoped that he was right, that the tightening in his gut meant what he thought it did. There was something missing, something that tied the two cases together, something that made Urquhart and Knox sound less incongruous when mentioned in the same sentence, but he couldn't see what it was. Valentine knew that once all the pieces of the puzzle came into view it would be obvious, it always was, but right now he saw no way through the forest of question marks.

Valentine helped the car's momentum to drop by lowering the gears on the way into Cumnock. When the car ahead's tail lights glowed red, he applied the brakes and brought the Vectra to a standstill. He lowered his window and the smirr on the air revived him. The town was his father's home: not his, it had never been his even when as a boy he had lived there. Cumnock was one of those stations where no new recruits wanted to be posted. It was a rough place: in Ayrshire they called it Dodge City – a nod to its Wild West similarity and the fact that so many of its inhabitants were on the dole. In the last few months, as he recuperated from his injuries, Valentine had totted up innumerable grievous crimes on the nightly news, all committed in Cumnock. It was customary, in the district, to see head shakes at the merest mention of the town, perhaps a berating of the Thatcher years that saw the pit closures and the vast majority of those employed in the mines made jobless. But there was more to it than that, thought Valentine; Scotland's post-industrial population had changed. Where once stood a working class was now an underclass. Things like self-respect, pride, any sense of community or belonging, had long since evaporated. The inhabitants of places like Cumnock, and much of Ayrshire, were increasingly growing to look like members of a separate race: drug-addled zombies wading through life like it was slowly drowning them, guided by full-time carers who were there to tell them how to put their trousers on, how to feed themselves, how to swallow their methadone, to shut up and slump back into stupor so the rest of us could get on without thinking what to do about them.

The curtains were drawn as Valentine pulled up outside his father's home on Keir Hardie Hill. He wound up the window and felt the stirring in the depths of his chest that occurred each time he came back. He collected the small carrier bag he'd filled with goods from the Spar store and opened the car door. Valentine stood in the street for a moment, watching the rain clouds looming over the rooftops. A cold wind rattled down the road and whipped at his bare throat; he turned up his collar as he walked towards the house. The gate screeched like an early warning of his approach, but as he raised his head to take in the window once again, the curtains remained still. He returned the hasp and headed towards the doorstep, knocked twice and reached for the handle. The door was open.

'Hello . . .' Valentine called out as he stood in the hallway. The carpet was faded and worn beneath his feet – he remembered the day when it had been taken up and turned round to allow the less worn end to bear the brunt of the front-door traffic.

'Dad . . . are you in?' His voice echoed off the walls; the

place was cold, damp and musty. He opened a window and made his way through to the living room. As he went through the door he heard some stirring in the next room. The noise of feet on boards and a wracking cough brought him a deep sense of relief. He made his way through to the kitchen, deposited the bag of groceries on the table, and started to fill the kettle; it was beginning to whistle as the thin frame of his father appeared, haunting the doorway like a ghost.

'Hello, auld yin.'

'To what do I owe the pleasure?' His father seemed several shades whiter than the last time he had seen him; Valentine wondered if it could be the case. Had it been that long?

'I brought you some rolls . . . and bacon. Thought I'd do you a bit of tea.'

His father started to tighten the belt of his dressing gown as he watched the goings-on in the kitchen. He seemed thinner too, more gaunt, and in possession of a stoop that shrunk his frame to boyish dimensions. 'You've been talking to that wife of yours.'

Valentine placed a mug of coffee in front of his father. 'Yeah, well, we do exchange words now and again.'

'I don't need looking after.' He raised a bony, gnarled finger and wagged it in front of him. 'Never taken a handout in my life . . . not even in the strike.'

Valentine's will to challenge withered and died. He lowered his shoulders and turned towards his father with the frying pan in hand. 'Don't start about the bloody strike again . . .' – he lifted the frying pan – 'or you'll get a clout off this!'

His father pinched his gaunt face and the white bristles on his chin pointed towards his son. 'Wouldn't be the first clout I'd got from a polisman.'

Valentine turned back to the stove and sparked up the gas.

He ignored his father's goading; time-worn experience had taught him that indulgence and ignoring him were the fastest route from the conflict.

His father sipped the coffee and continued. 'Summer of '84, after Thatcher had stockpiled enough coal, that's when I first faced down a polisman on a horse . . . Shields and sticks they had. They were all pally with us before that, joking and laughing away, but it got nasty quick enough . . . Did I ever tell you they used to come down and wave five-pound notes at us, those polis . . .'

'Once or twice, Dad.'

'Aye well.' He eased back in the chair and looked out of the window. 'Bloody coal board took full-page adverts in the paper, said we were blocking essential supplies of coal to the hospitals and the schools and the old folks' home.' He made a spitting sound, and sighed. 'Utter rubbish. I went up on the hills howking coal for the wee wifey who lived next door . . . Never saw anyone go short.'

Valentine turned round and presented his father with the bacon roll he had prepared. The plate clattered off the tabletop as he put it down. 'You want any sauce on that?'

He shook his head. 'I'm all out.'

'I could nip down the shops . . .'

'No. Be cold by time you got back . . .'

The pair sat in silence as the old man ate his bacon roll. Valentine watched his father raising his thin arms and thinner fingers towards his mouth as he ate and wondered what had ever became of him. This was the man who had stood in the Cumnock Town Hall to hear Mick McGahey proclaim the strike was theirs to win. Six hundred souls believed him and thousands paid the price of the fight that had no winners. The police suffered too. Valentine had listened to those stories when he had joined the force, but his father didn't want to hear about female officers getting booted in the face or local boys having their cars torched. It all seemed such a long time ago now that Valentine found it hard to understand what kept the flame alive in his father. Was it his war? He remembered his grandfather talking about his days in North Africa chasing Rommel and seeing the lights go on in his eyes; he was still there, even as an old man, back in his youth, in his prime. Was this what old age did to you? Was this what it was for: to regale yourself with the flashpoints, the highs and the lows of your life?

Valentine took in his father: the slow masticating of his thin jaws and brittle teeth looked a trial to him. He grimaced on each minute swallow of food. Did it have to be so hard, this life of men?

'How have you been keeping?'

His father moved his head from side to side in lieu of a shrug. 'So, so.'

'Clare worries about you. The girls are asking for you.'

The mention of his granddaughters brought a smile to the old man's face; his eyes lit up. 'There's no need to worry about me . . . I've never died a winter yet.'

It struck Valentine that the optimum word was 'yet'. 'Well, is there anything you need?'

'Not fussing, anyway!'

'Dad . . . please.'

'I'll be fine with some peace and quiet; get back to that wife and those daughters of yours and fuss over them.'

Valentine felt his father's inscrutable gaze burrowing into him and for a moment he was a small child once again. He had never managed to understand his father's complete rejection of all affection shown to him, but he knew it sprang from

158

the same source as his own overweening pride. He couldn't criticise him for it, but he wondered if he could target some censure at himself for perpetuating the fault. He took a deep breath and turned away from him, catching sight of a pile of library books in the corner of the room as he did. 'Do they need to go back?'

'Aye, they do.'

Valentine picked up the books: two detective novels by William McIlvanney sat on the top. 'What's this . . . Are you reading up on the police now?'

'He's a Kilmarnock laddie, the writer.'

'I know, I read the books years ago . . . Set in Glasgow, mind you.'

His father slouched forward in his chair and spoke with his finger tapping out his main points on the table. 'But it would take an Ayrshire man to make sense of that place, you realise.'

Valentine smiled. 'The son of a miner, no doubt.'

'Are you making assumptions?'

'Me, Dad? No . . . never.' He picked up the other books and turned for the door. 'I'll get these back. Do you want me to pick up some others?'

The old man nodded. 'Aye, you can get me the third one in the series . . . *Strange Loyalties*, I think it's called.'

'The police again?'

'They make good reading.'

It was the closest Valentine had ever heard his father come to a compliment.

22

DI Bob Valentine spent the night in fitful dreams with familiar figures, some of whom he knew, while others were mere phantoms that had come to assail his sleep. The small girl with the white-blonde hair was there once again, alongside his own father and late mother. It made the detective feel uneasy to dream of the dead; they somehow came alive once more, became animated in dreams as they no longer did in waking reality. It unsettled him, made his chest constrict and put winding bales of barbed wire in his stomach.

As he made coffee, said goodbye to his family and drove to the station, Valentine tried to downplay the significance of the night before. By the King Street roundabout he had put the entire situation down to the stress of the case: his unconscious mind wrestling by night with the problems he couldn't find solutions to by day.

Since dispatching Paulo with a suspension, Valentine knew he had unsettled the team: he would need to work twice as hard to get them to bond as a unit now. And with so few leads on the Urquhart killing and nothing to tie it to the murder of Knox, it would be difficult to find something to stoke their enthusiasm with. There was the added uncertainty of the chief super – a loose canon at the best of times – and how she would ultimately react to the team being a DS down. The ever-present threat of the whole investigation being turned over to Glasgow CID was a pressure Valentine could do without but, for the time being, was one he knew he would have to live with.

'Morning, Jim,' he said as he entered the front door of the station.

'Oh, it's yourself . . .' The desk sergeant leaned over conspiratorially and beckoned Valentine with a nod. 'Big Dino's in already, I see.'

Valentine approached the counter and lowered his briefcase to the floor. 'Starting early isn't she?'

'Aye, and that's not the all of it . . .' Jim looked back towards the staircase as if to set the scene for his next announcement. 'She's got some new blood up there with her now.'

'New blood?'

'Young one, twenties, never seen her before, but she's polis . . . got it written all over her.'

Valentine felt the barbed wire he carried inside him turning again: it was a call for caffeine, or something stronger. He didn't know who the young police officer was, but he had his suspicions already. 'Did you catch an accent?'

Jim frowned, the creases in his brow making his skin look even more like old leather. 'No, afraid not . . . What you thinking?'

If Valentine had learned one thing in his time at King Street station, it was to keep what you were thinking to yourself. 'Who knows with Dino . . . Could be my replacement.' He let the implication hang, then struck again: 'Or yours, pal.'

On the stairs, Valentine felt Jim's eyes on his back. He knew he'd set the cogs turning in Jim's mind and that he'd be paying close attention to their every revolution until something like thought ignited. The detective knew if there was any hope of the new officer's identity being revealed in a hurry then the desk sergeant would be the first to know; with any luck, Valentine thought, he would be the second.

161

In the incident room, he hung up his coat and carried his briefcase down towards the glassed-off office. He allowed himself a glance towards the whiteboard to discern any new information, but spotted little save a few additional jottings about the Urquhart post-mortem report in red marker pen. Before he had closed the door, the telephone on his desk was ringing.

'Hello, Valentine.'

'Morning, Bob.' It was Chief Superintendent Marion Martin, her voice high and chipper – too cheery by far. It unsettled him.

'Yes, Chief, what can I do for you?'

'Anything to report since yesterday?'

An inverted smile crept onto his features. 'I need to get an update from the squad before I can brief you; I had them on a number of specifics so I'd be hoping to be edging closer today . . .'

'Closer to what, Bob . . . the door?'

It was a glib remark and he ignored it.

'Anyway, I'd like to see you in my office when you have a moment.'

'Oh, yes . . .'

'Yes, Bob . . . In fact, right away.' The line clicked off.

Valentine held his hand in mid-air for a moment, staring at the receiver. He couldn't quite believe that he had reached his time of life and was still susceptible to the taunts of so-called superiors. The thought that there was anything, in any way, superior about Chief Superintendent Marion Martin brought a moment of levity to his thinking: the woman was deluded, she had ascended the ranks with such alacrity that daily nosebleeds were the norm at her altitude. The detective knew exactly what she was playing at too: she was frightened of being found out, of being found wanting because she was a mere interloper in the force. The consequence for Valentine, however, was that as the investigation's profile ramped up, the chief super's need for a speedy resolution intensified. She would spare no one in her quest for results because the results were the thin carapace she hid her true form beneath.

Valentine booted up his computer, waited for the Windows icon to appear and sat in his chair; its back creaked behind him as he twiddled frustratedly with the mouse in his right hand.

'Right away . . .' He repeated the words, but couldn't quite take in that she had said them. She had taunted him like a new recruit who needed to be shown the lie of the land. He reached for the telephone receiver and pressed the speed-dial for the press office – the line was answered on the second ring.

'Hello, media relations.' It was Coreen's assistant. Valentine struggled to remember her name but then it came back to him.

'Debbie, I was after your boss . . . Is she about?'

'Who's speaking?' She sounded aloof, and there were officers who would have been offended – served her her arse in parsley for questioning – but Valentine guessed it was Coreen's training coming to the fore: the girl had obviously made the mistake of handing over stray calls once, but she wouldn't do it again.

'It's Bob Valentine from CID . . . detective inspector.'

A rummaging on the other end of the line was greeted with a sharp intake of breath, then a gap stretched out that had Valentine tapping his fingertips on a pile of blue folders.

'Bob . . .' It was Coreen.

'Good morning.'

'And what can I do you for?'

163

Valentine leaned forward and rested his elbows on the desk. 'Have you heard anything about our man, Sinclair?'

Coreen cleared her throat. 'I thought that's what you might be interested in . . . Yes, suspended on full pay, I hear.'

A smile crept up the side of Valentine's face. 'Nice one.'

'I wouldn't put out the bunting quite yet.'

'Oh, no?'

'Definitely not . . . By all accounts he went ballistic.'

'So what? Paulo's on the record with the finger pointed squarely at Sinclair.'

Coreen sniggered. It was a fake laugh, more for effect than anything. 'If I know Cameron Sinclair, he'll have a bloody great hard-on for all of us now, Bob . . . Don't expect we've heard the last of him.'

'Just you let me know the second he comes anywhere near you with that hard-on, love . . . You hear me?'

As Valentine lowered the phone, the computer screen lit up and little icons formed themselves into neat rows on his desktop. He clicked on Internet Explorer. When the search engine appeared, Valentine dragged the drop-down menu to select his daughter's Facebook account and waited for the page to appear. The network was slow, but he conceded that might have something to do with the number of pictures on Chloe's timeline. His daughter was sixteen and not quite an adult, but seemed to be living a kind of sophisticated social life that he couldn't comprehend. He justified the intrusion into her life as a necessary evil in today's world. Valentine no more wanted to snoop on his daughter than anyone else, but it was a means to an end: the conclusion of a nagging feeling that something wasn't altogether right with her.

He checked her posts, all innocuous enough: pictures of puppies with pop-philosophising captions, links to music videos, adumbrations on the week's highlights to come. Only one remark struck him as worthy of closer scrutiny: 'Daddy's becoming a popular man . . .' A hyperlink followed. Valentine clicked on it and was brought to the website of the *Glasgow-Sun*. As he scrolled down he quickly identified Cameron Sinclair's byline on the article his own name featured in.

'What the hell is this?' He couldn't understand why anyone would post the link on his daughter's timeline, but conceded much teenage behaviour was inscrutable to him. Then a thought struck him. He returned to his daughter's stream and checked for the post's author. Hot needles pressed on his eyeballs as he took in the almost unidentifiable thumbnail picture of a blurred male. As he read the same name he'd seen on the byline only a few seconds ago, his hand constricted tightly round the mouse.

'You've crossed a line, Sinclair.'

The DI closed down the webpage and rose from the chair. He surmised that the Facebook post was some kind of mocking taunt: parents were good value on the embarrassment scale for youngsters, and seeing Dad on television or in the paper was something like incitement; it invited attention from other teenagers. It was a move meant to embarrass his daughter and create some tension at home for him. But Sinclair was sailing close to the wind assuming he wouldn't check his daughter's web usage. Either that or he was a more reckless idiot than he had previously given him credit for.

As Valentine opened the door and made his way to the chief super's office, he hoped he hadn't misjudged Cameron Sinclair. If he was as rash as his latest action indicated then he would need even closer scrutiny than he had afforded him so far. If it was simply an escalation, an act of desperation, then this was, he conceded, perhaps even more concerning.

The thought that his daughter was now seen as a legitimate pawn by Sinclair was something else altogether. If the hack's intention was to blunt his edge, he was in for a shock: it would have the opposite effect.

He knocked on the door, twice, and took firm hold of the handle as he stepped into the chief super's office. Dino was standing by the window with a coffee cup in hand; in her other hand was the elbow of a young woman who she seemed to be keen to impress. She threw back her hair and laughed as if the scene merited a kind of cocktail-party bonhomie.

Valentine took two steps and coughed into his fist. 'Good morning.'

'Ah, Bob . . . Thought you'd lost your way.' The thought was there to confirm that he may indeed have lost his way, but not in the manner she meant. He let the rejoinder lie.

'You wanted to see me?' He found his gaze shifting towards the young woman, who turned to face him and nodded. It was a polite nod, almost conspiratorial in its suggestion that she had the chief super's ersatz demeanour in hand.

'Oh yes indeed, Bob, I want to see you.' CS Martin motioned the young woman to the front of her desk and walked round the other side herself. 'I'd like to introduce you to Sylvia McCormack if I may . . .'

Valentine put out his hand. The woman reached out and shook it enthusiastically, a wide smile filling her face. 'Hello, sir.'

Dino stepped between them and made her way towards the coffee pot for a refill. As she poured, she spoke loudly, her words bouncing off the wall. 'Sylvia is one of Glasgow's finest young detective sergeants . . .' She continued on, but by the time Valentine had heard the words 'Glasgow' and 'detective sergeant' he knew exactly what was afoot.

He cut in. 'Am I to assume Sylvia has been seconded to Ayr?'

The chief super turned round, held up her coffee cup and dipped her head towards it. 'You assume correctly, detective.'

Valentine's pulse jolted; his heart rate increased. His jaws clenched and the familiar taste of a bitter pill being swallowed passed down his throat. Martin had gone behind his back; she hadn't consulted him but instead had presented the solution to Paulo's absence as a fait accompli. He knew it was her right to do so, but he also knew better people would have played it straight. He ran a finger down the crease of his shirtsleeve as he tried to find his response. DS Martin walked before him and the light from the window silhouetted her frame on the grey wall.

'The investigation is at a crucial stage. I'm not quite sure how an officer from another force will improve the dynamic,' said Valentine.

The young woman stepped forward. 'I've been brought up to speed.' She snatched a blue folder from the desk and opened it up. 'I've sketched out a profile on the kind of individual that might . . .'

Valentine cut in. 'That might impale a man through his arse with a piece of 4x2?' He had tried to ruffle her, but was unsuccessful.

'I have profiling experience, and I've worked a number of similar cases in the Central Belt.'

'Similar?' His intonation suggested the idea was ludicrous, that it resembled reality in much the same way as a model aeroplane aspired to manned flight.

'By that I mean serial mutilation.' The young woman lowered her head and stepped back. It was a retreat that signalled she thought Valentine's truculence was insurmountable.

The chief super pitched in with an act of consoling deference to the DI. 'Bob, I think Sylvia is trying to say that her experience might be useful to the team. A fresh pair of eyes and an outside perspective may pay dividends.'

'This is not a serial killer we're dealing with here: there's no trophy taking, there's no mutilation, sexual interference or anything else to suggest we're dealing with an abnormal psychology. This is calculated and precise, yes, but it's not a pattern killer, and I'll stake my reputation on that.'

Valentine sensed the air being sucked out of the room. His voice seemed to have risen higher than he'd intended; he was playing to the gallery and when he stopped speaking the audience fell into a stunned silence.

CS Martin fanned the lapel of her jacket in an animated manner. She turned to DS McCormack and made a lullaby of her voice. 'Perhaps you'd like to go and acquaint yourself with the incident room, Sylvia.'

The young woman's stone-grey eyes flashed. 'Yes, of course.' She was bright, had caught the hint immediately, and gripping the folder she eased herself towards the door with a smile for Valentine on the way out.

The DI felt a pang of guilt: she was an unwilling pawn in Martin's machinations and he'd been harsh on her, but life was harsh, and life on the force as harsh as it got.

'What the hell are you playing at, Bob?' Her sweet tone evaporated as quickly as a morning mist.

'I'm not sure I know what you mean.'

'Don't play wide with me, pal, I'll give you your head in your hands to play with if you start that patter in here.' She pointed to the floor as if it indicated a marker of her territory.

Valentine brought his hand up to tap a finger on his cheekbone and affected a look of stupefaction. 'If you're referring to the fact that you've parachuted a new DS into my team with no prior notice then I'll put my hand up to not being overly chuffed about it.'

'I gave you plenty of notice: how many times did I tell you, now let me see?' She walked over to her desk and opened her diary. She was hiding behind the rulebook, a favourite tactic of all bureaucrats.

Valentine turned where he stood and marched towards the desk. He leaned forward and directed his rant towards CS Martin. 'I'm referring to specific discussions, not veiled threats to pull the rug out from under me.'

The chief super's eyes narrowed, her mouth opened and closed like she was exercising her jaws and then her lips formed themselves into a thin pout that precipitated a gale-force blast to come.

Two loud reports on the door shattered the momentary silence.

The officers turned to hear the hinges creaking and saw Jim from the front desk bounding in like a tired marathon runner. 'I think you should see this . . .' He held out a copy of the *Glasgow-Sun*.

23

LEANNE DUNN EASED HER hands beneath the tabletop and fixed her stare on Danny Gillon. As their eyes met the pimp smiled, and then the action seemed to prompt a hacking cough that ended with him reaching for a cigarette. When he brought the filter tip to his mouth, Leanne seized the moment and leapt from her seat. The sound of the chair's back clattering off the wall startled her, she shot her arms towards her ears, but her mind was set and she ran from the kitchen with wailing, frightened screams. As she moved, her vision started to blur; she was light-headed and nauseous and each barefooted step on the floorboards sent a jolt of pain through her ankles that fled all the way up her leg to her hip bone. She was unsteady and nervous, and when she looked back to see Gillon jumping into the hallway, her balance deserted her. Leanne fell to the floor, her knees taking the brunt of the impact before she crashed onto her front and smacked her head off the wall with a solid thud.

Gillon halted where he stood and laughed. 'Oh, dear, Leanne . . .'

Her position on the floor beneath Gillon made her feel even more vulnerable, but the stinging pain that had begun deep in her brow was somehow working its way into her stomach. She raised herself on one arm, but as the weak elbow buckled beneath her there was a turn in her intestines and she vomited where she lay.

'Oh, man . . .' Gillon was laughing harder now. He walked towards the tangled mass of limbs and grabbed a handful of Leanne's lank hair. 'Going somewhere?'

A long trail of bile spooled from her mouth; she tried to speak, but her words were in competition with the vomit and the blood evacuating from a burst lip. 'No, Gillon . . . no.'

'What? What you saying?' He leaned forward, made a show of bringing his ear towards her mouth.

Leanne tried to speak again, only one word came: 'No . . .'

'No? I'll give you fucking no. You don't say no to me.' Gillon yanked Leanne from the ground, and the movement caused her to grimace as she was pulled skywards by her hair. Another scream bounced off the narrow confines of the hallway and Gillon brought a fist up to her face. 'Are you going to make me belt you, Leanne . . . Is that it? You want a belt, want reminding who you're dealing with?'

Leanne's eyes followed the left-to-right of her pimp's balled fist, she started to tremble, tears ran down the sides of her face. 'Please, please, Gillon.'

The fist disappeared from her line of view and for a split second there was a sense of relief, but it was soon replaced with the agonising realisation that Gillon had buried his fist in her stomach. Leanne folded over and tasted the salty blood in her mouth; then she started to panic as she was dragged towards the bedroom. Her knees were torn on the uneven floorboards, but the pain didn't seem to matter now that she saw what was coming. As Gillon threw her on the bed she tried to curl over, even though she knew it was a futile act: there was no escape, no avoiding the inevitable.

'Get on your back,' he roared.

Leanne was too weak to move, holding her stomach where the blow had toppled her.

'On your back!' Gillon grabbed her and slapped her twice across the face. Leanne felt her legs rising. She bent her knees and tried to kick out, but he was too strong for her, pinning her legs down to the bed and ripping open her dressing gown.

'You've got scrawnier than I remember,' said Gillon as he stood unbuckling his belt. 'Have to get a few burgers or that into you . . . Nobody likes a scrawny whore.' He rolled down his jeans and underwear and eased himself over Leanne. 'Not heard that the bigger the cushion the better the pushing?'

Leanne shut her eyes tight and felt her throat constricting as Gillon raped her. She was frozen, unmoving, like someone tied to the bed. She imagined herself as another person, as if she wasn't Leanne any more, as if she had somehow left her body and was standing in the corner watching Gillon thrust himself into someone else. She heard his guttural heaving, the shortness of his breath, the belt buckle banging off the bed frame and the floorboards with a metronomic rhythm. She felt the dampness of his sweaty brow on her cheek and the tightness of her lungs as he laid himself heavily into her, but she wasn't there. Leanne had long ago learnt to disengage herself from the physical act, the violence, the pain . . . If she didn't acknowledge it to herself then it didn't happen. She had told herself that as a child – it could be blocked out. Everything could be blocked out if you tried hard enough.

When Gillon raised his jeans and belt, his lower lip drooped and sweat hung from his eyelashes. He ran the back of his hand over his brow and smiled towards Leanne where she curled up on the bed. He pointed towards her as he spoke. 'You need to get your act together . . .'

She didn't reply, just moved herself to the edge of the bed and fastened her dressing gown.

'You hear me? You need to start paying attention to your

punters . . . I wouldn't pay for a ride like that.' He shook his head as he fastened his belt. 'No way would I pay for that . . . You need to start thinking a bit more about the punter and a bit less about scoring.'

Leanne stared out the window; the gloom of the early evening sky had settled above the flat rooftops and a small white moon sat low and stark in the sky. It seemed shocked to see her.

'You hearing me?'

'What?' She turned towards Gillon, who had his hand out to her as if offering to help her from the bed.

'Come on, get yourself dressed,' he said, nodding towards the door.

'Why?'

'We're going out . . .'

Leanne rose from the bed and tightened the dressing gown around her waist. 'Going out?'

'So you're not deaf then.' Gillon clapped his hands together. 'Come on, move it, move it, move it!' He pulled her towards him by the shoulders, then spun her to face the wardrobe in the corner of the room; the dressing gown was yanked clean from Leanne's back as she took her first step.

Gillon laughed. 'Christ almighty, need to put some meat on those bones . . .' A faint gleam entered his eyes as he made for the door. 'Going for a fag, be dressed and ready by the time I've finished or I'll drag you out in the buff and show the world that skanky arse!' He was still laughing as he made his way to the kitchen.

Leanne's mouth drooped. She wanted to speak but was too clogged with emotion to utter words. Her eyes studied the wardrobe: the hangers and few items of clothing inside were like alien relics to her; for a moment she wondered about the concept of clothing, of life, and then as she swayed the bare

173

boards beneath her feet cried out as if to issue a reminder of herself. Her eyelids twitched, jerking her gaze towards the rail; she reached out and began to dress for Gillon.

In the hallway, Leanne leaned against the wall and listened to her pimp stubbing his cigarette; the ashtray clattered off the tabletop as he dug the butt into the glass. When he was finished, he started whistling: his mood was light, and Leanne knew that was something to hold on to – she didn't want to be around him when his mood was dark. If she could keep him this way then Leanne knew that she would likely avoid any more conflict, any more kicks, punches, or any of the kinds of actions that reminded her of her lowly station. She was a tart, Gillon's tart, and when she forgot that she felt pain. It was better not to think about those things, though.

'Right, you set?' said Gillon.

'Where are we going?'

'To see a man.'

Leanne's pulse jerked. 'Who?'

'Who . . . ? Are you questioning me?' His bottom row of teeth were bared. 'Eh?' He reached out and grabbed Leanne's face in his hand and squeezed it. 'Eh? Is that it, you're questioning me?'

'No. No . . .'

He pushed her head away; she stumbled.

'Good. Just keep it that way.'

Gillon went for the door and Leanne trailed behind him. Her heels clacked on the concrete steps of the stairwell and she wondered if the noise would set Gillon off again. She toyed with the idea of removing her shoes and walking in her bare feet, but she worried that he might object to that; he didn't like seeing his girls barefoot, she'd seen others slapped about for being outdoors in bare feet before.

'Come on, move yourself,' he yelled as he reached the bottom of the steps.

'I'm coming.'

'Aye, not bloody fast enough . . .' He held out his hand and grabbed Leanne's arm when she came into reach. 'Move it.' He pushed her towards the door.

Gillon's van was parked on the other side of the road, she recognised it at once. As they headed for the van, she wondered if she was going to be forced to turn tricks in there; he had made her do that before. There was a mattress in the back of the van, an old, dank-smelling item that had been out in the rain once, before Gillon had found a home for it. The thought of spending the night on the mattress made Leanne's stomach lurch. She looked down the street and thought about running but at once knew she had nowhere to go. She was trapped.

They drove to Ayr Road and over Tam's Brig before heading out to Prestwick shore, at the end of the esplanade, where the walkway ran into an expansive car-parking area. Gillon pulled up the van. As the engine stilled, he removed the keys and reached out for a packet of Club that sat on the dash. He lit up and offered a cigarette to Leanne.

There was a car on the other side of the van, about forty or fifty metres away, and as she lit her cigarette she saw a man opening the door and heading towards them.

Gillon turned and wound down his window. He waved to the man and he reciprocated.

'What's going on?' said Leanne. She peered past Gillon's shoulder towards the approaching man. He looked to be no threat. There was nothing to him: thin shoulders, a chubby face with glasses; he wore a pair of comfortable, sensible shoes and his clothes looked to have been picked out by a wife or mother.

'This is a mate of mine,' said Gillon. 'I want you to have a word with him . . .'

'What about?' Leanne's voice revealed a rising panic.

Gillon spun round to face her. 'Whatever he wants to know, you tell him.'

'I don't know anything.'

His eyes widened; she sensed a threat. 'Look, don't mess me about, I want you to tell him about that fat paedo and your other pal . . .'

'What other pal?'

The man approached the window and smiled. He nodded to Gillon, then waved a hand towards his passenger. 'You must be Leanne?'

She raised the cigarette to her mouth and drew the nicotine deep into her lungs. An uneasy tremor passed from her stomach to her chest and neck, which made her feel like her heart was in her mouth. She watched Gillon reach for the door handle and step outside, and as he did so the man leaned forward and extended his hand. 'I'm Cameron Sinclair and Danny here's told me a lot about you.'

As Sinclair stepped into the van and closed the door behind him, Gillon took himself for a walk, back towards the esplanade.

24

DETECTIVE INSPECTOR Bob Valentine didn't realise his posture was so stiff, his demeanour so harsh, until he crossed his legs and caught sight of the rigid angle his foot made to his ankle. He stared at his shoe, pointing upwards towards the desk, and wondered if it might snap off, it looked so brittle, like it was the frosted, frozen branch of a tree that threatened to fall. He ran a finger down the crease of his trouser leg and then found himself scraping the stubble on his chin with a fingernail.

'Is everything all right, Inspector?' said Carole-Anne. Her voice was a low, flat monotone that never contained any inflection: a professional contrivance, no doubt, thought Valentine.

'No, everything's . . . just fine.'

The therapist's eyes seemed to be measuring him. 'Perhaps you could tell me what it's like being back to normal duties . . .'

Normal duties – what were they? thought Valentine. Was it normal to find an esteemed member of the public had been impaled on a wooden spike at the communal tip? Was it normal to find a repeat sex offender – one who had never expressed an ounce of remorse for the children he abused – executed in similar fashion? Oh yes, it was all another day at the office. He girded his jaw and let his gaze shift through the woman who was perhaps young enough to be his own daughter.

'Inspector, are you uncomfortable speaking to me?' She started to fan the yellow pencil in her fingers; the rubber tip became a blur.

Valentine knew he was in a no-win situation. CS Martin had made it clear the therapy sessions were to be a trade-off: a return to the training academy at Tulliallan was the alternative. If that happened, he knew also that the case would be turned over to Glasgow CID. He thought of the latest addition to the murder squad – DS Sylvia McCormack – and his throat constricted, numbing his clenched muscles.

'Look, I don't want to appear . . . uncooperative.'

'But . . . ?' She presented the one-word interruption like a uppercut. He took it on the chin.

'But . . . I really do feel that your experience could be put to better use elsewhere. I'm fine, I told Marion Martin as much.'

Carole-Anne put down the pencil and eased herself back in her chair; a reporter's notebook that sat in her lap followed the pencil. 'Bob – you don't mind if I call you Bob, do you?'

Valentine shook his head.

She continued. 'We have to get something straight. I'm doing a job. I know you know how to do yours, but you need to appreciate that you've been referred here by a senior officer with, it must be said, good cause.' A narrow smile eased over her face and he noticed that the smooth skin of her cheeks contrasted starkly with the dark crenulations beneath her eyes, which seemed to remove her from the vicinity of youthfulness.

'I understand that.' Valentine paused, then planted his foot down firmly. He could see there was no point in parrying her questions. 'What would you like to know?'

'Why don't you tell me how you feel about what happened to you?'

A tut, followed by a long exhalation of breath. 'You mean how I felt about being stabbed in the heart . . . ? You can say it, y'know.'

178

She pressed out another smile, a weaker one this time, but no words followed.

Valentine continued. 'The physical aspects are impossible to describe. I mean you can appreciate, I'm sure, what it feels like to have a piece of cold metal thrust into your chest cavity, but the shock almost cancels that out . . . I remember the blood, the sight of the blade sitting there – in my chest – they say your whole life flashes before you and by Christ it does . . .'

The therapist shifted uneasily in her seat; her face seemed to slacken and her mouth dipped towards her neck. 'Perhaps not the physical aspects, I was alluding more to the way you were affected psychologically . . . that's what I'm here for.'

She was there to make notes in her little book, to tot up the pros and cons of keeping him on the force, thought Valentine. He suddenly felt an almighty enmity towards her, but it seemed to wash over him and disappear as quickly as it had appeared. She wasn't a bad person – that much he knew – she was just, as she had said, doing her job.

'I thought I wasn't going to see my children again . . . and my wife.'

'You have two children, Bob, is that right?' She reached over to retrieve a stack of notes from her desk.

'Two girls.'

'It must have been hard for them . . . and your wife.'

The mention of Clare seemed to disrupt the image he was carrying in his mind of the girls as they were when he woke up in the hospital after surgery. He wondered now if the image was real: was any of it? He had officially died and been revived; he was a man risen from the dead – how real could that story be? And yet he knew it was him. He was the man his doctors said was 'lucky to be alive'. And he was, he

179

knew it. But he couldn't escape the feeling that he had been brought back for a reason. He wasn't the same Bob Valentine who had gone out to work that morning looking for a lead on a drug cartel and ended up stabbed in the heart with a nine-inch blade. No matter how many times he relayed these facts to people, or replayed them in his own mind, something out of the ordinary had happened that day and he hadn't been the same man since.

'I'd sooner not talk about my family,' said Valentine.

Carole-Anne's cheeks flushed. 'Of course, we don't need to discuss them if you don't want to.'

The detective felt a pang of guilt; they had only just thawed the room. 'Maybe next time.'

A car passed by the window outside; its shadow washed over the battleship grey walls. 'It's later than I thought ... perhaps that's enough for a first session, enough for one day.'

Valentine felt relieved, as if he had been released from a straitjacket. He exhaled a long breath and rose from the chair. Carole-Anne was standing to meet him with her hand outstretched.

'Thank you, Bob.'

He shook her hand and turned for the door.

In the corridor, Valentine caught sight of the cleaners wheeling a Henry hoover towards the main incident room and the image brought him back to reality with a shudder.

'No you're all right there, love . . .' He started to jog towards the cleaner, who dipped back her head and eyed him from beneath her heavy glasses. He grabbed the door from her. 'Maybe leave this one till last, eh, got a couple of things to tidy up in here myself.'

'If you're tidying up, son, I'll give you the trolley and the dusters!'

Valentine smiled, but the cleaner pressed out a frown, which suggested she wasn't joking.

'I'll only be half an hour . . . if you don't mind.'

She retreated a few steps and made for the chief super's office, shaking her head and trailing the vacuum cleaner like it was a badly behaved child.

When Valentine got inside the room the light outside was dimming. He reached out for the row of switches by the door and pressed them down. The strip bulbs buzzed and then illuminated the broad room. He was about to walk towards the glassed-off office at the other end when some movement caught his eye.

'You're working late, aren't you?' he said.

DS Sylvia McCormack sat behind a pile of case notes. She patted the top folder and peered over. 'Maybe not for much longer . . .'

Valentine approached her. 'What are you doing anyway?'

She shrugged. 'Oh, good question.'

He could see she was doing something; he didn't need to be a detective to work that one out. Her body language belied any wrongdoing, though he conceded that he might have preferred to catch the Glasgow detective in a compromising situation so he had the choice of removing her – and her department's – involvement in the case. He walked towards the desk and picked up a file. 'Knox . . . You're going over his record?'

'I'm sorry, I don't mean to be stepping on any toes; if someone else has this in hand . . . It's just . . .' She cut herself off.

Valentine returned the folder. He had a twinge in his back; he'd been in the office too long and needed to find some time to release the tensions. He wondered how it felt for DS McCormack on her first day in the post. 'No, you're all right . . . I was going to give this to Phil or Ally, but they've both got pretty heavy paper rounds as it is. And what with this morning's press kerfuffle . . .'

The DS nodded. 'Yes, sir.'

He knew when he had hit a raw nerve – the press situation was a bigger embarrassment than he thought if the squad's newest member already had the good grace to look ashamed at the mention.

'I should probably get off.' The DS reached out to retrieve her handbag from the back of the chair and eased past the detective.

'Hang on . . . *It's just* – what?'

She stopped and turned. 'Sorry?'

'The files.' Valentine turned towards Knox's case notes and tapped the top. 'You had an idea about these.'

'Oh right.' She brought her hand up to her head and grabbed a stray bunch of hair from her fringe. As she stood the strap of her handbag worked its way off her shoulder, but she caught the bag before it hit the ground. 'Yes, the name Knox . . . It rings a bell; I don't know from what, though.'

Valentine thinned his eyes and took two steps towards the DS. 'The name Knox rings a bell with you . . . What do you mean?'

'I don't know, I just thought I'd come across it before.'

'Where . . . Glasgow?'

She started to play with the buckle on the outside of her handbag. 'I don't know, sir . . . It might be nothing.'

Valentine saw his hopes, at once raised so high, now dropping back below the horizon. 'It's a pretty rare name . . . You'd think you'd remember the case.'

The DS shrugged her shoulders again. Valentine felt a twinge of anger and locked it away – it had been a long day. 'Right, get off home . . .'

'Yes, sir.'

'But before you go . . .' He turned towards the desk with the large pile of blue files and picked them up. 'Here, take these with you . . . If there's something in there that jogs your memory, you can tell me about it in the morning.'

'Yes, sir.'

'Oh and this is your personal obsession while you're in Ayrshire – get to know Duncan Knox inside out. I want to know all there is to know about him – if he traded a jelly-trifle for a bag of snout in Peterhead, I want to know who with. Get me?' He placed the pile of files in her arms and held the door open for her.

'Yes, sir . . .' She collected the files on her way through the door. 'Thank you, sir.'

As the door's hinges let out a sigh, Valentine sat down on the top of the desk. Where he had removed the files sat a copy of the *Glasgow-Sun* that seemed to have passed through the hands of the entire murder squad. He picked up the newspaper and turned to the story Jim Prentice had brought to their attention at first dawn. The paper was dog-eared and tatty, beyond any doctor's surgery or barber's shop waiting-room offer. There were smudges of ketchup and the ringed remnants of coffee cups all over, but none of it altered the contents or the headline:

AYRSHIRE POLICE HUNT DOUBLE MURDERER

'Bastard . . .' Valentine felt like spitting on the paper, but he resisted. The article's subheading had drawn his attention away:

KNOWN PAEDOPHILE FOUND AT RACECOURSE

183

Valentine had read the article already, but he passed his eyes over it again: if nothing else, it would reassure him that he hadn't imagined it – the newspaper had indeed identified Duncan Knox as the murder victim.

'That's twice they've shafted me now.'

Valentine closed the paper and shoved it into the wastebasket.

25

DI BOB VALENTINE KNEW he was an uxorious husband at times and a proprietorial father all of the time. His family meant more to him than anything, perhaps more than it did to other people – at least that's how it felt to him. There was no escaping the link between his family and his profession: on one cold night in desolate woodland he had watched the brittle white corpse of a fourteen-year-old girl cut down from the branch she had hanged herself from, and he had become like his daughters' stalker around their home. He found himself listening in on their phone calls to friends, tracking their Facebook posts and once – bizarrely, in retrospect, he conceded – checking Chloe's pulse as he found her asleep in front of the television. He couldn't detach fully from what he saw in the job. The curtain that cops pretended to lower behind them when they returned home wasn't a portcullis; it was permeable, porous, and often at the moments when it was least expected.

Valentine knew he had once been the typical, gruff hard man from Ayr – all bluster and gumption – but having children and watching them grow into near adulthood had changed him. He'd seen his daughters' struggles in the adult world and knew he could no longer slap down his damning authoritarian observations on shop girls, waiting staff or even his own employees. Valentine suppressed his emerging sensitive side when he had to – to get the job done – but at such times it felt at odds with the man he should be. He still remembered his own early mistakes, his faux pas on the force. It was difficult to go from being indulged as a child to barely tolerated in the workplace, but that was life. That was growing up, and he worried about the hard years his daughters faced in the transition to adulthood. None of us had it easy, but Valentine knew he had it in his power to make it a little easier for some, though he worried he was going a little soft and how that might impact on the job.

As he pulled the Vectra into his driveway he gave a wave to his neighbour, Brian, who was mowing the lawn. Valentine felt the guilt over his own shabby yard distil in him. Brian's manicured lawns and carefully tended shrubberies were a constant source of shame: it was as if they were planted to taunt him, a reminder of his own tardiness in reacting to the sprouting of weeds and rapid skyward acceleration of his grass.

'Hello, Brian,' he called out.

The cachinnating mower whirred to a slow stop and his neighbour straightened his back. There was a nod above the noise of the stilling mower and then he made his way towards the edge of the lawn with a wave. Valentine watched Brian hoisting up his trousers before brushing grass clippings from the flattened bulk of his belly. His T-shirt was sweat-stained and a spray of grass cuttings clung with grim resistance as if pasted there.

'Only been out half an hour and I'm like Albert Steptoe already,' he said, before leaning over the party wall and smiling.

Valentine liked Brian but had always found it difficult to bond with neighbours; having a police officer in the street made people watch their words, act cautiously. Some went to the opposite extreme and acted as if the street possessed a personal watchman to whom they could deliver suspicions and seek instant solutions to all manner of law-breaking accusations, like he was a resident judge and jury. It was a strange state of affairs: people didn't treat you like one of them – you were an outsider wherever you went.

'You must think my garden's been abandoned.' Valentine turned towards his lawn and shook his head. 'I just can't find the time to get into it, thinking of getting a gardener in . . . at least temporarily.'

Brian nodded and eased himself back from the wall with a sigh. 'Well, you've had your hands full of late.' He seemed at once in sympathy with his neighbour. 'I saw you on the news the other night . . . terrible business.'

Valentine drew a deep breath. He didn't feel comfortable discussing the case with Brian, but the subject had been raised and it would look haughty to dismiss it. 'No, not a pleasant state of affairs, but we're on top of it.'

'I was just saying to the wife, I don't know what this town's coming to.' Brian gripped the bevelled brick at the top of the wall, and his cheeks flushed red as he started to speak again. 'I mean, if you'd said to me a few years ago we'd see that kind of thing, a bloody execution no less, in Ayr, I'd have been waiting for the punchline . . .'

Valentine felt the handle of his briefcase growing damp; he would have to find a way out of the conversation before he became compromised.

'Aye, Brian, the auld town's not what it used to be . . . If I had a pound for every time I'd heard that recently.'

'But this bloke, the first one, he was in the bank . . . Not the kind you'd expect to see, well, y'know, how he was done.'

Valentine's skin was prickling on the back of his arms. He made a half-smile at his neighbour and pointed his briefcase towards his home. 'It's getting dark. Going to have to get myself fed, Col . . .'

'Sure, of course, I'm the same . . . My belly thinks my throat's been cut!'

Valentine closed his mouth and breathed out slowly through widened nostrils; it struck him as surreal that his neighbour could go from talking about the death of Urquhart to making a joke about his throat being cut: had everyone become desensitised or was it him who was oversensitive? The answer eluded him.

On the way into the house, the DI lowered his briefcase and leaned onto the banister to check for movement upstairs; if the girls were home they were being uncharacteristically quiet. As he headed towards the kitchen, a shrill voice cut the air like a saw-blade.

'Bob . . . Is that you?' It was Clare.

As he opened the door, his wife abandoned her search for an answer to her last question and began to blindly ramble. Her speech was fast but lacked any context or mooring; it was as if she had shaken a ragbag of words and scattered them to the four winds. Valentine removed a chair from beneath the table and watched his wife preparing dinner accompanied by the rapid tremolo of her inane chatter. He picked up odd grains of minutiae that were scattered in the direction of his interest, but mostly the talk was of people he didn't know, places he never went and all points in between their confluence. She was on a high. As she paced, he noticed she stood beneath a shadeless bulb – a new light-fitting sat on the work surface. She had been spending again, easing her weary place in the world with money. He felt a sickening in his heart that there was nothing he could ever do for Clare that would come close to the presenting of a credit card on a store's counter.

'Where are the girls?' His words sliced the room like the crack of a whip.

Clare halted where she stood and turned towards him, pitching her voice as high as a jazz horn. 'They're out.'

Valentine's mind skimmed the possibilities, but after a long day and the strange encounter with his neighbour that had brought recent events a little too close to home, he was impatient for a response. 'I gathered that.' He snatched his words. 'Where are they?'

Clare opened the oven door with gloved hands and reached in to retrieve a Pyrex dish stacked high with lasagne. She raised the dish in her husband's direction and presented it with a smile. 'I made your favourite . . . and there's a Key lime pie too.' Her smile evaporated into a scowl as she took in her husband. 'Do you have to wear that old sports coat every day, Bob? I'll have a look for a new jacket for you, there's some nice stuff in Slater's just now . . .'

Valentine absorbed Clare's words like a blotter, but they were not the words he wanted to hear; he wanted to know where his daughters were and why his wife's shaky grip on the last wrung of normalcy seemed to have slipped. He wanted to know what he had missed when he had been away at work, conducting an investigation into two brutal murders in their own home town. His mind filled with possibilities, but none of them addressed the uneasy doubts that were filling his consciousness.

'Clare, stop fussing over the dinner for a moment and come and sit down here.' He reached to pull out the chair beside him. 'Come on . . .'

Clare moved slowly towards him, folding the oven gloves as she went. For a moment she stopped and swayed before him as she placed a hand on the fridge door, and then she reached in to remove a bottle of wine.

'Do you want a glass?'

'I want you to sit down.'

Her drowsy eyes flickered as she poured the glass of Chablis; her frame seemed suddenly shrunken and tired. When she walked towards the table the chair caught on the table leg and she tugged at it impatiently, a glower growing on her features.

Valentine rose. 'Here, I'll get it.' As he pulled the chair out, he watched Clare slump on the cushion and raise the wine glass to her mouth. 'What's up, Clare?'

His wife touched the pendant round her neck and began to play with it as she spoke. 'People are talking, and I don't just mean people on the street . . .'

'About what?' Valentine's shoulders tightened as he watched his wife take another sudden gulp of wine.

'What do you think . . . ? About you.'

He was confused. What did she mean? He had been used to them talking about his time in hospital, everyone knew about that, they had been kind. But he sensed she meant something else. 'What do you mean, Clare?'

Her forehead creased and then her voice trailed off into a dull drone. 'What do you think, Bob . . . ? This bloody case. You've been in God alone knows how many newspapers and on the television. People are asking me about it, and do you know what? They're asking the girls.'

Clare turned away from her husband and the wine glass started to shudder in her grip. Valentine watched the pale liquid shiver and swirl around the glass and reached out to steady her hand. 'Clare, where are the girls?'

She slammed down the glass; some wine spilled over the rim and pooled on the tabletop. 'Oh, calm down. Where do you think they are? Packed off to the country . . . ? They're at the pictures, I gave them a treat to take their minds off things.'

Valentine didn't get it. He was ashamed not to have noticed the impact the case was having on his family. He wanted to see his daughters, to hold them and try to explain that everything was all right. 'Who's been talking to them?'

'Not both of them . . . Well, Chloe told Fiona, but only because she's been getting some stick at school . . .'

The DI's shame turned to simmering contempt, a vague undirected anger at anyone who would upset his daughter. 'Chloe's had trouble at school?'

'Yes, Bob, your daughter's been having the rise taken out of her.'

The strange remark he'd seen on Chloe's Facebook page flashed before him. 'What have they been saying?'

'Just kids' stuff. You know what they're like: they're cruel, you dare not stand out in the crowd or attract derision.' She touched her forehead and seemed to slump further in the chair. 'I think it's worse now than it ever was, worse than in our day. They used to just follow you around the playground then, but kids can't get away from the bullies now . . . It's the texts and the websites they post on; there's nowhere to hide now. It's such a mob mentality too, one gets on it and they all join in, all bloody little shits together!'

He understood. His mind flashed over the list of possibilities that might have been thrown Chloe's way. He didn't want his daughter to be another victim of the investigation. It was too painful for him to contemplate any hurt being done to his daughter.

Clare spoke again. 'Bob, what's going on? Are you going to catch someone soon? Because people are scared now, and I'm scared what's going to happen if this goes on any longer or gets worse . . . We'll have people knocking on our front door demanding you stop it.'

Valentine rose from the table and walked towards the patio doors. His heart was pounding hard, deep inside his chest, and he knew he needed to calm down. He looked up to the darkening sky: there were black clouds sitting there like precarious boulders waiting to fall. His gaze dipped as a cat leapt onto the back wall and just as quickly disappeared over the other side. He watched the gaps in the gate for the cat's reappearance in the shaded back wynd beyond, but it never showed.

'I don't know, Clare . . . I don't know about anything any more.'

26

FEW OF THE OLD PREOCCUPATIONS meant anything to Valentine now. The idea of chasing rank, climbing the career ladder, seemed preposterous. Why – for what? Would a bigger office or faster car make him feel better? Would it change how he saw himself, or others for that matter? He had seen what putting on rank had done to some people, and even with the extreme example of Chief Superintendent Marion Martin excepted, it had not been appealing. Of course, the financial rewards would be welcome, were always welcome, but at what cost to his sense of self, his well-being? Valentine knew he couldn't give any more to the job – he could not take on further responsibility without sacrificing something of himself to the force. He had to concede he was not a careerist, he was a man first and foremost, and he needed to live and act according to his rules. His priority might well be the job, but he had more to consider and the idea that he could shunt those concerns in favour of damming the rising tide of crime was anathema to him. He would start with his contribution to a better world one step at a time and the first step needed to be taken in his own home – with his wife and daughters. If he couldn't do that, he didn't know what he had to give elsewhere.

His family, his home, was the life preserver he clung to amidst the storm without. Coming home and being able to close the door on the outside world was a fallacy, he knew that, but he liked to fool himself that he and his family were different. They were shielded, cosseted almost, protected certainly from the horrors he had witnessed and knew existed on the other side of the door. If he achieved nothing else, he wanted his home to be an island retreat from the oceans of misery. He didn't want Chloe or Fiona or Clare to have to think about the evils that lapped at their shores – he would force them back, keep them at bay, because the reality meant conceding that what happened to families like the Urquharts could happen to them. And that was a possibility he could never countenance.

The detective had called the squad to gather at 9.15 a.m. By 9.20 there was still no sign of DS Sylvia McCormack and the mumble of judgemental voices around the incident room was steadily on the rise. Valentine stood by the board and drew a line down the side of the crime-scene pictures of Duncan Knox's corpse; beside the line he made a list of bullet points that he copied from the post-mortem report. When he was finished, he picked up the red marker pen and circled the words 'depressed skull fracture', drawing a line to the matching words under the image of James Urquhart.

'Right, listen up, everyone . . .' Valentine returned the top to the marker pen and clasped it in his hand, then pressed the pen with his thumb as he spoke again. 'As you can see there's a distinct correlation between the two post-mortem reports.'

DS McAlister spoke. 'We're looking for the same man, obviously.'

'It would seem that way, Ally . . . The MOs are almost identical, though we probably didn't need the pathologist to tell us that.' He paced the front of the board and the squad followed him with its collective gaze. 'Brutal, ritualistic murder on public ground – carried out twice, if not at the locus then with the intention to make us think so – one victim a privileged figure and the other the polar opposite . . . Right, what have we got?'

As he turned to face the squad, the hinges cried from the door at the other end of the room. DS Sylvia McCormack entered with her jacket on the crook of her arm and proceeded to the coat stand.

'Sorry I'm late . . . Traffic.'

A few tuts followed her explanation and then everyone returned to the DI.

'OK, Phil, so we're all on the same page, what have you got for us on James Urquhart's history?' Valentine eased himself onto the edge of the desk and gave DS Donnelly the floor.

'Right, thanks, boss . . . Well, I've spoken to the bank and the staff he took with him after the buyout, and I have to say there's no sign of any ill will. This is a man who seems to have made few enemies. Certainly in his professional life, there were a few dissenters . . .' The DS turned over a page in his notebook. 'One of the former partners, Carter, thought they should have held off before selling, but he admits he did very well out of the buyout and I don't think there was any bad blood between them . . . far from it, actually. That's the picture I got across the board, really.'

Valentine folded his arms and fixed the DS in his stare. 'What about clients, employees?'

'Yeah, very little to go on there. The phrase "kept himself to himself" cropped up a lot . . . I got the impression that he held his social life and his family life totally separate from his business affairs, but again, no troubles bubbling up to the surface . . . Sounded like a decent enough boss really.'

'Well, he pissed someone off, Phil. Are you forgetting how he met his end?' Valentine shook his head and scanned the crowd. 'Right, Ally, you're up . . . The buyout, you took that from Paulo, yeah?'

DS McAlister frowned and shook his head. 'Eh, no, Phil took that since he was looking at the employers and employees . . .'

'Jesus Christ, is that it? We've even less to go on than I thought . . .' Valentine pushed himself off the desk and stood with his hands empty in the air. 'Well, what have we got?'

McAlister spoke. 'I took the neighbour from Paulo – Ronnie Bell . . .'

'Yes, what did you unearth?'

The DS opened a blue folder and turned it over. 'Well, he's retired, had a string of pound shops but sold them off . . .'

'A pound a go, eh?' said Valentine.

A smile. 'Er, no, bit more than that . . . quite a few million as it happens. He's certainly not short of a quid and he did invest some money with Urquhart's brokers before the buyout.'

'Tell me he lost his hat.'

'No, seems to be quite the opposite actually.'

'Money goes to money.' Valentine had a knot of tension building in his chest. He dropped his chin to his shoulder and looked out of the window towards the street. A slow, somnambulant trail of hunched youths was working its way to the riverbanks, where they would spend the day in the kind of inebriated mischief the town knew well. For a moment their plans looked under threat as a loud siren emitted from the station and a police car cut a swathe through the hum of traffic. As the car sped off towards Tam's Brig, the youths gestured behind it, then regained their swagger like they had just put on armour.

Valentine turned back to the squad. 'So that's a blank on the work colleagues and the neighbour . . . Any more good news?'

DS McAlister hoisted up his belt and spoke. His voice was

quieter than it had been before, the timbre more drawn out, almost a drawl. 'Well, it might be nothing, but I checked out the Rotary Club and one or two other things.'

Valentine's eyes widened. 'Go on . . .'

'Urquhart was not a regular at the Rotary: he'd show for a Burns' Supper and a couple of other highpoints in the year, but that was it.' McAlister found his stride and started to punctuate his words with hand gestures. 'He did attend a regular bridge night and Mrs Urquhart mentioned a weekly model enthusiasts' club that he went to, he was into trains and the like . . .'

The DI raised his arm. 'Ally, is this going somewhere? I just don't know that I can take much more excitement.'

As the squad laughed, McAlister fixed his stare; his face looked solemn, as if he might begin to chant. 'No, this is my point, sir . . . The model-railway club was a weekly thing, met on a Wednesday night . . .'

'Don't tell me, like clockwork!' said DS Donnelly.

McAlister started to look nervy, his skin as pale as cheese, as the room erupted into more laughter. 'No, listen, what I'm getting at is . . . Mrs Urquhart said her husband went to the model club every week without fail, but when I spoke to the bloke in charge . . .' He started to turn pages rapidly in his spiral-bound notebook. 'Yeah, Mr Forgan, he told me he'd only seen Urquhart a handful of times in the last three years.'

Valentine's thoughts started to swirl in his mind. The roof of his mouth suddenly dried over; his lips were parched. As he looked at DS McAlister fingering the edges of his notebook, he noted he had the pleased look of a dog that had just retrieved a stick for his master.

'Ally, are you saying Urquhart was AWOL every Wednesday night?' said the DI.

He nodded. 'More or less.'

Valentine folded an arm across his stomach and rested his chin on the knuckles of his fist. As he fastened his eyes on the squad, tight radial lines appeared at their edges. He made a half-smile, not because he was happy, but because he couldn't help it. 'Right, listen up, all of you: I want to know where our murder victim was on all those Wednesday nights. I want bank cards, visas, petrol receipts checked and mapped . . . If we can pinpoint his whereabouts, I want uniform door to door with photographs and dates. I want CCTV footage taken from shops, garage forecourts and bloody eye-in-the-sky traffic reports if necessary. I want his car circulated, and registration, and I want all of this yesterday. If there's something unusual, anything – be it a trip to a toy store or a hotel that charges by the hour – I want it on that board!'

The team moved away from the whiteboard and the room filled once again with the familiar sounds of chair legs scraping the floor, telephones being raised and filing cabinets opening and closing.

Valentine looked out the window towards the cloud-crossed sky and saw weak sunrays patting the rooftops with bouncing light. For a moment he felt uneasy, like his grip on reality had been loosened; as he stared out, the world was a confusion to him. He felt hollowed out, a husk, as he thought of the case and how far they were from a resolution. He knew he needed something solid, something that would link Urquhart to Knox and unlock the investigation, but he felt a long way off. When he turned back to the desk to retrieve his notes, DS McCormack was standing there.

'Sylvia, glad you could join us . . .' It was sarcasm, and he almost regretted it.

'Sorry, sir . . . I had a late night last night with the Knox files.'

'Oh yes, did you remember the case you thought he was linked to?'

The sun's glare crept up behind her and a pair of drowsy eyes flickered. The chatter and fuss of the busy office seemed to subside as she spoke. 'That's what I wanted to see you about.'

27

As VALENTINE WAITED FOR DS McCormack to retrieve the paperwork she wanted to show him, he stood in the glassed-off office at the end of the incident room and stared out the window. The youths he had spotted earlier were still in the vicinity, still behaving like little more than unruly apes. He watched them, worked up over who knows what, smacking walls and doors. They attacked with fist, foot or forehead any number of inanimate objects in their path. Injury seemed an irrelevance. When a car's horn sounded in their direction, one took a swing at a moving windscreen. Another let fly at a lamppost. Valentine had seen it all before, seen them swinging bottles like clubs. Had any of them progressed from troglodytes? They ranted, shouted, screamed, poured recriminations in every direction, and why? To draw attention to themselves? To assert their authority within the pack? To test their virility? The answer didn't matter, he no longer needed to divine a reason: he had reached the conclusion that youths off the estates were feral. The detective had seen footage on television of Indian apes terrorising city dwellers and he had made the connection. He knew what it was like to face off gangs acting out their primal instincts, terrorising people who lived quietly in their homes, he'd even been on the receiving end of blows and blades, and he had little desire to repeat either. He had never felt the need to act in such a way, never felt the want to strike out, to attack the weak in order to assert a sense of superiority. As he watched them, the actions of the youths disturbed Valentine. Their behaviour was bestial, and it both repulsed and unsettled the detective to think that he shared a world with them. He didn't want to think of himself as being part of the same species as those swaggering apes he had cause to lock away in cells for their own good, week in and week out, since he had joined the force.

'All kicking off, is it?' said DS McCormack as she walked in clutching a bundle of blue folders and peering out the window to the street.

Valentine greeted her with a thin smile. 'No, it's just Ayrshire rites of passage.'

The DS placed the folders on the desktop and took in the view properly. A thin beanpole of a youth batted his chest and made a Nazi salute. 'Shouldn't we tell uniform?'

'Are you kidding? This is a daily occurrence . . .'

'But in front of the station?'

The detective tipped back his head and laughed. 'That's the reason for it: it's posturing to the powers that be . . . like an Orange walk. Don't worry about it, Sylvia, by lunchtime they'll all be full of Buckfast and basking in the warm glow of their own bullshit.'

She didn't look convinced. Valentine wondered how it must appear to an outsider, even someone from Glasgow, the infamous 'No Mean City' where there was no shortage of louts and yobs. He concluded inwardly that the sea air, or the water, or those inveterate west-coast genes were to blame, but really the cause didn't bother him: it was the effect that struck a chord. He folded the thought away and stacked it neatly with a host of other wearisome observations.

'Right, what have you got for me?' he said, drawing out a chair and positioning himself behind the desk.

DS McCormack stood before him and tapped two fingers on her cheekbone before inhaling sharply and bursting into lyrical speech. 'Right, you remember I told you that I thought I knew the name Knox . . .'

Valentine cut in. 'And do you remember I told you I wanted a complete case file on him, not just chasing rainbows?'

'You have it.' She rummaged in the pile of notes and presented the DI with a blue folder.

He took the folder and opened it up; he was scanning the contents as McCormack started to talk again. She seemed animated, keen: he liked to see that in his squad, but he knew enthusiasm was no substitute for groundwork, she would need to impress him with her police work over any desire to shine.

'Knox has spent more time inside than out in the last thirty years, some hard yards as well,' she said.

'Took a chiv in the back in Peterhead, I see . . .'

'Yeah, it was a sharpened chicken bone, I believe. He did the rest of his stretch in isolation, but still managed to get his top row of teeth knocked out.'

'Popular bloke . . . Can't say I'm welling up with sympathy, mind you. This record's horrific; I'd have knocked his teeth out myself.'

McCormack bunched her brows and then her expression gave way to a more understanding look. 'Never expressed remorse once, never submitted fully to any treatment: I think it's fair to say Knox was a serial paedophile without contrition for his crimes.'

'He was bloody well committed to it. He was a beast, nothing more.'

The DS nodded. 'There are psych reports in there, but they don't make for pretty reading.' Her eyes darted. 'Sir, if you don't mind, I'd like to make a point about Knox's time in custody.'

Valentine closed the folder, leaned back and laced his fingers across his stomach. 'Go on, then.'

'I listed the times Knox was inside and plotted his known whereabouts when he was at liberty ... Not always easy, because a few times he managed to slip under the radar, but in the main, save a period of about six months I couldn't account for when I think he was in the north, he stayed in and around greater Glasgow.'

The DI edged forward in his seat, placing his fingertips on the rim of the desk. 'Are you going to tell me you remembered the case?'

McCormack smiled. 'Better than that, sir.' A gleam entered her eyes as she reached for another folder. The desk was becoming messy. 'I found the case by cross-referencing all of Knox's offences with all of those of a similar nature stretching back through his period of offending.'

'Thirty-plus years – you trailed that last night?'

'Not exactly ... I subtracted the times he was inside and only looked at what was left, which cut it down by a massive amount.'

'Sylvia, I'm guessing you still had quite a few cases to wade through, but are you going to spill the beans?'

'Yes, sir ... I'm getting to it.'

'No, DS McCormack, spit it out ... I'm not a dentist, I don't pull teeth.'

She took her hand away from the blue folder and stepped back from the desk. She was pacing as she spoke, finding the exact words clearly a struggle for her. 'There was a case in Partick and a case in Shawlands, so two cases with the same MO, and Knox was living in a bedsit on Jamaica Street at the time of them both.' She paused. 'Boss, Urquhart was in Glasgow then too ... This is the only time outside of their recent past in Ayr that I can pinpoint them in the same locality.'

'And years later, they both turn up on wooden spikes in my patch . . .'

The DS nodded. 'This could be the link.'

'Tell me they took him in?'

She sighed, stopped pacing. 'Not for the Partick one . . .'

'Glasgow questioned Duncan Knox for Shawlands?'

'Yes. I checked just five minutes ago, sir, the Partick case was closed anyway, but the one they quizzed Knox on is still open.'

Valentine rose from the desk and put his hands in his pockets; his throat constricted rapidly as he tried to still his mind. He walked towards the window and stared out at the grey wash of sky. It was raining now, and a flooded culvert seemed to swallow all the detective's instincts whole.

'Right, Sylvia, give me the details . . .'

The DS reached for one of the folders and removed a single sheaf of paper. 'A missing Shawlands schoolgirl, Janie Cooper . . .'

The girl's name made Valentine reel. A knot twisted in his stomach and his breathing stilled. He had never heard the name before and his reaction puzzled him; it was as if he had been told of the death of a relative. A lightness in his head sent his balance askew and he reached out to steady himself on the filing cabinet. He felt like all the air had been sucked out of his lungs, like he existed in a vacuum. It was a strange feeling of weightlessness, of being a soul separate from the physical body.

'Is everything OK, sir?'

His mouth was dry, a lofty anger exuding through his pores; it was as if the current of his thoughts had accelerated.

He nodded and heard the blood pounding in his eardrums. 'Yes, go on . . .'

'She was only six, a pretty wee thing by all accounts . . .'

'Do we have a picture?' He didn't know why he had asked. He was magnetically drawn to Janie Cooper's plight; it felt as though their thoughts had become synchronised the second he became aware of her.

'No, not a hard copy, I'll print one up . . . It was twelve years ago now that she disappeared.'

'He did it . . . Knox.'

'What?'

Valentine moved away from the filing cabinet and placed the flat of his back on the bare plaster wall. His mind dawdled through a field of immense possibilities; his pulse beat harder when he thought of finding justice for Janie. 'Don't ask me how I know, I just know.'

DS McCormack double-blinked and looked away. 'Erm, Glasgow questioned Knox, but he was released soon after.'

'He did it.'

McCormack closed the folder over and started to tidy the notes on the desk into their respective piles. She tried not to look at the DI as she spoke. 'I know at least one of the officers is still on the force, sir. I could arrange a meeting.'

'What about Janie's parents?'

'I don't know . . . I could find out.'

Valentine nodded. 'Yes, do that. I want to meet them.'

'Is that a good idea, sir?' The DS seemed to be overwhelmed by the reaction the information had generated in the detective. 'I mean, won't that be like building their hopes up?'

Valentine pushed himself off the wall. The room felt suddenly small and insufficient for the knowledge he carried inside him. 'It's twelve years, Sylvia, did they ever find a body?'

She shook her head. 'No, sir. The remains of Janie Cooper were never recovered.'

Valentine crossed the distance to the door and opened it. He felt enveloped in a void of helplessness, detached from the reality he knew. He yelled out to the room, 'Ally, get in here!'

McCormack looked panicked as she picked up the files and headed for the door. 'I'll get onto Glasgow, get images.'

'Right, and get onto the parents: I want to meet them as soon as possible.' He drew deep breath and exhaled slowly. 'Maybe want's too strong a word.'

28

DIANE COOPER STARED OUT of the broad bay window of her childless home at the rain-washed road as if it held some secret that would never be given up. The street lamps had started to deliver an umber burnishing to the paving stones, but their filaments were not in full flow; when they were, the road would be smeared in an orange oil that Diane knew well. From the top-floor tenement building, the broad sweep of the long, straight street stretched out like a horizon she surveyed with weary eyes. Every inch of the view – a mile long to east and west – was familiar to her. The huddled, amorphous masses of people that passed by were not known by name, but each one was identifiable on sight. The old woman with the water-bag legs, trailing her tartan shopping trolley, was running late – she'd be lucky to catch the butcher's shop before closing. The broad man with the blazer – it was a blazer today, a change from pinstripes – sheltered under a raised newspaper outside the estate agents; had he left his briefcase behind? The *Evening Times* seller beneath the clock was never bothered by the rain, just let it plaster his hair to his head and collected his dues, crying, '*Times . . . Times . . .*'

It was starting to get cold, a change in the weather. There would be no more good drying days, her mother had said just that morning. Seasons changed overnight in Scotland: you woke up and suddenly the sun of summer was gone, replaced by winds and wet and the promise of frosts of winter to follow. Diane didn't like the nights drawing in, the cold, the wet. She didn't like to see the people rushing in the streets to get indoors, bumping into each other with elbows aloft beneath umbrellas. She didn't like to see the cars with their lights on when the day wasn't even halfway through. She didn't like to see the children coming home from school waiting at the crossing for the green man to appear. The younger ones would shiver in the cold; she feared for them. It was cold and flu season. Some didn't have proper coats. Children needed proper coats in this weather: it was Scotland, and four seasons in one day wasn't unheard of in summer, never mind winter. People needed to look after their children, needed to take care of them. Children were a gift: Diane knew this, sometimes, she thought, like no one else.

'She's a wee angel, so she is . . .' Her mother had said.

She could still hear the words, see the faces around the hospital bed. Billy had wanted a boy, but when he saw her his heart melted.

'She's perfect,' he said.

He had tears in his eyes when he held her. He didn't want to hold her, hardly ever wanted to pick her up because he was frightened that he'd drop her.

'Take her, daftie,' Diane told him. 'You'll not break her.'

He took her in those big builder's arms of his and held her in a way she'd never seen anyone else hold a baby: out in front of him, like it was an angry cat or laundry being delivered. It had made her laugh; she still laughed now.

'Oh, Billy, hold her to you,' she'd said. 'She needs to get the scent of you, get used to you, you're her dad.'

'I just don't want to drop her or, you know, hurt her.'

'You'll not drop her or hurt her.'

He held her tighter and smiled and stared at her. 'She's just so . . . perfect.'

And she was: Janie had been perfect. There wasn't a day went by that Diane didn't remember her daughter and thank God for the time she'd had with her. It was a short time, far too short, but the memories of that time burned like an eternal flame in her mind. She could still see her the day they brought her home from hospital – just a baby then – and then there were her first words, her first steps, her first day at school . . .

Diane felt pressure building in her chest and retrieved her gaze from the street. It was as if she had been staring into complete darkness, and the return to the dimly lit room required some adjustment. She reached out and took hold of the back of the sofa to steady herself. How long had she been standing there, staring out? She didn't know. The sense of time seemed to have deserted her; she was unsteady, woozy. It was as if the laws of gravity had altered when she was in her daydream. She pressed both palms onto the sofa's soft moquette and stilled her breathing. She'd been told about this before; she worried that the panic attacks might come back. Today she worried about them more than she had before.

'Jesus, Billy . . . Where are you?'

The room spun now, little blotches of iridescent light appeared on the rain-splattered window, the street seemed like a poorly lit circus, all loud noises and rushing, whirring bodies and vehicles she couldn't quite focus on. Diane folded over, balanced her brow on the back of her arm and then tried to straighten herself. She made for the kitchen and retrieved a tall glass from the draining board to fill with water. The city water wasn't the best, carried the taste of old pipes with it, but she gulped down a mouthful, and then another. When she was finished, she placed the glass on the drainer and turned her back on the window that overlooked the communal yard of the flats. Janie had played there, in the yard, as a little girl. Diane could still remember calling out to her on a spring morning to come inside and put on a cardigan. She was just playing, though, just playing with her little friends. Diane sighed, a deep, care-worn exhalation; she still saw Anna and Michelle, and the other little girl, Tammy, still lived across the close. She was eighteen a little while ago, the stair was trailed in bunting and banners, big keys . . . the key to the door, the keys to the outside world, the adult world. Life. Diane's heart stilled at the thought. Janie would have been eighteen this year, a grown-up, a woman.

'Twelve years . . .' She dropped onto her haunches and cried. 'Twelve years since . . . Janie . . . Janie.'

The kitchen linoleum was cold beneath her feet, but she didn't care. She toppled over and lay on her side where she fell; her bare arms touched the cold floor, but she didn't care. Janie was cold. Somewhere. Wherever her daughter had met her end, she was cold, dead. The tears became harder, stronger, more rhythmic. The tears shook her whole body and gathered in a shallow pool beneath her head. There had been so many tears, so, so many. There had been years of crying and recriminations. Years of hurt and hoping for better days to come, but they never did. Nothing repaired the damage done to a family by the death of a child, of a much-loved daughter who could never be replaced. How did they go on from that? How did she? The tears intensified once again, but the rictus of her contorted, agonised mouth refused to allow the deep wails of hurt that she held inside. It was something she couldn't share, not after twelve years, not even with her husband.

'Billy . . .'

Where was he?

She wanted her husband. She wanted him home, to hold her. To say he understood. To tell her that wherever Janie was, she was safe. She was with angels. She couldn't hurt any more. She couldn't feel pain, the pain they felt, because she was in heaven. It was all words, all Billy's timeworn words that he repeated to reassure her that she didn't need to see the doctor again, didn't need to have her prescription antidepressants increased from three a day to four. She could leave the flat, she could leave the building, she could, maybe, one day, if she felt like it, go into the real world, back to work even.

'No.'

Diane shook herself. She eased her elbows out from beneath her and pushed herself from the grimy, cold floor. It was dark now, completely in blackness, save the glow of a dim and distant moon that shone with weak luminescence over the back yard and was reflected through the window.

She wondered how long she'd lain there, like a rag wrung out. Her arms were cold, the white flesh horripilating. She rubbed the forearms and shook her head again. The kitchen table seemed like a great distance away, but she knew she had to get off the floor. She didn't want Billy to see her this way; he would have his own worries. He tried to brush things aside, tried to make light, to look on the bright side, but she knew he was full of hurts. He played the big man, but he was as broken as she was; he just didn't show it. He didn't dare reveal it, because he still needed to be strong so that she could be weak.

The sound of a key in the lock startled Diane.

'Hello, love.'

He was home.

She wiped her face with the back of her hands; her knuckles were raw, rough. How had her skin become so coarse, she wondered? She hadn't been looking after herself.

Billy's heavy boots trailed the corridor, then a light went on. The brightness burned her retinas, and she raised her arm to shield her eyes.

'Love . . . What are you doing on the floor?' His voice was calm; it was always calm.

'I–I . . .'

'It's OK, no need to speak.' He knelt down beside her, placed an arm around her shoulder and slowly began to raise her from the floor. 'Come on, love, I'll make you a nice cup of tea. How would that be?'

Billy set about filling the kettle in the darkness. He seemed used to it, like it was the room's normal state.

'You can put the light on . . .' said Diane.

'Are you sure? Your eyes look red raw.'

'It's OK . . . I don't want you burning yourself making me a cuppa.'

Billy grinned, and his broad face gleamed. She wondered why he hadn't asked her what was wrong. Did it mean he didn't want to know? Or did it mean that there was so often something wrong that he didn't feel the need to ask?

'Billy . . .'

'Yes, love.' The kettle started to whistle, he had the teabag and the spoon in his hands.

'I want you to come and sit down.'

He turned to face her, and for the first time since he'd arrived she noticed a look of concern on his face. He put down the teabag and the spoon, then crossed the floor towards her. 'What is it?'

'Will you sit down, please.'

His broad brow became furrowed, and the thin lines beneath his eyes, darkened by the dirt of the building site, deepened. 'Diane . . .'

She raised a hand to his lips and bid him quiet.

'I had a call today, when you were at work . . .'

'Oh, aye.'

'It was the police.'

Billy's mouth widened. 'The police?'

She could feel her lower lip start to tremble as the words passed. 'There's a police officer, he's investigating a murder.'

Her husband seemed to sense how difficult it was for her, he reached over and grabbed her hands in his. 'Hey, look, whatever's happened, it's OK.'

Diane looked towards the window, which reflected the interior of the room. She looked back to Billy. 'He's called Valentine and he wants to come and see us . . . about Janie.'

Billy gripped his wife's hands tighter. 'Why? Why now? After all this time?'

'I don't know, he just . . . asked.'

'Do they have someone?'

'No . . . I mean, I don't think so.'

'Then why?' He rose from the chair, he seemed agitated. Diane knew he liked to lock things away, keep them inside. If he didn't look there, they didn't exist, not really: at least that's what he could pretend.

Diane turned in her chair. 'I said he could come . . . I said we would speak to him.'

Billy walked towards the kettle; its whistle was piercing the air as he picked up a spoon and clattered it into a cup.

29

SINCE THE INCIDENT OF HIS stabbing, Valentine had become aware of a distant, almost imperceptible, ticking. There was a clock on him now. He had never thought of it before, even at forty, which may have been the logical time to detect its presence. At forty you may safely look back, then count the years forward to assume – bearing in mind some luck of genetics – you have lived longer than you have left to go. Valentine's father would not see out his sixties, his grandfather had gone in his fifties; how long did he have left?

When he pondered the prospect of the diminishing count of years, he took pause. His previous decade – his thirties – had passed in a blur. He could remember turning thirty clearly, as it was the time of the millennium celebrations, but had it really been so long ago? He couldn't believe all those years – all that time – had really passed. What had he done with it? The incidents of memory were few: his daughters' birthdays, a couple of holidays, the surgery. In the main, it had been a period of drudge: of paying his way in the world, playing to a set of rules he had nothing to do with establishing. It seemed a waste.

His twenties, though further away in time, conversely seemed closer in memory. He could remember them with more clarity and with more affection. On turning twenty, he'd seemed charged with a burning sense of excitement. He'd thought the world held something special for him, but of course he had been dispossessed of that notion now. Youth was a ruse that lulled you into maturity, aided and abetted by the self-serving ego. There was no special people, at least, precious few – enough only to be the exceptions that proved the rule or to act like a spur in your back, a reminder of your posting in the chain gang.

When he thought about the days of his distant youth, Valentine always alighted on his own children. They seemed so naïve. Had he ever been so naked in the world? At no time had he felt it. The detective smirked to himself – there was that egomania again – two decades on and he could still fool himself that what went on inside his head was different to everyone else's. It was pathetic: we were all no more than meat and bones controlled by urges and impulses we knew little or nothing about. If indeed there was more – a heart, a soul, a sentient mind – it mattered nothing. Our fate remained the same: the rotting meat on the decaying bone dictated that.

There had been a time, once, that shook him from the slumber of so-called waking life and made him question his perceptions of the world he inhabited. Was it really as cut and dried as he supposed? Who was he to assume anything? He was just a man, a speck of dust on the great plain of the Earth. Surely he was fallible. When he had taken the call from David, a friend of many years standing with whom he had attended Tulliallan as a cadet, with whom he had spent time in uniform, and who he knew better than anyone else alive, he had known at once it was the last time he would speak to him.

'I'm coming back to the old town for a few days,' David had said, his voice high, full of spirit.

'Great, I'll tell Clare. She'll be over the moon . . . You'll stay with us, of course.'

David had said he would stay, since he'd moved to the north

of Ireland he'd become a man of note, a VIP no less; it was almost an honour to have him stop by. They'd kept in contact, but David's visits had become sparser than his own hair now. Yet they were something to look forward to.

'Grand, I have a couple of days spare. We could go up the coast, see the countryside,' he said. 'I just feel like I need a dose of it, being away from the auld country gets you that way.'

'I'll pick you up at Prestwick Airport . . .'

As Valentine said it, he'd known it was a lie. He'd welcomed the idea of playing host to his old friend, but as he'd prepared the house, planned day trips to Culzean Castle and Burns' Cottage he found himself in deep reminiscence of days long gone. He'd known, in the recesses of his mind, that he would not be doing any of those things he wrote down on paper, because he knew David would not be coming. He didn't know why or how he knew – and this is what he examined now – but for some reason he'd felt – no, he knew for sure – that he would never see his friend again. When the call came from the RUC to say that David had died, it had not shocked Valentine; he felt as if he'd known all along. The first ring of the telephone confirmed it. As he replayed the surreal time of David's passing once again, he couldn't shake the thought that he'd been in touch with some otherworldly messenger. He found the assumption absurd, but there it was.

The living room door eased open and Clare appeared with a glass of wine in her hand. 'You look deep in thought . . . Penny for them.'

Valentine looked at his own glass; the ice was melting over the Grouse. 'Yeah, you could say that.'

She sat down in front of him, balancing her elbows on her knees. 'Well, do I have to shake it out of you?'

Valentine took a sip of whisky and the ice clattered. 'I was thinking about David.'

Clare's face creased and her voice became lyrical. 'David Patterson that you trained with?'

'Yeah . . . Don't know why, just thinking of him.'

His wife reclined, crossed her legs and balanced the wine glass on the arm of the chair. 'You always said you knew it was coming . . . David's death.'

He could still taste the whisky on his lips; his breath was warm. 'I don't want to talk about it.' The words seemed to come out sharply; he noticed their barbs register on Clare's face and tried to retract them. 'I just mean, you know, I'd sooner not rake over it.'

'What's wrong, Bob?' She seemed calm, wearing her concerned face. There were no neuroses on show, none of the nervy gestures of late, like tucking hair behind her ear over and over again. It was late, too late to be getting into a metaphysical conversation with his wife. He pressed his back deeper into the chair and tapped a fingertip off the glass he held. Yet before he realised it, he'd removed a photograph from his shirt pocket and passed it to Clare.

'Who's this?' She turned the picture over as if hoping to find the answer to her question written on the back.

'Her name's Janie Cooper.'

'She's a pretty wee thing.'

'Was . . .'

Clare's eyes widened. He thought she might throw the picture at him and storm out of the room; she didn't like hearing about his cases. 'This wee one's dead?' She seemed saddened. 'This is an old picture, must be a few years ago now.'

'Twelve years.'

'That long? Then why are you carrying her picture around?' She placed the photograph on the arm of her chair where the wineglass had been resting a moment ago.

Valentine sighed. He didn't think he had the right words to explain what he was doing with a photograph of a murder victim who may not even be related to the ongoing investigation that he was involved in. The idea was absurd; even to those he knew who relied on their gut instincts, it would still be regarded as such.

'Do you remember a few nights ago I woke you, wanting to talk?' He touched the edges of his mouth. 'You said I was sweating . . .'

Clare glanced at the photograph on the arm of the chair. 'Yes, I remember . . . you'd had a turn.'

'It was a dream . . . or something.'

'Hang on, you said you'd had a dream about a girl with hair like . . .' She retrieved the picture. 'You said she had hair like Chloe and Fiona at that age.'

'She does remind me of the girls at that age . . . They were like wee angels.' Valentine caught himself smiling into the past.

'Bob, what is going on with your job?'

The reverie was broken. 'What do you mean?'

She put down the photograph and sighed, sitting forward in her chair once again. 'Something is wrong. You're under too much stress if you're having nightmares about children that have been dead for twelve years.'

'No, you don't understand . . .'

Clare put down her wine glass and held her face in her hands; she depressed her temples with the tips of her nails. 'Is this about you feeling different, about having changed once again?' She dropped her hands and stood up; the empty wine glass fell over. 'No, don't answer, I don't want to know . . .'

218

'Clare, please . . .'

His wife left the room before Valentine had any further chance to explain himself. He raised the whisky glass to his lips and drained it. What he had wanted to tell her, to make her understand, was that he hadn't seen the photograph of Janie Cooper until today. The fact that he already had seen her in a dream was as much a mystery to him as anyone else; he couldn't explain it. But there she was, or had been, laying flowers on the dead corpse of James Urquhart, dancing round him at the scene of his murder. The image caused a shiver to pass across his shoulders and he tensed as if caught in a shrill breeze. It was like something you read about in cheap magazines or found on late-night television when flicking through the channels. None of it made a modicum of sense, it was all alien to him, to his reasoning and sense of self. The detective wondered what had become of his life, of his perceptions; he questioned his sanity. He knew he should relieve himself of his duties, tell Chief Superintendent Marion Martin that he was not fit for purpose, because surely this wasn't normal, but something told him that wasn't an option. The picture of the young Janie Cooper and the image of the girl in his dream had fused now, and his sense of purpose had crystallised with it. If anyone was going to find James Urquhart's murderer, or that of Duncan Knox or Janie Cooper, then it was going to be him. He believed it, no matter what he had to base his judgement on. He steeled himself for the moment when what he had seen and felt would be understood with some form of clarity – because wasn't that the way it always was? Afterwards, everything made sense. After the case was closed. After the evidence gathered, the clues followed. He told himself that. He longed to believe it, but there was an ache in the pit of his stomach that asked if he would ever really know anything ever again.

He rose from his chair and placed the empty tumbler on the coffee table. The ice had melted into a smear on the bottom of the glass. He walked towards the door, put out the lights and carried on to the staircase. As he ascended the stairs to bed there was a lightness in his head that he put down to the whisky but hoped was a thaw in his thinking. When Valentine reached his bedroom the door was closed. He depressed the handle and walked in – the room was in darkness and only a few stray glints of light emanated from the edges of the heavy curtains. He had enough vision to see his wife lying in the bed, her back to him.

'Clare, look, you need to bear with me on this one.'

She remained silent for a moment, then turned to face him. 'This one? They're all the same: every time you go out that door you become a basket case with the stress and strain . . . For God's sake, Bob, have you forgotten just a short time ago you took a knife in the chest?'

He reached up to massage his eyes. 'You don't sound overly bothered about that.'

'Maybe it's because you don't sound overly bothered about me, or the girls. We need some of you too, but there never seems to be enough to go around.'

'Clare, just let me get this investigation out of the way and then we'll take a holiday, you and the girls and me . . . All together.'

She sat up in the bed and brought her knees towards her chest. 'A holiday? You think that's going to cut it, Bob?'

'What do you mean?'

She shook her head. 'This isn't working . . . We're dysfunctional.'

The word sounded ridiculous to him, like a term from a self-help manual. He let a laugh emerge that, at once, he knew he should have suppressed. 'Oh, come on . . .'

She looked at him, and the whites of her round eyes shone in the darkness of the enclosed space. There was no mistaking her ferocity when she replied.

'Go to hell, Bob, just bloody well go to hell.'

30

DI Bob Valentine woke from cautious sleep with aching bones and the scent of whisky on his breath. He removed his hand from the duvet and collected up the alarm clock – the exposed flesh of his arm told him at once that there was colder weather in store. He took time to focus on the burn of the digital clock's message, but when it registered he let out a sigh and padded towards the bathroom. Clare had risen early; her side of the bed was empty. There was a nip in the air already, he hoped it wasn't time to put on the central heating: the tired old boiler wouldn't last another year. Surely it was just that period of adjustment when the body gets used to a drop in temperature from the sun of summer to the smirr and wind of an approaching winter. As he ran the taps, Valentine let the sink fill up and then slowly splashed at his face cautiously with the warm water. He saw himself in the mirror: the tired eyes and sunken jowls of a man racing through middle age struck like a lash, but their impact was lessened by the sudden alteration in the appearance of his chest. The scar, the long, invasive mark that signalled like a beacon to him every morning, had gone from its usual pinkish-red to an altogether less harmonious hue. The scar's colour was now a pale purple: there was still a hint of red at its edges, but the predominant pigment now seemed blue. He touched it: the thick ridge of flesh felt the same and Valentine at once was compelled to ask himself what he was doing.

'Christ, man, get a grip . . .' He leaned over the sink again and splashed more water on his face and neck. It was all an effort to shake him from introspection, from the concerns of the overactive mind towards the here and now.

When he was dressed the DI took himself downstairs, collected a cup of coffee from the pot and greeted his wife with a cordial, 'Good morning.' There was a package waiting for him on the kitchen counter and the outside of the brown envelope indicated the contents at once.

'What have you been getting now?' said Clare. It seemed a surreal remark, as if he was the one who was continually running up the credit card bills.

'It's something for my dad . . .' Valentine opened the package from Amazon and removed the worn copy of McIlvanney's *Strange Loyalties*. 'He's been reading detective novels, can you believe it?'

Clare collected the book from the counter and creased her nose. 'Couldn't you have got him a new one?'

'It's been out of print, I had to shop around for this.'

'I'm surprised you had the time.' It was a calculated remark, and one that Valentine had no reply for.

He sipped his coffee and watched his wife return to the morning newspaper and her glass of orange juice. 'Could you drop it off later today, Clare . . . ? He's just sitting about up there on his own, I think he'd appreciate it.'

She turned and put widened eyes on him. 'Well, you'd think he'd appreciate a visit from his son, then.'

Valentine put down his coffee cup and raised his briefcase; he wasn't prepared to pick up where he had left off the night before. 'I'm off to work.'

Clare had returned to reading the newspaper as he closed the kitchen door and headed towards the car in his shirtsleeves. The air outside was too sharp to be out without a jacket, he realised as he opened the door and flung his grey sports coat on the backseat; it covered the dark patch he still winced to see and still couldn't quite believe existed. As he pulled out, the sky was an infinite grey smear and the road still glistened from the recent downpour; the contrast struck Valentine as the natural bedfellows of the Ayrshire setting – bleak and bleaker. The Vectra's engine grunted all the way to the first tailback, which stretched from the junction all the way down Beresford Terrace. When he depressed the clutch the car steadied and he became aware of the fetch and miss of his breath. He gripped the gearstick as the lights changed and drove on to Burns Statue Square, taking a slow glance towards the High Street as he turned left at the Ayrshire and Galloway.

The town was a huddled hoard of bodies, all bared elbows and blunt shoulders. It was as if either the order 'eyes down' had been given or to a one they feared a glance to the grey skies would strike them blind. The traffic soon slowed to a stop once again outside the old market and Valentine found himself staring aimlessly as a torn poster waved to passers-by each time the breeze picked up. There were children on their way to school wailing with siren-like voices as he took off again, glad to be moving forward. The hotel where DS Sylvia McCormack stayed was in front of a roundabout. He knew it as the Caledonian Hotel: it had changed its name several times since then, but to Valentine it would always be the Caly. He pulled up outside and waited for his colleague to appear.

Valentine realised that he liked DS McCormack because

she thought for herself – she utilised some form of judgement, not just in the job but in life too. Most people, most of the time, were just trying to fit in. They were trying to make themselves more like everyone else at the expense of any of their own uniqueness. Being different, even in a small way, made the majority uneasy. Difference was something to be hidden, locked away and secretly challenged: 'Why am I not like everyone else?' was the modern preoccupation. It took guts, beyond confidence or any self-assurance, to stand out from the pack and say, 'No, I'm doing this my way.' Valentine admired that in DS McCormack: she acquiesced her own self to no one. If it set her aside from the others, so be it.

He imagined what the DS's school days must have been like – that cauldron of conformity where every transgression from the norm was an offence worthy of public hostility. Did she spend those days alone? Annexed from the others in the playground, in the dining hall . . . He caught a vision of a young Sylvia McCormack and smiled to himself.

'I'm sure it wouldn't have bothered her one jot!' he said.

Many years ago, someone had called Clare 'contrary', he remembered. It had been intended as an insult, a youthful dig, but at the time he thought it was the greatest compliment. To be the opposite, to be blindly accepting, was the true insult. She had been contrary because she'd had a mind of her own and guile enough to use it. He wondered now what had happened to all that: did the world really break us all? He certainly didn't see too much evidence of it making us stronger.

The car door opened. 'Hello, boss . . .'

Valentine reached for the gearstick and nodded towards DS McCormack. 'Right . . . Glasgow, here we come.'

She beamed back at him, and what he thought had been

a cruel, unsmiling mouth gave way to an otherwise pretty face.

'It's dreich enough out.'

'Aye, well, that'll be the summer by with.' He indicated on his way through the roundabout and onto Barns Street. He could already see the Sandgate clogged with cars. 'The traffic's a nightmare . . . When are they expecting us?'

DS McCormack was shimmying out of her raincoat. 'Any time after ten.' Her voice trailed off, fell into a deep well. 'That's what Mrs Cooper said . . . when I called.'

Valentine noticed how tense her face had become. 'How did she seem . . . Mrs Cooper?'

The officer sat in silence for a moment and appeared to be considering her response. She said: 'Empty.'

Valentine repeated the word. 'Empty.'

She turned to face him. 'It's the best I can come up with to describe the woman . . . It was like talking to a shadow on the phone when I mentioned Janie.'

Valentine stored the response away; he didn't want to give too much importance to the DS's observation, though he knew it was likely to be accurate. He felt somehow his own perceptions would overrule anyone else's. 'What did you tell the Coopers?'

She started to cough on the back of her hand. 'Hope that's not me coming down with the cold . . .' The coughing fit passed and she got back on track. 'I told them that we were investigating a murder.'

'Did you mention Knox?'

'No, I didn't think that would serve any particular purpose at this point.'

'Good. If we bring the Knox angle into play, I'd like to see the reaction.'

DS McCormack squinted. 'What are you hoping to gain from this meeting, sir?'

Valentine was pulling onto the main arterial road to Glasgow; the stretch of single carriageway was busy but allowed him to reach 50 mph. 'If I knew that, Sylvia, I'd send you and save myself the bother . . . Trust me, if there's a link to Knox and Urquhart, I'll find it. Of that I've no bloody doubt.'

'You seem very sure of this lead.'

'Knox was questioned at the time Janie Cooper went missing and the bank's confirmed that Urquhart was living and working in Glasgow at the same time. Call me an optimist, but I'm betting this is our link.'

The Ayrshire countryside stretched out on either side of the road, green fields washed in buckets of rain. A few cows, Friesians, made mud-splattered tracks towards a copse of trees. A grey half-moon still sat in the morning sky; there was no sign of the sun.

'You think they knew each other, Knox and Urquhart, don't you?' said DS McCormack.

Valentine tipped on the blinkers and made to overtake a Nissan Micra. 'Think . . . ? I know.'

'But how can you know?'

At once the detective realised the pomposity of his statement. He had never dealt in what ifs or casuistry; he reasoned and made use of the facts – at best, he interpreted. 'Do you doubt me?'

McCormack smiled again. 'That's not an answer, that's a question.'

'OK, then ask me once we've seen the Coopers . . . You'll have your answer then. Knox knew Urquhart and they both ended up dead because of that association. I don't know how they came to know each other yet, or how they came to know

Janie Cooper, but I know someone else on the force took a similar line of reasoning twelve years ago when that wee girl went missing. Knox was in the frame then and I doubt he's blameless now. Urquhart might have slipped under the radar at the time, but whatever went on has well and truly caught up with them.'

31

THEY WERE EVERYWHERE IN Glasgow, the poseurs. That was the trouble with the big city, thought Valentine, it attracted types prone to reinventing of themselves. It didn't matter what they had been before – accountant, plooky teen, quantity surveyor – in the city they imagined they could excoriate the skin of the past and start anew. The detective alighted on a man: balding, bad fifties, clearly fighting middle-aged spread. He had squeezed himself into the latest fashions from Top Man: had the term 'skinny' jeans not been a warning sign? Valentine fought an urge to shake his head, to frown disapproval, but settled for a disdainful glance towards his own M&S flannels. The bald man was sipping a latte in one of the long glasses that Valentine always sent back, telling the staff that it was a sundae glass and that he wanted a cup of coffee. The man he observed now seemed to relish the effeminacy of the receptacle; it was then that the DI came to the conclusion that the man might be gay. He turned his eyes away quickly, an atavistic fear from his Ayrshire youth firing inside him. When he was growing up in the auld toun, homosexuality was deemed a curse worse than any gypsy's and attracted the same hysterical, pernicious demonising.

A thought soon lit in Valentine: he couldn't grudge the stranger his new life. A vague, nauseating wave of guilt hit him for having judged someone who had likely faced harsh judgement his entire life. If he had just moved to the city, reinvented himself as a fifty-something Top Man, then so what? He had every right to his trip, as much as – maybe more so than – the middle-class teen who fancied himself an artist or a musician or a boulevardier hanging louchely on a Gitane somewhere in the Merchant City. People were strange and did even stranger things to escape the fact. Valentine realised that part of his aversion to the big city was the idea that he was confronted with such strangeness wherever he looked. He was overstimulated by the fact, like some hyperactive terrier let loose in a barn full of rats. He longed to be home, back in Ayr, where being normal and bland was a given because straying from the narrow path of conformity led only to the steep cliffs of derision.

DS Sylvia McCormack appeared clutching two paper cups filled with coffee. She smiled towards her boss as she placed the cups down on the Formica tabletop. The liquid let off a slow flare into the brisk air that signalled its unsuitability for bodily contact.

'Watch, it's hot,' said McCormack.

'I see that.'

'Aye, well, I felt it when I was stupid enough to take a sip.'

'It'll not be long cooling down. I swear Glasgow is the coldest place on the planet . . . Vladivostok doesn't get a look in.'

He watched the DS huddle her hands around the paper cup like it was a mini-brazier she had acquired for the purpose. There was a lot of people around, people just milling about – old men and youths alike. Valentine wondered where they came from and why they seemed to lack all sense of purpose in where they were going.

'Like the land of the living dead around here,' he said, glancing over McCormack's shoulder.

She took her cue from the DI and revolved her eyes over the scene. 'The jakey brigade . . . You get used to it.'

He knew she was right. He could remember a time when there was one tramp – they called them tramps then – in Ayr and one in Kilmarnock. They were well-kent faces; the towns had complete genealogical records on them, knew their previous lives and ultimate falls from grace as the stuff of legend. Not now, though. Valentine couldn't keep pace with the number of the fallen in Ayrshire; their toll increased almost daily, it seemed, certainly they were not faces with names – they were not unusual enough any more to be afforded any special status.

The DI ventured a sip of coffee. It wasn't as warm as it looked or as inviting as the idea suggested – the greasy rainbow swirling on top made his nostrils flare.

'Pretty dire, isn't it?' said McCormack.

Valentine stuck out his tongue. 'Did you buy it from a mechanic?'

She smiled. 'No, I did not . . . You saw me going over to the counter.'

'Maybe they do oil changes as well . . . Think we got the Castrol instead of the Nescafé.' He stood up and fastened the button of his grey dog-tooth sports coat.

'Are we off, boss?'

He nodded. 'Come on, you can bring your coffee with you . . . Might run into an AA man you can give it to.'

The officers left the car in a side road between a kirkyard and playing fields and made their way to Pollokshaws Road. Janie Cooper's school was a short walk from the car. An imposing stone building, it reminded Valentine of the way schools used to be made. It looked like Ayr Academy, not some prefabricated box that had been flung up in five minutes flat.

231

The windows were tall and thin, newly replaced but sustaining some grandeur of times past. He knew that the reality of the place would be somewhat different from his perception of solidity and that great Scots record on education, but he couldn't help feeling comfortable standing in front of the impressive façade. On the other side of the road sat a tacky, flat-roofed oblong of flats that looked to have been built in the seventies – the decade that style forgot – and now housed a children's play centre below and brutally exposed balconies replete with peeling paint and plastic furniture above.

'So, this is where she . . .' Valentine couldn't bring himself to say the words, to complete the sentence. They both knew where they were and what had happened to Janie Cooper that day twelve years ago when she never made it home from school.

'The Coopers still stay in Bertram Street.' DS McCormack indicated the direction of the route the young girl must have walked.

'Hardly any distance at all,' said Valentine. 'Come on . . .' He paced himself as he walked towards Bertram Street, taking in the scene of utter simplicity – an anywhere road in any town in Scotland. He knew why the Coopers had never moved: where could they go that would not remind them of the utter normality of the place?

As they reached the corner of Bertram Street, the detective stopped in his tracks. They stood beside a low verge and boxy hedgerows that edged the communal gardens of tenement flats. He was overwhelmed by the singular feeling that he had been there before.

'How many streets are there just like this?' he said.

McCormack pulled a stray strand of hair from her mouth; the wind was picking up. 'At least a million, we could be anywhere . . . Edinburgh, Inverness, the Borders . . .'

'We could even be in Ayr.'

The DS nodded. 'That we could, sir.'

They progressed down the street and made their way to the front door of the Coopers' tenement. As they stared at the rows of buttons on the outside wall, the plastic coverings on a host of nametags – all familiar to anyone accustomed to perusing a Scottish telephone directory – Valentine paused.

'I've a very strange feeling about this . . .' The words were out before he realised what he had said, and the DI made a sudden and sharp intake of breath. He wished he could have swallowed his last utterance.

'Sir . . . What do you mean?' McCormack's eyes thinned as she stood granite-firm on the path beside her boss and stared into him.

Valentine shook off the enquiry and reached forward to depress the buzzer in front of them. 'Nothing, just thinking aloud . . .'

'Is there something you want to tell me?'

He shrugged and turned back towards the door. 'Like what?'

'I'm not sure, anything . . . If you don't mind me saying, you seem a bit . . . jumpy.'

Valentine grinned, a wide headlamp smile that he knew he always reserved for such situations. He was cornered and had nothing to say that would get him out of the trap he'd sprung for himself.

The buzzer sounded and the detective lunged for the handle and stepped inside.

'Saved by the bell, eh,' said McCormack.

The stairwell was dark and dank. A mountain bike sat tethered to the railings of the banister; two stanchions had already been cut, and Valentine wondered how long the bike

233

would last under such flimsy security. There was a door that led out to a back green flapping open, banging soundly on the jamb every time the wind picked up. The plaster was crumbling from the damp walls and sat in dusty flakes on the stone steps. Some had made its way to the corner of the first floor – likely on a dustpan – and sat in a white cairn that poked at Valentine like a reminder of his visit. He ran a finger along the wall and inspected the blackness, simply as a distraction for himself, before rubbing it on his thumb and then the fronts of his trousers.

'Here it is, this is us,' said McCormack. She turned to face her boss, then spoke again with her hand poised over the door, ready to knock. 'Will I do the honours, sir?'

Valentine nodded and took a step back, making sure his mobile phone was switched off. They faced a faded net curtain in the door's window; its movement was almost imperceptible as the DS made two delicate taps on the doorframe and retreated to stand beside her boss. As a light went on behind the curtain, the net went from a dull grey to a luminous yellow and then the silhouette of a man appeared in the frame. Valentine's stomach clenched and then released, and he brought the flat of his hand up to his chest in an almost Pavlovian response to the unknown. The musty smell that percolated the stairwell seemed to vanish as the door opened and Billy Cooper waved them in.

Billy's face was stolid as he closed the door behind the officers and began to run the palms of his hands over the sleeves of his T-shirt. He was nervous, clearly, but this was someone who had learned to deal with simple emotions and some that were obviously far more complex – that much was displayed in the way he took control of the situation, extending a hand to the officers and flashing blue-grey eyes tinged with both a welcome and forlorn sadness. He was broad-shouldered and angular, but his frame looked burdened with the approaching bulk of middle age and the strains of a life given to manual labour; it was, again, a cross he bore lightly, almost blithely. The city could fall, nations and empires crumble, but Billy Cooper would be unmoved by anything else this life of man had to offer, not now, not ever again. He had survived a hurt that few would dare to imagine and there was nothing left for the fates to throw at him while he endured the remainder of his time in this existence.

The officers stood facing Billy for a moment, Valentine was unsure how to effect introductions: were they even there on official business? He doubted it and knew CS Martin would doubt it too. He was following a hunch that was more visceral than anything else, yet he believed he was in the right place to advance the case.

The DI dipped his head. 'Can I introduce myself – Detective Inspector Bob Valentine.' He turned to face his colleague. 'And this is Detective Sergeant Sylvia McCormack.'

Billy Cooper took the hands as they were offered, but his face told them that no connection had been made beyond the surface of the skin. He was a man who had cut all ties to the outside world, even the most ephemeral.

'My wife's through in the front room,' he said.

'We'd like to meet her, Billy,' said Valentine.

As they walked towards the living room at the top of the flat, the detective became vaguely aware that he was not in a home. It was a shrine to the memory of a home. There were pictures on the walls that would have been out of fashion a decade ago: rural scenes of hunting, shooting and fishing set in gaudy brass frames – they were the type of pictures you saw in charity shop windows, or cheap student bedsits, certainly not anywhere where people would want, or choose, to live. The carpets were threadbare and coated with such a heavy layer of dust that they would have greeted a vacuum cleaner as a long-lost stranger. As they rounded the hallway into the living room, a shelving unit made of chrome and smoked glass spied on them from the facing wall. Valentine at once gazed directly at the row of pictures that had been lined up like unholy babushka dolls in ascending height. To a one they contained photographs of Janie Cooper. She had a broad, say-cheese grin that shouted her personality to the world at large. Her round eyes were a violet-blue and shone beneath the shock of white-blonde hair that hung in a heavy fringe and was long enough to be tied in a neat ponytail. In every image the girl proclaimed her love of life, she brimmed full of it, looked in awe of an awesome world where she was happy to exist in the company of her beloved family. The sight of Janie jolted Valentine's senses and a deep, yet somehow hollow, pain erupted in the depths of his chest, telling him he was in a new place now, somewhere he had never been before. The detective felt like he stood at the threshold of the kind of life discovery that changed a man, made him anew, and not always for the better. He knew this, and yet despite all his reservations, all the consequences he foresaw, he was compelled to cross the line. As Valentine turned to Diane Cooper where she sat huddled on a corner seat, she seemed held together by only a thin thread of life, which, under tremendous stresses already, threatened to snap.

'Hello, Diane,' he said. 'The pictures of your daughter are just beautiful.'

32

THE AIR IN THE ROOM WAS still, almost felt lacking after the musty enclosure of the stairwell, but there was more to it than that, thought Valentine. The atmosphere of the house was different, had the quality of a tomb. Did he imagine it? Was it because he knew he was visiting one of the last places where Janie Cooper was seen alive? He knew there were others who had seen her afterwards, but they didn't count, not really. The Janie they had seen was not the same little girl. He tried to put out of his mind the degradation, the pain and the hurts that he knew must have befallen her, but he couldn't do it. Being there, in her home with her parents, made the realities of Janie's end seem only too real. Valentine felt his connection to the girl's passing intensify with each new second. He was tense, uneasy; his heart rate increased and there was a dull but persistent drumming beginning in his temples that he had never felt before now. It worried him; would he be able to do this?

'Can I get you a cup of tea, Inspector?' said Billy. He stood in the doorway with his hands in his pockets, tipping his head towards a small kitchen where a kettle had just boiled and an assortment of mugs clustered around its base as if interested in the rising steam.

'Erm . . .' Valentine had no words; his throat tightened like there was a rope around his windpipe.

'Yes, that would be lovely, thank you.' DS McCormack seized the reins and moved herself between the detective and the deceased girl's mother.

Valentine followed her lead and lowered himself onto the couch as Billy went into the kitchen. He positioned himself somewhere behind DS McCormack and tried to listen to the conversation she began, but the words became of little meaning after only a few brief moments. As the trail of slow seconds became more substantial minutes, Valentine removed his handkerchief from his trouser pocket and dabbed at his moistening brow; he was confused and uncertain of himself, like he was not the same man who had passed through the door only minutes previously.

'Inspector . . .' Billy Cooper held out a mug of tea before him. Valentine stared at the mug like it was an antediluvian conundrum before he was prompted again. 'Your tea, Inspector.'

'Oh, thank you.' His voice came like a low rasp and it shocked him out of his introspection.

'Can I ask you, Mrs Cooper . . . Did you ever have a feeling, I mean an instinct, that there was anyone around you who would harm Janie?'

The woman's face tensed and the hollows of her cheeks darkened. Valentine wondered if he had overstepped a mark, gone too far: could it be that after twelve years the woman was still unable to speak about it? She was her mother, though, and what was twelve years or twelve centuries to deal with that kind of grief?

'Did I suspect anyone, is that what you mean?'

The detective nodded. 'We visited her school, before we came here; it looks a good school.' Valentine paused, drew solemn breath. 'But perhaps there was someone there, or

238

on the periphery of Janie's life, who would have made you cautious around them.'

Billy had disbursed the mugs of tea and joined the others in the seating area of the living room, where he stared distractedly at the goings-on. He looked like he had heard it all before, like the officers were going over old and very well-trodden ground.

Mrs Cooper answered. 'No. There was no one.'

Valentine lowered his tea towards the floor and placed the mug on the carpet by the sofa. He had conducted interviews, informal and otherwise, with hundreds, if not thousands, of grieving and aggrieved parents in his time as a police officer, but there was something strange about this encounter. He felt like he was visiting with grief – the actual ethereal body of the pain and misery endured by families of the departed. He saw the injury in their eyes, but beyond that he felt their pained cries ringing in his ears like they were his own. The thought that he would intrude on such a personal hurt filled him with self-loathing, disgust, a desire to abandon himself. As he looked at the couple in their distress he knew they longed for one thing, and one thing alone, but there was no one on this mortal coil who could deliver it to them.

'Why?' said Mrs Cooper.

'I'm sorry, I don't . . .'

Billy spoke, his voice a lesser force than it had been. 'She means why did you come here? Has something happened?'

Valentine froze. He was rigid in his seat; his spinal column was locked to the ground beneath him, immobile.

'We are investigating another case, a murder,' McCormack's words were antiseptic, professional. At once the tone of the room seemed to be drawn back to a recognisable place. 'We don't know if it's related, but one of the victims was questioned twelve years ago about the disappearance of Janie.'

'He's dead?' said Billy.

DS McCormack nodded.

'Good.'

'You don't know who it is, Mr Cooper.'

'What does that matter? If he was caught before and questioned about my daughter, he was nothing. Worse than nothing. I'm glad he's dead.'

Diane Cooper sat perfectly still, like a pale marmoreal monument to her deepening sadness. When she spoke, the almost imperceptible movement of her lips seemed like a trick of the light. 'Who was it?'

DI Valentine sensed some semblance of composure returning. 'He was called Duncan Knox.'

The name sat between them like a small explosion that dictated they wait for the dust to settle before dealing with the fallout.

'We don't know him,' said Billy.

'Are you sure?' Valentine addressed the husband but kept his stare fixed on the wife. She held still.

'Why would we?'

'There's no reason that you would . . . We just hoped.'

Billy Cooper's colour seemed to alter: he became darker. He gnawed on his fingernail for a moment before he spoke again. 'You're on a fishing trip?'

'Excuse me?' said Valentine.

Billy rose, his inoffensive demeanour seemed harder now. His jaw jutted as he spoke with a finger pointed towards the detectives. 'You came here with nothing and now you're leaving with nothing . . .' He pointed to his wife, who had her head bowed. 'And it's the pair of us that'll have to pick up the pieces.'

Valentine stood up. The blood was surging in his veins as he presented his open palms towards Billy Cooper. 'I'm sorry, I know those words won't help a lot, but I do genuinely feel your loss.'

Billy shook his head and shot a hand to the side of his face. His nails dug into the fleshy part of his cheek for a moment and then he lunged forward and closed down the detective. 'Don't give me your shite!'

'Sir, can you step back, please . . .' DS McCormack jumped to her feet and tried to get between the two men.

'Sylvia, no . . . It's fine, sit down.'

Billy stepped back, but his chest was still inflated, his eyes burning with anger. 'You bastards don't care one jot about our loss; if you did, you'd have caught the freak that took our wee lassie.'

Valentine was unable to hold Billy's gaze. He looked away and caught sight of Mrs Cooper, sitting statue still. He wanted to leave their temple to the memory of their daughter, not because he felt unwelcome – though he assuredly did – but because he saw now that it was all they had. Something precious had been taken from them, something more than their daughter, even – their will to go on.

Valentine motioned DS McCormack to the door as he extended a hand to Billy Cooper. 'I'm very sorry to have intruded like this, I hope you can forgive us.' He stood with his hand in the air for a moment and then withdrew it. As he did so, a sharp pain shot up his opposite arm and he jerked to grip his arm tightly.

As they paced into the hallway, Valentine heard McCormack's heavy footfalls on the thin carpet behind him, but his eyes were drawn to an open door at the far end of the hall. He tried to focus, but his vision blurred like he was underwater and he grew suddenly cold, as though the temperature in the flat had plummeted sharply. With the next step, his knee locked mid-stride then suddenly gave way; his blurred vision disappeared into blackness as he fell first into the wall and then dropped to the hard floor with a thud.

Where he lay, Valentine saw the cornflower-blue walls in the facing room reflecting a luminous light that was streaming through the window in denial of the dreich day's setting. For a moment, his chest tensed to a sharp pain and he heard the blood pulsing in his ears like a cacophonous hammering. He made a deep wheeze of indrawn breath and time slowed to the dull pace of a mill wheel as a small, white-haired girl appeared in the doorway of the room. A deep spring of sorrow was tapped in Valentine as he stared at the girl in a red duffel coat, swinging a doll in her hand. She was smiling at him. Blood ran hot in his cheeks as he tried to speak, but words wouldn't pass his lips. He turned back to face the way he had come, hoping to see the Coopers, but there was no one there. When he spun back to the front he felt a warm hand on his face.

'Boss.' DS McCormack was facing him, her voice loud in his ears. 'Boss, are you all right?'

He gazed over her shoulder, towards the bedroom with the blue walls. The door was open but the room was empty.

'Boss . . .'

The Coopers had appeared now. 'Is he all right?'

'What happened to him?'

Valentine eased himself onto his elbow, then pushed away from the floor with the flat of his hand. 'I'm fine . . .'

'Oh, I don't know about that, sir.' McCormack placed a palm on his shoulder and withdrew her phone.

'What are you doing?'

'Calling an ambulance . . .'

Valentine snatched the phone and eased himself off the ground; his head started to spin as he got to his feet. 'You're overreacting . . .'

'Sir, you passed out.'

The DI grabbed her hand and slammed the phone in it. 'I'm fine!' Valentine staggered past her and opened the front door.

As he headed for the stairs, his shaky steps became a brisk duckwalk. By the tenement's entrance, he was breathing hard and a glaze of sweat had formed on his forehead. He pushed open the door and gulped for air as he flounced onto the front path.

Valentine was making his way to the edge of the garden as DS McCormack appeared. 'Wait, sir . . . Please.'

He carried on to the edge of the road, his legs unsteady beneath him as he glanced back at the deep ploughline of confusion he'd just dug. He could see McCormack sprinting after him and decided he couldn't outrun her; he stroked his now aching chest as he settled onto the low wall skirting the communal garden.

'Where's the fire?' said McCormack as she caught up. A trace of a smile sat on her lips, but a serious tone betrayed her thoughts.

Valentine cleared his throat and tried to cache his emotions. 'We should never have gone in there . . .'

'We needed to check it out.'

He looked away, caught sight of the wind taking an empty takeaway carton down the wide curve of the street. 'The last thing they needed was us stirring everything back up for them.'

McCormack joined him on the wall. She unhooked the strap of her bag from her shoulder and balanced it on her knees. 'We weren't to know. It was twelve years, sir.'

Valentine turned on her. 'Do you think that makes any difference?'

'No, but . . .'

'But what?'

Her cheeks flushed. For a moment she looked like she might answer his question: a reply queued behind her eyes and then she looked away. She clamped her teeth for a moment and then tilted her head back towards Valentine. 'What happened in there?'

He didn't respond. Birdsong sat dulcet in the air between them.

McCormack tried again. 'I know something happened, I saw it in your face.'

'Nothing happened.' His words came like hammer blows on the back of her sympathetic tones.

She picked herself from the wall and stood before him. 'I'll go and get the car.' As the detective made to stand, McCormack planted her hand on his shoulder. 'No, you stay . . . You're in no fit state.'

'I'm perfectly fine.'

The DS took two steps before she turned and lunged at him. 'You're far from fine.' A curl unfurled itself from her hair and lashed at her brow – it seemed to signal an alteration in mood. 'I wish you wouldn't treat me like such a bloody idiot!'

Valentine watched her heavy steps on the concrete slabs as she went. She wrestled with the strap of her bag and then gave up trying to get it to sit on her shoulder. She was frustrated and angry, and he knew dismissing her questions was not going to be an option. He was acting like a child sticking his fingers in his ears. It didn't faze the detective that the DS was capable of having his position called into question, because he had already started that process for himself. The thought gripped like a cincture round his chest and sent a spasm into his numbed arm. He gripped his fist above the edge of the wall and tried to hold firm – the short, stabbing pain below his breastbone passed, but he knew it wasn't going to be the last he had to endure. His breathing constricted and then, just as quickly, eased into a steady rhythm that seemed to calm him. He looked up. A weak sun divided the street into pale light and dark shade. McCormack had turned the corner now, was out of sight, but he could still see her scowl-crossed face and accusing eyes.

33

CAMERON SINCLAIR STOOD outside the Wellington Café watching the early evening punters shuffling onto the street with their tightly wrapped packages of fish and chips. There was a crowd, a queue out the door, and the ice-cream shop beside was picking up the passing trade of those walking by shaking their heads. Sinclair checked his watch, scrunched his brows to remove the glare of a low and weak but persistent sun from the face. His impatience was a display he couldn't have compounded with a stamping foot and fist shaken at the heavens. He moved away from the gathering of Ayrshire heifers that barged and bullied their bulk to get to the feed trough. Weren't they fat enough without all that starch and dripping, he thought. He didn't like the town, or the people. He had told his boss on the *Glasgow-Sun* – when he still had his job – that Ayr was too blue-collar for him.

'You're just a bloody snob, Cam,' he'd replied.

'Well, what if I am . . . Is there something wrong with having standards?'

'Aye there is, it's called looking down your nose at people . . . or being a snob.'

'That's a reductive argument,' he snapped, he knew at once it was the wrong tack to take with Jack Gallagher.

The older man laughed in his chair, rocked backwards, and pointed to Sinclair. 'When you're at that big dictionary next, look up the word "irony", eh.'

Gallagher had laughed him out of his office and the move onto the crime beat in Ayr was no longer up for discussion. Ten months he'd slummed it with the proles now, and all it had earned him was a handful of page-one splashes and a dubious suspension for bending the rules when Gallagher had himself stated the rules were there to be bent.

'Nothing wrong with bending the rules . . . Getting caught bending the rules, now that's another matter.' He could still see the ruddy cheeks resounding in broken veins, the raucous half-laugh, half-cough that rattled off the walls every time the editor found himself amusing.

'Bastard . . .' said Sinclair beneath his breath. Gallagher would be laughing on the other side of his face when he brought in the real story behind the Ayr murders. 'Bloody right he will . . .'

'Say something, mate?' It was just another pleb in a Rangers top.

'Sorry . . . you got the time?'

'You just looked at your watch!'

'It's bust . . . Battery must be flat.'

The man seemed suspicious, but rendered the time and walked away, glancing over his shoulder through slitted eyes as he went. Sinclair nodded his thanks and made a brief wave that skated so close to the common touch that he thought he deserved congratulations. He was still waving after the man when he noticed Danny Gillon's white van pulling up outside the bus station on the other side of the road. He jogged towards the roundabout, then slipped into the slow traffic on his way to the vehicle. The van's door dragged heavy in his hand and jammed a little; he applied another hand and tugged harder. The passenger seat wore a dusting of white powder, plaster perhaps. Who knows what he had been moving in the vehicle:

it was filthy, chocolate bar wrappers and empty cans littering the foot well. Sinclair shook his head, hoped his tetanus shot was up do date, and moved inside.

'This is a bloody mess,' he said.

Gillon grinned. 'It's my office.' He was holding a cigarette in his hand as he spoke, but he was also holding court, waving the cigarette expansively and feeding the wheel with the lightest of fingertip touches from his other hand.

'Calling this an office doesn't lend legitimacy to your ... business.' Sinclair spat the last word like it was the epitome of disdain, a fishbone that had lodged in his trachea.

Gillon over-revved the engine and pushed through an amber light; there was a hail of loud horns as he turned the corner with Sinclair gripping the dash. He smiled as the journalist straightened himself and brushed his hands on the front of his trousers. 'Try and not get us killed.'

'Oh, I'm always very careful in that direction,' said Gillon, the grin returning to his face.

Sinclair caught himself staring at Danny Gillon's teeth: they were not like any normal teeth but tiny yellow stumps, cracked and chipped like old headstones. Had he ever visited a dentist? How did these people live, here? He couldn't believe that he had grown up in the same country as some of the invertebrates he was brushing shoulders with now. They were a class above maggots, but only just. He had an overwhelming urge to wind down the window and vomit his objections onto the street.

On Racecourse Road, the conversation took a turn. 'I hope you had a word with that bloody whore of yours,' said Sinclair.

Gillon pressed the cigarette to his lips and exhaled the smoke in his passenger's direction as he replied. 'Oh, I had a word with her all right. But not the way you're thinking.'

Sinclair contained the urge to laugh. 'What would you

know about what I'm thinking?' He turned his eyes to the side window; the grass on the old racecourse was brighter than it had been in the summer months.

'See that?' Gillon raised a hand from the wheel and drew a fist: his gnarled knuckles were bruised and reddened. 'That's the only language she understands.' He dropped his hand and grabbed his groin. 'That, and this!'

Sinclair felt a queasiness rising in his stomach. He knew he had reached a new low with Danny Gillon, but he also knew that the pimp had something that he wanted. The whore had been reticent at their last meeting, but Gillon obviously had ways of getting information out of her that Sinclair didn't. For a moment he thought to ask of Leanne Dunn's condition, but when the thought of her bruised and bloodied features flashed in front of him he found his real feelings were only of distaste.

'This better not be another wild goose chase,' said Sinclair.

Gillon riled. 'Are you saying I don't know what I'm doing? Are you saying I can't make one of my own whores say what I want them to say?'

'I'm sure you know your business very well, Gillon, but is the information going to be any use this time?'

He wagged a finger in the direction of the dashboard. The green Magic Tree air freshener hanging from the rearview mirror came within reach and he pulled the tree down, crunching it in his hand. 'Look, I told you she knew the fat paedo they found out at the track with a plank up his hole.'

'We established that last time . . .'

'But she knew the other one, the banker guy as well . . . Urquhart . . . Not even the police know this. I could be getting myself into deep water just talking to you: it's two bloody murders we're going on about here.'

Sinclair turned his attention to the driver as he gesticulated above the wheel once again. 'Keep your eyes on the road.'

'Are you hearing what I said . . . ? They knew each other.'

They'd reached the edges of Alloway, heading in the direction of Monument Road.

'And do you think the police haven't asked the Urquharts about that? It would have been their first question. What in the hell makes you think us turning up on their doorstep is going to make an ounce of difference?'

They'd reached the Urquhart's home. There was a man at the gate pouring petrol into a ride-on mower, and he stared at the van with thinned eyes then raised a hand and walked towards the passenger's door.

'Yes, can I help you?' he said.

Sinclair peered down the bridge of his nose and sharpened his already cut-glass vowels. 'I'm sorry, and you would be?'

'My name's Bell; I'm a very close friend of the Urquharts.'

'Then you had better let us in, Mr Bell . . . We're here on a pressing matter.'

The man retreated a few steps, seeming somewhat stunned to be greeted by Estuary English in such plain wrapping as a white Bedford van. As he placed the petrol canister on the path, he released the gates and the van started to roll up the drive.

Sinclair waved regally as they passed the first hurdle and returned to his earlier conversation. 'Well, you still haven't answered me.'

Gillon brought the van to a halt in the gravel driveway. There was a scrunch of tyres and then he lunged to his left and yanked on the handbrake. 'I'm sure the police have asked the Urquharts if they knew Knox and I'm just as bloody sure they got a well-rehearsed answer . . .' He paused to flick a cigarette butt out the window. 'But have the police asked them about Leanne?'

Sinclair allowed a slow smile to creep up the side of his face. 'You may have something there, Gillon.'

'I know I have . . . and so do you, mate, or you wouldn't be coughing for the information in such a tidy manner.'

'I'll see you all right, don't worry about that.'

Gillon unlocked his door and inched towards the opening. 'Oh, I know you will. Of that I've no doubt at all, Cam boy.'

When the pair met on the driveway, they faced each other for a brief moment until a wide grin spread over Gillon's face. He left the expression to hang between them for a moment like a statement of intent, and then he turned and made for the front door.

'Some gaff, eh?' said Gillon.

Sinclair was still translating the pimp's expression into his own language: he couldn't find the correct words but knew somehow that there was a veiled threat in there. It was concealed about his person like a sheath knife, but it was there: of that he had no doubts whatsoever.

Gillon was the first to the door of the house. He leapt forward, delicately balancing on his toes like a comedy ballet dancer, before depressing the button that rang the bell. As he spun round, another broad grin crossed his face like the mark of an invisible cleaver and he rubbed his hands together in a sudden gesture that incorporated both his glee and gallusness. His demeanour put Sinclair on edge.

'I think you should leave the talking to me,' he said.

'How?' A new tone entered his voice: mock indignation.

'Because I know what I'm doing, what I'm looking for . . . I do this sort of thing for a living.'

The bigger man tipped back his head exposing a meaty

neck. 'Oh, aye . . . We don't want to mention what I do for a living.' He looked away, then turned briskly. 'Or maybe we do.'

'Just leave it to me, OK?'

Gillon kept his eyes front. There was the sound of door fastenings being moved, a key turning in the lock. 'Whatever you say, Cam . . . Just shout if you get into trouble, if there's any rough stuff.'

Sinclair had his reply paused on the tip of his tongue as the door opened and a figure he recognised as Adrian Urquhart took them in with a raking gaze. The young man seemed perplexed to see them at first, but soon gathered his composure.

'Yes?' he said.

'Hello, Adrian . . .' said Gillon. He was still smiling, dripping a false avuncularity that slightly embarrassed his associate on the doorstep.

Sinclair stepped forward. 'My name's Cameron Sinclair, I'm a writer, a journalist . . .' The name didn't register on Adrian's face. 'You might have been reading my stories in the *Glasgow-Sun* about your father's passing.'

'I've nothing to say to you.' The door moved towards the jamb; their view of Adrian Urquhart's features receded into a thin oblong.

Sinclair pressed the heel of his hand to the door front. 'I think it would be in both our interests to talk.'

Adrian's eyes widened as the door receded towards him once again; it was as if the shock of seeing a reporter on his doorstep had been compounded by the fact that they really didn't take no for an answer.

'Do you mind taking your hand off my door?' said Adrian.

'Oh, Jesus Christ.' Gillon's guttural voice sounded enough to force the door backwards, but for the avoidance of doubt he

252

pressed his shoulder to the heavy wood and stepped inside. A brass knocker in the shape of a lion's head that had previously looked like an immobile ornament let out a clattering roar as the door sent a shudder through the house and had Adrian back-pedalling on the polished-wood floor.

'What the bloody hell do you think you're doing?' said Adrian as the two men walked into the wide hallway.

'Oh, stop playing the innocent,' said Gillon. 'We're here to talk to you about Leanne Dunn . . .'

Adrian Urquhart's pallor lost some layers of its ruddy flesh tone, became almost a reflection of the white walls. 'I've no idea who you're talking about.'

Sinclair stepped out of Gillon's shadow. 'I think you might want to reconsider that stance once we set you straight on some stuff, Adrian.'

He backed up a few steps. His hands caught the banister behind him and he stopped still; only his eyes darted down the hall towards the sound of a television playing the evening news theme at some volume.

'Look, my mother will be back soon, she'll go to the police.'

Sinclair found himself turning to Gillon as if to share just how ridiculous the remark sounded; the pair started to snigger.

'Oh, I'm sure the police will be the last port of call in this storm, Adrian,' said Sinclair, who nodded to Gillon. 'What do you say, Danny?'

'Probably more chance of us calling them, once you hear what we've got to say.'

Gillon headed down the hallway, in the direction of the blaring television. Sinclair took a few steps in the same direction, then turned back towards Adrian. 'Come on, son, we've some talking to do.'

34

VALENTINE RESENTED THE downtime forced upon him; it seemed a waste of precious moments that could be better utilised in graft. He knew, of course, it came from the same Calvinist dirge his father had sung to him in childhood that awoke during these moments. Life was not supposed to be idle, it was for toil, and it was time away from toil that blackened the soul. Eating and sleeping were permitted – in moderation – and even rest was OK, but only so much as it was utilised to renew strength for more work.

He remembered his father, back from the pits, black as night – just two white eyes and a moist mouth indicating he belonged to the human race and was not some beast sprung from the dark earth. He would gulp his meal – because eating itself was an indulgence, a wasting of the portion of precious time we were allowed on the planet – and then he'd spend an hour reading the newspaper from cover to cover. He didn't feel his father enjoyed his hour with the *Chronicle*; he would shake his head over the pages and spit in the fire if the stories were particularly displeasing to him. But there was a use in it – those nights under the bare bulb at the kitchen table furnished him with some kind of knowledge, some kind of information, which however slight may indeed be useful in the outside world, the workaday world. Knowledge for knowledge's sake was another matter: if it didn't have a practical application, a clear use for the time burned in acquiring it, then it was mere decadence.

Valentine knew he had absorbed his father's views through the twilight osmosis of those late nights at the kitchen table. He could still see him folding the paper reverently and appointing it on the mantle like a trophy of his distinction before taking to the tin bath – filled with water his mother had spent the last hour boiling and pouring – in front of the fire. These were early images, from his formative years, perhaps even pre-school when he thought about it, because there had been a big bath in a proper bathroom by the time he'd reached school. Something was gained but something was also lost when the tin bath went. He smiled at the memory. His father had feared his boy would be brought up soft – he recalled the very words, 'You'll have that boy a jessie' – but nothing was further from the truth. His father's work ethic, his pig-headed stoicism, was seeded early in the young Valentine to the point where even now he found the weight of idle time on his hands too much to bear.

The detective seemed to have spent the day in introspection – never a good state of mind – navel-gazing rarely led to solutions, merely more thinking. He understood most of his breakthrough thoughts had arrived, fully formed and unbidden to his conscious mind, as the result of the deeper inner workings rumbling on while he was preoccupied with the immediate task at hand. He preferred to be busy, because the busier he was the more he got done. But today had been a day for deep ratiocination: he was examining his soul. He didn't know what had happened at the Coopers' home, and he wasn't even sure he wanted to, because the truth – he was man enough to face it – was that it frightened him too much. There had been the stabbing pain that twisted like a hot wire all the way down his arm and into his middle finger – that was frightening enough – but then there was the loss of consciousness and the resulting visions. He was not right in the head: that was the only answer he had to the question of why he'd seen the young Janie Cooper from the photographs in the crime file. He was losing it, seeing things. The job was pulling him apart, his body had been weakened, attenuated by the trauma of the knife in his heart, and he was no longer capable of making sense of anything. It was all too much for him, it was like a psychic defence mechanism: his body presenting apparitions, a variant on the black dots in front of the eye, to tell him that something wasn't right, to tell him he needed to withdraw for the sake of his health. But then there was the little girl, Janie Cooper, who seemed to be telling him the opposite. She was intoning him to help, to help her because nobody else could and because nobody else had. She had been abducted and murdered and her family had been denied even a Christian burial for her immortal soul. She was telling him that. Janie Cooper was telling him that her parents deserved to be able to get on with what remained of their lives: she wanted that, she was begging him for it.

Clare brought through their coffees and placed them on the table in front of Valentine. She eyed her husband with a cautious glare; she looked unsure how to tackle him where he sat in deep thought.

'You're doing it again,' she said.

'What . . . ? Sorry.' Valentine felt as if he'd been shaken awake.

'It's this case, isn't it?'

'No, well, yes and no . . .' He sat forward and retrieved his coffee cup. 'I was thinking about Dad, among other things. Tell me what happened again.'

Clare watched Valentine press the cup to his mouth and then she followed his actions like a mime. 'Well, there's not that much more to say: I took the book round and found him moaning at the bottom of the stairs.'

'So he must have fallen down the stairs?' Valentine creased his nose and raised a hand to touch his forehead. The information didn't seem to be going in at all; there had been too much put up there already today.

'He didn't know, he was very groggy, but he didn't remember falling, so that's when I thought: stroke.'

'And the ambulance crew, what did they say?'

'Nobody knew anything, Bob, that's why they've kept him in overnight. They'll do a scan and we'll know better in the morning when they see how he is . . . It's not good, though.'

There was no avoiding the fact that his father was advancing in years. He had always been so hale and hearty, so capable, but those days were passing. Valentine noted how suddenly life brought these surprises to you: one day everything was as it had been – the daily treadmill of existence turned as it always had – and then there was a gear shift and all of the old markers changed at once.

'I should be at the hospital,' he said.

'You can't, visiting time's over . . . If you'd had your phone on you might have been in a position to visit earlier.'

'I'll go tomorrow.'

'And you know what he'll say – why are you taking time off work?' said Clare. 'He'll be here by the time you get in, and I'll call you if anything comes up, just see him when you get in.'

'He probably won't be able to go back home to Cumnock, you realise.'

Clare crossed her legs and balanced the coffee cup on her knee. 'I know that. I've told the girls they'll need to share a room for a while.'

Valentine made a sharp intake of breath. 'Oh, they'd have loved that.'

'They were fine, actually . . . Well, Fiona was, thinks of it as a wee adventure.'

He smiled. 'And Chloe?'

Clare took up her cup, sipped. 'I don't want to talk about, Chloe . . . Not tonight.'

'Why not? I need to know if there's anything wrong, Clare.'

She dipped her head and scratched at her scalp, as if there was a way of expressing herself hidden there that might be of use. 'She's still getting trouble at school . . . but . . .'

'But what?'

'Look, can we do this another time, Bob? I can see you've had a long day and the news about your father isn't helping . . .'

He shook his head. 'No, Clare . . . I want to know.'

She sat forward and held her cup in both hands. She looked at the cup as she spoke, but her gaze seemed to be focussed on the middle distance. 'She's still being bullied. I went to see the headmaster before your dad and I told him how concerned I was, but he seemed to think it was all an overreaction . . .' She turned towards her husband, her focus back. 'I am not overreacting, I know my daughter.'

Valentine rose from his chair and went to sit beside his wife. He placed a hand on hers as he spoke. 'How is she?'

'I don't know. She's very quiet, doesn't tell me a thing. We'll have to wait and see what happens. The headmaster said he'd have a word with some of her teachers and see if there's anything amiss.'

Valentine gripped her hand tighter. 'It'll be OK, Clare . . . Chloe's a tough cookie.'

'Like you, you mean?'

He didn't have an answer for that.

Clare picked up the thread of her conversation. 'The other night you were trying to tell me something, about that girl in the picture.'

The detective sensed the blood draining from him. 'It's nothing.'

'No, you said it was important.'

Valentine withdrew his hand and slunk back in the seat. 'It's not.'

Clare twisted her body in order to face him. 'No, you were agitated and I was tired . . .'

'Clare, leave it.'

'Leave it?' Her eyes lit with indignation. 'I'm trying to help.'

Valentine could see his reaction to Clare's olive branch had been to hack it down with a chainsaw. 'I just don't feel like talking right now. I'm sorry.'

She kept her eyes on him for a second, and then she drew in her bottom lip and her face became a hard set of angles. 'OK, fine.' She stood up and turned towards the kitchen door. 'I'm sorry too, Bob. I really am.'

He listened to his wife loading a few items into the dishwasher and then he heard the light switch and knew she had headed upstairs to bed. It was early, even by Clare's standards. She would watch a little television and then, hopefully, nod off before he went up. Valentine realised he had started to avoid his wife, certainly any intimate contact. It wasn't that he didn't still care for her, he did, perhaps more now than ever, but the relationship had changed these past few years. There had been a time when sharing their thoughts with each other was part of being a couple, but those days had gone. He didn't want to unburden his mind and his work on Clare because the consequences led to the kind of painful vivisection he would sooner avoid. If she would just listen and take what he

259

had to tell her and store it away, that would be fine, but she wanted to solve things. Clare was all about solutions – even when there was not necessarily a problem – she imagined that talking things through led to the best outcome. For reasons he left unexplored, Valentine knew there were very few hard and fast outcomes in the world. Even when it looked to be patently black and white, there were shades of grey that had been missed. He looked up to the ceiling as his wife's footsteps sounded in the room above and then he heard the television set going on. He imagined Clare's night-time ritual of removing make-up and moisturising, brushing her hair and fluffing her pillows. It was the same every night. The routine had started out as unusual, then it became just another part of the decor that surrounded them, but recently it had borne a new significance to him: each swipe of cotton wool, each turn of the head, each swab of cream was a tick on a clock. It was almost as if he couldn't bear to watch the day's final gasps, as every one signalled fewer to come from the imagined store of their future.

Valentine rose and took himself through to the dining room. His grey sports coat hung on the facing chair and he dug in his pocket for the mobile phone that had been switched off as he stood outside the Cooper's front door. He pressed the on button and watched the screen light up; a few seconds later, the missed-call icon started to flash. He ignored it and went to his contacts.

DS Sylvia McCormack's phone was answered quickly. 'Hello, boss.'

'Hello. Look, I thought I should give you a call.'

'Really? Sounds ominous.'

Valentine sighed. He pulled back the chair in front of him and sat down. He rubbed at his forehead with his fingertips as he spoke. 'This situation we . . . I mean I found myself in today . . .'

She let the silence linger for a moment. 'Uh-huh . . .'

'I didn't want to say anything, at the time.'

'Because you could see that I knew full well what was going on.'

'I'm sorry . . .' Valentine raised his head, lowered his hand from his brow. 'I don't follow.'

Sylvia's voice dropped to a low whisper. She sounded concerned, but, beyond that, compassionate. 'When you took me on I presume you looked at my files.'

'Yes.'

'So you know about my previous cases?'

Valentine searched the recesses of his memory for the file he had skimmed on DS McCormack's background but had to concede that he hadn't taken much of it in. 'Sylvia, this case has been a belter; if I'd had the time to carefully go over every file that crossed my desk . . .'

'Right, well, if you don't know then I'll tell you now. I worked with Colvin Baxter on the Reece disappearance.'

The Reece case was familiar to Valentine: she was a mother of five who had vanished, and several weeks later her children found out she was buried in a ditch. The other name meant nothing to him. 'Who's Colvin Baxter?'

'He helped locate Karyn Reece. We had nothing on that case until he got in touch. We all thought he was taking us off on a wild goose chase, but we soon changed our minds . . . Anyway, I think the official term we use is a "precognitive", but you'd likely call him a psychic.'

Valentine waited for the DS to stop speaking. When he was sure she had finished he felt a strange impulse to drop the phone and step away, but he resisted.

'I'm not sure that I see the . . .'

'Oh, come on, boss, I saw your face . . .' Her voice sounded lyrical and high on her youthful enthusiasm. 'I know the look because it's the same one Colvin wore when he was in the zone.'

Valentine sensed the consequences of what the DS was saying, perhaps in a way she hadn't given any thought to. He saw her claims seeping out into the public domain and panicked.

'No, Sylvia . . .'

'Good officers, sir, senior police, went public with Colvin Baxter's help. Do you think that they'd expose themselves to that kind of scrutiny if they didn't think he was on the money?'

The DI's imagination lit up now: he saw the squad taunting him, he saw his reputation in tatters and he saw his income, the tenuous string that supported Clare and the girls, vanishing. The thoughts scalded him, but they were all just flights of fancy: what really concerned him was the impact on the case. He was already under psychological assessment: he couldn't afford any more questions being asked about his mental health, because if that did happen he was sure he'd be abruptly removed.

'I think you've got the wrong end of the stick, Sylvia.' There was a pause on the line, he wondered if his voice had sounded too harsh, if he had damaged the thin patina of familiarity they had been building up.

'But, sir, you can trust on my discretion if . . .'

The DI felt a cold needle turning in his stomach. His breath became heavy, and as he tried to speak his voice came weaker than only a moment ago. 'Sylvia, no ifs.' He cleared his throat and raised his tone again to signal the conversation was now closed. 'The reason I was calling is I want you to go back to

262

Glasgow tomorrow and speak to the officers on the Cooper case who interviewed Knox. If there are transcripts, bring them back.'

'Yes, sir.' McCormack's big talk seemed shrunken now.

'I have a sneaking suspicion what they might tell you, and if I'm right, we've found the link between Knox and Urquhart.'

'Yes, sir.'

He sensed his composure returning. 'And Sylvia, keep your feet on the ground and remember who's running this investigation.'

35

AYRSHIRE TOLERATED PRETENTIOUS self-aggrandising in much the same way as a pack of dogs tolerated the suggestion that butcher meat was for sharing. A remark extolling the lavish extent of a mortgage or a proclamation of an exalted family lineage was likely to be greeted with the same disdain as a public proclivity for coprophilia. There were some things best left unsaid in certain company. There were those who traded Range Rover purchases like football stickers, they carried a great wad of swaps to taunt the rest of the playground with their purchase power, but to the vast majority they were seen for what they were: shallow puddles of vapidity and deeply deserving of censure. There was always more kudos attached to behind-the-fan remarks about a fur coat and nae knickers or – a favourite the detective reserved for parvenus – 'I kent him when he had holes in his gutties'.

You didn't talk yourself up in the town of Ayr, or its surrounds, without ending up being talked about. There was no real benefit to getting ahead, getting away from the pack, because the pack always followed wherever you went. There was no escaping yourself, no pretending, because if you inflated the balloon of pomposity you could be guaranteed that a prick was waiting nearby to burst it. So people played themselves down; all but the most guileless and moronic made a virtue out of self-deprecation. Sons who got to university were lucky; well-earned promotion was to a job you wouldn't be thanked for; and a hard-won foreign holiday was for the wife or the weans, because it just wouldn't be the done thing to be seen basking in your own success.

As Valentine stood with the car keys poised before the door, he watched the builders unloading the sand and bricks into his neighbour's drive. Something told him his wife had known about this already but hadn't mentioned it for the obvious reason that she wanted to wait until the work began. With the builders on site, her remarks would carry more clout, because a constant visual and aural reminder just wasn't enough. The fact that his own home had become more cramped now – the girls sharing a room to accommodate his father – would make Clare's onslaught seem even worthy. It wasn't an option for them, though: he couldn't afford it on a public servant's wage – it was as simple as that.

'Hello, Bob,' his neighbour Brian called out as he navigated the building materials that sat between his lawn and his car.

Valentine nodded. 'Looks like a bit of work for you.'

Brian reached the wall and flagged a desultory hand towards the goings. 'Aye, we're opening up the space above the garage to give us a wee bit more room.'

It was a double garage, and judging by the hordes of materials the building work would be extensive, but at least Brian had the good grace to look almost embarrassed about his conspicuous consumption. Valentine knew Brian's wife would not be so modest, and it would be from her that Clare garnered all the details she would be firing in her salvos of envy later.

'It'll be nice to have more room.' He found himself glancing desolately towards his own front door, as he spoke his words trailed off into a forlorn organ peal. 'We could do with more space . . .'

As if sensing his neighbour's discomfiture, Brian changed the subject as abruptly as a hand-brake turn. 'You were a bit of a celebrity down at the Chestnuts last night; they had you on the late news again.'

The change of tone from glum resignation to chipper pontification seemed out of character for Brian until Valentine caught sight of the jocular wink on the end. Brian went on: 'Yeah, it was some kind of case round-up.' He fanned his fingertips either side of his mouth for emphasis. 'A special investigation, no less!'

Valentine didn't know whether or not to be glad that he had missed the programme, sometimes it was better not knowing, but then it was also good to be forearmed when dealing with CS Marion Martin.

'I must have missed it.'

The neighbour leaned forward, balancing a hand on the wall. 'This second victim, he seemed a piece of work.'

The detective directed the key towards the door of the car and opened up. 'I can't talk about it, Brian.' As he uttered the words he wished they were retractable; his neighbour wasn't officious, just curious, just making conversation. Valentine caught Brian's expression change: his face lost its animated, interested look and became glum, and he glanced towards the builders reversing into his driveway. It was as if he was inferring with his eyes that the sharpness of Valentine's tone was to do with the extension more than anything.

'Look, I don't mean to sound short with you, Brian, but this case is . . . Well, you can imagine it's at a pretty sensitive juncture.' He scrunched his brows. He was on edge, resorting to management speak before he'd left his own driveway.

Brian waved him off. 'No need to explain . . . I'll try and keep this disruption to a minimum.'

Valentine nodded and turned the key in the ignition. The drive to King Street station was a slow trial he set up for the prosecution of his own personality. He was judge and chief executioner and had decided that he needed to wear the black cap more often when presented with his own failings. He saw the evidence that he had isolated himself from his wife, children, father and colleagues, and now his neighbour had good cause to step away from him. But the case that burned him the most was that of the Coopers; he knew he had served nothing by visiting them and conceded that Billy Cooper had had every right to attack him the way he had. It was a trip that had served only Valentine's curiosity, after all, and had done nothing to palliate their hurts. If he could change that, he would, but as he walked into the station and headed for the incident room, the detective felt an empty void spreading inside him and he didn't know how to fill it.

As he hung his coat, Valentine noticed CS Martin was already grilling DS McAlister, by the looks of things, over hot coals. The DS seemed to be feeling the heat, sticking a finger in the collar of his shirt and working the top button loose. He was nodding in line with the chief super's Gatling speech as Valentine drew into their orbit.

'Morning,' he said.

'Well, look who it is, Ayrshire's very own silver-screen star . . .' Martin wore a smirk that could have passed for an incitement to riot.

'You as well? They'll be calling me DI Valentino next.'

McAlister started to laugh, a deep gut laugh that he cut off abruptly as he assessed the chief super's lack of response.

CS Martin stooped over the desk. She closed a blue folder and straightened her back. 'I'm glad you find it so funny.'

The detective was in no humour for the kind of gum-bumping

that Martin specialised in; he had far too much on his mind with the case in its advanced stages and the returning image of Janie Cooper spooling in his imagination.

He replied, 'Well, as you know, boss, I'm just the kind of arsehole to laugh at my own jokes . . . Most of the time nobody else will.'

She seemed to be having trouble processing Valentine's self-mockery, it was as if her own scale of self-awareness didn't reach those levels and it baffled her. 'Right, well, now you're here you can fill me in on the case instead of Ally.' She waved the DS away – he inverted a smile as he passed her eyeline.

'Right, my office or yours?' As the question was posed, he realised how much like the offer of a date it sounded; his throat constricted as if it was trying to swallow the words in a hurry.

'Yours . . . Lead the way.'

As the DI turned, the chief super uncrossed her arms and trailed behind him. The rest of the incident room was empty, except for McAlister and a couple of uniforms who seemed content to examine either the sheen of their shoes or the texture of the carpet.

'Right, this better be good, Bob, because I don't have to tell you how anxious all this media attention has made me.'

'Look, I didn't know anything about the special news report . . . It sounds like a mash-up of all the stuff they already have.'

'Oh, it was that all right, and more besides. The thing that worries me, Bob, is the fact that those telly people are taking it so bloody seriously. Normally they can't bother their arse coming down here, but – and you can call me an old cynic – they think there's something sexy about the fact that a banker and a paedo have been shoved up on spikes in my patch.'

Valentine was drawing out his chair; he eased himself down before he spoke. 'They mentioned Knox?'

268

'Oh, aye . . . Had pictures and everything. Old case stills and a screen grab of him at the High Court . . .'

'Christ almighty . . .'

CS Martin had her hands on her hips: on anyone else it would appear an overly fastidious approach to affectation, but it seemed to fit her perfectly. 'Can it get worse, Bob? I mean, is there anything else you should be telling me before I have to get on the phone to Glasgow and ask them to chuck us a lifeboat?'

The DI brought his hands above the line of the table; a yellow pencil with a pink eraser on the end became the focus of his attention as he tried to weave a response from the stray ends of thought that were flowing from his mind. 'Oh, I think it can . . .'

'What?'

He dropped the pencil; it started to roll towards the edge of the desk and he slapped the palm of his hand over it before it fell. The noise acted like a clapperboard in the room. 'I have Sylvia McCormack in Glasgow today . . .'

'Bob, are you shunting that girl out of the way?'

'No. Not at all . . .'

A hand shot from the hip and a ragged red fingernail pointed at the DI. 'I mean it, she's to be given full responsibility, I don't want to have her scratching at my door next week telling me she's been sent for a long stand or a tin of tartan bloody paint!'

Valentine reclined in his chair and laced his fingers across his chest; he became vaguely aware of the strength of his heart beating beneath his shirtfront. 'I took Sylvia to Glasgow myself yesterday; we were exploring a link between Knox and a previous case, the disappearance of a schoolgirl in Shawlands twelve years ago.'

'Name?'

'Her name was Janie Cooper.'

'It doesn't ring any bells, was it high profile?'

'It was a big case, yes.'

'There was so many of them around that time, wee lassies snatched every other day of the week, you couldn't keep up . . . Anyway, what's the connection?'

The DI felt his breath still. He wet his lips with his tongue and then wiped the back of his fingertips over his mouth. 'Knox was called in, they questioned him over the disappearance of the Cooper girl, but they released him.' Valentine's voice became reedy and slow. 'We haven't got anything solid yet, but Urquhart was living in Glasgow at the time and I think there may have been contact. I'll know for sure when I get the Knox interview transcripts today.'

There was a moment of stilled silence in the room as the chief super started to pace towards the window. She still had one hand on her hip, but the other pinched a dimple in her chin. As he watched her, Valentine felt the air packed in his lungs crying out to be released, but he held back and tried to remain as stiff as possible. He had extended the known facts of the case now, embellished even, to make it sound like he was making progress, and he knew – with the proper questioning – he could be found out. But he knew also that CS Martin was likely to be some distance shy of the required yards to keep up with him.

'So, you're saying that Knox and Urquhart knew each other from before, from the Janie Cooper disappearance?'

'No. Not exactly . . . I'm saying I suspect that.'

She turned and cut in. 'Right, let's not quibble over the wording, Bob . . . You think we have a predatory paedophile connection to the killings on our turf?'

He rolled eyes and permitted himself a half-nod. 'It's possible.'

CS Martin's features solidified into a delicate mask. She looked like she might shatter before him if she hadn't spoken and broken the spell. 'Well, if we thought we had some press attention before, what the hell's it going to be like when they get hold of this?'

Valentine raised a hand. 'No, there's no chance of that . . .'

'You don't know that.' She jutted her jaw. 'You've no way of knowing that.'

'Well, I believe I'm quite confident in declaring myself some way in front of the press pack on this one, because the only way they would know what I know was if they were involved in some way.'

'Or had an inside track . . .'

Valentine shook his head. His chest inflated as he rose from his seat and placed his palms on the desktop. 'We had one mole, Paulo, and he got his. Nobody out there would be so bloody stupid to jump into his boots.'

'You hope . . .'

'Do you have some information you'd like to share with me, or is this just scaremongering?'

Her face said she didn't like the detective's tone. 'I don't scaremonger.'

'Then my original suggestion stands.' He picked up the telephone's receiver. 'Shall I call in the rep?'

Martin crossed the floor towards the desk. 'Don't think about taking me on, Bob, or you'll be back teaching cadets how to wipe their arse before the day's out.'

He lowered the phone into its cradle – something told him he'd come too far with the investigation to risk losing it. The recent talk of Janie Cooper pushed her image back into his mind. 'My squad's watertight: I won't tolerate leaks and they know it.'

'Glad to hear it.' The chief super kept a firm stare on the DI for a moment and then turned for the door. As she reached for the handle, she called out. 'I want a full report of what we've just discussed on my desk by close of play tonight. With Sylvia's transcripts from Glasgow . . . If it sounds at all promising, you might not have to look out your tracksuit and whistle again.'

36

VALENTINE WATCHED THE chief super strut through the incident room and then stand and wait, regally, as the door was opened for her. When the door closed, he mouthed the word 'bitch' under his breath and then he found himself following her footsteps into the main room. Some more officers had appeared now and he nodded to DS Donnelly and some uniforms he recognised from the murder scene at the racetrack. The DI stood before the board and took in the information, which consisted of scrawled notes and mugshots, scenes of crime photos and long, looping delineations that may or may not indicate links. He brushed at the sides of his mouth as he took it in and then he picked up a black marker pen and drew a thick line between the two victims: Urquhart and Knox.

'Looks definite enough,' said DS Donnelly.

'Bloody sure it is, Phil,' said Valentine. 'That pair were in cahoots: I can feel it in my blood. They knew each other, they were connected, and they preyed on children together.'

'Whoa ... Step back a bit,' said Donnelly. 'We've got nothing to put Urquhart in the same league as Knox.'

'Oh, come on ... He's textbook. He never had so much as a casual acquaintance with anyone he worked with. Kept himself to himself, always. He had no critics, but he had no admirers either ... Wonder why? Because he was keeping a low profile, he was leading a double life and was frightened that if he revealed even a little of himself he'd be found out.'

DS Donnelly didn't look convinced. He seemed to be letting the DI speak himself out in the hope that he would say something he agreed with.

'Boss, I don't know ... You always say we can't make assumptions; this just seems a bit against the grain.'

Valentine turned from the board and replaced the top on the marker pen. He tried not to look at the DS because he knew his run of untrammelled confidence would be shattered by a single glance. He dipped his head towards the desk. 'OK, then what have you got, Phil?'

'Well ...'

'Squat ... Same as everyone else.'

'Sir, I'm not playing devil's advocate here, I'm just saying show me the evidence.'

'Are you saying that there's no evidence, just because we haven't found it?' He raised his head and took in the DI. 'Because that doesn't wash either, Phil ... In the absence of what we'd like, we have to make do with what we've got.'

DS Donnelly drew his lips into a tight aperture; he raised his hands and then folded them behind his head. It was a gesture that told Valentine he wasn't retreating any time soon; it also told him that if he was going to press the case against Urquhart then he was going to need more than blind loyalty to get the squad to go along with him. Was he losing it? Was he really letting his imagination take over from the rational part of his brain, the part that admonished officers like Donnelly when they made the kinds of lunging assessments he had just made? He was tense: the muscles of his shoulders ached like he had been carrying a loaded backpack, or the weight of the world perhaps. He was looking for answers where there were none, and he knew it. The earlier run-in with CS Martin had acted like a lash on him: he felt pressured, and that was never a good way to be. He knew police officers under pressure made mistakes, made the wrong moves; he had done that once before and nearly paid for it with his life.

Valentine peered over DS Donnelly and called out, 'Ally . . . Over here a minute.'

The DS closed the top drawer in his desk and pushed out his chair; as he walked towards the two officers he put his hands in his pockets. His expression was calm, blank almost.

'Yeah, what's up?'

'Ally, tell us what you got with the club you were checking out.'

He looked perplexed. 'Club?'

'The model-railway club . . . the Wednesday night thing that Urquhart was supposed to be going to but never showed up at.'

'Oh, the railway, sorry . . .' He trotted back towards his desk and reopened the drawer he had just closed; when he made his way back to Donnelly and Valentine he was carrying a notebook.

'Right . . . Here we go.' McAlister flicked through the first few pages. 'OK, nothing from the first credit card. Well, it was used on a Wednesday night at the Tesco Express on Maybole Road . . .'

'That's almost on his doorstep, doesn't tell us much,' said Donnelly.

'At what time did he use it, though?'

'Ah, don't know . . . Have to get the file.'

Valentine sighed and touched his forehead; moisture was pooling in his deep-furrowed brow. 'Well, check it: if it's late at night it could be because he was coming back home from somewhere else . . . What about the other stuff?'

He turned the spiral pages over. 'Yes, here we are . . . got a bank-card transaction on three successive Wednesdays at the off-licence on the Prestwick Road.'

'Why's he going to an offie?' said Valentine. 'I'm presuming these are nights he didn't make the railway club?'

'Er, yes . . . All those nights were no-shows. So the question remains: where was he going with the booze?'

'He bought alcohol?' said Valentine.

'Yes, same every night a bottle of Châteauneuf-du-Pape . . .'

DS Donnelly curled down the corners of his mouth, then shot them up in a smirk. 'Very nice indeed.'

'Well, I don't think James Urquhart has the type of palate to tolerate Blue Nun . . . He's drinking that, but who with?'

DS McAlister turned a few more pages in the notebook, then reversed the spiral and returned to the front cover. He let the pad flap open for a moment and then, as if overly conscious of its presence, he turned it behind his back.

The DI spoke. 'Right, that's three Wednesdays on the trot he's buying expensive plonk when he's supposed to be at some old-boys' model club . . . What the hell is he playing at?'

'It's a bird,' said Donnelly. 'It's got to be.'

'I'd have to say you're right.'

'But doesn't that rule out your earlier theory . . .'

Valentine shook his head. 'Are you saying he can't have an interest in birds too . . . ? He was married, you know.'

'Yes, but that could be a front, boss.' Donnelly positioned himself on the edge of the desktop. 'If we're following your line of thinking.'

'What's this?' said Ally.

Valentine flagged DS McAlister down. 'In a minute . . .' He turned back to Donnelly. 'My point exactly. This is a man, a predator, who likes fronts. Perhaps the wine was for someone who had something he wanted . . . A young daughter, perhaps.'

276

Donnelly eased himself from the desk. 'We need to check the rest of those cards.'

The DI nodded. 'And we want the CCTV footage from this off-licence and anywhere else within a country mile of Prestwick Road.'

'We should run the same checks on Knox too; I don't think for a second he's likely to have been as careful as Urquhart.'

'You're right . . . You got that, Ally?'

DS McAlister returned to the notebook and stood poised with a pen over the paper. 'Before I do anything, is someone going to fill me in on what we're talking about?'

Valentine patted Donnelly on the shoulder. 'That's one for you, Phil . . . and when you're done with that, you can put a summary on the board. There's been far too little going up there of late and Dino's starting to get nervous. She'll be in here pissing on the table legs to assert her authority if we're not too careful.'

McAlister and Donnelly were smiling as Valentine retreated to the glassed-off office at the end of the room. His mind was racing with the possibilities, but there was something sticking in there like a sharp splinter of ice. He didn't want to believe that he was being overtly influenced by forces he didn't understand, but he knew he was. He was being led by the thought that he might solve the Janie Cooper case if he could solve the murders of Urquhart and Knox. To a seasoned detective it was absurd, he was being led by instinct and avoiding the facts, but he couldn't deny that every significant development in the case had come as a result of throwing the rulebook out and following his gut, not from carefully acquired factual knowledge of the evidence.

As he sat down behind his desk, Valentine removed the blue folder that had the details of the Janie Cooper case that DS

McCormack had compiled. He turned over the first page and skimmed the others until he found the photographs. There were pictures he had seen already, newspaper cuttings he hadn't seen before and a selection of lab pictures that were tagged and bagged, but only the one numbered 14 stuck out. The item was a small blonde-haired doll, a Sindy doll like his eldest daughter had once owned. He had seen it before, though: not one like it, not a similar one. It was the doll Janie Cooper had been swinging in her hands when he'd passed out and seen her in her parents' home.

'Christ . . .'

Valentine picked up the picture and read the description on the label that was attached. The doll had been found a few streets from Janie's school on the day she disappeared; it was the last artefact to be uncovered before the girl was declared missing.

The DI felt his thoughts being dragged away by a wild river. The sound of footsteps, cabinets closing, telephones ringing and all the shrill din of noise from the office around him became a cacophony that filled his ears. A dull pain was beginning to form in his arm, which told him he needed to alter his breathing and find calm. As he did so, the room lost its foggy haze and he felt the truculent ache in his chest subside. Despite the shock, both physical and mental, Valentine felt invigorated. He let the thought of his growing confidence settle on his mind like a warm glow, and then a smile replaced his frown and he stored the knowledge of Janie Cooper and her doll in the new and rapidly expanding niche he had reserved for the unexplained.

37

IT WAS LIKE THERE WAS A scale inside of him, a see-sawing balance of weights and measures that divided the good and the bad from each other. At normal times, when all was well and as it should be, the scale registered an equanimity that was imperceptible to Valentine. But when his world was at odds, his children unsettled, his work life tiresome or over-challenging, then the balance tipped. He found himself stacking columns of pros and cons on each side of the fulcrum. It was a demonstrably divisive enterprise, or game, if you preferred, because there was little tangible benefit, save amusing himself. The silver plates he weighted with the good and the bad formed a snapshot of his existence, but sometimes it was lopsided. A positive representation of his wife, for example, with due credit given to her dogged support over the years of their marriage may be pitted to the negative, the diametric opposite, of her own selfish indulgences at scent counters and homeware stores. At times of true passivity, when he had given over to life's buffeting like a leaf on a breeze, he became a mere spectator – watching one side of the scales afflicted by an avoirdupois he was incapable of controlling. At such times, Valentine lost faith in the future and became submerged under the grim burden of an unsympathetic fate.

It was the gloom, the black dog, the Scots' bleak penchant for predestination. It didn't matter what you called it, or if you even subscribed to its existence, because the entity – and it felt like a separateness, a spectre – was no respecter of opinions. The black dog roamed wild, brought misery to bear wherever it touched and left the same in its wake, like messy paw prints that served as warnings of an imminent return. But why was there no white dog – an antithetical beast that brought some levity to the world? He smirked at the thought. It was not in the Scots' make-up to invent an antidote; and why would they? Surely that would merely deprive them of the very real aspect the black dog bestowed: identity. We wanted to be miserable, we wanted to watch the black dog bay at the moon because it was who and what we were. We found our definition in the dreich skies and desolate landscapes; we lived for the light touch of smirr blown from the sea; the jagged, rocky outcrops glimpsed through the gloaming sang to us – they were the ghosts of our souls and we would no more part with them than an arm or a leg because they were such an integral part of who we were. And, he knew, it was certainly who he was.

Valentine tried to comprehend what his wife was saying, but the words wouldn't go in. He stood in the hallway with his grey dog-tooth sports coat still on and his briefcase in hand, with Clare resembling a harpy before him, castigating and caterwauling.

'He's your father. How?' She shook her head and brought hands to her brow in a dramatic flourish of pique. 'Tell me how you managed to forget that?'

He didn't reply, because, although it was a question – posed in her own singular language – he didn't feel an answer was required. When Clare became rhetorical it was for effect, for show. She liked to repose in movie-star-style indulgence of her whims at every opportunity. And missing his father's return from hospital was an opportunity not to be passed up, even though he suspected her ire had more to do with the neighbour's new extension. Valentine took his wife's castigating blows because they had little impact on him now; he shook them off in the same way he brushed raindrops from his shoulders and with just as much care. He could let her go on all night, talk herself hoarse, as it barely penetrated the epidermis he would doubtless slough off in the next downpour. He wondered why his expression wasn't a giveaway to her. Why didn't she see her words were falling into a black hole of disinterest? He assumed it was because she didn't really care: he was just the target, it was the releasing of barbs she was concerned with. If it helped her deal with being Clare Valentine then he could stand there and take them all night.

'Clare, I'm sorry . . . I intended to be home earlier, but I've had a very busy day.'

She brushed her fringe from her eyes. 'It's not me you should be apologising to.'

Valentine sensed an unscripted break in proceedings; he lowered his briefcase and started to unbutton his coat. 'I'll go up now.'

'No. He's sound asleep, they gave him tranquilisers.'

'Is he OK?' He hung his sports coat on the banister.

Her fingertips flew from her fringe to the coat on the banister. 'The scan was clear. It doesn't look like a stroke, but he's not a well man.' She picked up the sports coat in thumb and forefinger like it was the discards of a leper colony. 'And this is ready for the bucket!'

Valentine snatched back his coat. 'Leave it, Clare.'

Chloe appeared in the hallway wearing her pink polka-dot dressing gown and pyjamas. Her Bart Simpson slippers looked like she had stuck her feet into a pair of cuddly toys. Valentine smiled at the sight of his daughter.

'Hello, Princess . . .'

She grimaced, turned to the side and made a wave across the glass of milk she held in her hand. 'Oh, please . . .'

He had an urge to scoop his daughter in his arms, but her teenage diffidence to the approaching adult world flashed like a warning light from her. 'How's school, love?'

She closed her eyes, let the lids hang in exaggerated fashion for a moment and then put a crick in her jaw. 'I'm going to bed.'

His daughter squeezed past them, sullen and disconsolate, and took to the stairs with heavy steps. Valentine saw his wife drawing a bead on him; he knew at once he had said the wrong thing, but his mind was so tired it required a back-up generator to keep body and soul together at this hour.

'I take it my dinner's in the dog?' he said.

Clare waited for Chloe to close the bedroom door. 'Why did you say that to her? You know she's not having the best of times at school, and you know why . . .'

He was re-hanging his coat on the banister as he replied. 'I wasn't thinking . . .'

'Well, perhaps you should start, Bob!' His wife pushed him aside and followed Chloe up the stairs.

'Where are you going?'

'To see if our daughter's all right.'

Valentine touched the edge of his jaw and felt the emery wheel of his unshaven chin. He opened his mouth just enough to call to Clare again, but something stopped him, an instinct perhaps, the thought that he could more than likely increase his trouble. He collected his briefcase, removed the blue file with the transcripts from the Knox interviews that DS McCormack had delivered, and headed for the kitchen. The down lights beneath the kitchen cabinets were burning, lighting the worktops but little else. He turned to the light switch and pressed it with his shoulder. As the room was illuminated, Valentine lowered his paperwork and started to make coffee. There was a plate sitting out, with what looked like a dinner of mince and potatoes blurred beyond recognition by its cling covering. He wasn't hungry now anyway. He had passed the point where food was something that would sustain him, it would merely bring dyspepsia at this hour. He took his coffee, retrieved the blue folder and made for the dining-room table.

As he read the notes, the detective was nostalgic for the time when he would have filled out the same forms. The paper case files had lingered in a few of the smaller stations for longer than they should have. Everything was committed directly to computer now, but the touch of paper felt more personal, reminded him of a time when the world itself seemed to care a little bit more. As he read on, however, Valentine realised his mind was just playing tricks on him: the world was a brutal place and always had been. The investigating officers were not the best communicators, few police were, with most resenting the task of note-taking as no more than a necessary evil at best, a bureaucratic time-suck at worst. He had learnt early on to take his time over the files, because they had a way of coming back to bite you if alternative meanings could be construed from the wording. He smiled as he recalled the incident his late colleague David Patterson had recounted after coming across a cow in the road.

'She'd been hit by a car or a truck.' He heard David's voice now, the rich inflection of his tones, the crooning cadence of his Ayrshire accent that had never left him. 'I swear the beast was half dead . . .'

'You're sure it wasn't half alive?' he'd tested.

'OK, smart-arse, three-quarters dead . . . There was nothing for it but to put the poor beast out of its misery.'

'That's not something they teach you in the Boy Scouts.'

David laughed. He had been a man who liked to laugh. He'd had a buttoned-up side too, but he didn't like to overexpose that part of his nature for fear of being taken too seriously. 'Well if they had a cow-shooting badge, I didn't get it.'

'Hang on, you shot it?'

He nodded rapidly, like an excited child. 'Two bloody rounds and it was still moaning . . . I swear you have no idea of the paperwork required for the discharge of two rounds of ammunition in the RUC.'

He was still laughing, shoulders rocking above his broad belly as he pointed his fingers into an imaginary gun and took aim at an invisible cow. Valentine found himself mouthing his old friend's name, and for the first time in years he felt the warmth of a friendship that could never die.

'Oh, Davie . . . We had some times.'

His friend was gone, and many more besides, but he didn't want to become morose thinking about his loss. As quickly as he had chided himself, his mind was wiped clear by the sound of his mobile phone. He reached into his shirt pocket and answered. 'Hello . . .'

It was DS McCormack. 'Are you reading the files?'

'Er, no . . . Just about to.' He looked at the clock; it was nearly midnight. 'I presume you're calling because you've found something.'

Her voice rose in pitch, put on running shoes. 'Go to page nine, second interaction from DI Fitzsimmons . . . Have you got it?'

'Hang on . . .' Valentine turned over the file and thumbed his way to page nine. 'Right, what am I looking for?'

McCormack's impatience poured from every word. 'Skip the top paragraph . . . Read the next one, how it starts . . .'

The detective ran his gaze down the page to the point she had indicated. 'OK, here we are . . .'

'He's addressing Knox, by the way.'

'Yes, got that . . .' He read the DI's words: 'Who are you working with, Duncan? You might as well tell us, because if they're on our books we'll be talking to them and they might not extend you the same favour . . .' Valentine brought his knuckles of his right hand to tap on his chin; he was drinking in the significance of the statement when DS McCormack spoke again.

'Sir, are you there?'

'Yes, yes . . .'

'Then you got that . . . You see what he's saying?'

Valentine rubbed his knuckle into his tired eyes and felt a change in the rhythm of his thinking. 'Fitzsimmons thought he had an accomplice.'

'Yes, but he was looking for someone like Knox, a sex offender.'

He clamped his teeth, when words came they trawled the room in a soporific drawl that indicated an overburdened mind. 'They had no chance of finding Urquhart in that case.'

'They were looking in the wrong direction, that's why.'

He pushed the folder away. If there were more gems worth unearthing they could wait another day – he had the Cullinan Diamond already. 'How much of this have you read?'

'I'm well on with it: there's a few things we need to look at, boss . . .'

'It's midnight, Sylvia, and I have a wife who thinks I'm a part-timer in this marriage as it is.'

'Oh, of course. I'm sorry to call so late, I just thought . . .'

He cut her off. 'You did the right thing, I needed to know. I'm glad you called, but tomorrow's another day.'

285

'I'm going to stick with it. I'm not tired and I'm all pumped up for this now.'

He admired her enthusiasm and envied her youth. 'Goodnight, Sylvia, I'll see you at the station tomorrow.'

'I'll keep notes . . . But at least we've something else to add to the board!'

'We have that.'

A faint gleam of optimism entered his weary eyes as he rose from the table and closed the blue folder.

38

DANNY GILLON OVER-REVVED his van on the road outside the doctors' surgery on Cathcart Street. By the time he had reached the Tourist Information centre there was a cloud of black smoke following him onto the Sandgate. He didn't care what the woman waving her hand in front of her thought as he passed, because the town of Ayr was nothing to him. Who were they? Old scrubbers and junkies. Streets full of mug punters rolling drunk to the bookie's or the Bridges Bar. He despised them all; none of them were worth the steam off his piss. He believed that, because, in his world, he was an undisputed potentate. He was a small-town Stalin, or might well have been for all the opposition his girls could muster against his authority.

A Stagecoach bus heading for Kincaidston pulled out in front of the van and Gillon cursed the driver and every one of his passengers. 'Bloody bunch of scruffs!' He raised a single-digit salute. 'Get out to your council rabbit hutches . . . Don't know why you're in such a rush, bloody sure I wouldn't be.'

By the roundabout at the top of the Sandgate his blood had cooled a little, and he smiled at a pair of young girls standing outside the bus station. One of them had spotted him, but pretended to be wall-eyed. He rolled down the window as the traffic stalled.

'Hello, darlings, and what are you lovely little ladies up to today?'

The girls were no more than fourteen or fifteen, and the

sheen of their overtly straightened hair and heavily mascarad eyes belied their attempts to convince anyone of the contrary. They giggled as Gillon leaned a hand on the edge of the window and winked. They were bait – jailbait, of that he had no doubts – but fresh meat in the town always attracted big game.

'And what brings you to sunny Ayr, eh?' He scrabbled on the dash for a packet of Embassy Regal and offered the girls cigarettes.

'Thanks.' One was gamer than the other. She'd be full of lip, thought Gillon.

'You sound like a wee handful.' He smiled at them and the girls turned to each other and giggled..

A car's horn sounded behind him, which seemed to startle the girls. They turned and headed back to the bus station at pace.

'Aye, all right! All right!' He smacked his hand off the steering wheel and pulled out from the roundabout. 'Bloody scared the horses now anyway . . .'

As Gillon turned for Wellington Square he cast a backwards glance in the mirror, but there was no sign of the young girls. He shook his head and cursed but opted only to depress the cigarette lighter and clamp a king-size in his mouth; after all, girls were ten a penny in this town. The coast attracted them, the sea air and the holiday atmosphere, the hotels and pubs calling for fodder to pour drinks and wash toilet bowls. It was a move that soon turned sour: he knew that, and relied upon it. The service industry's loss was his gain, because there was always work for young girls with Gillon. The trick was to paint it as something else at the start, fire them up, make them think life was one big party with him, and then once they were hooked, get them hooking. He smiled to himself because life was that simple: it was only square pegs and stupid lassies that made it complicated.

When he returned to the block of flats in Lochside where he had set up his working girls, he parked and stilled the engine. The exhaust rattled a little after he had stopped and he knew that it would soon be costing him money. He gnawed the tip of his cigarette and stepped out, looking towards the rear of the vehicle: a sooty black cloud was hanging in the air. The exhaust pipe was still in place but looked precipitously close to coming off. A bad speed bump or a clipped kerb and he'd be forking out for a new one. He scrunched his eyes and tried not to think about it. There was the payday from the hack coming; all he had to do was get Leanne prepared for the next stage in Sinclair's wee plan.

As he walked through the empty car park, Gillon kicked out at a stray can of Export and sent it into the air. The can spun all the way to the pinnacle of its grand arc and then plummeted like a stone onto the tarmac. The shaken remnants of the can spilled onto the street in a bubbling foam that looked at home in the litter-strewn surrounds. When he reached the door of the flats, the pimp pressed the buzzer for Leanne's apartment, but there was no answer.

'Come on, Leanne . . .'

He pressed the buzzer again, but there was still no answer.

'Come on! Come on!'

He stepped back and fastened his eyes on the kitchen window that faced out into the narrow courtyard: there was no sign of movement.

'Where the bloody hell are you?'

He had another girl set up in the same block. He returned to the buzzer and pressed for Angela.

She answered quickly. 'Hello.'

'It's me, Danny, buzz me in, eh.'

'Danny?'

'Aye, Danny . . . You wanting a picture sent up first?'

The buzzer sounded, the lock was released, and he walked through the door. The stairwell stank of urine and stale cigarette smoke. The combination was enough to put him off his Embassy Regal and he flicked it onto the ground. He grabbed the banister and loped up to the first floor of the flats.

Angela was waiting outside her door. 'Something up, Danny?'

He grabbed her thin white face in his hand and pushed her back towards the door. 'Who said you could come out?'

'I was just . . .'

He pointed at her as he walked to the foot of the next set of steps. 'You were just getting into that flat and getting on your back . . . I'll be round after for my money.'

The girl turned her black hair behind her ear and retreated into the dim hallway of the flat. She peered out from behind the narrow gap between door and jamb for a second, but as Gillon hit his stride on the steps she disappeared.

'Leanne . . .' He battered on the door but there was no answer.

'Leanne . . . come on, open up.' For a moment he had the notion that she might have collapsed. He leant down to look through the letter box but saw nothing unusual. The door to the kitchen was open, as it always was; the bedroom door was closed, but she never spent time in there unless she was on her back and there was no sign that she was with a punter. The place looked empty.

He banged on the door again. 'Leanne . . .'

It was a futile gesture, and he knew that. But at least she hadn't shot herself up and carked it on him. That would be messy: he'd have to take her to casualty and drop her at the door, or pay a cabbie, and that was never cheap these days.

Gillon punched out at the door again. The resounding sound of bone on wood rung through the empty hallway and brought a thin eye-slot to the neighbouring door.

'Hey, hey . . .' Gillon ran towards the chink of light that had appeared in the doorframe. He could see the outline of an old woman. He pushed himself towards the door and she shrieked.

'Do you know where Leanne went?' He kept his hand pressed firmly on the front of the door.

'I don't know.'

'Well, when did she go out?'

The woman smelled like an old chip pan, all burnt charcoal and dripping fat. 'We don't speak.'

'I didn't ask if you were best mates, I asked you where she went . . . When did you last see her?'

She raised a thin hand, and the spotted flesh hung over the bulbous fingers as she gripped the buttons of her cardigan. 'She went out last night, I think . . . I never saw her after that and I haven't heard her today.'

'What . . . Last night?'

The old woman nodded. She cast a glance into the stairwell as if looking for help. 'Yes, that's right . . . I haven't seen her since.'

Gillon started to drum his fingers on the door, a rough percussion that signalled his growing impatience and dissatisfaction with what was being relayed to him. 'And was she alone, or with someone?'

'A man . . . A young man.'

Gillon stared at the woman. Her eyes were moistening and she looked ready to keel over. He slapped the door and stepped back. She had the wood in the frame and the mortise turned in the lock by the time he could blink.

None of it made any sense. The pimp felt a mix of emotions and thoughts flushing through him. As he descended the stairs, he tried to put the facts together. She was with a punter, surely. But where had she gone? If the punter had turned up on her doorstep then why hadn't they just done the business in the flat? It didn't make sense, unless he had a kink for the outdoors, but then she'd be back by now, would have been back last night, surely. He didn't see anyone paying for an all-nighter with a skank like Leanne: she was strictly disposable.

Gillon rattled the knocker on Angela's door once again. When she appeared, gripping a brown dressing gown around her thin shoulders, he felt the need to draw a fist. 'Get inside . . .'

Angela gasped for breath as he pushed her inside. Her face indicated she would have preferred to scream, but she knew that wasn't an option worth pursuing.

'Right, speak . . . Where's Leanne?'

'What?' She was trembling.

'That tart upstairs . . . She went out with some guy last night.'

'I–I don't . . . I haven't seen her for a couple of days.'

Gillon flashed his bottom row of teeth the second before he fired his fist into Angela's belly. She folded like a hinge and then collapsed onto the floor.

The pimp crouched onto one knee and grabbed her hair. 'Am I supposed to believe that?'

She tried to speak, but merely spluttered.

'What . . . What are you saying to me?'

'I–I said it's true. Honest, Danny, I wouldn't lie to you.' She

292

brought her hands together as if about to pray. 'Danny, do you have anything . . . ? Just a wee bit, just to see me through.'

He smacked her head off the wall. As she yelped, her shoulders slid down the plasterboard.

There was a rage building in Danny Gillon's head and heart as he stamped down the steps towards the entrance to the flats. In the car park, the sight of the can of Export sent him lunging with a kick once again, but there was none of the playfulness of his earlier shot. The can fired into the air and smacked off the side of the flats, dislodging some roughcast with the force of impact.

'Bloody hell, Leanne . . . I will kill you for this.'

When he reached the van, Gillon removed his mobile phone from the inside pocket of his denim jacket and scrolled the contacts for Cameron Sinclair.

The reporter answered straight away.

'Yes, what's up?' he said.

'You're not going to like it.'

'I don't think I do already and you haven't even told me what's happened.'

'It's Leanne . . . She's jumped ship.'

'What?' Sinclair sounded incredulous.

'You heard, she's done a runner.'

There was a pause on the line. 'I don't believe this.'

'Believe it, I don't make up stories.'

He could hear Sinclair sighing down the line. When he spoke again, his voice had an angry quiver he hadn't heard before. 'You've done this . . .'

'What's that supposed to mean?'

'You're trying to bump your price up, aren't you . . .' He sounded like he was speaking through gritted teeth.

'Wait a minute . . . I'm as pissed off about this as you, mate.'

'I'm not your bloody mate.' Sinclair ranted now. 'And I'm not someone you can jack up for a few quid. I told you what the deal was, Gillon: now get me that girl or you won't see a bloody penny.'

'Now hang on . . .'

'I mean it, Gillon. You think you can mess me about, you're in for a shock.'

The line died before he had a chance to reply, but as he stared out of the dirt-scarred windscreen into the fast-darkening Lochside ghetto, Danny Gillon knew there was nothing to say anyway.

39

DI Bob Valentine sat on the edge of the bed with his hands gripping the sides of his head and his elbows balanced precariously on his thighs. He didn't know how long he had been there, but the birdsong beyond the window – a recent alert to his senses – suggested some time. He lowered his hands and sat upright, staring towards the closed curtains: a thin bleed of light from outside had started to seep along the top and at the edges. For a moment he wondered about the time of day. It still felt like night, but it couldn't be, surely. The desire to know sent him glancing towards the bedside clock. It glowed back with 6.05. He raised himself onto his feet and felt slightly uneasy – not dizzy, but in the neighbourhood – when he walked towards the bathroom door. The flick of the light switch sent his eyeballs running for cover in the back of his head. He couldn't understand this. For some hours his eyes had been preoccupied with what seemed like Technicolor film-reels. It had been in sleep, or something like it, he knew that – but the shock of returning to reality and the limitations of the physical world, things like recoiling from bright light, seemed utterly alien to him. He wondered where the world of dreams ended and the world of reality began. If he kept company with the incubus inside his head for much longer, he feared he might not be able to tell. The line between the two worlds felt like an infinitesimally thin membrane, and if he succeeded in piercing it then where would he be? Trapped

– neither here nor there. But then he felt that way now. He was lost to himself and feared the very real consequences of an unreal situation.

When he was showered, Valentine dried himself in the bathroom and then returned to the bedroom to dress. Clare was still sleeping, her head dug into the pillow and covered by her blonde hair. He watched her at rest for a moment as he tied his tie and wondered what occupied her thoughts. He smiled to himself. She was always so keen to know what was going on with him and what he was thinking about, and yet he couldn't remember the last time he had asked how she was, how she felt? Was he a good husband, he asked himself? He didn't have an answer to hand. He was a contented husband and father, he loved his family and would be lost without them, but the way Clare acted told him that her experience had not been the same. She didn't work and occupied herself with inanities – he couldn't do that – so he afforded her some latitude as a result. Life was hard enough for those who went out into the world and became inured to its workings, but to be sheltered from it, only glimpsing the insanity from a window or a television screen, must be difficult. You needed to be equipped with experience to make sense of the place and Clare was without any, so she occupied herself with the surface trivia of shopping and competing with the neighbours. He felt sorry for her because she had never had the chance to toughen up, to test the real value of all the junk she cluttered her mind with. But at the same time he envied her insularity; when he compared Clare's daily preoccupations with those of Diane Cooper – someone who had assuredly seen the worst the world beyond the window had to offer – she seemed trite and unreasonable. He was nobody to judge, though he knew just one gramme of the dose of life that Diane Cooper had been given would fell his wife, completely and resoundingly. She thought she was missing something, but in the final assessment Valentine was glad she didn't know just what that something was.

In the hallway, the detective checked the door to the room where his father had been sleeping, but the bed was empty. He was always an early riser; he remembered his father dressed and ready for him every morning when he was at school. Even after, when his father had retired from the mines, he was still the first of the household to rise. It was a strange comfort to have his father, and his old ways, transplanted to his home. He didn't know why it should be a comfort, but it was: it gave him a warm glow of nostalgia for times past; he remembered the feeling of security his father's presence brought to the household. He had been relied upon, a feature of his childhood that was as regular and dependable as the sunset. His father was known as the source of the household's income – he paid their way – and though it was never mentioned, it was an unspoken knowledge that bestowed an incogitable grandeur on him. He remembered the sight of his father walking the back lanes in the evening light, a piece box and Thermos slung over his shoulder, an inclination to a tired stoop the only giveaway of the day's duty done. When he came closer, un-hasped the gate and walked the path, the blackened features of his face, contrasted with the white creases of his eyes, detailed how hard the task had really been.

Valentine smiled to himself as he descended the stairs. He couldn't have lived his father's life, he knew that, but then how could one man live another's? Through the door that linked the living room and dining room, he spotted his father's thin shoulders poking beneath the paisley dressing gown that must have been at least thirty years old.

'Hello, Dad,' he said.

His father turned briskly to face the source of the greeting. 'Oh, it's yourself . . . I was wondering if you still lived here.'

'Don't you start!'

His father was smiling, an indication he had picked up Clare's earlier unease. Valentine looked the old man over: he seemed pale, gaunt. There was a little bruising on his forehead and white sticking plasters crossed his temple like a mark on a pirate's map. He could sense his unease. His father didn't want to be there, he wanted to be in his own home, but there was a weariness about him now that suggested he was tired of fighting the reality, or perhaps was ready to give in.

'Did you not get yourself some tea or coffee?' said Valentine.

'Och, I'm not raking about in Clare's cupboards.'

The old assumption that the kitchen was a wife's territory raised a smile with the detective. 'Well, I know my way about . . . What can I get you?'

'Tea . . . You remember how I take it?'

He shrugged. 'I think she's got it written down somewhere . . .'

'Milk and two sugars . . . and leave it some time to stand.'

As he clattered with the cups and kettle, Valentine called through to his father. 'So how are you feeling anyway?'

'Oh, you know . . .'

His father was never a man to bemoan his lot; he would be half-starved before he'd ask for a scrap from another man's plate.

'You don't remember what happened?'

'Well, I do and I don't . . .'

The kettle boiled and Valentine popped his head round the door. 'What?'

His father was rising from the chair a pained expression crossed his face as his slow gait took him to the kitchen. 'See, the thing is, I'd need to swear you to secrecy.'

The detective felt like his stomach was dissolving into his backbone. 'I don't like the sound of this, Dad.'

He reached out a hand, slapped it on his son's shoulder and gripped tightly. 'Oh, God, no . . . It's nothing like that!'

The kettle boiled, prompting him to pour out the tea. 'Well, what is it then?'

His father's long fingers, gnarled and toughened by a lifetime of manual labour, tapped the keys on an imaginary piano, then shot upwards to the waves of white hair on his head. It was clearly very difficult for him to find the words. 'Well, son, you see I was given this gift . . . A beautiful gift it was too, and I was very grateful for it at the time.'

Valentine clattered the spoon off the counter with impatience. 'Look, will you just tell me?'

'It was the slippers . . .'

'What?' Nothing made sense. He wondered if his father was going senile.

He sighed, reached out for the cup and turned for the dining room. 'You see, Clare bought me these lovely slippers the other day, grand they were, nice and comfy with the fur inside . . . but . . .'

The two men sat facing each other over the table. 'But?'

'They were too big, son . . . I didn't want to hurt her feelings, but I did myself a turn in them.'

Valentine started to laugh. 'You tripped over your own feet?'

'Oh, bugger off . . . They're size tens, I'm only an eight . . . Took a nosedive down the stairs, so I did.'

'And you didn't want to tell, Clare . . .'

'God, no, she'd be heartbroken . . . It was a lovely thought.'

The detective looked at his father, a wide smile crossing his face; he was delighted that there was no serious damage done. The thought of the old boy going for a day of scans and

299

having to keep his mouth shut for Clare's benefit was comical to him.

'You know she has you shipped upstairs for good?'

'Oh, Christ, you'll have to set her straight.'

'Me?'

He drew his hands from the sides of the cup. 'I need my own space; I can't be stopping in the youngster's room.'

Valentine took a sip of coffee, then made his way back to the kitchen to collect his coat and briefcase, but kept his stare on his father. 'I'll see what I can do. I don't think you're getting off that lightly, though, she'll keep you under observation for a bit longer.'

His father was on his feet, waving him off as he opened the back door. 'Aren't you going in a bit early?'

'I've got a lot to do, Dad. I'll see you tonight . . . Mind how you go, especially on those stairs!'

'Och, bugger off . . .'

Hillfoot Road was so quiet that he gave serious consideration to leaving the house at an earlier hour every day. There were still plenty of Glasgow commuters about, and maybe even a few late starts to Edinburgh. You could pick them by engine size, or marque: to a one they were Mercedes or BMWs, with a suit jacket hanging in the back window, perhaps a hard hat on a parcel shelf to signal a property tycoon, businessmen with beer bellies and fully laden egos to match. He shook his head and tried to take in the thought of what a two-hour drive at the start of every day, and again at the end, would feel like. What kind of vanity compelled them? It was insane, he thought, but that's what Ayr had become – a commuter town where shiny-arsed cogs in the capitalist wheel travelled for hours to have a bigger house at a better price than in the city. It would continue, because there were more houses going up all the time – fields given to foundations and the telling scars of heavy infrastructure; he'd even heard of people commuting to London now on the cheap flights from Prestwick Airport. He couldn't imagine it did much for the town's social cohesion, but then there was very little of that left anyway.

As he reached King Street station, Valentine ascended the stairs to the incident room and slid backwards through the swing door as he wrestled himself out of his sports coat. The lights were out. He fumbled for the switches on the wall and soon the room was flooded with the familiar bright, blinding whiteness that would burn throughout the working day. He didn't know why they needed to have such powerful, searing light – the place was lit up like a supermarket or one of the bigger branches of Boots – but nobody seemed to complain, so he felt stuck with it. On his way to the far end of the incident room, the detective glanced at the whiteboard to make sure DS McAlister had added the results of the credit card and CCTV sweep: he hadn't.

'Bloody hell, Ally.' He would call him on that later – if the chief super hadn't already. She was becoming more than a worry to the DI now. She was fickle at the best of times, but when she was under pressure, or in anyway exposed to censure, she became erratic. Dino could just as quickly divest Valentine of the case as she had delivered it; he knew that, and the added pressure was a weeping sore he felt the need to pick at constantly. One more piece of bad press, or another line of inquiry drawing a blank, and she was liable to wobble. He'd seen it before, she was prone to it, and when she did wobble he knew to get out of the way or she would use him to break her fall.

When he reached his glassed-off office at the end of the incident room, Valentine's eyes were drawn to a set of blue folders. He flipped the first one open: an old VHS videotape sat on the tip with a yellow Post-it note attached. The note was in Ally's spidery scrawl: 'Interesting viewing, boss!'

At once the detective felt a gnawing pang of guilt for having cursed the DS about his progress. A smile spread up his face and settled like a surreal scar as he thumbed the rest of the pages. Ally had indeed come up trumps with the credit search: two more successive Wednesday-night purchases attributed to James Urquhart in the same locale. But it was the CCTV footage from a Prestwick Road twenty-four-hour garage that intrigued him. Valentine took the tape and slotted it into the TV-recorder in the corner of the room. The dust on the screen fizzled as the tube heated.

'Right then, Ally . . . Let's see what you've got here.'

The tape was set a few minutes before the point of interest that had been marked by the DS. Valentine watched the grainy image of the petrol station forecourt. There appeared to be one car parked at the pumps and another just arriving but making its way to the parking bays next to the bags of charcoal and the long-past-their-best bunches of flowers. He thought he recognised the second car from somewhere, but he couldn't place it.

'Interesting . . .'

The screen changed again: a white band descended diagonally, splitting the image in two and merging with a new screenshot of the interior. A clock in the lower left corner ticked away the hours, minutes and seconds. It was 7.15 p.m.

'Hello . . .'

The first man to the counter was stocky and broad-shouldered but carrying a heavy paunch. His hair was short and cropped close to his scalp. As he handed over his money to the teller, there was no mistaking Duncan Knox.

Valentine nodded. 'Nice work, Ally.'

He let the video play a little longer and watched Knox leave the shop, and then the screen flipped back to the forecourt and he watched him getting into his car and driving away. He reached out to pause the video recorder. For a moment, the detective let his thoughts breathe. This was evidence placing Knox and Urquhart in the same vicinity at the same time, but it was far from the conclusive stamp he needed. Valentine knew Knox and Urquhart were connected – to have his suspicions almost confirmed was tantalising, but added little to his overall knowledge. Would it be enough even to convince the chief super of a link? He doubted it. What it presented was an interesting proposition, a list of more possibilities but little else.

He returned to the blue folder on his desk and removed the yellow Post-It note on which DS McAlister had written the next screen time he wanted him to view. He pressed the fast-forward button and watched the counter reach the requisite number. As he pressed play once again, the picture had jumped back out to the forecourt but was obscured by two jagged diagonal lines. He could see the door of the other car – the one he thought he recognised – opening and a figure stepping out. The screen jumped again, back to the interior, and Valentine leaned forward to better view the figure going into the store and approaching the counter. He had his head down, towards the counter; the rim of a tweed cap obscured the man's face. He was buying cigarettes. He paid cash and then as he collected his change he tipped his head towards the camera.

Valentine leapt to press pause on the video recorder.

As the screen stilled, there was no doubt in his mind the man in the tweed cap was James Urquhart. He stared at his face and

303

tried to process the information it provided. The detective felt like he had tapped into a secret signal from satellite orbiting in space and he needed someone to translate the raw binary code of the message into English for him, but his thoughts were already buzzing with the possibility of what it might say and what it might mean, for not only the investigation but for the case of the missing Janie Cooper.

40

THERE WAS A TYPE IN AYR, as common as paving weeds, that turned up just to proclaim their opposition to the world and all its inhabitants. They wore a look, an atavistic west-coast sneer that signalled a gruff indifference to all efforts to appease them. If you gave up a parking space at the supermarket for them, they'd sneer – perhaps also shake their head – because of course they deserved no less than special treatment from the masses that inhabited their planet. If you stood in front of their ilk in a newsagent's and ordered a broadsheet, they would sneer and say something about the wee papers not being good enough for some people. In any social gathering there would always be an abundance of Ayrshire's sneerers. At a wedding, the bride's dress – to them – was deserving of derision because it was too short, too long, too plain, too ornate, too expensive or too cheap. The exact criticism didn't matter; it was the opportunity to voice a complaint, to point out a flaw, real or perceived – it didn't matter, because to them everything and everyone was flawed and their mission was to make the world aware of this, like rubbing a dog's nose in its own dirt.

Conflict followed this lot like the stench of a rotting carcass. There were always raised voices, raised tempers and raised fists in Ayrshire. There was no need for an explanation to those who lived there. It was the way they were and had always been: rebarbative, belligerent and first to fly behind any perceived slight from this unforgiving universe that had the impertinence to test them. It could be exhausting to observers like Valentine, who had long since learned to turn the other cheek, keep eyes tight shut and the mouth tighter yet. There was no debating the issue: it was beyond discourse, beyond the pale, really. Valentine knew by ignoring the practitioners of the sneer that he was tacitly giving approval – good men speak out against bad deeds – but he stayed the course because wrestling with pigs only took you into the muck and there were just too many pigs to ever contemplate a positive outcome.

The detective had decided Adrian Urquhart was a sneerer the first time he had met him. He shouldn't have been, he was of the wrong class for a start, but the trait did not abide by such simple distinctions. The boy had obviously had contact with many classes, or perhaps he was just one of the lucky ones who inherited the talent for such idiocy full-blown.

DS McAlister and DI Valentine stood facing Adrian Urquhart across the threshold of his late father's home like opposing forces meeting in no-man's-land. The second he had opened the door, Adrian lifted his eyes skyward and sighed – all that was missing was a stamped foot to complete the image of petulance. Valentine wondered if their arrival had come at an inopportune time: perhaps he had somewhere else to be? Or was it they had been mistaken for unwelcome cold-callers – perhaps peddling double-glazing or religion when he clearly had no use for either. It unnerved the detective that he should react in such a way, his father's demise being so recent, but it didn't shock him, because he had Adrian Urquhart's measure.

'It might be better if we came inside; there are some new developments we need to talk about,' said Valentine.

Adrian stepped back into the hallway and flagged them in. His eyes were rolling again, not towards the sky but inwardly, as if in a show of deep disappointment.

'It shouldn't take too long,' said McAlister.

Adrian didn't acknowledge the DS, just closed the door and turned to face Valentine. 'Will you need to speak to my mother, because she's in the kitchen.'

The detective nodded. 'If it's no trouble.'

'Right, I'll get her . . . Just go through. I'm sure you know the layout of the place by now.'

The officers proceeded down the hallway towards the living room and stood before the fire. It was a large room, elaborately and expensively decorated, but the chintzy feel belied any real personality. It was as if the room had been decorated from magazines or coffee-table tomes; there was no feeling of a home about it at all. As he looked around and gauged that the footprint of his own property might fit comfortably into this one room, Valentine conceded a bias for what was and was not a home.

'Hello again . . .' Mrs Urquhart was rubbing her hands on a tea towel when she appeared from the kitchen.

The officers turned to face her and nodded in unison.

'You could have taken a chair, gentlemen,' she said, directing them towards the sofa and flicking the tea towel over he shoulder.

Adrian joined her on the adjacent sofa. The additional bodies did nothing to diminish the room's extent. There was a lulled silence that sat heavily between them, and then, like a moment of clarity descending, sighs were wrung out. The four faced each other over the rug's gloomy brocade like opposing, and slightly surreal, tag teams. All the previous goodwill that had been extended by the Urquharts seemed to have vanished, and Valentine suddenly wondered why. He was still searching for a killer – that hadn't changed – and it was too soon for the conclusion of hope. In his experience, the families of victims tended to reserve resentment until a case was closed without a proper solution being found.

Valentine leaned forward, clasping his hands above his knees. 'How have you been, Mrs Urquhart?'

She tilted her head to the side, and her reply came in a drawl. 'Did you come here to inquire after my health, Inspector?'

The DI's face tightened into a grim mask – one that might be useful to deflect derision. 'If you don't mind me saying, Mrs Urquhart, I detect you might be a little uncomfortable with the investigation.'

'Oh, really . . .' She crossed her legs and snatched the tea towel from her shoulder as if it was the arm of an assailant. There was no disguising her anger and frustration as her hands clasped the tea towel at either end and twisted a tight coil.

DS McAlister spoke. 'Have we come at a bad time?'

'Oh for God's sake,' said Adrian. 'My father has been murdered, do you think there is a good time for any of us?'

Valentine unclasped his hands and waved McAlister down. The tone of the interview had been well established now; he hadn't expected it to reach its nadir so quickly, but the turn of events presented an interesting possibility for a more direct approach. 'We won't take up too much of your time. I hope you'll appreciate that this murder investigation is a top priority for us and there are certain aspects of the case that have caused us some concern recently.'

Adrian snatched the tea towel impatiently from his mother's hands and slapped it on the arm of the sofa, out of her reach. 'Such as?'

'When we last spoke, you may recall I mentioned the name Knox . . .'

Mrs Urquhart's voice pitched higher, reaching the level of imperiously clipped tones. 'Yes, the other unfortunate victim.'

'That's one way of describing him.'

'Well, how would you describe him, Inspector?'

Valentine watched as a scowl crossed her face. He kept his words low and calm but avoided a direct answer. He saw no need to submit himself to an interview – that was his job. 'You said you didn't recognise the name . . .'

She cut in. 'I've had no cause to change my opinion.'

DS McAlister spoke. 'We didn't ask if you had . . .'

The Urquharts turned to each other. Adrian tightened his mouth as he took in his mother, but no words were exchanged. They seemed to both be concentrating on saying as little as possible. Their actions might have been rehearsed, but that was unlikely, thought the detective. Mother and son seemed to be adept at communicating without words: not telepathically, but like creatures in a zoo whose forced union had bred an infallible understanding of each other's ways and wiles.

As Valentine assessed the pair, he leaned back in his chair and rested his chin on the back of his hand. He could tell that he had crossed a chalk line with them, but he had no idea where it was or what it represented. Was it a personal animus or a more vague scattering of the seeds of disapproval in his direction? Either way, he didn't judge them for it – at least, not too harshly – because when he found himself perplexed by people he knew the only route to understanding was observation. To jump to the conclusion that they merely found his questioning – or, indeed, himself – coarse and impertinent would be like snatching assumption from the lucky-dip bag marked delusion. As he prepared to pose his next question, there was a sound like cups clattering in the kitchen and then the heavy wooden door opened.

Ronnie Bell looked to be dressed for country pursuits, a shiny wax jacket and Chelsea boots beneath corduroy trousers. He walked to the middle of the room, then approached the mantle, where he stood facing the officers, firm-footed and sure.

'Hello again, Mr Bell,' said Valentine. 'I hope you'll appreciate we're in the midst of a delicate discussion . . .'

Mrs Urquhart interrupted. 'No need to bother about Ronnie . . . He's fine where he is.'

The neighbour removed his outdoor jacket and flung it over the back of a chair, then joined the others on the sofa, sitting stiff and proud. He smiled to Valentine but did not open his mouth.

'All right, if you're content with the situation,' said Valentine. The Urquharts' actions seemed unusual to the detective, but not out of the ordinary. He had seen grief and the aftermath of trauma affect people in many ways. To take against the police was a common enough choice; he just couldn't figure out what the driver was.

'I think it might be best if you asked what you came to ask and were quick about it,' said Ronnie. 'This family has been through enough, and what with all the media attention, it's been far from pleasant.'

'Media attention?' said McAlister.

Adrian stood up, his voice rising like a slow siren wail. 'Look, what is it you want?'

Valentine's shoulders tightened beneath his grey dog-tooth sports coat. 'We'll try not to take up too much more of your time.' He motioned to the sofa. 'If you don't mind please, Adrian.'

He shook his head and sat back down.

The DI picked at the edges of composure. 'Mrs Urquhart, do you think there is a possibility your husband may have known Duncan Knox from your time in Glasgow, perhaps?'

She massaged her wrist. 'Well, I can't see how.'

DS McAlister spoke again. 'The Inspector asked if it was possible, Mrs Urquhart.'

'Well, anything's possible in theory . . . Are you asking if I knew that my husband was an associate of this Knox person when we were in Glasgow? I don't know. I certainly don't think so.' She dropped her wrist suddenly. 'I told you before, I have no idea who this man is.'

Valentine tried to remove the veil of apprehension that Mrs Urquhart was hiding behind but was unable to. He could see the answers were not going to change, no matter how he posed the questions. 'This model club that your husband attended on Wednesdays . . .'

'Yes, what about it?' Her voice edged higher and became almost staccato in its delivery.

'He went every week?'

'Yes. Why?'

'And you're sure of that?'

'Yes, I told you before, he went every week.'

Valentine glanced at McAlister and the DS seemed to intuit the passing of the baton. 'That's not what the club told us,' said Ally. 'In fact, he was rarely there at all. Have you any idea where your husband might have been going on those nights?'

Adrian reached over to touch his mother's hand. 'Why are you doing this to us?'

'I'm sorry?' said Valentine.

'You're upsetting my mother. This is an interrogation . . . Don't you see we're the victims here as much as my father?'

'This is all routine questioning, Adrian . . . We're trying to establish the facts, that's all.'

It was Ronnie Bell's time to stand up now. He pushed away Adrian's hand and made to grab Mrs Urquhart's elbow. 'I think that's enough for one day, gentlemen . . .'

The Urquharts raised themselves from the sofa in time with Ronnie, and the police officers followed. They all stood facing each other across the broad room.

'Thank you for your time,' said Valentine. As he started to fasten his sports coat, to walk for the door, he turned. 'We have James Urquhart on camera in the vicinity of Prestwick Road on one of those Wednesday nights . . . Any idea what he might have been doing there?'

'No. None.' Adrian's voice was blunt and sure.

Valentine held his gaze. 'Duncan Knox was there too.'

'It's a very small town, Inspector,' said Adrian.

Ronnie stepped between them. 'Right, that's it, no more questions. If you keep pestering this family then I'll be directing you to a legal professional.'

Valentine retreated to the door. In the hallway, the DI spoke out once more. 'It is indeed a small town, Adrian . . . and secrets aren't kept long in small towns. I'll be in touch.'

'I'm sure you will, but my mother is leaving for the Highlands in a little while.'

'The Highlands?'

'She wants some peace and quiet. You don't grudge her that, do you?'

'Not at all,' said Valentine, almost deferentially. 'That's not something I would grudge anyone.'

41

DI Bob Valentine knew he belonged to a nation that lauded its landscape of battle-scarred castles and limpid lochs with an almost mordant fascination. The Scots drank copious whisky and danced dizzying ceilidhs. They revered long, dark nights and their literature revelled in justified sinners and mean cities. Their history reviled the blood of ancient forebears: their wars were all lost and their slim victories were dressed as defeats. In short, we were a queer lot, the Scots.

There was no lust for life in Scotland: that much had been confirmed for him on those rare occasions he visited foreign shores and saw how differently life was lived there. Scots couldn't look forward because they were always too busy looking back and castigating themselves for past mistakes. How could a nation like this have arrived at any other place? Towns and cities blighted by the ignorant and drug-addled. Pushers, pimps and gang masters holding sway over great swathes of an isolated and abandoned society. The Scots killed themselves in countless ways because they were a defeated nation, a colonised country that had abandoned all respect for itself generations ago. Scotland's sins were compounded by the political class that ruled from afar, uncaring, uninterested and unwilling to treat their neighbours like anything other than the barbarians at their door.

Valentine knew he was fighting a battle he had no chance of winning because the people who should have been marching beside him had already given up. He'd once been told, many years ago when he was still in uniform, that his job was like mending cracks in a dam. Police were Polyfilla, masking tape, multipurpose emulsion. But that was then; he knew that now the dam had burst and all thoughts of repair had been replaced by one almighty scrum for the lifeboats.

The detective stood in front of his desk, staring out to a slate-grey street being washed by wind-driven rain. The diluted blue of the skyline was a dreary indicator of his mood, a fulminating composition of oppressive conditions he could never escape, even if he wanted to. There were people there too, hurried and harried by the elements into shop fronts and wynds where they might once have passed a pleasantry, shared in their dismal fate to inhabit a land lashed by downpours day after day after day. But not a glance was exchanged between the long retinue of wet coats and dripping umbrellas; they passed each other like phantoms from other worlds, unaware of each other – or, in reality, ignorant.

When had it become like this? thought Valentine. At what point did we all become so separate from each other? There seemed to be no sanctioned contact, no public nexus. No one wanted to be part of a wider collective. We wanted our own selves and our own homes and our own flat-screen televisions to while away the long hours of self-delusion. That's what we wanted. We didn't want each other because, if we were honest, at this point we didn't even like each other. Not as a people, not as a race. If there was a defining trait that we all subscribed to now, it was separateness. But we were amorphous in this nascent sense of ourselves. It was not an individuality, because that carried a certain connotation of self-assuredness that we lacked entirely – our desire was only to trade our culture and heritage for the same bland swill that encouraged us to take no responsibility for anything beyond our own immediate needs and wants.

Valentine couldn't look out the window any more. The world outside repulsed him. He felt a quickening of his pulse and a dull twinge in his chest that suggested he had allowed his adrenaline to spike in an unhealthy manner. Just a short time ago, he had been dead. No longer of this world. And through the miracles of modern medicine he had been brought back. He tried to remember why that was a good thing. He tried to think of the infinite perfection of life, how overjoyed he had been to hear that he and Clare had first created life, and there was his answer: his family. If it wasn't for the others he shared his life with, then what was this world to him? The answer was beyond the window that he could no longer bear to look at.

DS Sylvia McCormack was standing outside the glassed-off office at the end of the incident room. She seemed to be holding some files, the thick blue files that they stored the case notes in but also a collection of loose sheaves of paper. In her left hand, pressed tight to her side, was a mug that looked like it might contain coffee. Valentine crossed the floor and opened up the door.

'You weren't thinking, were you?' he said.

'About the handle you mean?' She nodded to another mug sitting on a table by the door. 'I made us coffee, can you take this?'

'Aye, sure.'

The detective took the mug from her hand and watched her wrestle the bundle of files onto her hip; she retrieved the other mug and walked through the door. The job of closing it behind her seemed to require another set of arms, but she didn't look fazed or in any way like she might welcome assistance.

315

'I take it you heard about the trip to the Urquharts?' said Valentine.

She placed the folders on the desktop and flicked her fringe from her eyes. She was breathing heavily as she spoke. 'I saw Ally in the cannie . . . Pretty grim, eh?'

'Oh, it's that all right.'

'I wouldn't let it get to you.' She dropped herself in the chair and watched as a swirl of coffee was evacuated from the brim of the mug. 'Shit!'

Valentine grinned; he thought that Sylvia had a way of ingratiating herself with people that was nothing short of a blessing. She was what his late mother would have called soulish. He had met precious few people who had set him in mind of his mother; herself perhaps the antithesis of the word soulish.

'Are you OK there, do you need a hanky?'

She shook her head and sneered at him over the bridge of her nose. 'I've survived worse.'

As he took in her self-deprecating scowl, he knew she wasn't milking the moment for herself, like others might have. 'I'm sure you have.'

Valentine retreated behind his desk and removed the chair. As he sat down, he raised the coffee mug and tested it for warmth. As he returned the mug to rest, he rifled the files and the pile of paper on top.

'What's this?' he said.

'The full Knox transcripts from Glasgow . . . I've marked up the highlights.' She crossed her legs and balanced the coffee on her knee. Her breathing had stilled now. 'That other stuff, the bundle of papers, is just something I thought might interest you.'

Valentine picked up the top sheet, which looked to have been printed from the Internet. The website seemed official

316

enough, but the content of the page was an excursion to new territory for the detective. As he read the top line and glanced over a sidebar, he knew the DS was dragging him towards something he didn't want to face. He certainly didn't want to face it on his own, although the thought of facing it with a colleague some years his junior, whom he had only known a short matter of time, might be even more worrisome.

'Look, Sylvia . . .' His words trailed off as he was caught in her eyeline.

'I'm only trying to help, sir.'

Valentine lowered the printout and gripped the tip of his jawline in his hand. 'So, tell me about this Reece case, the mother of five.'

The DS smiled. 'God, where to start . . . ? We had nothing until Colvin showed. He had images in his head of Mrs Reece in a field; he knew she was dead, but that was it. Most of the stuff he gave us was fragmented, patches of words and pictures of her children crying and so on . . .'

Valentine had heard of instances in the past where quite incredible messages had been delivered to police from people with no apparent knowledge of the case at hand; they had always struck him as slightly suspect or, worse, as frauds.

'Was he looking for money?'

'No, not a penny. He made that very clear from the start.' She tilted her head at a strange angle, as if searching the far reaches of her memory. 'The thing was, he was desperate . . . It was like he had to get this out of his system because it was, I don't know, haunting him.'

The detective shifted uneasily. He didn't want to be drawn into believing in psychics helping police with their clear-up rates, but something about McCormack's story poked at him and drew his attention into new areas.

'So you took him on?'

She thinned her eyes. 'More like took him in. As soon as he got close to the investigation, the information just started spilling out of him.'

'He found her, then?'

She retrieved her coffee mug and took a sip. 'No, sir . . . She was dead.'

'Not a great success.'

'How do you mean?'

'Well, the crime had already been committed . . . Murder, I presume.'

'No, you miss the point. The investigation was cold. Colvin saw where the victim was buried and led the squad there. We'd never have found her remains without him.'

Valentine stared at his coffee. The grey liquid seemed uninviting, but he raised the mug to his mouth, more to pass time than anything else. He didn't know what to say to the DS. He didn't want to reveal how he truly felt – confused – or to say what he thought of her mother and her friends, for fear of upsetting anyone. The overriding feeling he noted was embarrassment.

'Sylvia, I don't know what you think you saw at the Coopers, but . . .'

She raised a hand, as if to punctuate his sentence for him. 'Boss, I know what I saw.'

'Sylvia . . .'

'No. Wait a minute.' She reached forward and clattered the mug on the desktop. It was still quite full and some liquid ran down the side. 'Have a read of the notes I printed for you – sudden precognition is a well-documented occurrence in near-death survivors.'

Valentine forced a smile onto his face. He felt his attention drawn to the activity outside the office; he hoped no one could lip-read. He touched his jaw again and sighed as DS McCormack stood up and headed to the door.

'Just read the notes, boss,' she said. 'And if it doesn't ring true then I'll say no more.'

He doubted that was true. 'Oh, really?'

'Keep an open mind, sir.' She reached for the doorknob and paused, and a smug gleam entered her eye. 'And remember there are more things on heaven and earth than are dreamt of in your philosophy.'

If she had appended a wink to the statement, Valentine couldn't have been more unsettled. He felt like she had something on him now, a hold over him that was as damning as incriminating photographs or drunken revelations spewed forth in a moment of weakness. He knew, however, that DS McCormack's intentions were nothing of the sort. They were pure, decent even – but that only added to the tension crushing him as soundly as he would a tack in the heel of his shoe.

The DI fingered the edge of the paper printout for a moment longer and saw himself reading it, perhaps even digesting the contents, and then he withdrew his hand as if testing a griddle plate. He stood up so sharply he heard the blood coursing in his ears as he returned to the window and the sight of the grey and rain-lashed streets of auld Ayr. For the first time, Valentine realised he was trapped: trapped in the town, trapped in his marriage, and trapped in a career he had no right to in his current condition. Most of all, and certainly the most worrying for him, was the fact that he was trapped in a mind and body that he no longer felt in full control of. It worried him in ways that DS McCormack seemed incapable of grasping. It was not a matter of glimpsing a quite useful and seemingly productive sixth sense, it was a matter of whether he could stop it interfering with his sanity long enough for him to solve the murders of James Urquhart and Duncan Knox and the disappearance of Janie Cooper. Valentine felt his chest tightening, his heart beating so hard that he had to press the flat of his hand to his breastbone. As he reached out to steady himself on the window ledge, his vision became blurred and blotched. The detective knew he had to sublimate these feelings soon, because if he couldn't, the danger was that he would lose his job or, worse still, his life.

42

DI Bob Valentine came to the conclusion that the only option left to him was to resign from the force immediately. As he kept his gaze on the rain-battered windowpane, the view beyond became a blur of indistinct shapes and fragmented iridescent light. He thought about the situation he now found himself in, and the move he knew he must make increasingly seemed like the only honourable course of action. He had failed to find a coherent way through the morass of his thoughts, and the investigation, he was absolutely sure, had suffered for it. His focus was gone, had completely deserted him; he was spending too much time going over irrelevancies in his mind. When he looked coldly at the situation and was honest with himself, the largest share of his attention was on finding a solution to the Janie Cooper case. All his attention, not just some diffuse part of it, should have been on solving the murders; he felt a deepening guilt for a justice that the victims and wider society deserved but which he hadn't seen fit to deliver. No wonder Adrian Urquhart and his mother had been so offhand with him; they knew full well he was letting them down. Valentine turned away from the window. The burn inside him felt like his innards were in meltdown.

He couldn't recall another time in his career when he had felt this way or acted like he had. He could only alight on the arrogance of youth for a parallel, but this was different. In youth you could be forgiven for not knowing any better

– what was his excuse now? Valentine's heart settled down to a low, pulsing beat that he no longer felt in his left arm like hot pins pressing insistently from inside his veins. He was calmed by the idea of relinquishing the case and his job, and he wondered if that was because he knew it was the right thing to do. Was his survival instinct kicking in? Telling him that if he went on like this then the solution he sought would be final, and fatal? He couldn't bear to put Clare and the girls through hospitals and him clinging to life once again. He could take a million more hurts, but not that. He knew now that Clare and the girls had suffered more than he'd thought – had he ever really considered how much? He knew the girls, and Chloe especially, would need time to get over it, but they were young and had so much of life still to come, which would distract them. Clare was more of a worry: she was older and far wiser, and yet she'd been felled. He knew his wife had never gotten over the initial shock of him being so close to death; he tried to put himself in her place and for the first time Valentine realised just how much Clare meant to him. She was as much a part of him as the sand in the sea; if he'd been damaged when his life was endangered, then so had she, because he was sure they shared that much. The way she had been lately – was it merely her way of protecting herself from the damage she knew he was inflicting on both of them?

There would be an assessment, a test of his psychological fitness that would likely find him wanting. Did he care? He could only focus on his family – he cared for them. He no longer felt anything for himself, because he no longer recognised himself. Who was he? Who had he become? If he was losing his mind then the man he thought he once was had surely gone. A vague moment of self-pity entered his thoughts: a 'why me?' moment. But he brushed it aside. Why anyone? What did he know? The answer was nothing – it was like DS McCormack had said:

'More things in heaven and earth . . .' The words came out flat, empty of all their true substance.

What mattered was his family and that they would be kept safe. If he came clean, admitted his physical and mental failings, then he would be granted a medical discharge. There might even be compensation, a lump sum to add to his pension that would help ease the transition into a more straitened way of life. Clare would be ashamed, and Chloe wouldn't like having her father around all day, but Fiona was too young to understand. The sudden image of the rows and recriminations to come flooded his mind. He felt a failure, not just as an officer, but as a father and as a man too. How could he ever look his own father in the eye again?

As Valentine walked towards to door he knew this was an ending. He had tried to return to active policing after the incident of his stabbing, but he had failed. For whatever reason, his own physical and mental frailty or something else that he didn't understand, it was an irrelevance now. He thought of the call from the chief super when he was at Tulliallan and the spark of ambition it had ignited. He knew that flame was still there, still burning – if weakly – and he wanted to apply the bellows to it, but didn't know how. His resolve hadn't altered any; he just wasn't able to do it.

Valentine walked through the incident room in a daze. He tried to maintain his usual posture, he kept his hands in his pockets and gave the odd, slouching nod to those who crossed his path, but he wasn't present. His mind was already in with the chief super, delivering his resignation. It seemed to be a long walk; his legs ached and the fronts of his thighs grew heavy as he dragged his feet over the grim, corporate-looking carpet tiles. By the time he reached the brassy nameplate that bore the name CS Marion Martin, his heart was pounding again, and a dry, acrid taste was sitting in his mouth.

He knocked once and reached for the handle. As he stepped inside he felt a flash of heat in his forehead and then he saw the chief super lowering the telephone in the most careful manner. Her eyes were wide, her skin pale and shiny, and her mouth a thin point that threatened to reveal a recent hurt. She sat down and slowly pushed herself away from the edge of her desk. The window behind her was a luminous white band that cut the shape of her shoulders and head into stark relief.

Valentine was first to speak. 'Something wrong?'

She remained still. A slow trail of words seemed to be coming from somewhere else. 'We have another one: a young girl out in Mossblown. Running club just about trampled over her . . .' She looked up, stared into the DI's eyes. 'Did you hear what I said?'

He nodded. 'Is it the same MO?'

She shook her head. 'No . . . No spike. Uniform say the scene looks like it was abandoned in a hurry.'

Valentine found a juggernaut of thoughts driving over his earlier intentions. As he looked at CS Martin, felled in her own office by yet another murder, he knew there was no one else who could carry the load. Resignation seemed his most insane thought now – how could he have conceded the investigation to such an incompetent? He might not solve the case in quick time, but he was confident enough in his abilities to see that Dino would fare far worse. The idea that he would lie down before her became another one of his bad moves. He was lurching from pillar to post, he knew that, but there was another victim to consider now and perhaps it would reveal some secrets that had so far remained hidden from the investigation.

324

'Mossblown? The others were in Ayr. That's worrying, a widening spread.'

'Probably thought the town centre was too hot now.'

'No. If it's a different MO then the intention will be different – Urquhart and Knox were impaled on spikes to attract attention; taking a body into the countryside says concealment to me.'

The chief super nodded. 'Why show off with the others and not this one?'

Valentine shrugged. 'I don't know. We don't even know that they're linked.'

'Oh come on, we treble our annual murder count in a matter of weeks and it's not the same perp?' She gripped the arms of her chair and the shape of her face changed.

'Maybe the motivation's different . . .' He leaned forward and balanced his body weight on his palm. 'Maybe this girl was done over because our killer wanted her out the way.'

'It's possible.'

Valentine felt his energy levels increasing. He pushed himself away from the desk and turned for the door. 'Running club?'

'Bloody Ayrshire Harriers . . . Twenty-six names taken by uniform.'

'Crime scene will be a mess.'

Martin shook her head. 'I'm more worried about the potential for press leaks . . . Won't take long to seep out with twenty-six tongues wagging.'

The DI dipped his brows. As he gripped the door handle he felt like he was entering a different station to the one he had crossed a few moments ago to offer his resignation. 'Look, I'll get out there and see what's what.'

She didn't reply. Valentine knew this was virgin territory

for the chief super, and if there had been a clock ticking on his efforts before it had just sprung into the red zone. He returned to the incident room and took a brief pause once inside the door. If his mind had been awash with thoughts before, it had stilled now: he grasped his newfound focus and stepped forward.

'Right, everyone, can I have your attention?'

The room seemed to go into slow motion and then freeze. A cup clattered onto a desktop like the last bell in a town-centre pub and then the only sound was that of the photocopier. A uniform reached out to remove the paper tray and then silence fell on the place like it was its natural state of being.

'Thank you,' said Valentine. 'I've just been in with the boss and have to report we have another body on our patch . . .'

DS McAlister called out, 'Another one . . . Where this time?'

'Mossblown, Ally . . . The details are still sketchy, but we'll know more when we get out there.'

'Right, then,' said McAlister. 'We should get going.'

The room's volume was suddenly turned up a notch; some shuffling and animated facial gestures spread through the enclosed space.

Valentine walked to the coat rack and retrieved his grey dog-tooth sports coat. 'Right, Ally and Phil, you can follow me out . . . Sylvia, you're with me.' He pointed to the DS and then he curled up his index finger as if reeling her towards him.

'Yes, sir.'

The sound of the squad's feet on the stairs came like a stampede. Jim Prentice looked up from the front desk and a woman struggled to hold onto what looked like a lost dog; it started barking as Valentine rushed past.

'What's all this?' said Jim. 'It's never another one . . .'

The detective held the door for DS McCormack and the others and managed to sneer over their backs towards the desk sergeant. 'Jim, try and keep it zipped, eh!'

In the car, Valentine depressed the clutch and pulled out before McCormack had a chance to put her seatbelt on. A red light illuminated on the dashboard and then a chime started to ping.

'It won't go off till you've got the belt on,' said the DI.

'I haven't sat down, yet . . .' McCormack turned towards the door and reached out for the seatbelt. Cars halted on the approach to King Street roundabout as the trail of police vehicles accelerated. They were halfway to the Tesco superstore before the conversation began again.

'What do we know about this one, sir?'

Valentine dropped a gear and changed lanes. 'Female and not the same MO.'

'How far out's this town?'

'About ten or fifteen depending on the road . . . There's nothing to the place. A few council houses and a couple of pubs. Farms all around and, if I remember right, a nursing home.'

'Sounds beyond glamorous.'

'It's beyond the beyonds . . . Nobody goes to Mossblown unless they have to, and even then you'd try to avoid it if you could.'

The traffic lights turned to green and the left lane cleared enough for Valentine to put the foot down. They'd passed Tesco and were well on their way to the bypass before the weather turned again. He put on the wipers and wound up the inch or so of window he had left open to the elements.

As they reached the Whitletts roundabout the traffic started to slow again; it seemed as good a time as any for Valentine to broach the subject on his mind.

'Sylvia, about that little chat we had earlier . . .'

She turned her head towards him. 'What about it?'

'I know you think you saw something, and I know you think you're helping me, but . . .'

She interrupted his flow of words. 'There's always one of them, isn't there?'

He glanced towards her. The expression she wore was the one he expected, a mix of disappointment and sadness tinged with no little hurt. 'I'm grateful to you for your concern, obviously . . .'

'Oh, obviously.' The tone lapsed into polished sarcasm; the change didn't suit her.

The lights on the roundabout were red; he came off the accelerator and pressed the brake. As the car slowed to a halt the tension inside was building to the level of nuclear fallout. 'All I want to say is, let me deal with this in my own way.'

She poked her jaw out and looked towards the wet fields in the distance. 'And you'd like me to mind my own business, I suppose.'

'Sylvia . . .' He didn't think he had said anything to merit this reaction; were they talking at cross purposes, he wondered?

She turned to face him as the car came to a halt. 'It's OK, boss, I know when to bite my tongue.' She looked away again. 'You've no need to worry about that . . . Consider your wee secret safe with me.'

43

CLARE VALENTINE REMOVED her wedding ring for the first time in nearly twenty years and stared at the white band of skin beneath. It seemed a strange sight; the pale, sagging skin that usually sat beneath the band of gold looked surreal exposed to the wider world. She grasped the ring between finger and thumb and held it up to the light, and myriad tiny scratches glinted before her eyes. Each scratch was a memory, an experience, and whether they were worth recalling or burying deep in her unconscious didn't matter: they were still there, they existed – perhaps more than she did now.

Clare returned the wedding ring to the dresser beneath the window and stared at it from the stool where she sat. It looked so insignificant, tiny. Just a piece of metal, really. But what significance they attached to it. She could remember the day she and Bob picked the wedding bands from the jeweller on New Market Street. She had thought about white gold, but on her finger it didn't look substantial enough. Her mother had a wide gold band that signalled solidity. She wanted that too.

'Isn't it a bit big?' Bob had said. 'Like something to go through a bull's nose . . .'

She smiled at the memory. There were many more like it, still stored away, secreted in the strangest of places, surfacing when you least expected them.

How could she bury those memories? Did she want to?

Clare turned away from the window and half-rose from

her seated position, then decided to sit down again; as she slumped back to the stool she sighed heavily. She felt weary, tired, more so than she had ever felt; it was like all vitality had been drained from her, sucked away to who knows where. She dropped her face into the palm of her hands and started to cry. The sobbing lasted only a few moments before she shook herself back to the reality of her bedroom and escaped the youthful flashbacks to better times. She didn't know how she had come to feel this way, how everything had changed, but changed it had.

Clare pushed herself from the stool and made her way to the wardrobe. There was not much left to pack: two cases full already was more than enough. There was just her coat, and she could wear that; nothing else would fit in her luggage. As she stared at the two full, bulging suitcases on the bed, they seemed to press on her mind, light the landing torches that were summoning in a descending guilt. She turned away sharply and touched the side of her face.

'Get a grip . . .'

The girls were older now. They were hardly children – more like young adults. They would understand. She knew they would. They might shed a tear for her the first night she was away, but that would be all. She'd seen their friends talking about their parents' separations like it was a trip to the supermarket; it was all just another rite of passage these days. But the guilt was still there, no matter what she told herself. There would be no more family Christmases, no more family birthday celebrations . . . no more family. Because, and she made no mistake, that's what Clare knew she was doing: destroying her family.

She flicked her fingers away from her face and tried to ball a fist. It was a pathetic-looking symbol of anger, but she felt the need to press it into her thigh and attempt to spark some dudgeon.

'You did this, Bob . . .' She shook her head. 'Not me.'

As she released the fist, she tapped the sides of her face and stared into the mirror. Her make-up had started to peel away from the edges of her eyes, thin flakes that failed to adhere to the thinner folds of older skin. She shook her head and patted at her cheeks. It would have to do; she would have to do because there was no other Clare Valentine on offer, and that was another blindingly obvious fact.

She turned back to the bed and latched her grip on the handle of the suitcase. It was heavier than she imagined, or perhaps she was weaker. Clare knew she was weak, but that wasn't why she was leaving her husband. She was leaving Bob because she was strong, because she couldn't bear what their marriage had become and how he had changed. She could no longer look at him and feel the same way: that she was somehow a part of him, a part of his life, like they shared something together. She felt lost to her husband, like she no longer recognised him. Who was he now? Who was Bob Valentine? There was a time when she could have reeled off a list of lengthy answers, but not now. She no longer understood him. He had become an automaton, a mere ghost in their lives. He went to work and he came home and inhabited their life like a stranger to her. She couldn't believe how many tears she had shed over his injury; he had died . . .

'Oh my God . . .'

She had said the words but didn't quite believe them.

It was true, though, Bob had died. Somewhere after that knife entered his heart, the old Bob had left. She didn't know this man that floated in and out of their home like a shadow. He stared at her, but she stared through him. Night after night he came home and there was no talk outside of work, no compassion, no shared sense of themselves. She'd lost Bob, and she knew it.

The suitcase made a loud thud when it slid off the bed and onto the carpet. She stared at the other case and knew it would make a similar noise; she couldn't alert Bob's dad to her leaving because she couldn't stand the explanation she'd have to give. Clare rolled the first case to the side of the bedroom door, glanced to the other, and pledged to come back for them both soon. In the hallway she wiped at her eyes and tried to assume a plausible smile. It felt painted there, but it would have to do. There would be a lot of times ahead when she would have to force herself to face people, she knew that, but she didn't want to contemplate the consequences of her actions until she had struck the final blow.

Clare descended the stairs and made her way through to the living room, where the old man was sitting. The television was silent; the only sound was from the goings of the builders in the neighbour's garden.

'I think they must be putting up the Taj Mahal next door,' said Bob's dad.

'Aye . . . Lucky them.' Clare moved towards the window and peeked through the blinds. A dumper truck laden with concrete slabs was being manoeuvred into the driveway accompanied by a persistent and repetitive beeping noise.

'I was saying to Bob . . . I'll not be under your feet much longer.'

Had her husband put him up to this? He was always very good at reading the advance signals of her intentions, but she didn't think he had been paying that much attention lately.

'What? Don't be silly.'

'I mean, it's been very nice of you and all that, but you need

332

the space and the girls need their rooms. You're a family, after all and I'm just a visitor.'

Clare felt his words were so pointed they might have been scripted. Her lip trembled and she fought to prevent a single teardrop being released from her eye. She touched the window ledge and tried to hold her composure as she spoke towards the blinds. 'You're part of the family!'

There was a gravid pause. 'Not really.'

Clare turned round and wiped her eyes. She knew at once that her father-in-law suspected something wasn't right.

He lifted his desultory gaze from the carpet and fixed his eyes on Clare. 'Is everything all right, my dear?'

'Oh, yes ... Quite all right.' She'd managed to inject some steel into her voice, from she knew not where, but her gratitude was boundless. 'Look, why don't you nip down to the Spar and get yourself a paper?'

'Och, I'm not bothered about a paper, love, there's very little reading in them these days.'

She smiled. 'Well, stretch your legs then, the fresh air will do you good ...' She turned back to the window again. 'It's a lovely day.'

'Maybe you're right.'

The old man raised himself from the sofa and strolled through to the kitchen. As Clare turned, she caught sight of him removing the cap from his jacket pocket and manoeuvring it into place on his glabrous head. When he had wrestled the jacket on and negotiated the awkward zipper, he turned and tapped the tip of his cap to her.

Clare waved and listened for the sound of the back door closing. She let Bob's dad get to the end of the drive before she moved from the window and went into the kitchen to retrieve the telephone. She was fighting a deep pang of conscience at the way she'd pushed the old man out the door, but she knew she couldn't face the recriminations right now. She didn't want to have to justify her actions to anyone and even though she knew the opposition he would have put up would have been slight, she just didn't have the strength to face it. The truth was, if she could be persuaded otherwise, she might not go. But her mind was set.

Clare removed a piece of paper with the telephone number for Station Taxis on it; the bigger black cabs would be better for getting the luggage loaded in a hurry. She dialled and ordered the cab and was told to expect it in ten minutes. She looked at her watch and nodded, then made her way onto the stairs and to the bedroom once again. She collected her coat first: putting it on was an act of resolve. But the second case was even heavier than the first. She couldn't believe how heavy they were, but it was too late to start unpacking; the castors screeched as she rolled the case through the bedroom door and bumped each step of the staircase on the way to the front door. She repeated the action for the second case and then, feeling warm from her exertions, removed her coat and placed it on top of the luggage.

As Clare sat on the end of the staircase, a sudden rush of emotion engulfed her and she burst into sobs. She couldn't bear to look at the house she had shared with Bob and her children all these years. She knew it would be her last chance, though, so she forced herself, still sobbing, to take in the familiar sight of the hallway with the hanging mirror and the new rug she had just bought for in front of the door. She could see through to the living room from where she was, and the pictures of the girls in their school uniforms seemed to scream to her from the top of the shelving unit. Her nails started to tap off her lips. She hadn't realised how hard this was going to be – would she spend the whole day in tears, or the rest of her life?

Her tears were heavier now; she could feel them on her cheeks and at once she knew she must be a sight. Clare moved to the bathroom, ran the taps and splashed water on her face. She was drying her eyes on the hand towel, smearing mascara on the white cotton, as the doorbell went.

'Right, taxi . . . Get a grip,' she told herself.

As she stared in the mirror, Clare recognised only a passing resemblance to herself. Her cheeks were red and puffy, her eyes spiderwebs of burst capillaries. She looked away; she couldn't bear to face herself any longer. She'd made her decision and she was determined to see it out.

As Clare opened the door, she felt like she'd been kicked in the stomach. Her quick breath subsided into a mournful sigh as she stared at her father-in-law.

'There's a taxi here, love . . .' he said.

'Yes . . .' She didn't know how to explain herself. 'I thought you were going for a paper.'

He held up a copy of the *Daily Record*. 'Builder next door gave me a lift there and back.' He peered round her shoulder and obviously caught sight of the suitcases. 'Clare, are you going somewhere?'

She didn't know how to reply, didn't think she had any of the right words.

44

IT WAS ALL A GAME, LIFE. What other way was there of describing it? He had been in so many strange places, met so many different people, that Valentine had stopped the dissolute notion that there was any alternative. We were born to power or pauper and we had no choice but to accept the hand we'd been dealt and play the cards. He'd heard of the Indian philosophy of lila: life as a divine game, life's energy in all its guises from man and beast to tree and even stone all containing the same life force and susceptible to its whim. It sounded right, seemed to fit the irrational and erratic pattern he knew so well. But there was something else too, a darker element that came into play. He hadn't always thought like that, however. Valentine could remember a time in his teens when, drunken insensate by a spirit he wasn't used to, he'd lain down on a bench in Ayr's magic circle – the town's less common appellation for Burns Statue Square. As he lay on his back looking at the stars, he saw Rabbie's head blocking out the constellation of Orion, or was it the Plough? He couldn't correctly recall, or care, now, but he had a feeling there was something up there for him, in the stars, beyond the grimness of the town. He knew now he had been wrong, embarrassingly so; the detective had pounded those streets, from brig to bar, for decades and knew there was no cobbled pathway or gilded ladder leading skyward – it was all a fallacy. And it was deceit. A lie told to gullible optimists in their tender youth, just to

336

keep their hand in the game. How else did you explain the disparity between James Urquhart's fortune and yet another poor lifeless girl's misfortune? There was no rubric within the game's rulebook to turn to for confirmation, but he knew the rule existed as a fatalistic law of life on Earth. Those who said otherwise were either fools or had an interest to preserve. There may once have been a greasy pole and it may once have even been climbed by someone who found it led all the way to a new galaxy of riches, but it was now long gone. If the pole existed still, it was truncated, cut down somewhere shy of ground level, as likely a declivity as a divot to remember it by. This pale-white murdered girl never knew of its existence, the town of Mossblown never knew of its existence, he was sure of that.

The detective crouched low to the ground and took in the tangled mass of thin white limbs, damp now with the downfall of a little rain. She was no more human than the bed of dirt she lay on. No more a life than any of us would be when the blood sat stagnant in our veins, that great pump stilled in our chests, all thoughts, all clocks, halted. He felt cold inside, cold enough for two people – he felt her cold too – but not because of the exposure of her bare flesh to the harsh elements; he felt the coldness of her loss. She had been someone, once. She hadn't always been so cold; she'd held the flame of life inside her, but it had been extinguished. Snuffed out, brutally.

'Look at those bruises,' said DS McCormack.

'On the neck or the arms?' said Valentine. 'The ones on the arms are older.'

'She's a junkie.'

The term turned a spike in the detective; she was a drug user, there was no mistaking it, but she was a member of the same race of beings as they were. She was someone's daughter.

She'd meant something to someone: if not now, then once. We all had, once.

He lowered himself on his haunches and picked a wet leaf from the white flesh. The contusions continued down her arm in consistently spaced points. 'Fingertips, she's been battered about.'

'Repeatedly, I'd say for some time. Look at the stomach distension, sir.'

'She's brass, I'll bet money on that.' Valentine rose and motioned to one of the uniforms. 'We got her printed?'

'Yes, sir. Going through now . . .'

'Well, that's something. With any luck we'll have her on our books and get a name before too long.'

DS McAlister and DS Donnelly approached the crime scene. They were ducking under the blue and white tape as Valentine turned away from them to take a closer look at a silver chain around the girl's neck.

'What's that, boss?' said McCormack.

'Don't know . . . Some kind of pendant.'

As he knelt down again, Valentine removed a yellow pencil from the inside pocket of his sports coat. He pointed the pencil towards the girl's neck and slotted the tip beneath the silver chain; as he rummaged for the pendant he saw a tangle of mulch around a silver clasp and then the item was sprung onto her chest.

'A cross . . .' he said. The detective almost felt like laughing. 'Where was her God?'

'It's just a cheapie,' said McCormack.

Valentine stood up and rolled his eyes to the heavens. 'Maybe He might have been pissed at her for that?' He shook his head. 'I mean, there's some things worth splashing out on.'

DS McCormack seemed unsure how to interpret the

338

detective's words. She held herself still as the wind took stray tendrils of hair in front of her face. Valentine turned away and walked towards the blue tape.

'A bloody cross.'

He didn't know why he had got so worked up by the sight of the small silver cross. It just seemed so out of place to him, so ridiculously trite. She was a young girl who hadn't had a chance from the day she was born, a prostitute who pumped her veins full of poison to numb the pain of being alive: what use did she have for God? What kind of a god could even she imagine had fashioned this hell on Earth for her? How long had she suffered? He knew her story all too well because it was the story of every young girl like her. Pain in childhood, and pain in bigger portions the older she got. There was no escape, no saviour for her. As he reached the edge of the clearing, he felt his throat freezing with an involuntary welling of unwanted emotion.

'Sir, have you seen the tracks?' One of the uniforms pointed to the broad-rimmed tyre marks in the wet ground. He was tall, his shoulders looked too square for his narrow hips, but he didn't seem the type to be concerned with his appearance.

'You better get those cast,' said Valentine. He watched the uniform dip his head and lower his gaze to the tracks. It was like watching a giraffe take a drink.

'Looks like a big vehicle, sir. A large saloon or maybe even a truck.'

The detective looked at the tyre prints; they were clear and fresh, and the vehicle seemed to have spun a little in the wet mud. 'Looks like they were in a hurry to get away.'

'Might have been the running party . . . Maybe saw them coming.'

Valentine turned back towards the crime scene. The SOCOs

had started to unfurl a white tent, and a noise like wind in a sail sent a wood pigeon scrabbling from the branches of a nearby tree.

The detective pointed to what looked like a steep gash in the ground. 'What's that, there?'

The uniform straightened his back and tipped up his head. 'That's like some kind of hole, sir . . . We think it's fresh too.'

Another interpretation made more sense. 'A grave, you mean.'

'Could be, sir.'

The DI was tired of the lopsided conversation; he had seen enough to know he didn't need to see any more. He turned for the car with his face set in a granite sneer. 'Tell the others I'm going back to the station.'

'Don't you want to wait for the fiscal, sir?'

He didn't think the question deserved an answer. Was the fiscal going to deliver some insight? Was the fiscal going to tell him how to do his job, how to solve another murder? As he reached the road, Valentine unlocked the car and kept his head low, facing off a fierce wind, until he had reached the vehicle. He got inside just as the rain was starting up again and sat with his hands in his lap, his knees locked at right angles to the floor. As he stared out of the car's window to the row of grim council houses he saw the stacks of chimneys stalking the grey horizon like weary sentries who wished to be anywhere but here. An old man stood in front of his home, leaning on a dilapidated garden gate with folded arms and furrowed brows. Valentine stared at the man for a moment, made an unfathomable connection with his dark eyes and felt them share a mute understanding of a world that had long ago ceased to make any sense to them both. The detective put the key in the ignition and set off.

The road back to Ayr was lined with fields, green and bright in the divisions that were spared the cut of tractor tracks. The march of yuppie commuter homes had started to spill into the fields skirting the bypass, and the heavy machinery of clearing vehicles and dump trucks chuntered behind drystone dykes. Valentine knew he was observing a rapidly changing landscape: the fertile fields of Burns Country were giving way to bricks and mortar, to tiled roofs and tarred roads. In another decade the small town would be swallowed up, along with a few others. Ayr would be a small city then – if it wasn't already in all but name.

At the station, Valentine approached the front desk and called out to Jim Prentice. The desk sergeant turned and nodded; he was holding the receiver of a telephone, but the conversation seemed to be coming to an end. His facial expression suggested there was a fence that needed mending sitting between the two men.

'Sorry to be barking at you this morning, Jim,' said Valentine.

'It's all right, I know how it is.' He clamped his mouth tight shut and removed the chair from beneath the counter. It slid out on its small castors. 'I take it that's another one to add to the tally?'

The detective nodded. 'Young girl. She's brass, but lucky if she's seen twenty summers.'

'Well, she'll not see another one.' He shook his head. 'What's this bloody place coming too? What happened to the days of lost bikes and kids raiding orchards?'

Valentine smirked. 'Long gone, Jim . . . Long gone.'

As he made his way onto the stairs, he caught sight of the chief super's chubby ankles on the floor above him heading for the incident room. The heavy thump of her footsteps suggested that she had some important news to deliver.

Valentine upped his pace and made leaps of two steps at a time. As he jogged in behind CS Martin's thundering footfalls, he was breathing heavily.

'Oh, you're back?' she said.

'Just . . .'

'Couldn't have been there long.' She ran her fingers through her hair as if it was an annoyance to her, perhaps even interfering with her thought processes.

'Long enough . . . She's a prostitute, a well-worked one by the looks of it, so she shouldn't be too hard to ID.'

The chief super raised her right hand and pinned a pile of papers to Valentine's chest. 'Get your laughing gear round that . . . We have an I.D.'

'The prints?'

'Yes indeed. We've pulled her up more times than a shithouse seat.'

Valentine removed his gaze from Dino, peeled the paperwork from his chest and scanned the contents. The printout wasn't the best quality: a grainy black and white photograph of the girl that looked to have been taken during a booking. There was no doubting her resemblance to the girl he'd just left lying in a cold field, though.

'That's her,' he said.

'You sure?'

'Certain.' Valentine held up the papers and slapped his other hand off them. 'The girl in Mossblown is Leanne Dunn.'

45

DI Bob Valentine spread the Leanne Dunn file over the desktop in front of him. His thoughts moved quickly as his eyes took in the details, darting like an agile little fish on a coral reef. She was an Ayr girl, had always lived locally, if you could apply that term to how her days had gone. He couldn't hide his sympathy for her; it all seemed such a tragic waste. The poverty and the deprivation she had endured since childhood had been compounded by a drug-addicted mother. She'd had little success with foster parents from an early age and ended up in care homes. He knew the types of places, had heard all the names before: they were the region's hate factories, churning out the types of conveyor-belt criminals he was depressingly familiar with. She suffered under what the social workers called a 'constellated disadvantage': a life of casual drug use and less casual criminality. Her death in a field before the age of nineteen could almost have been written in the poor girl's horoscope from the day she was born. What the detective also knew, however, was short lives like Leanne Dunn's were remarkable in being defined by their chaos. Murder victims mostly knew their killers and the likes of Leanne didn't mix with master criminals: they were the bottom feeders, the pond life, the scum that always left a sticky trail in their wake. He would find Leanne's killer – he knew it – because experience had taught him that unravelling the murder of a penniless prostitute was much easier than

343

that of a wealthy banker. Whoever her killer was didn't know it yet, but the DI was prepared to gamble on wrapping up more than one murder now; in that regard Leanne Dunn's short life and brutal death may yet serve some wider good.

Valentine had called the other detectives back from Mossblown and now they started to appear in the incident room.

'What you got there, boss?' said DS McAlister.

The DI took the page containing the picture of Leanne Dunn and pinned it on the board; he nodded to Phil and Sylvia as they arrived.

'This is our girl in the wood,' he said. 'Leanne Dunn, a prostitute who is well and truly known to us.'

'Local girl, then?' said Ally.

'Born and bred.' Valentine stood square-footed before the others. 'Right, you know what I want and you know I want it done yesterday . . .'

DS Donnelly stepped out from behind the filing cabinet he was leaning on. 'So, she's Ayr: then that narrows down the options.' He turned to Ally and showed his hands like he was testing for rain. 'We're talking one of Big Madge's girls or someone like Finnegan or Gillon.'

Ally nodded but Valentine halted him from speaking. 'Dunn was street brass according to her record, so that rules out Madge. I want all known bedsits, flats, bloody lay-bys used by Finnegan's girls and Gillon's looked at by uniform right away. I want the word out on this that I'm taking them all in, every last one. I want no brass in Ayr in any doubt that we will bust heads on this.'

DS McAlister seemed pensive, deep in thought, as he pushed his way to the front of the board and stood there.

'What is it, Ally?'

He pointed to the board. 'Here, sir: the tip murder, we were trying to trace a white van.'

'And?'

McAlister turned to face the team. 'Danny Gillon drives a white van.'

DS Donnelly nodded. 'He does too . . . Calls it his shagging wagon. And, boss, we had something like van tracks out at Mossblown as well.'

Valentine stepped away from the board and cut a path through the squad as he made his way towards the desk with the rest of the notes. When the DI collected the page he was looking for, he picked up his sports coat and started to slot his arms into the sleeves. His voice came loud and firm, followed by a wide-eyed trawl of the room: 'Right, Ally and Phil, I want you to take Danny Gillon's place right away. Get the word out to uniform too: I want all his known haunts dug up, and while we're at it every pub on the port . . . The Ship, Smugglers, the Anchor, the Campbelltown; anywhere I've missed, try there too.'

'Yes, sir.' The pair moved towards the door.

'Sylvia, you're with me . . .' said Valentine.

'Yes, sir.' She gripped the strap of her bag and turned to follow the DI as he made his way to the top of the stairs. 'Where are we going?'

At the first rung of steps, Valentine locked eyes with her. 'Leanne Dunn's last known address . . . It's in Lochside.'

DS McCormack tipped her head towards her shoulder and gripped the banister as the DI started to descend the stairs at speed. 'Right behind you, sir.'

The officers trailed the marked cars out of the station car park. A man with a dog made a sour look as he was flagged from the road, he leapt back to the pavement and the dog was jerked fast to his side by a tight leash. The persistent rainfall of earlier had diminished, but the road was still wet, and waterlogged potholes became short-lived geysers as the car's tyres crossed them. Valentine spun the steering wheel awkwardly and gunned the engine to keep pace with the marked cars. The houses and flats they sped past sat shrunken beneath an oppressive grey sky. A few heads turned, mouthed some words, but soon moved back in step with their drudge trails towards the town's centre. No one was heading to Lochside, it seemed, apart from the police officers; the grim council scheme was a place you went when all other options were no longer open to you.

Valentine glanced towards his passenger. DS McCormack's eyes flitted about the streets, eager for information. As they turned into the final road before Leanne Dunn's flat, an old man gave them a gummy smile then halted in the street and delivered them a V-sign salute.

'That'll be the welcoming party,' said McCormack, a smile sliding onto her face.

'We're as welcome as a dose of the clap around here.' He turned sharply into the parking area outside the flats and a spray of water was evacuated from a deep declivity in the road. As he parked up and exited the car, Valentine felt the tips of his fingers pulsating after the rapid friction of his movements. He broke into a jog as the uniforms congregated outside the door to the flats.

'What the bloody hell are you waiting for?' he called out.

The uniforms exchanged blank glances amongst each other.

'Put the door in for Christ's sake!'

An officer in a high-visibility stab-vest and protective helmet swung a small battering ram in front of him and charged the door. The rotten wood splintered and the weak lock retreated from the jamb as if backed by explosives. The squad piled onto the stairs.

'Right, up to the next flight,' said Valentine.

The sound of their boots on the stone steps sounded like an army manoeuvring. A door opened and a head popped out, then quickly retreated. The action was mimicked several times as they approached the flat that had been occupied by Leanne Dunn.

'That one . . .' Valentine brought the black mass of bodies to a halt outside the door. He moved to the front and battered with the heel of his hand. There was no reply. He made way for the officer with the battering ram once more.

'She's not in!' The words came from the flat next door. An old woman with a cardigan clutched tight to her chest stood half in the lobby, half out.

Valentine raised his hand to halt the uniform. 'Wait . . .' He approached the woman. 'What's that you say?'

Her hair was as white as cotton wool, sitting in limp curls around her heavily lined face. The long fingers worrying the seams of her cardigan were attached to liver-spotted hands. Her voice came quieter the second time she spoke. 'She's not there, hasn't been for days.'

The detective approached the old woman. 'This is Leanne Dunn we're talking about?'

She pinched her mouth, tightened her lips as if she was preparing to whistle. 'I don't know what her name is . . .'

Valentine removed the printout with the photograph from his pocket. His hand trembled a little from his recent exertions, but the woman didn't seem to notice. 'Is this her?'

She nodded. 'Yes.'

He looked back to the team and ordered them to go in. The sound of the wood splitting in the door caused the old woman to shrink further into her property. The detective stepped forward and adjusted his vision to take her in again. 'Can I ask, when did you last see her?'

She looked perplexed; her face became a ligneous mask and then her eyes flickered as if she sensed it was safe to proceed. 'There was a man round asking me that yesterday . . . He was screaming like billy-o.'

'A man?'

She nodded again; she was relaxing some now. 'He'd been round before.'

The sound of the officers in the next flat came through the thin plaster walls, and Valentine felt a sudden pang of sympathy for the old woman who'd had to endure the noise generated by the previous occupant. Is this how his country rewarded their elderly? A rathole flat in a drafty and decrepit ruin with prostitutes turning tricks a few feet away and their pimps shouldering the door whenever it took them? As his mind totted up the column of new facts, he knew at once who he was dealing with. 'A tall man, quite stocky?'

'Yes, he'd be about thirty or thirty-five . . .'

The thought that he was getting close to Gillon coalesced with an earlier emotion: there were three murders on his books and the disappearance of a schoolgirl from twelve years earlier. He didn't dare to think that he was close to a quick solution for those unsolved cases, or even getting close to finding the connecting link that might lead somewhere – a pointer to evidence or an indicator of what might have gone on. Right now all he had was questions and precious few answers. But the more he thought of Gillon, the more he felt he was the ice chilling his veins.

He turned for the other flat. 'Thank you . . . I'll send an officer round to get your details.'

As Valentine was entering Leanne Dunn's flat, he was distracted by movement in the corner of his eye. When he turned, he spotted someone on the steps, staring at him through the stanchions. She knew she had been recognised immediately and slunk back, running down the stairs.

'Hey!' Valentine's voice came like a howitzer. He ran to the top of the stairs and called again. 'Stay where you are.'

The thin girl in the tight blue dress froze on the spot. As the detective reached her, he took the last few steps slowly, then circled her like a lion taunting prey.

'Where do you think you're going, Angela?' he said.

The girl folded her arms, but seemed uncomfortable in the stance and unfolded them again quickly. As Valentine took her in, her lazy left eye drew the attention from her other features. She could have been described as pretty once, he was sure of that, but her looks had long since left the vicinity. No celebrity fitness video or cosmetics regimen was going to return them either; she'd gambled with what she'd been given and lost it.

'I'm not saying nothing . . .'

Valentine's chest was rising after the exertion of chasing her; his breath was heavy as he spoke. 'You know the drill, Ange: you can say what I want to hear now, or you can say it down the station.'

She shook her head. 'You'll get me killed, you will.'

'Oh, really . . . Like Leanne, you mean?'

Angela screwed up her features. 'What? I don't know what you're talking about.'

'That right? Funny you should say something like that when I've just seen Leanne cold as stone out in the wilds of Mossblown.'

349

Angela's mouth opened a little, but the corners stayed closed, stuck together by a heavy application of red lipstick. She stared at the detective for a few seconds then pressed her hand to the wall as if she was looking for support.

Valentine reached out to steady her. 'Here, sit yourself down . . .'

She folded her arms again, seemed to grip herself as if a saw blade was slicing through her middle. 'I need a fag . . .'

'Right, just wait.' He went to the top of the stairs and called out to the squad in Leanne Dunn's flat. DS McCormack came running, one hand in her bag removing a packet of cigarettes. Valentine caught the box of Benson & Hedges as she threw them and then nodded for her to join him on the stairs.

'Here you go, love,' he said.

Angela's long, thin fingers, the nails bitten to the quick, shook as she opened the packet and took out the pink plastic lighter inside. She drew out a cigarette and pressed it in her mouth, and instantly the filter tip became smeared in thick lipstick. 'I just saw her the other day . . .'

'Had she been arguing with Danny?'

The girl looked up; her eyes didn't seem to be able to focus. Valentine knew she would be needing a fix within an hour; her shoulders started to shiver as she spoke. 'No. Danny was with me.'

The DI looked towards McCormack and then back at the girl. 'Angela, I never asked you if Danny was with you.'

She flicked the cigarette ash on the stairwell, drew a deep drag from the tip. 'But he was, all day . . . and night.'

DS McCormack was moving her head from left to right as Valentine looked up from the stairs. He placed the sole of his shoe on the step Angela was sitting on and leaned forward. Before speaking, he pinched the tip of his nose between thumb

350

and forefinger and took a sharp breath. 'Look, Angela, I want you to think very carefully about what you're saying . . .'

She jerked her gaze towards him. 'He was with me.'

'Ange, I'm not buying that. It sounds too rehearsed to me.'

She returned her eyes front and brought the cigarette to her lips once more. 'I'm not saying any more.'

Valentine stepped away. He straightened his back and motioned for DS McCormack to follow him to the foot of the stairs.

'What do you make of that?' he said in a whisper.

'She's lying.'

'No kidding . . . Do you think Gillon's put her up to it or is she acting on instinct?'

McCormack turned to look at the prostitute. 'Hard to say.'

'Right, get her down the station and let her sweat for a bit . . . She'll be scratching at the walls for a fix soon enough. We can try her again then.'

'Yes, boss.'

46

VALENTINE WAS LOADING Angela in the back of the car, his hand pressed on the crown of her head to guide her in, as his mobile started to ring. He closed the door but kept an eye on her; she looked so thin and frail that he wondered if the handcuffs might slip off her delicate wrists.

'Yes, Valentine,' he said.

'Boss, we got him.' It was DS McAlister.

The DI turned away from the car. DS McCormack was getting into the passenger seat; she halted with one foot on the tarmac.

'Tell me you're talking about Danny Gillon.' He made a thumbs-up sign to McCormack.

'Picked him up at the Auld Forte . . . Had the van parked outside, which was a bit of a giveaway.'

Valentine thought to allow himself a moment of elation, but it soon passed; the squad was still a long way from where they wanted to be. 'Ally, what about the van?'

'What do you mean?'

The detective shook his head. 'The mud, Ally, was the van covered in mud from the field in Mossblown?'

There was a pause on the line. 'I can't see from here, boss . . . Do you want me to check it out?'

'It should have been the bloody first thing you checked out.' He reeled in his temper. 'Look, just get back to the station and fill me in there . . . but if there's mud on that van I want samples and I want it soil-matched with the tyre tracks at the Leanne Dunn site.'

McAlister's voice dropped; his initial enthusiasm seemed to have been drained away. 'Yes, boss . . . I'll do that right away.'

Valentine hung up. As he pocketed his mobile phone, he caught sight of DS McCormack's hungry gaze. He turned away from her and opened up the back door, the one through which a few minutes ago he had manoeuvred Angela. He raised his voice loud enough for everyone to hear: 'Good news, Ange . . . We have Danny to keep you company down the station.'

Her red mouth drooped. She seemed ready to allow words to pass her lips, but then she closed them tight and dropped her head towards her hands, which were cuffed in her lap.

'Nothing to say, Ange?' said Valentine. 'Well, I'm sure Danny will have plenty to say: that's always been my experience of the man, wouldn't you agree? Likes to try and talk his way out of trouble, Big Gillon, doesn't he?'

Angela sucked in her cheeks. When she turned to face the DI, she looked ready to spit. 'Leave me alone.'

'Oh, come on, Angela, you know there's no chance of that . . . It's murder we're talking about now, not just streetwalking.' He leaned back and slammed the car door shut. As he walked around the front of the vehicle, he kept his gaze firmly fixed on the prostitute; she followed him with her eyes.

Valentine got in the car and yanked on his seatbelt, then started the engine. He looked in the rear-view mirror as he spoke again. 'You better have a think about what you're doing, Ange. If Danny Gillon's going down for murder and you're telling me lies, then you'll be going with him. Think about that . . . and while you're at it, spare a thought for your friend Leanne, because if anyone needed looking out for, it was her.'

He turned the wheel and pulled out of the car park. He could see Angela staring out the window towards the block of flats and the group of uniformed police officers gathering in the street below. He tried to interpret her expression, but her face was unreadable. The detective knew things could get messy now: he was looking at hours wasted in interview rooms stringing together the stories of accomplished liars. It was a way of life to the likes of Gillon and Ange: their first instinct was to suppress the truth, even if it was in their own interest to reveal it. There was a buzzer that sounded in their heads when talking to police and it told them to revert to form, to obfuscate and to hinder. What he had in his favour, though, was the fact that they were both as likely as each other to sell out their own mother if it would save their skin. Angela was protecting her pimp now, but what did that really translate to? It was a sort of short-term self-preservation rooted to the fact that Gillon supplied her with trade and trips. When the reality dawned that Gillon was not going to be in a position to do either any more, then she'd see sense. At least, he hoped she would, and he hoped she would have something to say about Leanne Dunn's death.

Valentine followed a monochrome road beneath a blackening sky all the way back to the station. For no reason that he could pinpoint, the town of Ayr looked locked in an old movie, one that had been playing in his mind for as long as he could remember. The grim cast of characters made an almost motionless glissade through the wet and windy streets he knew so well. In the dying light they looked like shadows, or ghosts; they were phantom people trapped in a phantom reality that the detective had constructed for a town he took only an eschatological interest in. He couldn't quite recall having a need to escape before, but it was there now, fixed in his mind like it had been riveted there. He couldn't see how he had come to this point, or how the town had changed so quickly from a place people took holidays to a place where life was cheapened and degraded by a race into entropy. He'd once been amused by the recital of a local poet's tribute to Robert Burns, a fanciful recounting of his return to the town of his birth in the current day. Valentine had been amused by the poet's reaction to the one-way system and the out-of-town hypermarkets, but in retrospect those comments seemed nothing but the work of a churl – because if he came back now, Burns would be horrified; he'd gallop through the place faster than Tam o' Shanter haunted by any ghaists and houlets.

No words had passed between the occupants of the Vectra that was driven by Valentine, and when he parked it seemed almost an invasion of the enclosed space to open his mouth. He exited quickly and took two steps towards the back of the vehicle, where he motioned for Angela to get out. She slid herself along the back seat. She had the movements of a much older woman; her face was chalk white as she stood in the broad exposure of the car park.

'Come with me, Angela.' DS McCormack emerged from the car and beckoned the young woman towards the station.

Valentine nodded to the detective and mouthed, 'Thank you.'

He stood with the door open, a blustery wind picking up behind him, and stared at the dark patch on the backseat that he knew had been made by his own blood. The sight seemed to jolt him and he couldn't understand why; he had seen it so many times before that it shouldn't even be a concern. But it was, and he felt gripped by its strange sight: the long-standing stain hadn't changed shape or position, but somehow had more significance for the detective. As he stood, threaded to the image by his eyes, he had to shake himself out of a hypnotic trance. He slammed the door and walked towards the station, telling himself that to look back was to be lost. He needed to think about the future, about salvaging his career while he still could, and about securing the conviction of Leanne Dunn's killer.

In the open-plan station, Valentine caught sight of DS McCormack standing with Angela; she'd separated the prostitute from the other detectives and uniforms who had Danny Gillon handcuffed where he stood at the main desk. He seemed cocky and obstreperous as the officers booked him in. Valentine raised his hand and signalled to DS McAlister to separate from the group and join him by the stairs.

McAlister turned away from DS Donnelly and made his way to the DI.

'Hello, boss.' He smiled and tipped his head towards the crowd he had just left. 'Nice result, eh?'

Valentine held his face firm; his expression was immobile. 'We don't know that yet.'

'Well, we got him anyway . . . That's a start.'

'How's he been?' said Valentine.

McAlister inflated his cheeks and exhaled slowly before answering. 'Honestly?'

'I wouldn't want a lie.'

He looked away. 'Well, he's been playing the big innocent . . . and being really shirty with it.'

'What do you mean?'

McAlister scratched the top of his head and returned his gaze to the DI. 'When we clocked him in the pub he didn't even move, never got off his stool . . . He thought we were there for someone else.'

'He's acting it, Ally.'

'I don't know, boss, he looked rattled when we took him out . . . Quite a contrast to how relaxed he looked when we spotted him. If he's putting on an act then he's bloody good at it.'

Valentine put his hands in his pockets. 'I'll be the judge of that when I get him in the interview room.'

'You taking him down now, sir?'

He nodded. 'In a minute. Let them get the pair of them sorted first.'

DS McAlister turned back towards the others. 'OK, I'll get on with it.' As he went, he pointed a finger to the ceiling. 'Oh, and his van was clean.'

'How clean?'

'Spotless.'

Valentine shook his head and headed for the stairs. 'Aye, clean as one straight from the car wash, I'll bet.'

As he ascended the stairs, he met the chief super on the mid-landing. She seemed confident, almost jaunty. He didn't want to be the one to dispossess her of the notion since it was the first time in living memory he could recall seeing her this way.

'Good work, Bob,' she said. She was two steps past him and staring back up the stairs before she spoke again. 'I really didn't think you had it in you.'

If there was a reply queuing in his mind, it was some distance behind the other thoughts he had, ones like delivering her a lecture on the basics of policing and the finer points of employee etiquette. He resisted, however, because he had more important matters placing demands on his attention and any interaction would merely rob the CS of her misguided optimism.

In the incident room, Valentine rounded up the case notes and photographs he wanted for the interview with Danny

Gillon. He had already decided the questions he wanted answers to and how he was going to get them. Gillon might have been playing the innocent with Ally and Phil, but it would be harder to maintain in the sight of colour reproductions of recently mutilated corpses and the plain threat of a life sentence. Whatever it was that Gillon knew – and he was concealing something, of that Valentine had no doubt – the detective wanted it.

Valentine hung his grey dog-tooth sports coat on the coat stand at the end of the room and headed out to the vending machine to collect a cup of coffee. As he waited for the slow vend to materialise, the gurgitating coffee released its familiar aroma; it was enough to insinuate the hint of caffeine into his senses. He collected the cup and sipped. A long draft followed and then he made his way towards the interview room. Outside, a uniformed PC stood with DSs McAlister and Donnelly. The PC held out a packet of Club and a box of Bluebell matches for the detective.

'Thanks,' said Valentine. 'You pair set?'

They nodded, and McAlister spoke. 'I'll come in with you, sir.'

'Right, then let's get on with it . . . Phil, you and Sylvia get what you can out of Angela.'

'Yes, sir.'

As Valentine turned the handle on the door, he saw Danny Gillon raise his head from the small wooden table and let out a tut.

'I thought you were finished . . .' said Gillon.

Valentine smirked, then slapped the folder down on the table. 'You thought wrong, son.'

Gillon straightened his back and reclined in his chair; he eyed the cigarettes covetously.

'So, what's all this about?' he said.

'What's it all about?' said Valentine. 'Are you taking the piss, Danny?'

The stocky pimp rolled his eyes towards the roof beams. 'I told this one here that I don't know what any of this is about.'

'Aye, well . . . You might want to rethink that statement.' Valentine opened the folder and removed a picture of James Urquhart's corpse. He let the bloody and scarred flesh sit before him for a moment and then he removed another picture of the corpse of Duncan Knox and, finally, the picture of the corpse of Leanne Dunn.

Danny Gillon stared at the pictures; he seemed to have lost some of his assurance and several shades of his pallor. He opened and closed his mouth like a recently landed fish and then he pushed the pictures away.

'Not pretty, is it, Danny?' said Valentine.

Gillon was staring at the cigarettes; the detective picked up the pack and started to remove the cellophane wrapping. 'Where were you last night, Danny?'

He looked away. 'I was with Ange . . . You know that.'

Valentine started to laugh; McAlister joined him on a lower volume.

'Aye, you can laugh, but she'll back me up on that!'

'Do you think I care if you have a junkie streetwalker standing alibi for you, Danny?' said Valentine. 'This is a triple murder investigation, not a counter jump at the BP garage.'

Gillon stood up and hit his palms off the table. 'I don't know fuck all about that!'

The detective opened the box of cigarettes and slowly extended a single filter tip from the packet. 'Calm yourself down, Danny . . .' he said. 'Here, have a fag.'

Gillon snatched the packet and walked away from the table with the two officers. When he had lit up, he returned to his seated position and placed the cigarette box on the edge of the table.

'Ange's word's as good as anyone's,' said the pimp.

'Oh, aye ... and how do you work that out?' said DS McAlister.

'It just is. I mean, it's her word against yours.'

Valentine leaned forward. 'She's a drug-addled prostitute and you are her pimp who has form for beating the living daylights out of her ... What court are you putting this proposal to, Danny? A court of laughing gnomes wouldn't take you seriously!'

Gillon drew on the cigarette and the detective pushed the photographs back towards him. 'Think about it, Danny, think very carefully about what you're saying to me. Look at those pictures: three lives have been taken and we have to account for them. Now, so far I've got your face with a bull's eye on it pinned to my board and unless you convince me otherwise I'm sticking a dart in you.'

Gillon drew deeply on the cigarette. A grey trail of smoke escaped from the elongated ash tip as he spoke through his bottom row of teeth. 'I told you, I was with Ange.'

Valentine reached out for the photographs, collected them up and shuffled them into position in the folder. As he closed the blue folder completely, he pushed out the back of his chair and rose. He didn't look at Danny Gillon again. He turned to DS McAlister.

'Can you believe this idiot?' he said.

'You just can't help some people.'

'He thinks he's bulletproof, but he's more like the Yorkshire Ripper using Rose West as an alibi.'

McAlister laughed out. 'He's going down for the lot, boss.'

'Oh, I think so, Ally . . .'

The officers headed to the door and Valentine knocked twice. The PC opened up.

'Let us out, we're done with him.'

47

DI Bob Valentine stood outside the interview room and pressed his back to the wall. His shirt provided little insulation from the cold plaster and a shiver seemed to pass straight into his shoulder blades and down the thin sweat-line below. He widened the spread of his feet to add strength to his stance, but the detective didn't feel in the least way steady or confident. He'd thought he had something on Danny Gillon – they all did, especially the chief super – but now he wasn't so sure. Gillon didn't have the intelligence to bluff and yet he was assuredly defensive in his answers. There was no reason for him to keep what he knew to himself in the circumstances unless it was because he was afraid of greater consequences or was protecting someone. Neither of those two options made any sense to Valentine; there was no greater consequence than life imprisonment for three murders, unless you counted death itself. And Danny Gillon didn't regard anyone, save himself, as worth protecting; he wouldn't put his own neck on the block for anyone. Bits and pieces of thoughts crossed Valentine's mind like motes, but they were all indecipherable, fleeting particles of information. He needed to see the whole picture, not just isolated swatches whose details may or may not be of value when taken as part of the wider purview.

The DI's chest tightened and his breathing was stertorous as he paced the hallway between the interview rooms. There was a stopwatch on him now, he knew that. The latest murder in Mossblown would be latched onto by the press sooner or later, but if they got to it before tonight's news bulletins then he would face the likelihood of a full-scale press scrum in the morning. Dino had been on a melodramatic high since they'd pulled in Gillon, but that would become a crushing low if it yielded the wrong outcome. The case would be taken out of his hands – he could live with that – but any new investigation would go back to square one and there was no guarantee that his conclusions so far would be taken seriously. Valentine knew the murders of James Urquhart and Duncan Knox were connected – they knew each other – and something told him Janie Cooper and Leanne Dunn were victims of that association. He also knew that his instincts were less than worthless without any evidence to back them up, and he had nothing to place his finger on.

'Right, time to give Ange a rattle,' said the detective. He paced towards the interview room where DS Donnelly and DS McCormack had taken Angela. As he walked, he flicked through the blue folder trying to locate the one image that would deliver the most impact.

He thrust down the handle and the door screeched loudly as DI Valentine entered the room. He took firm and impressive strides towards the table in the centre of the room where the interview was underway. The officers eyed him with caution, but the predominant feature of Angela's look was fear.

'Right, I am not pissing about with you any more,' said Valentine, the heavy bass of his voice rattled round the room. 'Tell me how this happened now or I'm putting both you and Gillon away . . .' He slapped down the image of the bloodless face of Leanne Dunn.

Angela shrieked and turned away; her hands shot up to her face and she sobbed.

'Don't start with the bubbling, love,' said Valentine. He picked up the picture again and stuck it in front of her face. 'Do you see anyone crying for that lassie?'

'Get it away . . . get it away . . .' She rose from her chair and took two stumbling steps towards the shuttered window frame. Her arms went out to steady her when she reached the ledge.

Valentine followed her. 'This is Leanne . . . You remember her don't you . . . ? Leanne Dunn.'

Angela sobbed harder. 'Yes.'

'Then tell me where Danny Gillon's been and what he's been up to.'

She looked up through her reddened eyes. 'I don't know.'

'Say again . . .'

She straightened her arms in front of her. 'I don't know. All right? I don't know where he's been.'

'So you were bullshitting us?'

'Yes . . .'

'Once more, loud enough for us all to hear.'

'Yes. I made it up. I wasn't with Danny.'

Valentine turned away from her, as he paced towards the table he slapped the photograph of the corpse of Leanne Dunn back on top of the folder and paused before the officers. 'Get her cleaned up and get some coffee into her.'

'Yes, sir.'

'Then get out on that street and start rattling cages . . . all Gillon's known haunts. If he's been seen in the last few days I want the where and when in writing and I don't care if you have to smash teeth or heads to get it.'

Valentine left the room, closed the door firmly and returned to the hallway where DS McAlister was waiting. The DS had his hands in his pockets and quickly removed them as he spotted the detective; he looked as if he was getting ready to break into a run.

'Everything OK, sir?'

He pointed to the room where Danny Gillon was. 'Follow me.'

Valentine's footsteps sounded loudly on the floor as he entered the room. He closed the short distance between the door and the table where Gillon was seated with a cigarette in his hand – Valentine snatched the burning cigarette and threw it at the wall. He stood between Gillon and the table and folded his arms. He was sneering as he spoke.

'Right, Danny, seems like Ange has had a change of heart . . . You've lost your alibi.'

He sniffed. 'So . . . ?'

'Not good enough for you?' He turned to McAlister and held out his hand for the blue folder. 'OK, we've got more . . . Greta Milne, Angela's neighbour, has ID'd you as the bloke knocking ten bells out of her door the other night.' He slapped down the folder. 'Speak to me, Danny. Now.'

Gillon looked at the wall, and his eyes latched onto the point where the cigarette burned on the floor. For a moment, Gillon's mask of assurance slipped and he looked alone, without a friend in the world. An almost imperceptible tic started in his left temple and then he wiped away at his mouth with the back of his hand.

'I want a lawyer . . .' he rasped.

Valentine shook his head. 'You give me what I want.'

Gillon looked up; a grey tongue flashed on his parched lips. He shrugged. 'What's that?'

'Everything, Danny . . . From start to finish.'

The pimp turned away again, his shoulders drooped now. He seemed to be physically shrinking before Valentine's eyes.

'I want to know, if I tell you . . . then none of this comes back on me.'

'Danny, I'm not trading favours here. You start speaking or I walk out that door. It's your choice.'

Gillon took a deep breath and looked at the table. As he started to speak he sounded like he was reading from a prepared manuscript detailing his confused thoughts.

'See your murders, the guy from the bank and the other one . . .'

'Knox?'

He nodded. 'Aye, well, Leanne knew them.'

'What do you mean "knew them"?'

Gillon fidgeted on the chair. 'I want to know I'll be looked after if I talk.'

'No deals, Danny.'

He slumped closer to the table. 'She knew them from way back: well, the Knox one from when she was in that home place . . .'

'She knew him as a child?'

He nodded. 'She might have known them both, then.' He looked uncomfortable, as if detailing secrets that the dead would have preferred to take with them. 'They used to come round, like years back, when Leanne was . . . you know.'

'When she was working as one of your prostitutes?'

He crossed his legs and started to finger the hole in the knee of his jeans. 'Well, not really . . . She was only young.'

Valentine moved away from the table and retrieved the chair he had been sitting on earlier. 'Let me get this straight, Danny: you procured an underage Leanne Dunn for Duncan Knox and James Urquhart?'

'No, it wasn't like that. She wasn't working properly then . . . Just them, she knew them both from before.'

366

Valentine's palms started to sweat. 'So your involvement was what? Estate agent . . . ? Hotelier? This went on in your property, I take it?'

He grimaced. 'She went to work there in the end, yeah.'

The DI watched as Gillon avoided all eye contact. He was trash, worse than that. Valentine wanted to raise him from the chair and clamp his hands around his neck. He spoke about a young girl's life being ended before it had begun as if it was a just another transaction. He cared more about his shabby van or being kept in cigarettes than he did Leanne.

'Was Leanne the only girl you got them?' said Valentine.

'I didn't get a girl for them. Look, it wasn't like that . . . I don't deal with beasts.'

'Was there another girl, Danny?' The anger in his voice was unmistakeable.

'No. No way . . . Never.'

Valentine let the pimp's blood cool. He looked agitated, pensive as the DI spoke again. 'Who killed Urquhart and Knox?'

'I don't know who did that . . . How could I know that?'

'You don't know?'

'Of course I don't.'

'But you seem to know a great deal, Danny . . . Why am I only finding this out now?'

'What do you mean?'

Valentine leaned forward and flattened his palms in front of him. 'I mean you've known about these paedos for years and never told a soul. Where they paying you hush money?'

'No. I kicked them out. I didn't want any part of it, but they kept coming round to see Leanne behind my back. I told her it wasn't bloody on, but they had some hold over her.'

'What hold?'

'I don't know, just a hold; she said they were her keepers.'
Gillon seemed tired, his voice trailing now. He had the look of a man who felt repulsed by the discovery of his involvement with people he had nothing but contempt for. His self-esteem was slipping and sliding like lacustral sludge beneath him.

'Why didn't Leanne come to the police?'

He snatched an answer. 'I don't know.'

'I don't believe you.'

Gillon looked up from his misery. 'She wanted to. I–I . . .'

'What? You stopped her?'

He nodded.

'Why would you do that?'

Gillon shrugged; his mouth had started to twitch in time to the uncontrollable tapping of his foot on the floor.

'Oh come on, Danny, you must have had a reason, there must have been something in it for you . . .'

He stayed silent. Valentine understood how the criminal mind worked. He had spent years of his life dealing with people like Danny Gillon and knew he could second-guess them. There was no need to coax out a motive or search their psyche for reasons why or how: it was all about opportunity – if it existed, they would take it.

'I'm going to ask you again, Danny, because I can tell you want it off your chest . . . Why didn't you let Leanne come to the police when Urquhart and Knox were killed?'

'I don't know.'

'But now you know that was a mistake . . .'

He shrugged again. 'I suppose.'

'No suppose about it, Danny . . . If Leanne Dunn had told us what she knew about those murders, you wouldn't be sitting here. And Leanne might not be in the mortuary.'

He looked up. 'I wanted money for her.'

368

'What, who from?'

'I thought . . . the papers.'

Valentine's palms tingled a million pins and needles pressed on the underside of his fingers as he got up from his chair and approached Gillon. 'You went to the papers: who?'

'Just some guy . . .'

'Just some guy who?' Valentine's voice rose again; it echoed off the bare walls.

'Just a hack. He said he would pay. He spoke to Leanne a few times, I thought he would pay up . . .'

'A name, give me his name.'

'Sinclair . . . His name was Sinclair.'

The detective noted the name but felt a strange compunction to object. When it came, his voice didn't sound like his own: 'Cameron Sinclair . . . ? From the *Glasgow-Sun*?'

Gillon chamfered the table's edge with his fingernail. 'That's him, yeah.'

Valentine moved his head, turned his eyes away as if he was searching for something; he found a chink of light that sat in an oblong blur beneath the doorway. 'You spoke to him about Leanne?'

'Well, aye . . . but she spoke to him too.'

He couldn't take in what he was hearing. As he got out of his seat and edged forwards, Valentine's stomach cramped tiny arrows of pain jabbed at his diaphragm. His thoughts were working in reverse, moving backwards to the press conference where he'd seen Sinclair and the post he'd left on his daughter's Facebook timeline, then through to the bribery affair that had led to DS Rossi's suspension.

'When did you last see him?

'I don't know . . . Few days ago. I spoke to him on the phone; I told him Leanne had done a runner.'

'He knows she went missing?'

'Yeah, I just said that.' He leaned onto the edge of his seat. 'I didn't know she was dead . . .'

The DI struggled to rein in his thoughts as his intestines tightened. Nothing seemed to make sense. He rubbed at his ribcage as he headed for the door.

Gillon's voice rose, assailed the room. 'Hey, where are you going?'

Valentine banged on the door with the side of his hand, and as it opened he turned to Gillon and pointed. 'Don't worry, I've not finished with you, not by a bloody mile.'

The DI pushed the door and left the interview room, his mind thumbing a new index of possibilities. The feeling of getting close to a killer that had gripped Valentine when he'd first approached Gillon was gone now; he felt like he'd been dunking for apples in an empty barrel.

DS McAlister appeared in the corridor behind him, and he fanned a lapel nervously as he spoke. 'Well, boss, what do you make of that?'

'Make of it . . . There's nothing to bloody make of it, Ally.'

The sharpness of the DI's words hung between them. 'Do we bring in Sinclair?'

Valentine nodded. 'Of course we do . . . Now, Ally.'

The DS turned and broke into a jog. 'Yes, sir.'

'And, Ally . . . Get onto his paper. I want to know what kind of copy he's been filing lately. And if the editor's thinking of running anything like Leanne Dunn's last interview then read him the bloody riot act – he'll be grateful he got it from you and not me.'

370

48

DI Bob Valentine knew his options were rapidly running out. He couldn't count on Danny Gillon to reveal any more information, and what he had revealed was something and nothing. The nothing part of it was already knowledge to Valentine, of a sort, though the confirmation that Urquhart and Knox were connected through Leanne did little to further his understanding of the murders that had been committed. The something – that Cameron Sinclair had been probing the case's seedy underside – was, he supposed, to be expected. It would take a wilful naivety on his part to assume the Rossi affair and Sinclair's own suspension from the *Glasgow-Sun* would thwart his ambitions any; he was in too much of a hurry and too rash a man. Quite what the consequences of Sinclair's actions had been remained unknown – the detective knew it wouldn't be without recrimination, but questioned how far he would go.

The part that puzzled Valentine the most was Gillon's revelation about the length of time Leanne had been known to Urquhart and Knox. If he was to be believed then she had been abused in care when she was still a child, and the timing was close to the disappearance of Janie Cooper. Was there a wider paedophile ring in operation? If there was, and he felt certain of it, then it was on his patch and had some history. The roots would go deep. Valentine scrunched his eyes and tried to process the thoughts that were galloping through his mind. There would be another case now: a cold investigation of the children's home and the broad sweep of Urquhart and Knox's associations. He could see the helical strands of the cases intertwining, but he knew he must separate them. It was impossible to process so many possibilities, so many 'what ifs' and 'wherebys'. The detective's main target had to be the murder investigations that were in hand and the rest would have to wait, but the cries of justice for the children burned like a fierce acid corroding him from the inside.

The skies outside King Street station were already darkening as Valentine stood at the window stroking a deep ache inside his ribcage. He watched an old man navigate the road as the wind picked up, blowing a stray newspaper that attached itself to the man's leg. Another man, younger, made to wrestle the paper from him; the scene was almost comical, had the quality of slapstick, but the detective felt too raw to be amused. He turned from the window and walked back towards the main incident room. DS McAlister stood by his desk, deep lines standing out on his forehead as he crossed the floor towards the board.

'What's that you're sticking up, Ally?' said Valentine.

McAlister turned round to face him. A dull glaze had settled on his eyes. 'The Sinclair stuff, sir . . .'

'Give me that.' He snatched the papers from his hand. 'We'll keep that to ourselves for now.'

'But . . .'

Valentine cut him down. 'No buts about it, Ally, if Dino gets wind of Gillon's ramblings then she'll be on us like a dog on chips.'

McAlister bowed to superior wisdom. 'I called the paper . . . spoke to the editor.'

'What did Jack have to say for himself?'

'Hasn't heard from Sinclair since his suspension over the bribery allegations.'

'Did you believe him?'

He shrugged. 'Well, I'd no reason not to. He didn't go as far as calling Sinclair a square peg, but I got the impression he was a bit surprised that I seemed so interested in him.'

'Just because he's a public schoolboy doesn't make him as pure as the driven snow, Ally.'

'I know. Anyway, Phil and Sylvia checked out his flat and he's not there. They're going to check a few hacks' drinkers on their way back.'

'He's not there?'

'Aye, he gave a forwarding address of a guest house in Queen's Terrace, but he was only there for the one night.'

Valentine cached away a mounting frustration. He raised himself onto the edge of the nearest desk and listened to the hammering inside the smithy of his mind. 'Right, get onto all your touts, even the ones you haven't seen for a while, and find him. Bloody Ayr's not got that big and he isn't the invisible man.'

'Yes, boss . . .' He stood splay-legged for a moment and then eased himself onto the adjacent desk. 'What's going on, sir?'

Valentine threw up his hands. 'At this stage, Ally, who knows?'

'Do you see Sinclair in the frame?'

'What's his motive?'

McAlister shrugged and let his vision drift. 'Well, it's a cracking story whichever way you look at it.'

'Oh, come on, that's taking manufacturing the news a bit far.'

He slid off the desk. 'Well, maybe he had some connection

to Urquhart and Knox that we've not seen . . . We've not been looking at Sinclair.'

'So he's an unknown factor to us . . . So are you, Ally, we haven't looked into your background on this one: does that make you a suspect?'

'Get real, sir.'

Valentine smirked; he took the putdown because he deserved it. 'Who's to say you're not on the right lines, Ally? The truth of the matter is right now we don't know. There are too many variables. Has Sinclair been up to something? Yes, I've no doubt. And has Gillon been up to something too? Yes, I've no doubt about that.'

'So where do we go from here?'

'Where can we go? We can't magic up extra variables to the mix . . . we have to wait and see.'

'Dino will love that. She went out that door tonight expecting us to have it wrapped up by the morning.'

Valentine shook his head: the mere mention of the chief super's name stuck a spike in an exposed nerve. 'Bloody deluded bitch . . .'

McAlister gnawed his bottom lip as he spoke. 'You know she's going to drop the bomb tomorrow morning.'

'Not if we don't give her the chance.'

'Meaning?'

The DI raised himself from the desk and headed for the glassed-off office at the end of the room. 'There's more than one way to skin a cat. Get onto those touts now, and don't expect to get home tonight!'

DS McAlister collected his jacket from the back of his chair and headed for the door as Valentine stepped into his office. He stood for a moment in the centre of the room and dipped his head; there was a penny sitting on the ground that compelled him to pick it up. As he reached down for the coin he remembered his grandmother; he hadn't thought of her for a long time.

'Pennies from heaven . . .'

He took the penny, walked towards his desk, removed his chair and sat down. As he looked at the shiny coin, he turned it over in his fingers. It seemed to sing to him of times gone by. His grandmother had been a superstitious woman; she would never allow a hat on a bed or an umbrella raised indoors. If a cat crossed her path there was a reason for it and a spilled saltcellar took a pinch over the shoulder. He smiled thinking of her now: she had been a kind woman, he had always remembered her that way. She once told him, when he was a young boy, that when you found a penny it was someone in heaven's way of telling you that they were with you, thinking of you. He smiled at the coin, and the memory of his grandmother, and wondered who in the heavens would be watching over him now.

The blue folder containing the details from the Janie Cooper case was still sitting on his desk. He turned over the cover and saw the picture of the little girl staring back at him. The image of the doll was there too, sticking out from beneath a sheaf of notes. She had been swinging the doll and smiling at him when he passed out at the Coopers' home. Since that day he had tried to push the image from his mind and tell himself that it hadn't happened. He knew DS McCormack thought differently, but she had her reasons for that. There may indeed be more things on heaven and Earth, as she said, but he was a man of reason and hoped to remain so. Valentine didn't want to rely on guesswork to find the killer of three people and solve the disappearance of a schoolgirl more than a decade ago, but the more he searched the further he seemed to get from a solution. He leaned over the desk and put his head in his hands. The blood was rushing hot in his veins. For a moment the sounds of the street brimmed in his ears and then lapsed into no more than a dull humming. He could have been anywhere: at home, on a beach, it didn't matter. He was tired, he wanted to rest, and was ready to give in to sleep. He knew his body was not what it had once been, he was weaker now, perhaps too weak for the job he had taken on, but it was too late to make that conclusion. The detective would see the job out now, even if it killed him.

As he removed his hands from his eye sockets and allowed his gaze to take in the full extent of the incident room, he spotted DS Donnelly and DS McCormack walking through the door. A brief pang of optimism lit inside him and he rose from his chair and tapped on the windowpane to beckon them in. As he checked the clock on the far side of the room, he knew the evening news headlines were just about to start. He was leaning over to switch on the television as the officers came in.

'Hello, sir,' said DS Donnelly, his voice a low growl.

'Well . . . What did you turn up?' said Valentine.

Donnelly sighed and motioned to DS McCormack.

'Not good, sir,' she said.

'What do you mean, not good?'

'We did the usual points of interest . . . Nothing. No one's seen hide nor hair of Sinclair for days.'

'Have you rung the B&Bs . . . the hotel bookings?'

'Yes, boss, we tried that,' said Donnelly. 'What are the odds on him booking himself under his own name? He's not stupid.'

DS McCormack spoke up. 'And he obviously doesn't want to be found . . . Apparently he was a regular in the Phoenix

– there every night – and two days ago he vanished without trace.'

Valentine flagged the officers down. 'Right, shush . . . I want to hear this.'

As the news headlines played on the small portable screen, he reached down to turn up the volume. The familiar face of the early evening news anchor read out an abridged snapshot of the day's events: a fatal road accident on the A9 was followed by a Royal visit to Deeside and a factory closure in Broxburn. There was no mention anywhere of the west coast of Scotland; for once, Ayrshire was gratefully ignored.

'Well, that's something,' said McCormack. 'Gives us some breathing space.'

Valentine flicked off the television. 'Maybe twelve hours if we're lucky.'

The officers looked at each other with heavy eyes.

'So, what now, boss?' said Donnelly.

Valentine's answer was short. 'Nothing.'

'Come again?'

'Unless you're hiding something that's going to spark my interest, Phil, then nothing . . . You might as well both go home.'

They glanced at each other again.

McCormack pitched up on her toes and raised her voice. 'Well, we can keep searching the town for Sinclair.'

'And what makes you think you'll do any better than uniform? It's like Phil said: he's smart and doesn't want to be found.'

'So we just give up?' said Donnelly, his voice following the same peaks as McCormack's.

Valentine shook his head. 'I didn't say that. I said you both go home and get some rest; it's been a long day. If anything changes, I'll let you know. I'd sooner have you both fresh for tomorrow.'

Donnelly inflated his cheeks and exhaled slowly. He turned for the door and waved farewell to the others. When he had left, DS McCormack lowered her voice to a near whisper. 'Is everything OK, sir?'

Valentine turned back to the television screen and pressed the on switch. 'Perfectly, Sylvia. Go home.' He turned to wave her out of his office. 'You heard me, give me some peace to catch the headlines on the other channel.'

The detective reclined in his chair and raised his ankle towards his knee. He stared through the blinds towards the bottom of the incident room and watched Donnelly and McCormack put on their coats and make their way through the door. As he returned to the television screen, he lunged forward and flicked the channel to the other side. He felt sure that both stations ran with much the same output, but wanted to check. He sat through twenty minutes of trivia masquerading as news-entertainment, a schedule of football fixtures aimed at the recently lobotomised and a weather report by a glamour model in a cocktail dress. When he was sure Ayrshire was not making the headlines on any of the main stations, he switched the television set off and closed his eyes before lowering his head onto the desk and giving in to his exhaustion.

DS McAlister was arriving back in the empty office when Valentine next looked up. The large incident room was empty, with only the hum of strip lights and the occasional gurgle from the coffee machine attempting to suggest otherwise. McAlister didn't seem to notice the detective until he called out on his way to greet him.

'Any luck, son?' said Valentine.

McAlister stood silently, his face stone as he shook his head.

378

'Not a thing. I don't know what to say, boss.'

'You don't need to say anything.'

'Well, there's nothing to say . . .'

Valentine pulled out a chair and directed McAlister to sit down. He reached out for another chair and dragged it by its castors towards him, then sat with his chest leaning on the chair's high back.

'Look, Ally, I know you want this bastard as much as I do. I can see it: that's why I bumped you up to DS when Paulo lost the plot . . .'

'You're not wrong, boss.'

'But I don't want you to think you owe me for that. You deserved the promotion and it was coming your way sooner or later.'

He looked perplexed, shrugging and showing his palms. 'OK . . .'

'You see, I'm going to ask you to do something, but you don't have to say yes.'

His eyes widened. 'Do something . . . What?'

'Now remember you're under no obligation. You can say no and I won't hold it against you.'

'I understand what you're saying, boss.'

Valentine leaned back from the chair; he decided he might be more comfortable standing. 'You've got your whole career in front of you, son, and you have to think about that, but if you're game, and you trust me, I think we can close this case tonight.'

McAlister pressed the palms of his hands firmly onto his trouser fronts. His jaw was tight in his face as he spoke. 'Well, I'm in . . . Just tell me what you want me to do.'

The detective reached a hand out and placed it on DS McAlister's shoulder. 'Good, lad.'

379

49

DI BOB VALENTINE KNEW things weren't quite as they should be at home. He had taken on the case and returned to active duty without even consulting his wife, and she had every right to object. When he thought about Clare receiving the call to say her husband might not make it through the night, his low reserves of remaining strength left him. She was fragile, Clare, she always had been. He had noticed the trait early, when they were taking those first tentative steps together as a couple, but he had seen others like her shed the sensitivity when they settled down. Valentine wanted to provide the security of a home and children for Clare, he wanted to see her start to feel secure in herself, in her world, but it had never happened. She would always be highly strung or one of those types people spoken of as suffering with their nerves. He remembered her father had said it was an artistic temperament that afflicted her. At the time it seemed like a stigma, but his father-in-law joked they would always have a beautifully turned-out home, as if it was some kind of compensation. Valentine knew now that his wife's fragility was more than a trait, there would be a mental-health scale that some doctor or psychiatrist could place her on. She was depressive or bipolar or suffered from seasonal affective disorder. It didn't matter what the modern nomenclature was. She was still Clare, still the mother of his children and his wife.

Valentine raised the telephone receiver and dialled home.

The ringing on the line filled him with the same dread it always did now. There were simply no words to reveal to Clare that the job had won again, that he was not coming home as planned. She would be angry, at best; offhand with him at worst. Did it matter which? Sometimes the short burst of belligerent temper was preferable to the stony silence that left him wondering just where and when the blow would come.

'Hello,' he said. The line stayed silent. 'Hello, Clare . . .'

It wasn't his wife who had answered. 'Oh, hello, Bobby.'

'Hello, Dad . . . Where's Clare?'

He heard the old man negotiating the windowsill where the phone sat, unravelling the wires and taking a seat. The puffed cushions sighed at his back. 'She's, erm, taken a bit of a lie-down, son.'

Something didn't sit right with him. 'What did you say, a lie-down?'

There was a slapping sound on the other end of the line, and his father's tone changed. 'It's just me and Mr McIlvanney here just now . . . A great book this, *Strange Loyalties*.'

He knew all about those; his father was being deceitful, changing the subject. It was one of those perfectly honed skills of the experienced police officer to be able to detect lies, white or otherwise, in those with whom he had an intimate knowledge. There was no mistaking the twitching antennae. 'You wouldn't be changing the subject on me, Dad?'

He sighed, exasperated or too aware of the futility of his stance. 'Clare is, as you know, one in a million, but she has her little . . . moments.'

'What's happened?'

'Look, nothing's happened, she's fine.' His voice slowed into a reassuring drawl, extinct of all emotion. 'You know how

381

she gets: well, she had one of those days, but we had a little chat and now she's fine.'

Valentine read the gaps in his speech more than he did the actual words. He knew his wife, but he also knew his father's way was to adopt a less-said-soonest-mended philosophy. But something had happened, he knew that much, and it worried him. His mind batted out the possibilities like breakers battering the shore: they couldn't be ignored but nor could he do anything about them.

'All right, Dad, if you say so . . .' he paused briefly. His thoughts coalesced with some unspoken understanding he knew they shared. 'If you see her, tell her I'm thinking of her and I'll be home as soon as I can be. She's not to worry.'

'Yes, son, I'll do that.' he said. 'Goodbye now.'

Valentine lowered the receiver into its cradle and stood staring at his desk for a few seconds; he wasn't quite sure he had handled the conversation, or indeed the situation, effectively, but he knew there were few other options available to him. His fingers tweaked the corners of his mouth, as if sealing in words, thoughts. He would see Clare later and explain things, everything. If he could make her see what he had been through, spell it all out, maybe she would understand she didn't have the monopoly on life's defeats.

DS McAlister paused outside the door and gently tapped his knuckles off the glass. His neck, at full stretch seemed almost dislocated from his body. 'Is now a good time, sir?'

'Yes, come in . . . Sorry, Ally, I had a personal call to make.' He let his previous lines of thought turn to ashes and scattered them on the wind. Focus was everything.

'It's all right, I understand.' He took a step inside and closed the door behind him.

'So, about this grand plan of mine.' Valentine raised the

blue folder from his desk and turned it towards the DS. It sat between them, commanding the room like a model army. 'Take a look at that . . .'

McAlister leaned forward. 'A tyre cast . . .'

'From Mossblown.'

The officer looked at the pictures and read the accompanying notes, hungry eyes flickering like sparks rising from a campfire. 'Lab boys say it's not from Gillon's van.'

'That's right . . .' The DI paused, for effect mostly, but also on instinct. 'Which means it's from another vehicle.'

McAlister lowered the file. His gaze thinned now, his pupils pinpoints of concentration acting as the advance party of pertinent thought. 'Which means he's not working alone.'

'Exactly.' Valentine leaned his back against the window, and the Venetian blinds crumpled. 'Danny Gillon isn't going to win *Mastermind* any time soon, but he's not a complete idiot either. He knows about self-preservation and he knows when to keep his trap shut.'

'I think I see where you're going with this, sir.'

'Do you?' He eased forward, forcing the blinds to sing out again. 'I mean, Ally, do you really? I wasn't joking when I said I was asking you to put your job on the line.'

The DS remained silent. He pressed a crease into the corner of his mouth: it was an insouciant gesture, a glimpse into a mind that had ran the gamut of consequences and couldn't care less what they brought; it was the outcome alone that concerned him.

Valentine nodded and smiled when he saw Ally was onside. 'OK then, if you're game, here's what I'm proposing. We give Gillon his freedom tonight – let's see where he leads us.'

'Oh, Christ.' He nervously pinched the tip of his nose. 'I mean, yeah. Let's do it.'

383

'Are you sure, Ally?' He took another step forward, fixed him with a flat, expressionless look as devoid of coercion as he could manage. 'You won't get a chance to change your mind.'

'Sir, the way I see it, if we don't, then in the morning we've lost the case, and if Sinclair's still in town, this is our last chance.'

Valentine held out his arms, then brought his palms together in an ear-splitting clap. There was no going back now. 'OK, then. We let the bastard out . . . for a few hours.'

McAlister smiled, cautiously at first, but widening with a growing confidence he seemed uncertain of his right to possess. 'Aye, but he's not to know that.'

As the DI walked towards the door, he snatched his grey dog-tooth sports coat from the back of his chair. In the main incident room his strides were purposeful but his stomach churned with the uncertainty of the action he was taking. If he was to make this gamble pay off, however, he knew he had to convince himself otherwise. There was no room for detracting thoughts or the distraction of doubt. It was all or nothing, because if he looked at what was on the line, it was already over. On the stairs down to the cells, Valentine turned to catch sight of DS McAlister: his face was ashen and immobile, making him look younger than his years. The image struck the detective like a body blow; he knew there was more at stake than his own washed-up career, and the heavy responsibility unsettled him. He knew he needed to push all his cares and concerns away, however; the idea of gambling on such a grand scale without the nerve to back it up was lunacy.

Outside the cells he looked at the desk and summoned the custody sergeant. It was Alec Laird on duty, his deep tan and lightened hair proclaiming his recent visit to warmer climes like a billboard. He eyed the two officers and tipped his head in a knowing nod. Valentine hoped the holiday high hadn't worn off yet.

'Hello, Bob,' said the sergeant.

'Alec . . .' He picked up the duty log and ran a finger down the column of names and cells. 'Right, number four can breathe easy . . .'

Sergeant Laird recovered the logbook and presented Valentine with a narrow, searching stare. 'That's Big Danny Gillon . . . Thought he was in some hot water?'

The detective shook his head and snatched a pen from the desk without returning the look. 'Gillon's always in hot water. Not bloody hot enough this time, mind you.' He scratched his signature in the book.

'Danny's always been a daft boy.' The sergeant looked down at the logbook for what seemed like an eternity. If he chose to be difficult, thought Valentine, then everything would be ruined – the plan would go no further. He jerked back his head as the sergeant took the logbook and hung it on its brass hook, checking the clock on the wall behind him. 'His problem's that he likes to run with the big dogs . . . but he's just a bloody chihuahua!'

McAlister and Valentine emitted the usual drone of enforced laughter that was the accustomed response to such a remark and turned for the door. The DI spoke: 'He's got a van in as well, give it back to him. We won't be needing it now the trail's run cold.'

The sergeant nodded and raised a hand, still smiling at the plaudits to his humour. 'No bother. Goodnight, lads.'

On the way out to the car park, Valentine's knees were loosening, but he tried to keep his wilting resolve from McAlister. He knew he needed to convince him that their mission was at least partway capable of success; after all, the

DS had plenty at stake. Valentine was leading the way: it was his idea, his gamble, and he needed to present a confident front to get the result he wanted. Of course, it was all bluff, but he couldn't show that. Not for a second. He painted on his poker face and lengthened his stride in an act of mock defiance.

'He seemed to buy that well enough,' said McAlister.

'Why shouldn't he?'

The blunt rebuttal buoyed the DS. 'No reason, I suppose.'

On the way to the car, Valentine extended the remote locking and the indicator lights flashed at the vehicle's corners. It felt like a flag waving, a beacon: they were really doing this. When they got inside, the detective rolled down his window and craned his neck out. The air was cold and still.

'I can see Gillon's van from here,' he said.

'Where do you think he'll lead us?'

Valentine turned towards McAlister and dipped his brows, and the assuredness of his voice surprised them both. 'Well, I'll be bloody disappointed if it's back to the Auld Forte bar.'

'You and me both, sir.'

The night air defeated him and he turned up the window again, but kept a few inches of it open in the hope that some of the car's tension would escape. He had no reason to believe that things would go their way, but tried to tell himself that the bigger the risk, the bigger the reward. He had been backed into a corner and knew that there was only one way out. Had it always been like this for him, he wondered: the hard way or the harder way? He had taken risks before – even with his own life – but this was different, felt like something else. As his thoughts swam, he tried to avoid their desperate struggles, to rope in a port of calm. He needed to find some space to think about what he was doing, not what he feared might happen.

'No matter what happens tonight, Ally, don't let Gillon out your sight.'

'Christ above, I don't even want to think about losing him, sir.'

'And I don't want you to either . . . But if things go tits-up for whatever reason, stick with him.'

'Yes, sir.'

As they readied themselves for the night's eventualities, they seemed to come crashing down upon them like a violent hailstorm. There was no room for preparation now. There was no place to retreat and rethink the wisdom of what they were doing. The station doors swung open and a thickset figure in a denim jacket emerged into the darkness. He stood for a moment lighting a cigarette and then he loped down the steps, followed by a plume of white smoke. Danny Gillon looked over his shoulder as he walked towards his van, then spun the keys around his finger and started to jog. He looked cocky, confident. Like a man who knew he was to be feared and wielded the assurance like a claymore.

'Seems keen,' said McAlister.

'Let's hope so, let's hope he's bloody keen and bloody worked up.'

As Gillon started the van and moved onto the road, he indicated a right turn on the roundabout ahead. Valentine engaged the clutch and pulled out behind with a sense of dread building in the pit of his stomach. The white van followed the pothole-pitted road round to the traffic lights and took a left onto the one-way system of the Sandgate. As the van proceeded through the next set of lights and chuntered uphill towards Wellington Square, the route seemed to indicate the next move would be in the direction of the plush mansions of Racecourse Road.

'Where the hell is he going?' said McAlister.

'Well, it's not to any kip-house or B&B . . . Unless it's a very nice one.'

'He's heading out to Alloway.'

Valentine grabbed a glance at McAlister as the van crossed a box junction and proceeded past the desolate playing fields. The road widened, presenting snatches of shoreline and blue sea. From time to time the Isle of Arran came, cloud-wreathed, into view as wide driveways winked between Victorian villas. By the time the white van had passed the entrance to the rarefied echelons of Belleisle golf club, it was clear Gillon was either leaving town or heading to an address the officers had visited themselves only a short time ago.

'This is very odd,' said Valentine, drumming the dash.

'I didn't expect this at all . . .'

'Well, why would you . . . ? There's nothing to suggest Danny Gillon's had any contact with the Urquharts. But here he is . . .' His fingers rose from the dash and pointed, palm up, towards the unfolding scene. 'Pulling into their drive.'

Valentine depressed the brake and worked down the gears. He brought the car to a standstill behind the drystone wall and watched as the van rolled to a halt, spluttering black smoke onto the driveway. Gillon stalled momentarily, seemed to be gathering wit or wile, it was impossible to tell which, as the sudden parallax shielded his face from view. He exited the vehicle quickly, slamming the door loudly behind him, and proceeded to the front window of the property, where he started banging with the butt of his fist.

As the two officers followed his action from the car, Valentine spoke. 'He doesn't look too happy.'

'Well, you wanted him worked up.' Ally twisted in his seat. 'Should we get out?'

'No, we'll wait and see.'

As the door to the property opened, Gillon gesticulated wildly, waved his arms and banged a fist off the window ledge. The sound of raised voices, both men's, was heard by the officers, but from where they sat it was impossible to see who the other voice belonged to. As the men went inside a second door slammed, but the loud yells were still detectable in the street beyond, breaking the sombre peace of a place that was a stranger to anything but hallowed quietude. For a second, Valentine allowed himself to feel he had done the right thing by releasing Gillon, that he might actually get somewhere with the investigation, and then some long-lost philosopher's lines about hope prolonging the torments of man came back to him, stilling the thought, preserving it like a museum's extinct species section, never to return.

'Should we go in, boss?' said McAlister.

'No. Not yet.'

The raised voices could still be heard from the road. The DS stepped out of the car and made his way towards the edge of the garden. He moved like an automaton, an unsteady, ungainly figure on limbs too long for his stooped frame. As he leaned onto the wall, Valentine left the car and joined him in the cold, dark street.

'It sounds pretty tasty in there, boss.'

'You're right . . .' He looked down the broad, rain-washed street. It was empty. He knew they had brought a disturbance to the stolid neighbourhood, but nobody seemed perturbed – not a curtain twitched. It took some more time, and another sweeping glance at the terrain, before he realised the distances between the buildings were too great for the sound to travel. The price of that isolation was a life lived insulated from your neighbours; none of them knew, or could likely contemplate, what went on behind the topiaried fringes of this exclusive address.

The shouting stopped as abruptly as it had begun and the officers checked each other through widened eyes. Valentine felt the night air enclosing them as he watched McAlister brace himself like a buttress against the wall. The columnar row of trees that lined the driveway on either side started to sway in the wind and the large, old house etched its bulk against the moonless sky. As the detective focussed on the sturdy property it ceased to be a spacious home and symbol of guarded affluence and transmogrified into a tomb-like keeper of secrets. In the dim light, the building looked old and tired, its too-large windows like eyes scoping an outside world it longed to join but never could. It was an image of misery, a haunting sight that tugged some deep unconscious part of the detective's psyche where the souls of the past were stirred by the winds of the present.

'I'm going in,' said Valentine, his voice a faltering marker of doubt.

'Right, I'm coming with you.'

'No, you stay here.' He knew at once how ridiculous such a bold statement sounded from a man in his condition.

'You've got to be kidding . . . Do the sums, that's two against one.'

Valentine put his hand on McAlister's arm and turned him away. 'Think about it: if they drop us both, who's going to raise the alarm?'

The DS shook his head and made a show of digging in his heels. A defiant gleam entered his eye and then the sharp sound of a door slamming erased it as he turned his gaze back on the house. 'Wait a minute . . . Someone's coming.'

Valentine peered over the wall in the confusion, the scene

seemed unreal. He wasn't prepared to see Danny Gillon striding back towards his van with peremptory steps. He moved quickly, had the engine in motion and the wheels churning up the drive before he closed the door.

'Someone's in a hurry,' said McAlister.

'He's not the only one.' As Gillon manoeuvred the van through a rough three-point turn in the driveway, Valentine pressed his car keys into McAlister's hand. 'Right, follow him and whatever you do don't bloody well lose him.'

The DS looked unconvinced by the sudden decision, pinning back the edges of his mouth and looking like he was searching for the right words to object. 'But . . .'

'No buts, Ally.' The van screeched past them and into the road, and Gillon wrestled with the wheel, his features a stern grimace signalling a burning anger beneath. Valentine spun the DS towards the car. 'Get going before you lose him . . .'

McAlister turned for the car; he was no sooner inside than he had accelerated wildly in the direction of Danny Gillon's van. The back wheels lost some traction on the smooth, wet road and the car fishtailed for a few yards before righting itself.

As Valentine stood in the street, peering over the wall towards the large and uninviting house, his heart stiffened and the blood grew heavy in his veins. A dull ache set up lodgings in his chest and spread in numbing concentric rings throughout his body. It was instinctual – a physical reminder of emotional pain. He knew he had not been in a confrontation since he took a knife in the heart, and the thought of how he might react to such a test gripped him tighter than a straitjacket. It was just primal fear, he told himself, a self-preservation that he could do nothing about. But it prodded him, came with images of his beloved family, his wife and children: how would they cope if he didn't come home? This wasn't his own conscious thought, he hadn't originated it; it had floated in from God knows where. If he accepted that, then he could see it for what it was and face it down. As he took his first step towards the Urquhart's home, Valentine's heart pounded so hard in his chest he felt a cardiac arrest was surely lying in wait for him.

50

THE HOUSE LOOMED OVER the driveway with what seemed like a dolorous reverence for the detective's approach. Far from welcoming, the face it wore was one that could no longer find shock in the actions of men. He closed the one fastening button of his sports coat to ward off the smirring rain that had started and leaned toward the approaching gable. When he had driven up to the building before he hadn't taken the time to be awed by its imposing stature, and now he saw it was a much larger property than he had imagined, somehow. The place seemed to belong to another time, another era; surely by this point it should have been subdivided into half a dozen flats or adopted as the headquarters of a government quango. It looked wrong, it was plain wrong that one family occupied its interior, but more than that it looked like it was begging to be put out of its misery. The house was an anachronism, as strange on the eye as catching a procession of Model-T vintage Fords coughing and spluttering amidst the rude health of today's Toyotas and Audis.

DI Valentine became dimly aware of the sound his shoes made on the driveway scree and found himself almost proceeding on tiptoes. When he thought about the absurdity of his action, he stopped: what did it matter if he encountered the home's occupant out in the cold or inside under lamplight? If he was too infirm to defend himself or his ailing heart gave out then a few scatter cushions and a deep-pile carpet would make little difference to the outcome. He passed the first window and glared in: everything was as it should be; normalcy reigned. The flickering coloured shadows from the television screen leant a familiarity to the setting that seemed surreal. All was as it should be, prosaic: chintz and voiles carefully arranged, leather-bound books in order of height on parallel shelves. Convention predominated: it could have been the set of a costume drama or a well-to-do comedy of manners. He didn't know what he had expected to see. Human sacrifice? Pentagons drawn in blood on the walls? He cached away the suggestion, but whatever it was that waited for him inside he knew it contained an answer. That's what he was there for, that's what he had risked his career for and was prepared to risk his life for now. A whirring mist rose in his head, carrying the faces of Janie Cooper and the other victims. Even his own children appeared now; the case had touched so many lives.

Valentine's cold breath came in white clouds as he neared the front door of the mansion house. He could feel the icy fingers of the night on his chest and in his lungs. The rain, that insidious leakage from the sky that made itself into almost invisible droplets, had fooled him again; his shoulders were soaking, his hair stuck hard to his brow. He'd caught the kind of drooking that merited a night on the hills in only a few strides and he resented its sneaky encroachment. He felt fooled, deceived. Valentine wondered if his senses had taken such a battering that he was still recovering. At the foot of the steps he saw the door was open, only a few inches, but enough of an invitation for him to take the steps and ascend. As he touched the door, he expected noise – a loud evacuation from obstreperous hinges perhaps – but nothing came. He felt almost welcome, like he was walking with destiny. He stepped in and the squelch of his wet shoes on the hardwood flooring compensated his eardrums for their earlier disappointment. The sound rang out in the still emptiness. There was no sign of anyone. The staircase leading skyward was fully lit, as was the lobby entrance leading towards the living room. The detective stood still, picked up the minute burr of his breathing, but nothing else. He was certain no one had left through the front door, they would have to pass him on the driveway, so whoever had been remonstrating with Gillon must still be there.

His shoes continued to squelch as he turned on the hard floor, assessing his options on each step. There was a third hallway to the rear that he had seen on previous visits but never explored before, and it seemed to be singing to him. Where did it lead? What was in there? Something he'd missed perhaps. Valentine gave in to his curiosity; the unknown was now his favoured option. His pellucid trail of watery footsteps went with him as he approached the dark corridor. As he reached the wall he touched the plaster, searching for a light switch, but found only the flat of the wall. A few more steps into the darkness and he started to question the wisdom of his actions: was this wise without back-up? He spotted a thin strip of light glowing beneath one of the doors ahead. He was aware of his stomach cramping; the dull ache in his chest had become a concussed anvil his heart battered against. There was a dry, almost metallic taste that appeared in his mouth as he reached out for the door handle and slowly, almost wearily, opened up.

The room sat in stilled silence, almost a tableau of an old-fashioned study. There was an escritoire, a leather-backed chair on castors and a brass reading lamp burning away. It was James Urquhart's no doubt, and the sight of the large and detailed model railway encompassing three-quarters of the floor space confirmed it. There were no trains in motion, but he saw them there, in the station where tiny people huddled behind newspapers and tinier children rushed about the concourse. The sight of the miniature railway gripped the detective; like a strange message from childhood it seemed to call out to him to take a closer look, to come and play. How many others had felt the same compulsion? He resisted. His attention had already turned towards the open hatch bleeding light from the floor. There was a door from the hatch pressed up against the wall, and as he approached he could see there was a bright light burning in a room below, a white wooden staircase leading the way down. It looked like a cellar, or a basement perhaps, but why was it necessary to keep it out of sight? The rolled-up carpet that came out from the wall had been tugged and torn and now sat in a crumpled mass beside a hessian-backed rug. As he stared, he knew the steps down was the route he should take, but something stopped him. Valentine's throat tightened as he stood staring into the secret world below; his constricted stomach lurched with his thoughts. As he paused, he sensed a presence; he made to turn, but a heavy blow like a man's double-fisted punch struck his back.

Falling was a strange experience: the sudden loss of vision, the blurring of the familiar into the unfamiliar, and the way time seemed to float with your body through the air in a strange slowed motion. Valentine stretched out his arms to break his fall when the realisation dawned that he had been pushed down the hatch and was dropping several feet towards a stone floor. A loud retort like a gunshot signalled the end of his fall and the shooting pain in his wrist confirmed for him that bone did indeed make that loud noise when it broke. The pain arrived at once, in a sharp, agonising burst that repeated itself over and over, extending further along the arm and into his shoulder.

Valentine lay prone on the stone floor. After his arm, his nose and mouth had taken the brunt of the fall, and blood rushed from both. He spat it out: a mouthful at first, and then more drooled before him onto the dusty floor. There was a strange smell in the basement: not damp alone, but something that was definitely dank and something else like burning kerosene. He tried to raise his spinning head, to regain the rest of his blunted senses. The next to return was his hearing, alerted by the sound of footsteps behind him; that sensation was followed by the return of touch, and he was jerked backwards by a hand on his shoulder and spun round to face his assailant's wild eyes.

'You've broken my arm.' The remark was instinctual. When he heard it, he thought it might elicit a laugh, such was its absurdity at this point. When his vision drew the dark shape in front of him into focus, he could see laughter was not an option.

Adrian Urquhart was holding a knife in his hand. It looked like a dagger or a bayonet as he leaned forward and placed its tip on Valentine's shirtfront. His hardened features were separated by the thin slit of his mouth. 'Why are you here?' he said, a tremble rising in his voice.

The detective's eyes flitted between the blade and Adrian's hardened, immobile features. He saw there was no reasoning with him: he was lost to himself, a maniac had taken him over.

'Think about what you're doing, Adrian . . .' Each of the detective's words fell between a fresh grimace of pain.

Adrian removed the knife and stepped back. His dark gaze was as distant as another universe. If thought sparked there, beyond those impenetrable eyes, it was a mystery to even him. 'Get on your feet, Valentine.'

The detective pressed himself against the wall and slowly edged onto his feet. The pain in his arm came in shooting bursts, like he was being lashed with a steel baton, and it prompted waves of nausea from stomach to head. When he managed to stand, he took in the full extent of his surroundings for the first time. Adrian watched him, tapping the dagger off his leg like it was a stick he itched to throw for an impatient dog. He was anxious, but not in any normal way; his anxiety was formed out of despair for a burden he was soon to set down, and it put him on edge. He'd carried this weight with him for so long that it had become part of him; the option to release it had always been there, but so had the consequences, and he couldn't avoid them now.

'You want to know what this place is, don't you?' he said.

'What is it?'

He raised up the blade and pointed it at Valentine's chest once more. His mouth split into a nervous grin as he spoke. 'It's your final resting place is what it is.'

Thoughts eddied in the detective's mind like the confused cries of a drowning man. He thought he saw Adrian Urquhart standing before him with a knife in his chest, proclaiming his guilt of three murders, but he didn't look like a murderer. His piercing eyes and taut mouth, pressed over his teeth like a wire, painted him as an avenging angel. If he was in the wrong, he didn't know it. Valentine's gaze flitted about the room once more. In desperation he sought an escape, but his attention alighted upon a tiny red coat, a child's coat, hanging on the wall. As he stared at the garment, he knew he had seen it before, but he didn't want to believe it matched the connection in his mind. He felt himself drawn away from Adrian; the dagger became an irrelevance as his eyes fastened on the wall, on the child's coat and the pictures. There were

398

photographs stuck on a large frieze and more in boxes on a table. He turned from Adrian, pushed away the knife and walked over to the images. They were children. Their pale bodies exposed to the flashbulbs looked so thin and frail, but it was the pained cries on their faces that reached out from the prints and stung Valentine's eyes.

He turned back to Adrian, his voice a growl. 'What the hell is this?'

He didn't answer. Valentine saw a small pair of sandals on the table: they were tan with buckles, like the kind very young children used to wear to school. He thought he had seen the sandals before. He felt compelled to touch them, and as he did so he felt their inert power pass through his fingertips.

'Oh, Christ . . .'

A schoolbag, an old-style leather satchel, sat next to the sandals, and its buckles were opened. Valentine reached out for the bag and picked it up with trembling fingers. Inside were jotters, little notebooks from a children's school. All the pale, age-worn dusty books had the same child's name on them: Janie Cooper.

A flash of heat engulfed his head as he took in the name and then he dropped the satchel back on the table.

'Janie . . .'

In the box of pictures beside he saw a little girl wearing the red coat and carrying the bag, but it wasn't Janie. He picked up the top photograph and held it up.

'Who's this?'

'You know her too,' said Adrian, his monotonous voice seeming too droll for the occasion.

Valentine turned to face him. 'Who is she?'

'It's Leanne Dunn . . . in Janie's clothes.'

The detective turned back to the picture and stared. He

could see some hint of the young girl Leanne was then, but there was very little of the child left in her. She was aged, old before her time, her eyes wide, staring into a world she didn't understand but knew she was trapped in. The look she wore was of sheer pain and helplessness; it was beyond any of the myriad hurts a childhood could bear or move on from.

'You see, don't you?' said Adrian.

Valentine steadied himself on the table, acid bile rising in his trachea. He tipped out the box of pictures. There were many more images. Piles of them. Pictures of children with men. In focus, out of focus. Colour-bleached or bright, black and white. They covered decades: odd reminders of times past appeared in the backgrounds. A teak-trimmed television, a star clock, bright-red Kickers boots. One thing that never changed was the children's misery and pain: it was etched on their little faces like a first taste of fear. Valentine brought his uninjured hand to his mouth and gripped tightly; he couldn't stem the rising vomit, but he couldn't look away from his hurried search. He tipped over the box and spread out the pictures; it wasn't long before he alighted on the evidence and held its photographic form before Adrian.

'This is your father,' he yelled.

'It is.' He didn't move. A low-pitched sigh started to flow from deep inside him, like he was dredging for a dead emotion. 'That was my father.'

At once the detective understood; he didn't need to hear an explanation. The silence said it all. How could it be explained, anyway? There were no words for this. The true revulsion could never be expressed. He knew why the man before him couldn't face the shame of what inhuman acts had taken place, of the monstrous events his own father had participated in, the man whose blood he had running in his veins.

Valentine's heart pounded as he took in the sight before him; a million cruel images burned in his mind. He swayed as he wiped back sweat from his heavy brow. 'What happened to Janie Cooper?'

'You think I know that? I know she died. I know Knox took care of the remains. They kept her coat and things; I think they dressed Leanne in them to remind them of her. She was special.' His voice was so flat, so devoid of emotion that he could have been dictating a shopping list or any one of the mundane chores of life – not the brutal abduction, rape and murder of an innocent.

The knowledge was not new to him, brought no understanding, and somehow only served to blur his thoughts even more. He looked down to the picture in his hand of the little girl and felt a fierce wave of anger engulf him.

'But why Leanne . . . Why would you want to kill her?'

Adrian brought the dagger up to the side of his head and scrunched up his eyes into tiny knots of anguish as he spoke. 'I didn't want to kill her, I had to.'

'You had to?' Valentine's mind was a pit of confusion and darkening rage. The answers he'd sought came but brought no understanding or resolution. If anything, the reality smacked at him harder, drove deeper wounds in him.

'She was going to talk to that bloody reporter, wasn't she?'

'So Sinclair paid you a visit; you should have lapped that up!'

'What?'

'Oh come on, Adrian.' Valentine put down the picture and moved towards the murderer. 'That's what this has all been about, isn't it? Well, I've seen it now, and everyone will know about your father's secret.'

'It wasn't about that: they needed to pay.'

401

Valentine fronted up to him. 'Leanne Dunn didn't need to pay, she'd already paid, her and Janie Cooper and all the fucking rest of those kids!'

'Leanne was in the way. I didn't want to kill her but . . . she was going to talk to Sinclair.'

'And steal your bloody thunder. That's what you resented, isn't it, Adrian? Leanne was going to expose your father and you wanted to be the only one to do that.'

'No. You're wrong.' He steadied himself before the detective and brought the knife towards his chest once more, pressing the point of the blade into the fleshy part of the muscle.

'Did you really think he'd hurt you more than those girls?'

'Shut up . . . Just stop talking now.' He pressed the knife harder.

Valentine backed up, innate fear and painful memory rose in him. He tried to lift his injured arm to fend off Adrian, but a greater pain overtook him. 'You've got what you wanted, this is what it's been about, the whole world will see him for what he was now. Everyone will know about your father, everyone, Adrian . . .'

The sound of police sirens started to wail through the house, diffusing the intimacy of their talk, bringing back the outside world and its implications. Adrian looked up to the rafters for a solution but was greeted by the sound of pounding footfalls above. Yells and roars came on the back of the study door opening, and louder footsteps were heard on the boards of the staircase. Adrian jerked his eyes to the detective, but Valentine severed the gaze between them and looked up to see DS McAlister descending the stairs. He flagged him to a stop.

Adrian gripped the dagger tighter, held it in both his hands. He didn't seem to be there: like a spectre of himself, he haunted the room with all the other ghosts, all the other victims.

'Adrian, come on, it's over. Your work's done.'

He started to sob, raised his hands towards his face and let the knife fall to the stone floor with a dull clatter. Valentine reached out to him and brought his head onto his shoulder as the young man creased up before him and cried, deep heartfelt sobs tangled in anguish and misery and loss for the father he never had.

'It's all over now, Adrian.'

EPILOGUE

DI Bob Valentine had enjoyed another full, and uninter-rupted, night's sleep. The weeks since the conclusion of the case had served to build his strength and spirit. The worries he had once carried back and forth on the road to Tulliallan had faded into insignificance and the scar on his chest become a mark of pride he bore like a wound won in a long-ago war. He was not the same man, he knew that, but the preoccupation he had simmered in his mind about who the new Bob Valentine was no longer mattered. There was a word he wanted to use to describe how he felt now, but even that seemed an act of gra-tuitous self-absorption. 'Surrendered' was how he felt. He had surrendered to himself and to the world he lived in, because any other act was futile. There was a time, he knew – when he was still the old Valentine – that he would have considered surrender to be defeat, a weakness, but he would have been wrong. He had been wrong about many things: he conceded that, he surrendered it to himself. If it was his weakness then it was also his greatest strength.

The road to Glasgow was dry and fast, some late sun spreading through the cloud in crimson bursts. The sky above was an infinite wash of blue and white where a light aircraft buzzed like an irascible insect on high. There were still glass-topped puddles twinkling in the sunlight by the side of the road, but they were only there to reflect the day's glory.

'Isn't it lovely,' said Clare. 'It's too lovely for a funeral.'

Valentine glanced towards his wife. 'It's not a funeral.'

'I know, but it feels like one.'

The detective wanted to agree, but he knew he couldn't. It was the one hurt he harboured from the investigation: that he had been unable to recover Janie Cooper's body for her parents. That secret had gone with Urquhart and Knox to their graves.

'You look so smart in that jacket, Bob.'

It was good to see Clare smiling again. He hadn't given her much to smile about lately – it was his father's intervention he had to thank for her being there at all. He knew his devotion to the case had nearly cost him his wife and family, but that was going to change now.

He raised his bandaged arm from the wheel and proffered the nap of the cloth. 'I'm still not sure about pinstripes.'

'They suit you. They're distinguished.'

Valentine started a low, growling laugh. 'I liked the old sports coat, you know, it had seen me through many a tough time.'

Clare widened her eyes and laughed. 'Let it go, Bob, the old dog-tooth's where it should be, bloody landfill.'

The mention of the tip staled the detective's thoughts and brought him back to the grim find on the outskirts of Ayr that had led him to this day. He felt no remorse for the passing of James Urquhart, or even the indignity of his death. His sympathies lay with his wife and the children he had abused in life; wherever he was now, the world was a better place without him.

'That's our turn-off,' he said. His eyeline followed the dotted-white lines at the side of the road as it merged into the slower, more sedate pace of the city limits.

The contours of parklands soon gave way to slower roads and streets of shop fronts and pedestrians. The kirkyard, when it came into view, was dominated by a red-sandstone tower, almost spartan in its simplicity. The centuries had taught Scots not to build lavish monuments to worship in this life when the real rewards were in the next. If we could just believe that, ultimately, we all shared the same end, we would be content in our time in this world. Valentine knew it was a ruse. Anything man could contribute to the lionising of his God was an abomination compared to the misplaced faith his God had spent on him. We were not, and never would be, worthy inheritors of His Earth.

'There's Sylvia and Phil,' said Clare.

As Valentine parked the car, he was greeted by DS McAlister. They hadn't spoken properly about the night in James Urquhart's basement or in any great detail about how the DS had trailed Gillon to where Sinclair was holed up. He knew they were both still reeling from the gamble they had taken; it might be years till they fully digested the investigation and shared their thoughts. Today certainly wasn't the time or place. 'Hello, Ally.'

'Boss . . .'

'Looks like we're all here.'

'All except Dino.'

The detective smirked. 'Don't tell me she's developed a sense of herself.'

'It's your show, sir, everyone knows that.'

'No, Ally, it's that wee lassie's show.' He turned to the rear of the car and opened up the boot. Inside was the box containing Janie Cooper's red duffel coat and sandals, her satchel sat beside them.

DS McAlister looked into the box and quickly removed his gaze.

'Jesus, I can't look,' he said.

'You have to, son. You have to face it for them.' Valentine nodded to the Coopers as they waited by the edge of the burial plot.

'They're just the tip of the iceberg . . . the ones in plain view.'

'We can't bring any of them back, but there'll be no more now, not from that pair of evil bastards.'

McAlister leant into the boot and eased the box towards him. 'Here, let me.'

Valentine shook his head. 'No, it's my job.'

The pair walked from the car. As he wrestled the box onto his hip and walked towards the others, the DI eyed the Coopers being joined by the minister at the burial plot. The sun, high in the sky above, painted a white glow round their profiles. The mood was of perfect stillness.

'Boss, why did Urquhart do it . . . ? The son, I mean, why did he kill his own father?'

A deep breath was ingested, then words seemed to float on their back as Valentine spoke. 'He hated him. Hated what he was and what he stood for and how the world knew nothing of the real man, the father he knew.'

'But he was his father . . .'

Valentine's thoughts turned to his own parents for a moment. 'It's a good thing you find it difficult to grasp, Ally . . .' He halted his stride and turned to face the DS. 'I read a line in a background report once, I think it came from a German philosopher: when one has not had a good father, one must create one.'

McAlister stared back at the detective, seemed to be digesting the comment. 'Do you think Adrian was abused too?'

The DI shrugged. 'It seems more than likely, but who knows?'

'He sacrificed what was left of his own life.'